Dear Reader,

The editors at Harlequin and Silhouette are thrilled to be able to bring you a brand-new featured author program for 2005! Signature Select aims to single out outstanding stories, contemporary themes and oft-requested classics by some of your favorite series authors and present them to you in a variety of formats bound by truly striking covers.

We want to provide several different types of reading experiences in the new Signature Select program. The Spotlight books offer a single "big read" by a talented series author, the Collections present three novellas on a selected theme in one volume, the Sagas contain sprawling, sometimes multi-generational family tales (often related to a favorite family first introduced in series) and the Miniseries feature requested previously published books, with two or, occasionally, three complete stories in one volume. The Signature Select program offers one book in each of these categories per month, and fans of limited continuity series will also find these continuing stories under the Signature Select umbrella.

In addition, these volumes bring you bonus features...different in every single book! You may learn more about the author in an extended interview, more about the setting or inspiration for the book, more about subjects related to the theme and, often, a bonus short read will be included. Authors and editors have been outdoing themselves in originating creative material for our bonus features—we're sure you'll be surprised and pleased with the results!

The Signature Select program strives to bring you a variety of reading experiences by authors you've come to love, as well as by rising stars you'll be glad you've discovered. Watch for new stories from Janelle Denison, Donna Kauffman, Leslie Kelly, Marie Ferrarella, Suzanne Forster, Stephanie Bond, Christine Rimmer and scores more of the brightest talents in romance fiction!

The excitement continues!

Warm wishes for happy reading,

Marsha Zinberg

Marsha Zinberg
Executive Editor
The Signature Select Program

MINISERIES

DEBRA SALONEN

WINDOW
TO YESTERDAY

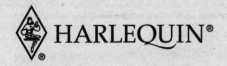

HARLEQUIN®

TORONTO • NEW YORK • LONDON
AMSTERDAM • PARIS • SYDNEY • HAMBURG
STOCKHOLM • ATHENS • TOKYO • MILAN • MADRID
PRAGUE • WARSAW • BUDAPEST • AUCKLAND

ISBN 0-373-21765-X

WINDOW TO YESTERDAY

Copyright © 2005 by Harlequin Books S.A.

The publisher acknowledges the copyright holder
of the individual works as follows:

HIS DADDY'S EYES
Copyright © 2000 by Debra Salonen

BACK IN KANSAS
Copyright © 2001 by Debra Salonen

www.eHarlequin.com

Printed in U.S.A.

CONTENTS

HIS DADDY'S EYES

CHAPTER ONE

SUPERIOR COURT JUDGE Lawrence Bishop III slammed his gavel. The three staccato repetitions dropped a curtain of silence over the proceedings. The opposing lawyers, who up to that moment had seemed poised for fisticuffs, turned to him with a combination of supplication and censure in their eyes.

As the third Bishop male to wear the black robes of a judge, Lawrence, who was "Ren" to everyone except his mother, had grown up hearing stories of courtroom theatrics. But in the two years since his father's death and Ren's subsequent appointment to the bench, he'd become weary of prima-donna headline hounds, such as defense attorney Steve Hamlin.

Hamlin, an up-and-coming name in Sacramento political circles, had a well-practiced smile that garnered female groupies. His defendant, a soon-to-be third-time offender, slumped in his chair like a lump of unformed clay.

Peter Swizenbrach represented the plaintiff—in this case, the State of California. If one believed the evidence—and Ren did—the lump was guilty of serial stupidity, which normally wouldn't be punishable by life in prison unless it included using a gun, which this did.

"Gentlemen," Ren said, his voice carrying as he meant it to, "do either of you see a jury in this room?"

The lawyers looked at each other as if suspecting a trick question. Tentatively, each shook his head.

"Then, who the hell are you playing to?" Ren barked, nodding toward the dozen spectators. "The audience?" Three young women—obviously Steve Hamlin groupies—in the front row squirmed as if he'd called on them to speak. "Because if you can't control yourselves, then I will ask them to leave. I," he stressed the word regally, for he was king of this particular corner of the world, "am not impressed."

The two attorneys scurried to their respective tables to regroup.

Ren stifled a sigh. The bench was every lawyer's dream job—and an important step in Babe Bishop's not-so-secret political agenda for her son—but some days Ren would have traded it for a window job at the post office.

Before he could muster enough energy to begin round two, his clerk, Rafael Justis, a bright, young Hispanic who took no small amount of razzing about his name, handed Ren a folded piece of paper the size of a postcard.

Ren opened it. The familiar scrawl brought a peculiar quickening of his senses even before he read the cryptic: *Gotta talk.* Ren swore softly under his breath, then lifted his gavel a second time. "We'll take a twenty-minute recess."

REN TOSSED HIS ROBE on the brass-and-mahogany coat rack that had been his father's, then paced to his office window. The view of downtown Sacramento from the third-story wasn't impressive—no prestigious law firm's corner office with a vista of the river. But it was an improvement over his previous digs: a tiny cubicle in the basement of a fifty-year-old federal building, where he'd researched environmental law.

Ren had chosen law school because it was expected of him, but he'd wound up falling in love with the law, not the circumspection of it. Although his favorite professor had urged Ren to take up teaching, Ren couldn't bring himself to disappoint his parents, so he'd sought a compromise: environmental law. The pay sucked, but it gave him a chance to champion a cause he believed in.

For fifteen years, Ren quixotically tilted at bureaucratic windmills. Then, to his immense surprise, a small court battle over salmon spawning grounds two years ago stirred a media frenzy, and Ren became an overnight celebrity. Pretty heady stuff at age forty, but damn unnerving, too. Looking back now, Ren understood the impetus behind his crazy lapse in judgment, which no doubt was the subject of this upcoming meeting—a meeting Ren hoped would bring resolution to two years of haunting guilt.

A noise outside his chamber door made his stomach clench, and he ran a hand nervously through his hair, causing a wedge of ash-brown hair to fall across his view.

A soft knock preceded the opening of the door. Ren turned, motioning the visitor to a chair. At five foot ten, one hundred eighty pounds, with sandy brown hair and hazel eyes, Bo Lester epitomized the word *nondescript,* an invaluable trait in his line of work.

"Howyadoin', Ren?" Bo called amiably before plopping like a sack of potatoes into the leather wingback chair opposite Ren's desk.

No more grace than when we were students, Ren thought, smiling. He quickly sat down in his high-tech desk chair—a Christmas gift from Eve, his future bride, and leaned over to shake hands. "Long time no see," Ren said.

"Did I pull you out of court? I told that Mexican kid I could wait. It's your money, and you know I don't mind wasting it."

Ren grinned. Robert Bowen Lester Jr., or "Bo," as he preferred, liked to come off as a redneck hillbilly. He was, in fact, the only son of one of the country's top financial gurus, Robert B. Lester Sr. But Bo had broken with his family shortly after college when he'd chosen law enforcement over what he called "legalized money laundering." Today, Bo was one of the top private investigators in northern California.

"You have some information, don't you?" Ren asked, feeling as if he were swimming in shark-infested waters.

Bo shifted positions, hunching forward to rest his elbows on his knees so he could face Ren eye-to-eye. Ren found the posture ominous.

"You found Jewel." Ren's comment was a statement, not a question.

Bo nodded.

"Where?"

"Here."

Damn. A worst-case scenario. He and Bo had discussed this possibility from day one. As long as Jewel lived somewhere outside the Sacramento area, Ren wouldn't feel any need to contact her. He could stay out of her life, as—*so far*—she'd stayed out of his.

But now that option was gone. This was a town that lived and breathed political scandal. What would happen to Ren's career if Jewel decided to embarrass—or even blackmail—him? His mother's hopes and dreams would be destroyed. Babe would kill him if she found out. And Eve…Ren didn't dare think what his future bride would do to him. But he could be sure that whatever form her retaliation took, it would probably wind up on the six o'clock report. Eve Masterson was the popular anchor of the Channel 8 news team.

Bo rapped his knuckles on Ren's desk. "Don't get too far ahead of me on this, old friend. That's only part of the news."

Ren sat back and took a deep breath. His friend knew him well. "So tell me." Ren was pleased his voice didn't betray the fierce humming in his chest.

"Well, I've got bad news, and even worse news. Which do you want first?"

"Cut the crap, Lester, just tell me."

Bo's wiry brows waggled, but his smile faded as he took a folded piece of paper from the breast pocket of his wrinkled cotton shirt. He slowly opened it. "First off, the name she gave you—Jewel—was pretty close. Does the name Julia Noelle Carsten ring a bell?"

Ren's heart thudded against his ribs. Jewel had a full name. His gorgeous sex goddess, his first-and-only one-night stand, had a name. *Julia.* Such a pretty, innocent name for someone with a body like hers.

"Julia Carsten," Ren repeated aloud. He searched his memory, which included a long list of miscreants. "Nope. Never heard of her."

Bo smoothed the paper across one knee, out of Ren's line of sight. "Her married name was Hovant," he added casually.

"Married?" Ren croaked, lurching to his feet. His chair crashed backward into the bookcase behind his desk.

Of course. Why else would she disappear without so much as a word? Ren retrieved his chair and sat down, feeling both relieved—Jewel couldn't very well resort to blackmail when her own reputation was at risk—and yet, let down.

Ren looked at Bo. The man who'd just simplified Ren's life and eased his guilty conscience wasn't looking very pleased about it.

"Oh, God," Ren groaned. "What else?"

"She's dead."

An invisible weight of some extraordinary measure pressed on Ren's chest making it impossible to draw a breath.

"She can't be dead. She's too young." Even as he said the words, Ren knew they made no sense.

Bo passed him the paper, which Ren saw was a copy of an obituary. Four inches of tiny print. A four-inch lifetime.

"How?" he asked hoarsely, trying to comprehend the unthinkable.

Bo cleared his throat. Ren felt himself tensing.

"The inquest called it—"

"Inquest? Why was there an inquest?" Ren asked sharply.

"Fancy speedboat. Too much power, not enough lake. Rammed an exposed rock and burst into flames—"

Ren shuddered at the graphic image.

"—the inquest ruled it an accident, but the investigating officer told me Dr. Hovant was known for his temper. Some people think he might have let that temper run away with him."

"Murder-suicide?" Ren asked, almost choking on the words.

"Something like that, but no way to prove it."

Ren tried to digest the information, but it wouldn't stay down. "Her husband was a doctor? What kind?" he asked, as if it mattered.

Bo shrugged. "A specialist with a whole bunch of letters after his name. Julia had been a nurse before she became Mrs. Hovant."

Questions percolated in Ren's head like toxic runoff, but Bo didn't give him time to sort through them.

"It happened last July. I asked around the marina. Everybody remembered the crash. One guy said the boat blew up like a grenade." Bo shook his head. "You could ask your fiancée. They probably have it on tape. The media eats up this kind of thing."

As usual, Bo didn't bother hiding his disdain for Eve or her job, but Ren ignored the jibe. "Why do they think it was intentional?"

Bo shrugged. "I guess that's what happens when you air your dirty laundry in public. According to my source, the

Hovants were known to get into shouting matches. Seems their marriage had been rocky for the past few years—which, I guess, might explain why Jewel-slash-Julia did what she did with you."

"This obituary says she was survived by her son, Brady. Stepson, right?" Ren asked, looking up. "The woman I made love to was nobody's mother."

His comment seemed to startle Bo, who frowned and tugged a small wire notebook from his hip pocket. After flipping through half-a-dozen pages, he looked up. "You're right. She didn't have the kid when you were together. He was born later."

Ren froze. "How much later?"

Bo fumbled with the notepad. "October? November?"

Ren and Julia's tryst had taken place the Friday after Valentine's Day. *February, March, April…*he mentally counted. "I repeat—how much later?"

Bo flipped pages. "Bingo! Brady Hovant. No middle name. Born November twelfth. Eight pounds ten ounces. I forgot to mention the aunt. I talked to her, too."

"What aunt?"

"The kid's aunt. Julia's sister. Sara Jayne Carsten, age thirty-one. Runs a bookstore near the K-Street mall. She's got custody of the kid."

Ren frowned, trying to wade through a river of swirling emotions.

Bo sat forward. "Hey, man, this doesn't mean anything. Think about it. Julia obviously slept around. And she was married. There's no reason to think…I mean, you didn't…hell, man, this is the age of AIDS—tell me you didn't have unprotected sex."

"Of course not." Ren glared at his friend. "I used a condom." He frowned, trying to remember. Not that it was hard to recall with photographic—some might say pornographic—clarity the night in question. "All three times."

"My, my, aren't you the stud."

"Shut up. She's extraordinary." *Was. Jewel is dead.*

Ren picked up his phone and pushed a button. "Mr. Justis, court is over for the day. We'll reconvene tomorrow morning."

Bo looked at him, frowning. "This has rocked you."

Resting his elbows on the desk, Ren put his head in his hands. "I never met anybody like her, Bo. Cool and direct on the outside, steamy and wild on the inside. Damn. She was incredible."

"You fell hard, didn't you?"

Ren looked up. "If you mean, was I in love with her?—no. Not even close. Love and sex are not synonymous, my friend. She was gorgeous, wild and hot, and I can definitely say I've never had sex like that before or since." Bo's hoot made Ren scowl. "That was not meant to demean my fiancée in any way. You don't marry a woman like Jewel."

"Dr. Hovant did," Bo said, rising. "Fat lot of good it did him. If the rumor mill is right, all they did is fight—right up to the moment he drove his boat into a rock."

Bo crammed his notebook into the back pocket of his rumpled canvas slacks. "Well, looks like your secret's safe. Bullet dodged. Case closed."

Ren picked up a pen and made a series of hatch marks on his blotter. Nine of them. "Are you sure?"

"Why not? If Julia knew who you were she obviously didn't tell anybody, because we haven't heard anything in two years. She never even mentioned your name to her sister."

"How do you know that?"

Bo produced a disreputable-looking cotton baseball cap from his other back pocket. "Because I'm a professional. When I visited Miss Carsten at her place of business last week, she never blinked when your name came up."

Ren's blood pressure spiked. "You asked her about me?"

Bo made a face. "I told her my friend collected first editions, which is true. I said he was pretty well known for his collection. True again. I said his name was Lawrence Bishop III, and asked if she'd ever heard of him." Bo smiled, apparently picturing the encounter. "She laughed and said, 'If any of my customers have numbers associated with their names, it's more likely the result of a problem with the law than hereditary honor.'"

Ren knew he should have been relieved, but for some reason felt more peeved than pleased. Bo turned to go. "Wait a minute. You're not done."

"Yes, I am. You hired me to find your love goddess. I did. It's not my fault she's dead." Bo wedged the cap on his head.

Ren rose and walked around his desk. "Bo, I need clarity on the matter of this child."

His friend snorted. "What kind of clarity? You used a condom. You were a good bad little boy. End of story."

"You don't find it the least bit unnerving that I spend the night in the arms of a stranger in early February and nine months later said stranger gives birth to a child?"

"But you said—"

"Condoms have been known to fail, Bo. And I was asleep when Jewel left, maybe she took the…evidence of our encounter with her. For what purpose, I don't know. Maybe hubby was sterile and she needed a sperm donor. I don't have a clue, but I'm uncomfortable with loose ends and this one seems like a big one."

"Actually, he's pretty little," Bo said, leaning down to demonstrate a height somewhere near his knees. "Cute as a bug. Curly brown hair. Big blue eyes."

Ren pictured a photograph hanging on his upstairs wall: his father leading a toddler—Ren—with curly brown hair .

and big blue eyes down a dock to the family boat. "You saw him?" he asked.

"Yeah. At the bookstore," Bo replied. "The aunt takes him to work with her instead of using a baby-sitter. Go see for yourself."

The idea made Ren's knees buckle. He parked his butt on the desk and gripped the edge while he forced his brain to re-call the paternity cases he'd tried. "What's his blood type?"

"I don't know. *A, B* or *O,* I suppose," Bo said flippantly.

"Could you narrow that down?"

"How? Medical records are confidential."

"Come on, Bo. You hack the telephone company's records all the time. All I want is his blood type, although I suppose I'll probably need a DNA match to go to court. Maybe you could ask the aunt."

Bo's mouth dropped open. "Have you lost your frigging mind? There ain't no way that woman would voluntarily give you a drop of that baby's blood if it meant you might wind up taking him away from her."

Lowering his voice, he added, "Listen, Ren, get a grip. Chances are, like, one in six zillion this could be your kid. Maybe Julia and the doc had a spat, and she ran up to Tahoe to get back at him—but odds are the kid's his. If not, she'd have come look-ing for you as soon as she found out she was pregnant, right?"

Ren had no way of knowing what Julia would do; he didn't know Julia—only Jewel—and their relationship hadn't in-volved much talking. "I never told her my last name."

"Big deal. If she didn't recognize you from the salmon thing, she sure as hell couldn't have missed your dad's funeral or when you were appointed to the bench."

"Maybe…"

"Not to mention the fact I see your ugly puss in the papers every few days thanks to that news bimbo you're engaged to."

"Eve is co-anchor of the Channel 8 news, Bo—I hardly think she deserves that kind of disparagement. But you do have a point. We are photographed quite often. If Julia had wanted to reach me, she could have found a way."

"Exactly," Bo confirmed. "My old man used to tell me 'Don't trouble trouble 'til trouble troubles you.'"

Ren snorted. "Very profound."

"Hey, people pay big bucks to hear Robert B. Lester Sr. talk. The point is, you've got a nice life. Don't rock the boat."

A part of him wanted to agree, but the problem with Bo's nautical metaphor was that Ren's boat was sinking fast from a broadside hit by an eighteen-month-old iceberg.

"SARA J., I'M NOT GONNA tell your sorry ass again, you can't be giving stuff to every person that comes asking!" Keneesha said with finality.

Sara ignored her friend and continued putting books into the box she was sending to the homeless shelter. Daniel Pagininni was due to arrive at the bookstore any minute to pick them up, and she wanted to be sure she included as wide a range of titles as possible.

"Leave her be, Keneesha," Claudie St. James said, rocking back and forth in the bentwood chair. "You know how she gets. Sara's a woman on a mission. And I don't mean position."

Claudie laughed at her own joke. Sara smiled, too. For her age, which Sara guessed to be twenty-five, and profession—prostitute—Claudie could, at times, be downright childlike. Perhaps that was what endeared her most to Sara.

Claudie rocked a little faster, her small feet coming off the colorful braided rug that delineated the story corner where Sara regularly read to her customers' children and to her eighteen-month-old nephew. At the moment, Brady was sound asleep in his soft-sided playpen behind her desk.

"Don't talk dirty in front of the child," Keneesha said, her tone surprisingly maternal. To Sara's knowledge, neither woman had children, but ever since Brady had arrived in Sara's life, the two hookers had become veritable founts of wisdom on how to raise children.

Claudie snorted. "The child's snoring like an old man, or is your hearing going?"

Keneesha drew herself to her very impressive height of six foot, her voluptuous chest swelling indignantly. "I hear just fine. I was referring to Sara J."

Both women laughed. Sara looked at them, her best—most unlikely—friends, and stuck out her tongue. The two laughed all the harder.

Sara had known Keneesha, a woman in her mid-forties, for almost ten years, which was how long Sara had been back in Sacramento. They'd struck up a conversation on a bus from Reno. Sara had been on the last leg of her journey, returning home after being summarily ejected from the Air Force. Keneesha, "Kee" to her friends, had been returning home after three days of partying with a group of high-rollers.

Kee had listened sympathetically to Sara's story of her aborted military career—destroyed by a boyfriend, who'd used Sara as a means to facilitate his drug sales on base. Kee had agreed wholehearted with Sara that the judicial system was deeply biased and routinely hung women out to dry.

Claudie had come along later, showing up one night, fiercely prepared to stake out her turf. Kee, who could act downright maternal on occasion, had taken the younger girl under her wing, and Claudie, too, became attached to Sara. To the casual observer, Keneesha and Claudie had only two things in common: their profession—which Claudie engaged in only to supplement low-paying jobs that never seemed to

work out, and which Keneesha did when she pleased, period—and Sara. They adored Sara.

Everyday the two women would make their way from their
rooms in the crummy hotel down the street to No Page Unturned, Sara's bookstore. They'd drink coffee at Sara's new
coffee bar, or, on nice days, they'd sit out front at one of the
three tiny tables and poke fun at the general populace.

Sara was content with her life as a single mother and small-
time bookstore owner. She'd inherited the store when her
long-time employer, Hank Dupertis, a gruff old widower with
no children or close relatives, passed away in his sleep. Brady
was a gift that accompanied the most grievous loss of Sara's
life—her beloved sister's death.

The book Sara was holding slipped from her fingers, just
as the bell above the door tinkled. When Sara straightened,
she saw Daniel stride into the shop.

"Hello, Sara love," Daniel said, his dark eyes teasing. "Will
you marry me today?"

Once—about three lifetimes ago—Daniel had proposed in
earnest. Fortunately, Julia had intervened. "You and Danny
both need to find out who you are before you jump into a relationship," Julia had told her. "Get out and live a little, girl."

For Sara that had meant a stint in the Air Force; Daniel had
headed to college, then to a job in Seattle. He'd returned to
Sacramento just after Julia's death, and although he and Sara
remained good friends, both knew his proposals were in jest.

"Sara J. don't need no stinking man in her life," Keneesha
said. "She's got us."

Daniel looked from the large black woman to the petite
blonde, then back to Sara. "Two hookers and a bookstore—
why does that not sound like everybody's idea of heaven?"

Sara laughed and pushed the now-overflowing box across
the display table. "I guess everyone's idea of heaven is dif-

ferent. Actually, I've been very blessed. I have three wonderful friends. And business is good. In fact, *Channel Eight News* is doing a show called *The New Downtown* next Friday. They want to interview me about No Page Unturned."

"Next week?" Claudie squealed. "I thought you said next month. Good Lord, Kee, how are we going to get her done by then?"

Daniel looked confused, so Sara explained. "They think I need a new look to be on TV." She glanced down at her calf-length cotton dress, a sort of wallpaper print with a pale rose background and tiny yellow flowers. Her white sneakers were gobbling up her anklets, heel first. "Who has time for glamour?" she said, tugging up her stockings.

"You're beautiful to me just the way you are," Daniel said. He tenderly reached out and tugged on a lock of Sara's shoulder-length hair.

Sara hated her hair. Bone straight, baby fine and the color of dishwater, her mother always said. Compared to her sister's vibrant red locks, Sara's always looked washed out. The idea of being interviewed by someone as beautiful as Eve Masterson left her more than slightly unnerved, which was why she'd agreed to the makeover.

"Yeah, but you're a man, so what do you know?" Claudie said spitefully.

Sara sighed. "Stop squabbling, children. I told you you could play with my hair, so be nice."

"And a new outfit," Keneesha reminded her. "I am royally sick of those baggy dresses. You need some color, girl."

Sara looked at Keneesha's leopard-print tank top plastered over fuchsia pedal pushers, and involuntarily cringed. "Maybe."

The bookstore bell tinkled, and Sara glanced at the nondescript gentleman in a baseball cap who quickly made his way toward the back of the building. The patron seemed vaguely familiar, but since he didn't seem to require her assistance, Sara turned to Daniel, who was talking.

"…and you can have first pick."

"What?" she asked, noticing how Claudie's gaze stayed on the customer as he meandered into the cookbook section.

"Jenny just cleaned out her closet. She never keeps an outfit longer than a year and she only buys the best. I was taking the bag to the shelter, but you can go through it first."

Daniel's sister, a true fashion diva, was Sara's size and had excellent taste. "That's fantastic. Thanks!"

"No problem," he said, giving Sara a hug. "Now, where's my godson?"

Keneesha scurried around the desk to stand defensively in front of the playpen. For a large woman, she moved with surprising speed. "Back off, light-foot. He's our godson, not yours."

"Do you have that in writing?"

"I'll show you writing, white boy," Kee said, her bluster taking on volume.

The noise woke Brady.

Sara hurried to the playpen and picked him up. "Hey, baby love," she said, kissing his soft, plump cheek. His sleepy, baby smell made her heart swell and her eyes mist. "How's my boy?"

Daniel walked over and planted a kiss on Brady's cheek. The sleepy child chose that minute to rub his eyes, and his small fist collided with Daniel's nose.

"See, there," Keneesha chortled, triumphantly, "he likes us better."

Sara saw a hurt look cross Daniel's face and impulsively drew him close with her free arm. "We both love you, Danny boy, you know that," she said softly.

"I know," Daniel replied. "I love you, too. I'll see you Sunday, right?"

Before Brady came into her life, Sara had participated on Sundays in a literacy program at a local shelter. Unfortunately, nowadays her free time was so limited, she seldom had the energy to join the other volunteers at the Open Door family shelter.

"I'll try, but Brady's cutting teeth, and my neighbors don't like the way my eaves look." She rolled her eyes. "I keep getting nasty letters from the Rancho Carmel Homeowners' Association."

Daniel gave Sara a peck on the cheek. "Don't sweat it. You've done your share." He picked up his box of books. "So? Who's going to fetch the bag of clothes?"

Claudie grumbled about being the company slave, but she followed him out the door.

Brady squirmed, so Sara knelt to put him down. His bare toes curled against the sturdy nap of the new gray-blue carpet. Until recently, the store's flooring had consisted of worn tile squares circa 1955—some black, some green, about half of them broken. Hank had refused to waste money on a building he regarded as "a piece of junk waiting for the wrecking ball." Sara never had the funds to redecorate, but finally decided to use some of the trust money Julia's lawyer sent each month to make Brady's play area safe and comfortable.

"Mine," Brady said, reaching for the bottom drawer of Sara's desk. She'd been careful to have all the drawers fitted with locks—except one, which belonged to Brady. She made sure a healthy snack was in the drawer at all times.

She couldn't help smiling at his triumphant chortle when he pulled a thick hunk of toasted bread from the drawer. His ash-brown curls, as thick and lush as his mother's had been, bounced as he toddled to his miniature cash register and sat down to play.

Sara glanced around; she'd nearly forgotten the customer now unobtrusively tucked in a corner near the cookbooks. *That's odd,* she thought. Her occasional male cook usually carried the tragic look of the recently divorced. This fellow didn't strike her as needy or interested in *cordon bleu* cooking. And he definitely seemed vaguely familiar.

She started in his direction, but was deflected by Claudie's loud "Whoopee!"

"Holy sh—shimany," Keneesha exclaimed. "Look at this, Sara J. Lord God, what I wouldn't give to be size eight!"

Sara joined her friends at the counter to examine Jenny's discarded clothes. It wasn't until the bell tinkled that she remembered the cookbook man.

BO POCKETED his palm-size camera and exited the bookstore, ducking into the alley. A mural of the store's name was painted in five-foot-tall lettering along the brick wall. *Clever name for a bookstore,* he thought. *I wonder if Sara made it up?*

Thinking of Sara made him scowl. Normally, Bo liked his job, but at this particular moment he felt like a piece of excrement wedged between the proverbial rock and a hard place.

Ren Bishop was the brother Bo never had, his one true friend, and Bo owed him more than he could ever repay—but he wasn't happy about the turn this case had taken.

I should have seen it coming, he silently groused as he opened the door of his car, a twenty-year-old Mazda with peeled paint and two primed dents in the fender. His work car, like Bo himself, knew how to be inconspicuous. "Two years without a goddamn lead," he muttered. "The only witness finally comes home after trekking through India, and what do I find? A dead Jewel and a kid that's got Bishop written all over his face!"

Lowering himself to the tattered upholstery, Bo pictured

the sideswiped look on his friend's face when he'd left the courthouse. It reminded him of that night two years ago when Ren had stumbled down the gangplank of Bo's houseboat, vulnerable, exposed and all too human.

"I screwed up, Bo," Ren had confessed, pacing from one end of Bo's tiny living room to the other. "Positively. Beyond all screwups."

"Did you kill someone?"

"Of course not."

"Then stop pacing. You're making me seasick." Bo had been surprisingly unnerved by his friend's agitation. In college, Ren had been known as Mr. Unflappable. Bo didn't like seeing him flapped.

Ren proceeded to spill his guts about the redhead who'd mysteriously disappeared after one night of passion. Bo recalled half hoping that Jewel was a blackmailer so he'd have a chance to meet her. But nothing happened. If that night clerk had stayed in India, Bo never would have had a clue to Jewel's true identity.

"That's Mrs. Hovant. Julia," the twenty-year-old clerk told him, after Bo gave her Ren's description of the woman. "She and Dr. Hovant used to come up from Sac five or six times a season, depending on the snow. Maybe they still do. I don't know. I don't work at the lodge anymore."

With a little cautious probing, Bo also found out that the day in question stuck in the clerk's memory because Julia had come to the lodge alone. "I asked her where the doc was, and she said something like 'Getting his rocks off at a medical convention.' She didn't seem too happy," the clerk told him.

The rest had been child's play for the PI.

Bo heaved a sigh, stirring the dust on his dashboard. He'd expected Ren to mourn Jewel's death, but this thing about the kid had caught him off guard. Bo had tried to downplay Ren's concern, but he had to admit the possible date of conception fell eerily close to the one-night stand.

Still, Bo had balked at pursuing it, partly because of what it might do to Sara, an innocent bystander in this little passion play.

"Even if, for argument's sake, the kid is yours," Bo had argued, "there's nothing you can do at this point. It's your word against the mother's, and she's dead."

"As the biological father I'd have more rights than an aunt."

"But it comes down to proof. How can you get the proof without admitting what you did? Which, if I remember correctly, was what you hired me to make sure never happened."

"I don't suppose there's any way I can. But regardless of how it affects my political future, I still have to know."

Bo sighed and started the car. A couple of discreet photos and the kid's blood type from his medical records. This Bo could do, but that would be it.

"You have to draw the line somewhere," he muttered to himself. "Even for a friend."

CHAPTER TWO

REN YANKED ON THE CORD of the wooden blinds with more force than the old rope could take. The handle came off in his hand and the heavy shades crashed back to the mahogany sill with an ominous *thunk.* He sighed and tossed the yellowed plastic piece on the sideboard.

I've got to call a decorator, Ren thought. Although he seldom used the formal dining room, he knew it would be called into play more often once he and Eve were married. At present, the room reflected Babe's favorite decorating motif: Ostentatious. The opulent crystal chandelier cast an amber glow across the Regency-style table at its eight saffron brocade chairs. Without benefit of the morning light streaming through its mullioned windows, the room's musty gloom matched Ren's mood.

Ren blamed part of his foul mood on his alarm clock. If he'd remembered to set it, he would have made his weekly golf game. Instead, he'd slept in till nine-thirty. Ren pushed on the swinging door and entered his kitchen, a pristine world of black-and-white tile—the first room he'd remodeled after he moved in.

His home had once belonged to his parents, but after his father died, Babe, wanting something smaller and more luxurious, sold the house to Ren. He loved the old beast, just as his father had, but the forty-year-old house needed work.

"Coffee," he mumbled, moving like a bear just out of hibernation. Ren took a deep breath, hoping to discover his coffeemaker was still warming his morning brew. His nostrils crinkled. No light beckoned from the stainless steel coffeemaker, but the smell of overcooked coffee lingered.

Ren microwaved a mug of the tar-like liquid and carried it to the small bistro table in the glass-enclosed breakfast nook. He sat on one of the waist-high stools covered in black-and-white hound's-tooth.

The wall phone rang before he could take a sip of his coffee. He stretched to pick it up. "Hello."

"Hi, handsome, sorry about last night. I'd have called, but you wouldn't believe how late we got out of the booth."

Ren had no trouble picturing his fiancée as she rattled off her apology. No doubt she was in her car, zipping through the light, Saturday-morning traffic on Interstate 80, headed back into town from her Roseville condo. Eve was ever a study in motion; she reminded him of a hummingbird with too many feeders to frequent.

"Don't worry about it," he told her, finally taking a sip of coffee. The brew—a shade off espresso—made him blink. "It's not like I was dying to go to the fund-raiser."

Ren heard a horn honk. Probably Eve's. She drove fast and had little tolerance for those who got in her way. "I know, but your mother won't be a bit happy. By the way, I went online and had a nice big basket of flowers delivered to her this morning with a note saying you'd be making a substantial donation to her cause—what was it, anyway?"

"League of Women Voters, I believe."

"Oh, damn. I wish I'd remembered that. Don't be too generous. They were particularly snotty to the media last fall."

Ren smiled—his first of the morning. His first since Wednesday afternoon, actually. Although he'd gone through all the motions for the past two days, his mind had been consumed by the thought of Julia. And her child.

He missed what Eve was saying and had to ask her to repeat it.

"Where have you been lately?" she exclaimed. "I'm serious, Ren. You always tell me I have too many irons in the fire, but at least I listen when somebody is talking to me. I asked whether Babe talked to you about setting a date for the wedding. She left a message on my machine, and it made me realize we really do need to sit down and talk about scheduling. You *know* what my schedule is like."

Ren knew. *Lesson One of celebrity dating: Everybody follows the schedule but the schedule-maker.* "You're right. We do need to talk." Ren recognized that although his affair with Julia had taken place before he and Eve started dating, she had a right to know what was happening, particularly if it turned out he'd fathered a child.

"Okay, then," she said. "Let's see…."

A loud engine noise came over the line, and Ren cringed, picturing her flipping through her thick day-planner while changing lanes. "Why don't you call me back?" he suggested. "I may go out later, but I'll take the cell phone."

There was a pause. "You hate cell phones. Ren, are you okay? You don't sound like yourself."

"I didn't sleep well," he admitted. A guilty conscience had a way of conjuring up the worst scenarios. For instance, what if the reason Julia's husband had driven into a rock pile was that he'd found out the child wasn't his? What if Ren was to blame for his son's mother's death? Would the little boy wind up hating him when he was old enough to understand?

"Maybe you need vitamins. Boyd did a piece on male vitality last Wednesday—did you see it?" Eve asked.

"Nope. Missed it."

"Do you *ever* watch my show?" she asked, her voice suddenly vulnerable.

"Yours is the only news program I watch, you know that. I just happened to be with Bo that night," he said in partial honesty. After Bo had brought him the news about Julia and the baby, Ren had driven to the American River and walked along the jogging trail until dark. It was either that, or do something utterly stupid like visit the aunt's bookstore and check out the kid for himself.

Eve's dismissive snort brought Ren back to reality. "I wish I knew what you see in that man. He's such a boor."

Ren grinned. He'd never figured out why the two people he cared for most couldn't stand to be in the same room together. "Bo did a little research job for me and brought me the results. He's the best in the business, you know."

"So you say, but…" The sound of squealing tires broke her line of thought. "I'd better go, sweets. I'm meeting Marcella this morning. We still have to go over my '96 and '97 tapes. You wouldn't believe what a fanatic this woman is. She makes *me* look laid-back."

Her musical laugh brought an odd pang to Ren's chest. He loved this bright, beautiful woman, but he had a feeling she wasn't going to be overly thrilled at his news.

"So are we on for tonight?" he asked when he found his voice.

"Maybe. Marcella is only in town for another four days. She flies back to New York on Wednesday. Would you mind if she joins us?" Ren and Eve had a standing reservation at Hooligan's. Since she worked weeknights, Saturday and Sunday were their only nights to dine together. Usually, they ate out on Saturday, and he cooked on Sunday.

"Naturally I'd prefer to have you all to myself," he said, hoping his tone was more romantic than peeved. "Let's leave it open for now. Call me later, and we'll figure something out. Maybe we could ask Bo to join us so we'd have a foursome."

Ren grinned, picturing Eve's face at the idea of introducing her famous New York agent to the Sacramento PI. "You're right," she said. "We'd better hang loose until I have a better scope on my time. See you later, sweetheart. I love you."

She hung up before Ren could tell her the same thing.

"Exactly what kind of foursome did you have in mind?" a voice said from the doorway.

Ren spun around, nearly dropping the phone. "Goddammit, Lester," he shouted. "Don't you know how to knock?"

Bo shrugged. His sloppy green-and-gold plaid shirt wasn't tucked into his pants, making him look as if he'd come straight from the bowling alley. Brown double-knit pants barely cleared a disreputable pair of saddle shoes, which he wore without socks. His flattened-out hat was the kind that snapped to the brim.

"I looked for you on the golf course. Your partner said this was the first time on record that you were a no-show. He even thought about calling the paramedics, but didn't want to miss his tee time." Bo's lips curled wryly. "Notice your *real* friend dropped everything and rushed right over to check on you."

Ren hung up the receiver and sat down. "Thank you for your concern, but I overslept." He took a sip of coffee, then frowned. "Did I give you a key?"

Bo ambled to the coffeepot, took a mug from the white oak cupboard and poured himself a cup. He added two scoops of sugar from the bowl on the counter, then carried it to the microwave. "Nope. I picked the lock. Gotta keep in practice, you know."

Ren doubted that. More likely he'd forgotten to set the alarm. He'd been doing a lot of irresponsible things lately.

"You got anything to eat?" Bo asked, poking his head into

the refrigerator. "Oh, Lordy, Revelda's apple pie," he said, referring to Ren's part-time housekeeper. "I swear I'd marry that woman if she'd have me."

"She wouldn't. She'd have a heart attack if she saw that floating hovel you call home."

"Actually," Bo said, talking through a mouthful of pie, "I found a lady to come in and clean for me a couple of times a month. Works great now that I've moved my computers to the office. Speaking of computers—" He pulled a manila envelope from his waistband and tossed it on the table.

Ren's gulp of coffee lodged in his throat. He strove for nonchalance as he opened the envelope and withdrew a half-dozen black-and-white photographs and a single sheet of paper.

He picked up the computer printout first, but his gaze was drawn to the photos. "Is this her? This can't be her."

Bo's mouth was full. "Uh-huh," he grunted.

Ren shook his head, his gaze darting from one photograph to the next. "There's no way this woman is Jewel's sister. She's so…plain."

Bo's muffled expletive made Ren drop the printed page and pick up a photo. Leaning forward, he studied it closely. While the image was a trifle blurred, it showed a woman whom, though nice looking, he wouldn't have looked at twice. How could he reconcile this image with the one he held of her sister, an Aphrodite with flaming red hair, lush curves and flashing green eyes?

Feeling a bit let down, like a child at Christmas who'd expected a bike and got a book instead, he sighed. "Her hair's straight, her dress looks like a discount store special and her figure…" Ren frowned, squinting. "Well, I can't tell much because of the dress, but she looks like a librarian."

Bo made a low, snarling sound and helped himself to a second piece of pie. "Close—she owns a bookstore."

"Owns it or runs it?"

"I didn't hack her bank records, but her business card says, Sara Carsten, Owner."

"She's pretty young to own a business," Ren said, mentally adding a point in her favor.

"The guy down the block said she's worked there since high school. In fact, she's turned it around from near-bankruptcy. The old man who owned it left it to her. She's kept up with the times—added a coffee bar and two Internet stations. And she's got a couple of book clubs that meet there." Bo made a sardonic sound. "The men's group is called The Unturned Gentlemen."

Ren added another point in her favor—literacy was a pet project of his. "Okay, she's a good person and a decent businesswoman, but I still can't believe she's Jewel's sister."

Bo scowled. Ren ignored him and rocked back, holding the photo. In the light from the window behind, he could see things he hadn't noticed before. Her smile, for one. It was a kind, gentle smile that made him inclined to smile back.

Ren focused on her eyes. Jewel's had been bright green, full of flashing sauciness and humor. If he squinted, Ren thought he could see humor in this woman's eyes, too. "What color are her eyes?"

"How the hell should I know?"

The downright angry tone could not be overlooked. "What is your problem?"

"You, man. You are my problem," Bo said, marching to the table. He ripped the photograph out of Ren's hand. "Here you are, poised to destroy this woman's life, and you don't think she's *pretty*. Well, f—"

Ren raised his hand in warning. He studied his friend as he might a criminal with a gun. Keeping his tone calm, Ren said, "I was just surprised that I couldn't see any similarities between the sisters."

Bo's shoulders relaxed visibly. "It's not a very good picture. She was talking to that guy when I took it." He put the photo on the table and pointed at a good-looking man standing at the edge of the photograph. "She even gave him a hug, and I heard her tell him she loved him."

A funny, totally unexpected twinge caught Ren in the solar plexus. "Her boyfriend?"

Bo shook his head. "No. I got his plate through the store window. His name is Daniel Paginnini. He works in the Building." Ren had met enough congressional insiders to know that meant the Capitol. "I'd say he and Sara are old friends. She's got a lot of friends."

Ren detected an odd inflection in Bo's tone, but he let it go, although he was curious why Bo was so defensive of the woman. Ren picked up a shot of her holding the baby. Her back was to the camera, but her upper arms looked firm.

"Does she work out?" he asked. Jewel had been in peak physical condition, he recalled, her long, lean body as finely honed as an athlete's. When he'd asked about her sleek muscles, she'd said, "My job keeps me in shape." When he'd inquired about her job, she changed the subject by putting her mouth on a part of his anatomy that drained the blood supply from his brain, waylaying any questions he might have asked.

"Yeah," Bo said snidely. "She lifts weights. I'd say forty pounds, about a hundred reps a day."

"What?"

"The kid, man. She's a single mom." Bo shoved another photo in Ren's face. All Ren could see of the child was a mop of curls and a pudgy fist clamped around a soft blanket. He missed the first part of Bo's heated litany. "…gets up at dawn and works around this ugly house in Rancho Carmel until it's time to go to the store, then she runs her business and chases the kid all over the place until after the noon rush. Then, she lets one of the hookers take over while she takes the kid to the park…"

The word took a couple of seconds to register. "Did you say 'one of the hookers'?"

"Yeah."

"How many are there? And what are they doing in a bookstore?"

"Two. The big one's black. The little one's white. And they're her friends. As far as I can see, they're there every day."

Ren sat back, letting out a caustic laugh. "Oh, that's a wonderful environment for a child."

Bo leaned forward, his lips curled in a snarl. "I knew you were going to say that. Like you have any business pointing fingers."

Ren's mouth dropped open. "Okay. That does it. What the hell's going on with you?"

Bo pulled out a second stool and hopped up to sit at the table. He dropped his chin into his palm and muttered, "I like her."

"The aunt? Or the hooker?"

Bo glared. "Sara."

Perplexed, Ren reached for the photograph again. He'd never seen Bo behave in this manner. When involved in a case, Bo rigorously maintained a hard-nosed impartiality.

"Have you actually talked to her? Since that first time?"

"Yeah, yesterday."

Ren's solar plexus took another hit. They'd agreed that Bo's surveillance would be from a distance. "Was that necessary?"

Bo sunk lower in the chair. "It wasn't my idea."

"Whose idea was it?"

"The hooker's."

Ren smiled at the embarrassment he heard in Bo's tone. Bo was a professional, one of the best. Ren could imagine Bo's chagrin if someone had blown his cover.

"The big one or the little one?"

Ren almost missed the mumbled answer. "The little one, huh? Hmm. What happened?"

"She remembered me, okay? I can't tell you the last time that happened. Maybe I need to work on my disguises—they get old, you know."

Ren nodded, trying to keep from smiling.

"I didn't think anybody noticed me Wednesday when I went back to take the pictures, but yesterday, right after Sara and Keneesha—the black hooker—returned from the park, I eased in behind a couple of shoppers—and *wham*. The little one—Claudie—nailed me. I thought she was gonna demand a strip search."

Ren diplomatically covered his grin with his hand. "There's an image."

Bo shuddered as though recalling a harrowing experience. "It was so sudden. One minute I was standing in the Mystery section listening to Sara explain about some drumming group when—boom—Claudie grabs my arm and spins me around, feet apart, back against the wall. My hand was going for my piece—"

"You were carrying? Around m—a baby?" he corrected.

Bo scowled. "No. But old habits are hard to break, and she knew what I was doing. Believe me. I saw it in her eyes. She knows people. And she pegged me." He sat back, shaking his head.

"What'd she say?" Ren was surprised when a smile crossed Bo's lips.

"She said, 'What's this guy doing back again?' And then Sara and the other one came up, and Sara told her, 'We really need to work on your people skills, Claudie. Let the customer go.'"

Bo sat up straight. "You'll never guess what happened next."

"What?" Ren croaked.

"Sara invited me to join her *gentleman's* reading group. Meets every other Wednesday at the store. So I figure I can keep an eye on things until you decide what you're going to do about this." Bo nudged the computer sheet toward Ren. "Have a look."

Ren's stomach contracted at the implication he read in Bo's words and tone. His heart thudded loudly in his ear as he skimmed the page. "*O*-positive," he said softly. "Same as mine."

"Yeah, I know. I hacked your file, too."

Neither man spoke. Ren stared out the window at a mockingbird strutting in his backyard. A black and white maître d' against a flawless green expanse. *What does this mean? Another coincidence or am I a father?*

Over the pulsing static of questions, strategies, legal precedents, moral obligations, terror and niggling hint of joy in his head, Ren heard Bo mutter something about reading books not being part of his contract.

Suddenly, the incongruous image of Bo in a literary setting struck Ren as hysterical. Laughing, he said, "A reading group. You?" The release loosened the pent-up emotions percolating in his chest, taking him beyond humor. Gasping for breath, he sputtered, "That'll have Professor Neightman rolling over in his grave."

Bo jumped off his stool and stalked to the door. "You know what you and Professor Neightman can do, preferably in public with your fiancée watching," he barked.

Sobering, Ren drew in a shaky breath and wiped the tears of laughter from his eyes. He regretted his jest. For a man who seemingly cared not a whit what people thought, Bo could be damn touchy about certain things, and his lack of formal education was one of them. Not that he hadn't had his chance. But Bo hadn't been in study mode during college; he'd been too busy partying.

"Hey, man, I'm sorry. I appreciate what you're doing, really. I know you're not crazy about this, but is there any chance you could get some better photos?"

"Why? You think she's gonna get sexier?"

Ren flinched. "I'd like a shot of the child. Type *O* is pretty common. It could be a fluke, but if he—"

Bo shrugged. "I'll think about it."

Ren would have pressed the point, but Bo didn't give him the opportunity. The heavy door swished closed, leaving Ren in silence.

He picked up the photographs and headed for his study, intending to go through his mail and pay bills. But once there, he laid out the photographs on his desk. Maybe his calling Sara plain had come from his need to see something of Jewel in her. According to the background information Bo had faxed him, the two women had different fathers. Julia's had split shortly after her birth. Her mother had married Lewis Carsten a year later and he'd adopted Julia. He'd died when Sara was a toddler. Their mother—an alcoholic—died when Sara was seventeen.

Ordering himself to put aside any memory of Jewel, he studied Sara's image. Her jawline was strong but not harsh, her nose perky and small. He liked the shape of her eyes, her thick lashes a shade darker than her hair. In the black-and-white picture, her heart-shaped lips reminded him of an old-time movie heroine—innocent yet sensual.

He could tell, even in the blurry image, that she wore no makeup—a practice that set her apart from other women of his acquaintance. Perhaps he'd done her an injustice. She was pretty, and if she changed hairstyles—hers was straight and plain—she could probably turn a man's head. However, that didn't alter the fact that she projected not one iota of the sexual chemistry her sister had exuded.

A sudden knife-like pain sliced through his gut, making

him bend over. Tears rushed to his eyes, and he choked back a cry that had been lurking in his subconscious for days. He lowered his head to his desk and wept—for the loss of someone he barely knew, but who'd touched his life with a kind of unfettered passion he'd never experienced before. He hadn't loved her, this enigmatic Jewel, but on that one night she'd given him…freedom.

THE RAUCOUS SQUABBLING of two blue jays in her neighbor's sycamore tree reminded Sara of Claudie and Bo, the most recent recruit to Sara's gentleman's reading group. It had taken Sara until this Sunday morning, when the mindlessness of scraping paint freed up her random access memory, to place him—the customer who had asked about first editions for his friend. At the time, she'd brushed him off with a flip answer.

"Sara, is it okay if I give Brady a peanut butter sandwich?" Amy Peters asked. The thirteen-year-old wasn't a terribly experienced baby-sitter, so Sara only used her when she was home and needed some relatively uninterrupted time.

"Sure. You know where everything is, right?"

"Yeah, but it looks like this will be the last of your bread."

"Darn. I forgot to buy some last night. Oh, well, Brady and I will walk to the market before his nap."

Amy dashed back inside. Brady was a pretty good toddler, but he had a mischievous streak in him—he loved to be chased. And just lately he'd discovered he could send Amy over the edge by hiding.

With a sigh, Sara tackled her task. A good mile of gutters encircled Hulger's house. Unfortunately, the original painter had failed to prime them adequately; the brown paint flaked like dandruff in some spots, yet resisted her most vigorous scraping in others. Another reason she hated her brother-in-law's house.

After the accident, Sara had given up her apartment, which was within walking distance of the bookstore, and had moved into Julia and Hulger's twenty-eight hundred square-foot house because she hadn't wanted to uproot Brady. Although it meant a difficult commute twice a day, she'd welcomed the security the gated community offered. But now she was regretting her decision.

"Hello, Miss Hovant," a grave voice said.

Only one person called her that—Mary Gaines, her neighbor to the left. "Sara, Mrs. Gaines. Please, call me Sara," she said, striving for patience. Sara didn't even bother trying to correct the woman on her last name.

"I see you're *finally* getting that gutter painted," the white-haired woman said. Her emphasis was clear.

"Just scraping. I'm still waiting for a bid on the painting. The painter was supposed to meet me yesterday but didn't bother showing up." After the scathing message she left on the painter's machine, Sara doubted she'd ever hear from him again.

"I can give you the name of a man, but he's not cheap," her neighbor said, turning to leave. "I just hope you get something done before the next association meeting."

Sara waited until the woman was gone, then sighed heavily. The homeowners' association took its job seriously—too seriously for Sara's taste. But she didn't think it was right that she had to pay for Hulger's mistakes. And in her opinion, the entire house was a mistake.

Hulger had had the house built as a wedding present for Julia. Then he'd devoted the five years before his death to imposing his taste on every decorating detail, inside and out. Sara still could never understand how a woman as strong-willed and self-sufficient as Julia had tolerated such an autocratic husband. Another mystery of life, she figured.

In many ways, Julia was an enigma. Sara blamed their

mother for that. When Audra was incapacitated by drink and couldn't run a can opener let alone a household, Julia had become a surrogate mother to Sara, making sisterly confidences impossible.

Julia's stormy relationship with her husband had never been open for discussion. Danish-born Hulger once told Sara his role in life was to make money and visit his parents once a year; Julia's duties, according to Hulger, included looking beautiful for his friends, entertaining in lavish style and accompanying him to Denmark.

Julia had tried to do justice to her role, working out at the gym to stay fit and taking exotic cooking courses, but she'd missed her nursing career. Sara had been privy to enough arguments between the couple to know this was a huge issue in their marriage.

Sara had hoped things would turn around once Julia found out she was pregnant, but Brady's birth seemed to add a new kind of tension to the marriage.

Sara sighed. She missed her sister every single day. Living in Julia's house was a mixed blessing—reminders of Julia abounded, but so much of her taste was overwhelmed by Hulger's bizarre, unwieldy legacy.

An hour or so later, Sara strapped Brady into his stroller and started down the street. Although she'd invited Amy to join them, the teen said she intended to use her baby-sitting money to take her mother to the movie as a Mother's Day treat. Sara had completely forgotten about the holiday.

"Well, Brady, love, what should we do to celebrate?" she asked, giving the stroller a jiggle. "Shall we buy an ice-cream cone?"

"Iceee," he cried enthusiastically.

She pushed fast to avoid looking at Hulger's unfinished landscaping. In her opinion, the empty concrete fishpond resembled a giant diaphragm, which complemented the stunted marble shaft that was supposed to support an ornate fountain. Sara had petitioned the estate lawyer—a close, personal friend of Hulger's who treated Sara like some greedy interloper— for the funds to complete the work, but he'd spouted something about long-term capital investments overriding short-term needs. Feeling utterly intimidated, she hadn't even bothered asking for help with the gutters.

Sara pressed down on the handlebar of the stroller, leaning Brady far enough back to look up at her. *"Whee,"* she said, pushing him over the speed bump. His high-pitched chortle made her heart swell. She loved the sound of his laugh. Her favorite time of the day was his bath. Invariably she'd wind up soaked, but it didn't matter because they'd laugh from start to finish.

"Fas," Brady demanded. "Mommygofas."

She took two quick steps. "This fast?"

He shook his head, his curls dancing. "Mo'fas."

She sped up. "This fast?"

He leaned forward, pushing his little body back and forth as if his movement could increase the speed. "Mo'fast."

His reward for saying the word right was an all-out run, which lasted until Sara became winded. Brushing her bangs out of her eyes, she hauled in a deep gulp of air. "No mo'fast. Mommy tired."

With a slower pace, she walked to the market, singing a silly song for Brady. *"When you're happy and you know it, shake your feet..."*

Brady's fourteen-dollar sneakers bounced just above the pavement. "Another 'short-term' need, I suppose," she muttered under her breath. *I wonder whether that lawyer would manage if he had my income instead of his.*

BO SQUEEZED OFF THE LAST of his exposures. Even through a telescopic lens, he could tell Sara looked tired, but the shots of her laughing as she pushed the kid in his stroller ought to get Ren's attention. With her hair pulled back in a ponytail, she looked like a teenager. Not exactly sex-goddess stuff, but he'd included a few shots of her nicely shaped legs displayed by snug denim shorts, for good measure.

After a stop at the one-hour processing lab, he could wash his hands of this job. It was one thing to tail a stranger, but for some reason he didn't think of Sara that way. Bo blamed that on her open, friendly manner. He had a feeling Ren would like Sara, too, but Bo doubted the feeling would be mutual once Sara found out about Ren and her sister.

Bo shook his head sadly. He wasn't the kind of guy who believed in happy endings, but this one looked worse than most.

CHAPTER THREE

THE FOLLOWING WEDNESDAY EVENING, Bo parked the Mazda a block-and-a-half from the bookstore, then hunkered down to wait. The Unturned Gentlemen's reading group was due to begin in fifteen minutes. His stomach rumbled—a two-front nervous rumble.

First, the more time he spent in Sara Carsten's company, the more Bo admired her. The duplicity of befriending her while running a background check seemed shoddy, but the longer Bo was around Brady, the more convinced he was that the little boy was part-Bishop.

Granted, Bo knew squat about kids, but Brady had an imperious manner that shouted, "I'm important!" Pure Babe, some Ren.

The second source of anxiety stemmed from the slim paperback resting on the seat beside him. He couldn't decide if he was more amazed by the fact that he'd actually read the thing or that he'd enjoyed it.

A rap on his passenger window startled Bo, until he saw the smiling face of Sara Carsten, who was bending down to look at him. Busted, he groaned silently. He picked up his volume of Endurance: Shackleton's Incredible Voyage, then opened the door and hauled himself to his feet.

"Hi, Bo. I'm so glad you could make it. Did you like the book?" Sara asked. At her side, a far less cordial Claudie watched him warily.

"Yeah," he admitted. "I liked it. Half the time I couldn't believe it was true, but no writer would be that cruel to his hero, right?"

Sara sobered. "True. Real life's often bleaker than fiction."

Claudie snorted. "The guy was a jerk. He deserved what he got. Why the f—heck would anybody go to Antarctica in the first place?"

"Challenge. Adventure. Accomplishment," Bo returned.

"Men things," she muttered. "Only men would be stupid enough to think those things mattered."

Before Bo could reply, Sara laughed and said, "Now, now, children, if you can't play nice, you don't get any cookies."

"Cookie?" a voice chirped from the navy-blue stroller.

Bo walked around the front of the car and squatted, eye-level with Brady. "Hey, kiddo, out for a ride?"

Brady kicked his feet and twisted to one side, shyly hiding his face in the soft fabric. "We had a picnic supper in Capitol Park. Brady walked all the way there, but petered out on the way home," Sara said.

"It was them squirrels that wore him out," Claudie added.

Sara poked at a crumpled bread wrapper stuffed in the top pocket of the stroller and explained, "He likes to chase the squirrels. Brady loves animals—but what little boy doesn't?"

"I bet he didn't," Claudie muttered.

Bo decided it was time to confront her. Rising, he faced her squarely. She barely came to the top of his shoulder, but she lifted her chin defiantly and met him eye-to-eye.

She wouldn't be bad looking, if she weren't so damn prickly, he thought, taking in her blousy shirt cinched at her very narrow waist by a black leather belt. Although her purple stretch pants showed every curve of her shapely legs and derriere, her running shoes were more Stairmaster than streetwalker.

"Night off?" he asked, and immediately wished he hadn't.

Her eyes narrowed viciously, and her red lips clamped together as if she'd tasted something bitter. "This ain't the safest area at night, so Keneesha and I take turns hanging out with Sara on book club nights. You got a problem with that?"

Not at all. In fact, he found it admirable. But he couldn't tell her that.

Sara relieved him of the problem. "I'm so lucky to have such great friends. Look what Claudie did to my hair. Isn't it fun?" She fluffed out her shortened locks. The style made her hair seem fuller, and it bounced in a girlish manner near her jawline.

"I like it," Bo said honestly.

"Who cares?" Claudie rejoined waspishly.

"I do," Sara said. "I'm vain enough to be pleased when a handsome man tells me I look nice." A blush brought up the color in her cheeks. "Well, my hair looks nice."

Handsome? Bo nearly stumbled backward into the gutter, but he managed to get past the odd compliment in time to add, "You definitely look better than nice. I'd go so far as to say beautiful."

Claudie frowned at him and gave Sara a push. "You better open up. Your gentlemen don't like to be kept waiting."

Sara, who was dressed in a simple sleeveless, teal-green sheath that cupped her bosom, then fell straight as a plumb bob to the tops of her canvas deck shoes, looked at the utilitarian watch on her wrist and gave a little yelp. "Good point. Come along, Bo. You don't want to be late for your first meeting."

"He'll be there in a second, Sara J. I gotta discuss something with your new gentleman."

Sara tossed a concerned glance over her shoulder. "Don't hurt him, Claudie. He's a paying customer."

Bo swallowed. He didn't like the way Claudie was looking at him. Like he was a wad of gum on the bottom of her shoe. "Okay, say your piece."

Claudie waited until Sara was inside, then asked, "Are you a cop?"

Bo blinked, astounded by her perceptiveness. "No."

"You move like a cop. You're always asking questions like a cop. If you're not a cop, then what are you?"

A PI looking into ruining your friend's life. The thought made his stomach heave, nearly recycling his hastily eaten burrito.

He moved past her, noticing for the first time how fragile she seemed. How'd you end up on the streets? he wanted to ask. Instead, he said, "Just a guy killing time 'til I get a job, but jobs ain't easy to come by when you got a record." He was good at improvising.

"What kind of record?"

D.U.I. in college. "None of your business," he said shortly, walking away. She dogged his heels, step for step, but stopped half a block from the bookstore. Reluctantly, Bo slowed, then turned around.

"I don't know if I believe you, but I don't really give a flying you-know-what. Keneesha and me look out for our friends, and Sara is off-limits to all losers," she said, her tone ominous. "She wouldn't be interested in you anyways."

Bo had no intention of making a play for Sara—no matter how cute she looked with her new haircut—but he didn't like being told what to do. He'd had enough of that growing up. "Oh, really? And why is that?"

Claudie waited until the man ahead of them was through the door of the bookstore before she said in a low voice, "Because she's…gay."

Bo's mouth dropped open. "Bullshit," he sputtered. "I don't believe you."

Her eyes narrowed. "Well, she is."

Before he could reply, Sara poked her head out the door

and motioned to him. "I need him, Claudie. The group's starting. Besides, this is your night off."

Bo's face heated up, even though he could tell by her tone,
Sara was teasing. His only satisfaction came from seeing
Claudie's face flush with color, too.

SARA TUNED OUT the low rumble of masculine voices emanating from the far corner of the bookstore. Years earlier, before Hank had died, she'd hauled in a couple of old couches
Julia was throwing out and some funky pole lamps to create
a "reading room." Hank had called it a waste of space, but had
let her have her way. Although he never admitted it, sales went
up—and the reading room stayed.

Closing her eyes, Sara gently rocked Brady back and forth.
If she let herself, she could drift off to sleep, too. She'd been
up since five, trying to figure out how to pay for the repairs
needed on Julia's house.

"Can I put him down for you?" a voice asked softly.

Sara opened her own eyes to a pair of remarkable blue
ones, as deep a hue as the pair she played peek-a-boo with
every morning—only this pair was attached to a stranger. A
very handsome stranger, who seemed full of concern for her.

That by itself was odd, but the sudden, shocking quickening of her senses left her speechless. In answer to his question, all she could do was shake her head.

"He looks heavy. Are you sure?" His voice was cultured,
rich as honey and faintly melodic. Its basic vibration caught
her somewhere between her breastbone and her belly button
and radiated outward in the strangest way.

She rocked forward, intending to rise, but her knees felt insubstantial, as if they might crumple if she put any weight on
them. He seemed to sense this, and plucked Brady from her
arms as if by magic. He didn't hesitate for a second but

smoothly transferred the sleeping child to the playpen with such fluidity that Brady didn't even stir.

Sara put her hand to her chest as if to capture Brady's warmth a second longer. Tears rushed to her eyes for absolutely no reason.

"He's a handsome boy," the stranger said.

"Thank you." Sara looked at him as he stood a few steps back from the crib. Suddenly she felt a deep primal urge to push him away. She rushed to cover Brady with a knitted throw that Keneesha had made for him.

Sara straightened, forcing herself not to be intimidated by the man's size or beauty. And he *was* gorgeous. His thick, wavy autumn-brown hair had a carefree quality that made her want to touch it. His skin was a healthy tan, not too dark, not too pale.

"Are you here for the group?" The inanity of her question struck her the second she took in his fine, navy pinstriped trousers, perfectly creased above Italian leather shoes. Even without a tie and unbuttoned at the collar, his smoke-gray shirt made a fashion statement: wealthy.

He shook his head. "No, I'm supposed to meet a friend, but I got here a little early. Do you mind if I look around?"

The bookstore owner in her wanted to offer him free reign, but some other part of her remained uneasy. She tried attributing her qualms to his proximity and his maleness, but somehow that wasn't enough. She had a store full of males, and none of them made her senses peak like this man.

"Be my guest," she said, faking a smile.

When he stepped away, she let out a long, silent sigh and turned to her desk. She had a hundred things to keep her occupied while the men talked, but couldn't for the life of her recall a single one. She was about to sit down, when the stranger called to her, "Have you read this one?"

His soft, husky tone made tingles run up her skin. Rubbing her bare arms—Sara told herself it was rude to ignore him—she walked to the cardboard display case holding the latest release from a popular, prolific writer.

"No, I'm not really a fan of horror genre."

He seemed surprised by her frankness. A blush warmed her cheeks. *Smart move. Knock a potential sale to a potential customer.*

"I once heard a fifty-eight-year-old man accused of killing his eighty-year-old parents say the reason he hacked them to death with a butcher knife was that they wanted to move into a rest home and he would have had to get a job." His serious, contemplative tone took her by surprise.

"Are you a psychologist?" Her first guess would have been politician.

A smile tugged at the corner of his thin, masculine lips, suggesting a dimple in his left cheek. "It sometimes feels that way. I'm a judge."

Sara reflexively took a step back. *A judge.* The word conjured up memories of a time she wanted to be excommunicated from her consciousness.

She started to turn away, but his next words stopped her.

"In law school they tried to prepare us for some negativity." He flashed her a beguiling, boyish grin. "Do you know the difference between a catfish and a lawyer?"

Sara shook her head, intrigued by the humor in his tone and the oh-so-human crinkles at the corners of his eyes.

"One's a scum-sucking bottom feeder. The other's a fish."

Sara tried not to smile, but did, anyway.

Oddly, his smile faded. "The antipathy changes when you become a judge," he said. "It doesn't go away—it just becomes more…judicious."

The wistfulness of his tone caught Sara off guard. The

only judge she'd ever met stood out in her memory as a Wizard of Oz kind of character. A big head and commanding voice, passing judgment on things he didn't understand.

"I'm sure it's not an easy job, in fact, I can't imagine one I'd want less."

Instead of being put off by her opinion, the man stepped around the display, bringing himself closer to Sara. It made sense since they were speaking in library-level whispers, but crazy alarms went off in her head, obscuring his reply.

"It wasn't high on my list, either, but when the governor asked me to fill a vacant slot, I felt I had to accept."

Normally, Sara might have credited his amiability to good manners and responded accordingly, but for some reason her long-simmering resentment over the justice system chose that moment to erupt. "You're talking politics. I'm talking human lives. What makes you—or anyone for that matter—think you're capable of deciding someone else's fate? Doesn't that constitute supreme ego?"

His brows sank together in a more attractive way than Sara wanted to admit. "No, I don't think so. Law limits a judge's powers. Any judgment is based on evidence, and the law as it applies to that individual case."

"But how can you read a few lines on a sheet of paper or listen to two over-priced lawyers talk for ten minutes, then decide a person's fate? Not everyone who breaks the law is a bad person," she added in an even softer voice.

His blue eyes were tempered with compassion, as if he knew she was speaking of herself. "I believe a person who breaks the law and pays his or her debt to society is a better person for it. The ones who break the law—from shoplifters to congressmen—and go unpunished are the losers. They have nothing to build on but guilt. What kind of legacy is that?" he asked.

His words touched her, as did his tone and some elusive nuance in his manner, something that made her think he might actually be capable of knowing her without judging her. How crazy was that?

"Ren?" a voice croaked.

Sara blinked, dissolving the mesmerizing connection between them.

The stranger straightened with such unexpected hauteur that Sara had to work at keeping her mouth from hanging open. He suddenly looked like a judge, not just some handsome man lending a sympathetic and understanding ear to her old grievances. Sara's heart boomed in her chest—what had come over her?

"Hello, Bo," he said, turning to face Sara's newest recruit. Bo hurried forward, displaying considerable shock at seeing his friend.

"What are you doing here?" Bo demanded.

"I had to work late and I remembered you were going to be here. I thought we could grab a drink when it's over."

Sounds plausible, Sara thought, *but it's not the truth.*

Bo squinted at his friend a moment longer, then looked at Sara. She read something sad in his eyes. Anxious to help, she reached out to pat his hand, which gripped his book like a buoy. "It's a very informal group, Bo. You can leave anytime. Besides, there's always next week," she said. "Did they tell you they're switching to weekly meetings? What do you think? Do you want me to get you the next book?"

His gaze flickered to his friend, whose grin provoked a snarling "Sure."

Confused by the antipathy between the two, Sara pulled back her hand. "Well…um, great. Stay put, and I'll be right back." She tossed a semi-smile in the judge's direction, then dashed to her storeroom. She didn't understand what was going on any more than she could explain what had come over her, but Sara cultivated new readers like flowers in a garden; she wasn't about to let this one wither on the vine. Not without a fight.

REN EYED THE BOOK in his friend's hand, damn glad it wasn't a gun. Prudently, he backed up a step, which also afforded a better view of Sara as she hurried toward a doorway marked Employees Only. His gaze followed the lithe form in the pale green dress. She moved quickly but with grace, back straight. Bo's last photos showed her to possess a very shapely body with sleek calves and a trim derriere, but her business dress was of Shaker simplicity.

"What the hell is this about?" Bo growled, taking a step closer.

Ren raised his hand defensively—not that it would have done any good if Bo Lester took it in his head to beat him senseless. Ren had seen him in action more than once during Bo's drinking years. "Pure impulse. I can't explain it. I guess I needed to get it over with."

"You could have warned me."

Ren shook his head. "I didn't know myself. I was supposed to meet Eve for dinner—she took the day off to drive her agent to the San Francisco airport, but she called from her car. Some big toxic spill up near Lake Shasta. I started home, then changed my mind."

Ren had only intended to peek inside the store, but something had come over him the instant he saw Sara Carsten—eyes closed, lips whispering a lullaby, rocking the sleeping child. The image was so ecumenical, so Madonna-like, that he felt drawn inside as if propelled by a force outside his body.

And then Ren took the biggest leap of faith in his life. He'd picked up the baby. A child that could be his own flesh and blood. It was an idea so staggering and life-altering that he should have run in the other direction, but holding that compact little body seemed the most natural thing in the world.

"Let's get one thing straight. You hurt her and you'll regret it." The threat was so serious, so unexpected, all Ren could do was nod, as Sara hurried to join them, a cardboard box in her arms.

"Sorry 'bout the wait. I've been hoarding these so long I couldn't remember where I put them." As she neared, she faltered a step as if sensing the primitive, masculine energy between them.

She set the carton on a display table and picked up one small paperback. "The title is *A.P.B.* It's a little police procedural—the first in a series. The rest of the group voted for something light this time."

Bo put out his hand. "I like crime novels. The good guys always win. The bad guys either end up dead or in jail. Right?" He shot a pointed look at Ren.

She glanced from Bo to Ren. "Umm…yes."

Ren regretted causing her added disquiet. "My friend's not a big reader," he said, picking up a book. "I can't tell you how great it is that you've been such a positive influence on him."

One slender brow lifted. "Bo may not read a lot, but he must like books. He's been here pretty often."

"Oh?" Ren asked.

She nodded. "In fact, the first time he came in was to ask about a rare book for a friend." She clapped her hand over her lips, a blush claiming her cheeks. "This is your friend, isn't it. The rare book collector. I've ruined the surprise, haven't I?"

Bo seemed momentarily taken aback, but he recovered. "Actually, this *is* that friend, but since I'm not sure he deserves a Christmas gift this year, don't lose any sleep over it, okay?"

She was obviously puzzled by Bo's response, but chose not

to question him. Instead, she smiled. "My sister used to tell me I was notorious for speaking before my brain could catch up with my mouth."

The word *sister* caught Ren by surprise, and he almost missed a step as he followed her to the counter. Now would be the perfect time to segue into that subject, but he found himself mute. So, apparently, was his private investigator.

While Bo paid for his new book, Ren studied the child sleeping so peacefully in the playpen behind Sara's desk. The little boy had turned slightly, curled protectively around a stuffed elephant he'd somehow found in his sleep. This image, as much as the one of Sara rocking the baby, wrapped itself around Ren's heart and squeezed.

"What's the baby's name?" he asked, not having known he was going to.

"Brady," Sara answered guilelessly.

She glanced over her shoulder and smiled. Ren, who was studying her face, saw something that had been missing from her photographs, even the ones from Sunday afternoon. A luminous quality that enhanced Sara Carsten's quiet beauty.

"Brady," he repeated. "That's…different."

She flashed him a grin that made him blink. "You're very diplomatic. Of course, that probably comes with the job. My sister, Brady's mother, had the name picked out even before she knew she was having a boy, but she could never decide on a middle name."

The duplicity of his inquiry made his throat dry and his jaw ache. "You're his aunt," he said, as if not framing it as a question could absolve the guilt he was going to feel if he took this inquiry forward. Since Armory, his lawyer, wasn't due back from Hawaii until tomorrow night, Ren had put off formulating a legal strategy.

Her lovely face changed. In sorrow it became vulnerable.

"My sister died," Sara said simply. "She was killed in an accident, but she left me Brady."

Tears glistened in her eyes. Hazel, not temptress-green, but beautiful nonetheless. *And I thought she was plain.*

When she looked down to count Bo's change, Bo shot Ren a dark look. It hadn't been easy convincing Bo to stay on the job, but Ren's promise to approach the matter slowly had helped. His impulsive decision tonight might have jeopardized things.

"Well, there you go," she said, tucking the book in a sack. "Thanks, Bo. I'm glad you came. And it was…um, interesting talking with you…"

"Ren Bishop," he added. "It's Lawrence, actually, but only my mother calls me that."

He held out his hand, and she took it, just a trifle reluctantly. Her hand was small, her grip slightly reserved. "Sara Carsten," she said, dropping his hand to reach for a card from a plastic basket beside the cash register. Her blush told him she'd used that as an excuse not to touch him any longer.

Ren took the card she offered. "I don't carry first editions," she said. "But I might be able to help if you tell me what you're looking for."

Ren was within a heartbeat of telling her the whole sordid story when the sound of men's voices indicated the readers' group was over. "We gotta go," Bo said, starting away.

As Ren followed his friend out of the store, he glanced back once and was surprised to find Sara's gaze still on him. She had a puzzled expression on her face. He lifted his hand to wave goodbye, but Bo grabbed his arm in one plate-sized fist and dragged him bodily out the door.

"You bastard," Bo muttered, stalking off down the sidewalk. "There's a right way and a wrong way to do this."

Downtown's daytime hustle and bustle had given way to

an empty-theater kind of quiet. Miniature lights peeked
through the new-growth foliage of the well-pruned trees. A
gold-hued street lamp spotlighted Ren's Lexus while ignoring Bo's Mazda one space ahead of it. The two cars seemed
a metaphor for the contrast between their owners.

Ren stopped beside the Mazda. "This wasn't planned, Bo.
It probably wasn't smart. But I needed to see him." *I held
him—the child that might be my child.*

Suddenly Ren's knees felt disconnected from his body. He
reached out to steady himself on the blistered hood of the car.
"Is there a bar around here? I really could use a drink."

Ren's response seemed to take some of the heat out of Bo's
anger. "Around the corner," he muttered, leading the way.

Bo didn't speak again until they were seated at a small
table. After the waitress delivered a light beer and a cola, Bo
said, "Okay, suppose you explain to me what happened tonight. I thought I was the inside guy, and you were going to
let the suits make contact when we all decided the time was
right."

Ren took a long draw on his beer. "I was in my office
looking at the pictures…the ones you took Sunday." He
paused, knowing there was no way to explain the sense of ur-
gency that had been building in him ever since Bo had delivered the color photos of Sara and the child. Yes, he saw a
resemblance in some of the shots, but this need to connect
went deeper than that.

He shrugged. "It had to happen sometime, right?"

Bo took a sip of cola. "This means you're going forward
with the paternity suit, doesn't it?"

Ren couldn't meet Bo's gaze. He didn't want his friend to
guess the truth: that deep down, Ren wanted the child to be
his. He *needed* the child to be his. As much as he loved Eve,
Ren knew her career was her primary focus. It might be years

before she was ready to have children, if ever. Ren was ready for fatherhood now.

"Do I have any choice, Bo? Would you walk away? Live the rest of your life wondering?"

Bo looked ready to argue, but in the end shook his head. "I guess not, but what about Sara?"

Ren's heart lifted, then fell oddly. He hadn't expected to like her, but he did.

"She's a good person and a wonderful mother," Bo said. "She doesn't deserve what this is going to do to her. It's bound to get messy. If she's smart, she'll scream bloody murder and hire some media shark like Steve Hamlin to make you squirm. Even if you ultimately win, you'll be scarred for life."

Ren took another swallow of beer. Bo's prediction threw him, but he pretended to shrug it off. "I wouldn't blame her for going on the offensive. She obviously loves the child, and I saw what mentioning her sister did to her." Ren's voice faltered; Sara's unshed tears had touched him deeply. "I don't want to hurt her, Bo, but I have to know. What if he's my kid?"

Ren didn't really expect Bo to understand. Bo's relationship with his own father was practically nonexistent. Ren doubted they'd exchanged more than a dozen words in the past year.

"Yeah, I get it. My old man may be a well-dressed rat, but I know he'd give his last dime to help me out," Bo said, surprising Ren with his insight.

Before Ren could respond, a voice said, "Don't tell me you actually have a friend."

To Ren's surprise, a woman in tight purple leggings and a blousy shirt pulled a chair from a neighboring table and straddled it, dropping her chin to the arched metal back. Her unsteady gaze flicked from Ren to Bo.

Bo groaned. "Go away, girl. Didn't you give me enough trouble earlier?"

"That's why I came over. To apologize." Her words were slightly slurred.

"Apologize for breaking my balls for nothing?"

Her eyelashes fluttered coquettishly. "Did I have my hand on your balls? I must have missed that."

This has to be one of the hookers. Claudie? And she's been drinking.

She turned her attention to Ren. "Oh, my, aren't you hunky—"

"You're off duty tonight, remember?" Bo barked.

"Working girls never pass up an opportunity to…work."

A sad little smile crossed her lips, and Ren was reminded of Sara's words. *How can you know the person behind the crime?* If Claudie were brought before him, what would he see?

"Not tonight, Claudie. Besides, he's taken," Bo told her.

"You could still introduce us. I don't bite. Well, I do, but it costs extra."

Ren put out his hand. "Ren Bishop."

"Claudine St. James. My friends call me Claudie," she said, giving him a suggestive look that came off totally fake. Ren decided he liked her pluckiness.

Bo coughed. "So what's the apology for, Claudie?"

She drew herself up fairly straight and said solemnly, "I told Keneesha what I told you, and she called me a dumb f— person. She said Sara would never forgive me if she found out, and I'd better tell you myself or she would."

Ren couldn't keep from asking. "Told him what?"

She shot him a poisonous look. "This is private. Just between the cookbook man 'n me."

"It's okay. Just say what you want to say." Bo brushed her arm with his fingertips.

Her automatic flinch made Ren's stomach clench. Men probably weren't very nice to her. He had heard his fair share of horror stories in the last two years; hers was probably no different.

"I lied," she said soberly—her intense scowl obviously a ruse to keep tears at bay. "Sara's not gay. I made that up."

"Hell, I knew that," Bo said gruffly. "I never believed you for a minute. You're a terrible liar."

"I am?"

"Yeah. And when you're that bad of a liar, it's like it never happened, so just forget it." Bo rose and motioned for Ren to follow.

She stood, catching the edge of the table as if her equilibrium had been shaken. "You know, cookbook man, you're not that bad, after all."

"Cookbook man?" Ren asked, as they exited the bar. He inhaled deeply, the brisk delta breeze a welcome change from the smell of stale beer and cigarette smoke.

Bo growled. "When I was taking your damn pictures the first time, the best view was from the cookbook aisle."

Ren studied his friend in the light from the neon Budweiser sign. Bo was a successful investigator who traveled all over the world, but in his private life he was a recluse who favored fishing and satellite TV over dating. Obviously, these women had somehow touched him. Ren didn't question his friend's loyalty, but he wondered if his decision to pursue the paternity issue would change their friendship.

They walked in silence. Ren used his remote to unlock his car. The double *beep-beep* pierced the quiet. "Bo, this isn't malicious," he said somberly. "I wish there were some other way, but I sure as hell don't know what it is."

Bo looked skyward. "Yeah, I know."

Ren waited a minute, then asked, "Do you have that background information on Sara yet? I'd like to read it before I see Armory on Friday morning."

Bo unlocked his car the old-fashioned way. The door gave an unhappy groan when he opened it. "It's at home. I wasn't expecting your surprise appearance tonight, remember?"

Before Ren could reply, Bo climbed into his car. Ren watched him start it and pull away. Obviously, Bo didn't understand the primal urge that had pulled Ren through the bookstore door. Ren wasn't sure he understood it himself.

He glanced up the street. A yellow glow spilled from the windows of the bookstore. *Why is she still there? She should be home, tucking Brady in bed.* Ren longed to walk back to the store to make sure she was okay, but the lawyer in him warned against it. *You're poised to change her life forever. And she's never going to forgive you.*

SARA EASED BRADY'S sleeping form to her left shoulder to better manipulate the key. She'd waited as long as she could for Claudie to return, but still had a long drive ahead of her.

"I'll do that," someone said behind her.

Sara recognized her friend's voice and immediately gave a huge sigh of relief. "Thank God, you're okay! I was worried about you," she said, giving the younger woman a quick, one-armed squeeze. The smell of alcohol and cigarette smoke made her recoil. "You are okay, aren't you?"

Claudie kept her head down as she took the key and finished locking up. "Yeah, I'm fine. Had one too many at Jake's, is all."

Sara's brows went up. "How come? You never drink."

Claudie handed her the keys with a look of profound weariness. "I drink. Just not when you're around. How else do you think someone like me lives with all this shit?" The last word was part whisper.

Sara put her arm around her friend's slim shoulders. "I didn't mean to sound condemning. I was just surprised. I know you're doing the best you can—so am I. That's why we're friends, remember?"

The two walked down the dark alley toward the employee parking lot. "Do you want to talk about what's bothering you?" Sara asked.

Claudie held her tongue until Sara had Brady strapped in his car seat in the back seat of her Toyota wagon. When Sara closed the door, Claudie melted to the curb like a marshmallow over an open flame. "I suck, big time," she wailed.

Sara sat beside her. "You don't mean that literally, do you?" she said, purposely injecting a spot of humor. Sara knew her friends liked to think of Sara as angelic, so her occasional forays into the ribald always cracked them up. This time the jest went over Claudie's head.

"I told the cookbook man you were gay," Claudie cried.

Sara grasped the odd confession immediately, but it took a second or two longer to figure out how she felt about it. Bo, her newest recruit, was a nice guy, but Sara felt no attraction to him. And even though she was attracted to his friend Ren Bishop, she'd never get involved with a judge, so what did it matter?

Sara shrugged. "Did he believe you?"

"No. I don't think the other guy did, either."

Sara's heart took an unwelcome jump. "The other guy? Tall? Wavy hair? Really handsome?"

Claudie looked at her strangely. "You met him?"

"He came into the store while he was waiting for Bo. Where'd you see him?"

"At the bar." Claudie turned to face Sara. "I 'fessed up like Keneesha told me. And Bo said he never believed me, anyway, because I was a terrible liar so it wasn't like what I said even counted. But Keneesha said a rumor like that could make trouble for you with Brady. If social services proved you were an unfit mother, they could take him away. They do that, you know."

Her solemn anguish touched Sara's heart. *Did that happen to you, my friend?* Sara wondered. She didn't ask; Claudine St. James never spoke of her past. Never. "Nobody's out there trying to take Brady away. Why would you worry about something like that?"

Claudie shook her head. "You know what life's like, Sara. Every time you get a sweet thing going, somebody comes along to mess it up."

An odd shiver passed through Sara's body. She prayed her friend was wrong. Life without Brady was unthinkable.

CHAPTER FOUR

REN SCANNED THE JAM-PACKED reception area located on the second floor of the courthouse. Potential jurors milled about waiting for instructions, praying, no doubt, for a quick release. To pick Bo out of such a crowd was like looking at a Where's Waldo? puzzle, Ren thought.

"So, what's the plan, Stan?" a voice asked beside him.

Ren glanced to his right. Typical Bo. Baggy, tan canvas pants. Navy T-shirt with some engineering firm's logo on the breast pocket. Scruffy running shoes.

"Lunch," Ren said shortly. "Let's beat the mass exodus."

They took the stairs, hurrying past the uniformed guards at the entrance. Neither spoke until they reached the plaza.

"Where do you want to eat?" Ren asked, jogging down the concrete steps to the street.

Bo shrugged. "The noodle shop?"

The thought of food made Ren queasy, but the instant the white hand appeared on the stoplight, he took off—a sprinter in street shoes. Dodging slow-moving pedestrians, he hurried toward the J-street locale, not paying attention to Bo until his friend grabbed his arm and hauled him to a stop in the shadow of the Union Bank building.

"Slow down. Sara doesn't get back for another hour, and we need to give her time to get Brady down for his nap. Tell me what Mason said."

"I gotta give him credit," Ren answered. "He didn't even blink when I told him about Julia."

Armory Mason, Ren's lawyer, had been his father's closest friend. Telling Armory of his affair was almost as bad as confessing to his dad.

He'd called Bo right after the meeting with Armory. They'd discussed the timing of this upcoming confrontation, and he'd asked Bo to accompany him to smooth the way with Sara.

"I'm a little nervous," Ren admitted.

"Well, duh. Who wouldn't be? But you gotta eat." Bo grinned. "Actually, I gotta eat. I don't care about you. You want moral support—it's gonna cost you lunch."

He started off at a more sedate pace which Ren matched. The four blocks to the café brought them closer to Sara's bookstore, as well. *Sara.* He'd thought about her almost non-stop since Wednesday night. Sara…and Brady.

Earlier, Armory had confirmed what Ren had deduced on his own. Before there could be a custody suit, they had to determine paternity. In other words, he needed a DNA test.

"I suggest you talk to the aunt first," Armory had told Ren. "You say Bo's obtained the child's medical records so you know the little boy's blood type is *O,* which is the same as yours. But that's a very common type. In fact, I'm type *O,* and we both know I'm not *your* father."

Ren smiled politely at Armory's attempt at levity.

"Perhaps if you explain the situation, she'll be agreeable. If she's unreasonable, I'm sure we can get a court order, but that will take time."

Unreasonable, Ren thought. What constituted "reasonable" when a child was involved?

Armory looked thoughtful. "You said she's a single mother. Do you know what her financial needs are? Maybe she'd be receptive to an offer of some sort of monetary incentive."

Ren knew his lawyer was only doing his job. But Armory didn't know Sara Carsten. Of course, Ren didn't know her, either, but he didn't think she'd take a penny from him. The only way she might consider his request was if she believed it was in Brady's best interest.

At the small restaurant, both men ordered teriyaki noodle bowls—Bo's with chicken, Ren's with broccoli. A smiling Asian woman took Ren's money, then told them "Number twenty-two." After filling their drinks, they sat down at a small table. Ren chose a chair facing the large, plate-glass window. Foot traffic surged and ebbed on the sidewalk. People carried take-out meals to the park across the street.

Does Sara ever take Brady to that park? Ren wondered.

Bo kicked Ren's shins to get his attention. "Lordy, they must have loved you in court today. Let any murderers go free?"

"All I did today was listen to lawyers with motions. Boring, long-winded motions." He sighed. "I don't know what's wrong with me, Bo. I used to love that part of the game—finding the best argument to prove my point. It took me back to my high-school debate team days."

Bo snorted. "Don't tell me you were that kind of geek."

"It was fun. Besides, the debate team got to travel all over the state."

"So did the football team, but we didn't have to wear sissy jackets and ties."

Ren couldn't help looking down at his Ralph Lauren suit. He poked his paper napkin at a faint spot on his red-and-navy striped tie. The lax dress code was one of the things he missed most about his days as an environmental lawyer. Tucked in a basement, no one had cared what he wore. Once he went public, dressing became a contest that both Babe and Eve insisted on his taking part in.

When their number was announced, Bo rose. He returned

moments later with two steaming bowls. The aroma tempted Ren despite his unsettled stomach. Ren half listened to Bo's tale of his struggle with an elusive catfish that had gotten away, but his nerves were slowly getting the better of him.

"Am I doing the right thing, Bo?"

Bo chewed, appearing thoughtful. He looked at Ren a long time before answering. "I've been trying to put myself in your place, and I guess I don't see how you've got any choice. But I'm not sure Sara will see it that way."

Ren's appetite vanished. He pushed his bowl aside and took a sip of iced tea.

"What else did Armory say?" Bo asked. "What are your chances of gaining custody if she fights?"

Ren shook his head and looked around, hoping Bo's words couldn't be overheard. "Paternity issues aren't his specialty. He's going to call a friend." Ren hated the idea of people talking about his life, speculating about what made him do something as foolish as having sex with a stranger.

"What did your mother say when you told her?"

Ren took a sip from his glass to avoid answering.

"You haven't told her yet, have you?"

He shook his head. "I need to tell Eve, first."

Bo stopped chewing. His look made Ren fidget with his chopsticks, poking at a blob of spilled teriyaki sauce. "I haven't seen her in over a week. She took her agent wine-tasting in Napa last weekend, and then she covered that big chemical spill up near Shasta. This isn't the kind of thing you discuss on the phone."

Bo's expression said he recognized an excuse when he heard one. "I thought you were staying at her place on weeknights," Bo said.

Ren stifled a sigh. While he and Eve had discussed moving in together, neither wanted to be the person to make the

DEBRA SALONEN 69

move. Ren felt her condo was too small, and she called his home a mausoleum. "Off and on. She didn't want me around when her agent was there."

He couldn't stifle the bitter chord in his tone. Eve had been so wrapped up in her plans, she didn't have a clue about Ren's impending crisis. During one of their infrequent phone conversations, she'd seemed to pick up on his tension, but attributed it to lack of sex.

"Don't worry, sweet thing," she'd told him. "I'll be home Friday night, then we'll have the whole weekend to play. We could go back to Napa. I have a coupon for a mud bath. Marcella loved it."

Ren hadn't liked Marcella, Eve's agent; he'd found her pompous and demanding. Eve, who called her a cutthroat deal-maker, was hoping the woman could steer her career to bigger and better markets—maybe even network television.

"Hang tough, honey," Eve had told him before hanging up. "We'll be back on schedule in a day or two." Everything was a schedule to Eve. When life was on track, everyone was happy. Being off schedule meant chaos. What would a paternity suit do to Eve's elaborate and carefully considered plans?

"I'll tell her tonight," Ren said decisively. "First Sara, then Eve, then my mother." A good, logical order.

Ren didn't try to interpret Bo's look; instead, he swiped his friend's half-finished bowl of noodles and carried it to the busing area. "Hey, man, I'm not done," Bo complained.

"Close enough. Let's go."

Despite his grumbling, Bo followed Ren outside and plunged into the throng. A few doors down the block, they passed in front of the bar where they'd talked two nights earlier. "Hey, cookbook man," Ren called, when Bo got sidetracked by an attractive young brunette in a tight skirt, "I thought you liked blondes."

Bo frowned. "Don't call me that. Claudie does it to get under my skin. I stopped by the bookstore yesterday to pick up the new reading list, and she went on and on about my culinary prowess—only she made it sound like I was cooking in the bedroom." He shook his head. "For a high school dropout, she's pretty snappy with the insults."

"How do you know she's a dropout?"

"Sara was quizzing her for the equivalency test when I was there. Sara says once Claudie has her GED, she'll be able to take some junior college courses and get off the streets permanently."

Ren paused. "Are you interested in her?"

Bo's face flushed red and he put on his sunglasses. "Of course not. She's a mixed-up kid, and I feel sorry for her, that's all."

They walked on in silence. A glance at his watch told Ren they were still too early, so he slowed his pace. A display in the window of an antique store caught his eye. "See that music box? Eve bought Babe one like it for Mother's Day."

Bo shrugged. "So?"

"She bought it for *me* to give Babe. Signed my name. Had it delivered. I got the bill this morning."

"How much?"

"That's not the issue. The point is, she didn't ask me first. She just did it."

Bo cocked his head. "Babe doesn't like music boxes?"

"It's not the music box." Ren sighed. "I might have picked it out myself. It's just…" He wasn't sure he could explain why this had him so pissed off. Eve was doing what she did best—organizing.

"Let me guess. You feel as if your life is out of your hands."

Surprised by Bo's insight, Ren turned. "I wouldn't go that far. I still have control over my life—" he ignored his friend's skeptical snort "—it's just that everything is a challenge with

Eve. She has her agenda, and if you want to be involved you have to stay on schedule." *Right down to having sex,* he added silently.

Bo cuffed him lightly. "Hey, man, welcome to the real world. Eve's a modern woman. She makes good money. She's got the car, credit, connections. If you think about it, she doesn't really need you. You're…what's the word?"

"Superfluous?"

Bo snickered. "Yeah, that's what Claudie called me the other day. She said once doctors figured out how to make test-tube babies, men were about as useful as tits on a boar."

Ren leaned one shoulder against the building and squinted at Bo, who had a bemused look on his face. "What about love?"

Bo's arched look summed up his opinion on that matter.

"Well, what about family, then? Children? Continuity?"

Bo shrugged. "I said the same thing to Claudie, and she pointed to a magazine with Rosie O'Donnell on the cover. Single and just adopted her third kid. Traditional families may not be a thing of the past, but there's a lot of single parents out there doing a better job than some of the dysfunctional mom-and-pop families."

Bo rolled his shoulders and took a step away. "The point is, you're engaged to a career woman and you haven't even told her you might have a kid. Eve's a beautiful woman, but she doesn't strike me as the motherly type. Am I right?"

Ren felt himself tense. "We've talked about kids. Nothing specific, but…" He tried to recall Eve's exact words on the subject. Something to the effect of "Everybody wants kids, right? Someday. But I'd have to be at a secure place in my career. Television viewers have short attention spans and very little loyalty."

Bo began walking but stopped. "Have you asked yourself what you'd do with Brady if Eve dropped out of the picture?

I mean, Sara's a terrific single mother. Do you think you could do that well?"

Ren had wondered the same thing, and he wasn't nearly as confident as he wanted to be. "I don't know, but I had a great role model growing up, right?"

Bo's attitude softened and he smiled. "Yep, that's true. They don't come much better than Larry."

Ren's father had taken Bo under his wing at a critical time in Bo's life. If not for Larry's intervention, Bo might never have kicked the booze.

The two walked in silence until they reached the entrance of the bookstore, where a circular emblem two feet in diameter and inlaid with mosaic tiles in the shape of an open book was imbedded in the sidewalk. Ren hadn't noticed it before. "I like that."

"Sara had it put in. She thought it would be a way to lure people. She said most people walk with their heads down, and they don't see the sign overhead unless they're looking for a bookstore. The mosaic catches their attention and makes them look up."

Before Ren could comment, Bo yanked open the door and marched inside. "Lucy, I'm home," he called in a pathetic imitation of Ricky Ricardo.

Ren squared his shoulders and took a deep breath. Best-case scenario, he told himself, she won't call the police and have me arrested. Worst-case? Years of litigation, family profiles, home studies, lawyers, judges, he thought, sighing. But in all honesty, he couldn't blame Sara. Any good mother would go to great lengths to protect her child.

THE TINKLE OF THE BELL over the door seemed to set off a frenzy of activity—an anthill gone mad, Ren thought as he stepped inside. Claudie and three strangers, two men and a large, colorfully dressed black woman, were moving chairs, tables and display racks to one spot, then picking them up and moving again. In the center of this chaos stood Sara, Brady in her arms.

At least, Ren thought it was Sara, although she certainly looked different. Instead of a shapeless dress, she wore a fitted suit of silver-green with a white silk blouse, shimmering hose and black pumps. Her hair was pulled back by a woven metallic band that emphasized her high cheekbones and arched brows.

"Hi, Bo," she called, glancing over her shoulder. She acknowledged Ren with an extra widening of her eyes, but turned away when Claudie called her name.

"Where do you want this one, Sara J?"

"Over there." Sara pointed to the far wall, below a poster that read, Read Now, Before You Forget How.

"What's going on?" Bo asked, walking to her side. Ren followed, unable to keep from cataloguing the changes he saw in her. Instead of soft and demure, this was a woman who knew what she wanted and had no trouble voicing her demands.

"Move the table a little more to the left," she ordered a harried-looking gray-haired man. "The gal who called said the more spacious a place looks, the more inviting it is. We want to invite people here."

When the change was made to her apparent satisfaction, she turned to Bo and Ren. "Isn't this exciting? The camera crew should be here any minute."

Her breathless, flushed excitement made her look younger. Her enthusiasm lifted Ren's spirits, making him want to grin, even though this wasn't at all what he'd expected to find. "What camera crew?"

"*Channel Eight News.* They're doing a feature on downtown businesses." Her cheeks bloomed with color. "I told

Claudie we'll be lucky to get a sound bite—but every bite helps."

Ren's stomach turned over. "Channel Eight, huh."

She shifted Brady to her other hip. "Eve Masterson herself. It's so exciting."

Ren and Bo exchanged looks. *Exciting* was not Ren's first choice of adjective.

"Hi, Brady," Ren said, smiling at the little boy who promptly buried his face in his mother's shoulder.

"Don't be shy, honey," Sara coaxed. "Can you say hello?"

Brady shook his head. His hair was lighter than Ren's and held a faint tinge of red, but the springy waves seemed so familiar that Ren almost reached out to touch them. Before he could, however, Brady squirmed to be let down. When Sara bent over to set the little boy on his feet, Ren couldn't help noticing the way her skirt outlined her shape.

"How's that?" Claudie asked, flashing a critical look from Bo to Ren. She handed Sara something, then pointed to the wall behind the coffee bar where a slightly lopsided banner was hanging.

"Wonderful," Sara exclaimed. "Is that the last of the reading posters?"

Claudie rolled her eyes. "Lord, I hope so."

Sara gave her a light cuff on the shoulder, then sent her off in another direction. To Ren, she said, "Are you here for moral support?"

He didn't understand the question, but before he could ask, she was called to deal with another crisis. Over her shoulder she called, "You're welcome to browse, of course, but we're closing down the register until after the interview."

"Actually..." Ren stopped when he felt a warm little body attach itself to his right leg. Smiling, he looked down. Brady had wrapped both arms around Ren's thigh like a monkey. He squeezed his arms tight, making a sort of grunt-ing sound.

Ren's laugh was aborted by a low bark of agony that stopped everyone mid-stride. "Argh…" He reached for his leg just as the little boy jumped back, a satisfied smirk on his face. "He bit me!"

No one moved for a full five seconds, then Sara leapt be-tween Ren and Brady as if separating two prizefighters. "Brady," she cried, dropping to one knee. "Did you bite?"

The little boy's face immediately registered his mother's distress. Instant tears appeared at the rims of his Delft-blue eyes. His bottom lip unfurled like a flower petal. Before she could reach for him, Brady darted away and crawled under her desk.

"I am so sorry," she said, rising. "He's never done that be-fore. I can't…" She shook her head.

Ren rubbed the throbbing spot on his thigh. "Don't worry about it," he said, but a dozen thoughts clamored for attention. *Does he hate me already? Do I really want to be a father?*

Sara lightly touched his sleeve, then dashed after Brady. "He's had all his shots," she called before ducking behind the desk.

Ren looked at the other spectators. The older man picked up a Raiders cap from the counter and headed for the door. "Guess you don't need me no more, Sara. See you Wednes-day. 'Bye, Bo."

"See ya, Frank," Bo called, as the man left.

A tall, good-looking man in a white shirt rolled down his sleeves and lifted his suit coat from a chair. "Sara, love, I'm leav-ing, too, but I'll stop by after work to watch you on TV, okay?"

Sara's head popped up above the desk. "Great, Daniel. Thanks so much for everything. See ya tonight."

Ren exchanged nods with the man as he left.

Claudie finished straightening a display, then walked to

Ren. "I'd be happy to check out that bite for you if you want to take off your pants."

"No, thank you. I'll be fine."

"Honey, you *are* fine," the large black woman said, pushing Claudie aside. "My name's Keneesha. I'd give you one of my business cards but I'm out right now."

"Better not," Bo said, giving the woman a dry look. "The man's a judge."

She eyed Ren skeptically before turning to Bo. "Cookbook man, what are you doing here?" Keneesha asked.

"I asked him to come," Sara said, joining the little group. Brady was plastered to her, his head pressed against her chest. "Remember? I wanted some of the readers to be here in case Miss Masterson had time to interview any of the Unturned Gentlemen."

By the look of horror on Bo's face, Ren felt it safe to assume Bo had forgotten about that little detail.

"And Claudie, you could talk about the books you've been reading to prepare for the equivalency test," Sara told her.

"Oh, no. In fact, I just remembered something I gotta do right this minute. What about you, Kee? You wanna be on television?"

Keneesha's eyes grew big. "F—Forget that action. I'm outta here."

Sara's face fell. "Come on, don't go. I need you. I can't face that woman alone. Claudie…"

Ren turned to watch both women scurry through the door. He realized at the same instant that Bo had disappeared, as well.

Sara looked momentarily dismayed, then sighed and hugged Brady. "Oh, well, we can do this, can't we?" she whispered softly. "But first we have to apologize to Mr. Bishop." She looked at Ren, as if to confirm his name.

Ren couldn't help smiling. She looked so earnest, so fresh

and real. "Please, call me Ren. You, too, Brady, even though we haven't been formally introduced."

He tried to keep his tone light, but could tell she was embarrassed. She stepped closer and turned so Brady's face was visible. The child immediately turned his head the other way. She bent her head and said in a low voice, "Brady, you need to apologize. We don't bite. Ever. You hurt Ren and you need to say you're sorry."

The boy turned his head and looked at Ren. The child's blue eyes—a dark, almost sapphire color—were luminescent with tears. He blinked twice and rattled off a string of gibberish made more unintelligible by the wet fist he kept in his mouth.

As the long explanation continued, Ren looked from Brady to Sara—her heart plainly on view as she watched the little boy's animated apology. Sara wiped her son's tears and kissed the top of his head.

"Very nice, love," she said. "You're a very brave boy to admit when you made a mistake," she told him, then looked to Ren. "I don't suppose you got that." He shook his head, mesmerized by the connection he saw and felt between the two. "Brady said he was sorry. Your pants are nice but they don't taste good."

She smiled. "I think he wanted to touch your pants and just got carried away. I'm very sorry. We both are."

She might have said more, but at that moment the door opened and a battering ram of mobile news equipment surged inward. At the hub of the onslaught stood Eve, who scanned the interior in a three-second sweep before focusing on Ren and Sara.

Eve's beautiful face, an exotic combination of Mediterranean skin tone, English cheekbones and Indo-European eyes, lit up with surprise and pleasure. "Ren," she cried, pushing past her colleagues. "What are you doing here? Did you call and get my schedule from Gloria?" Gloria was her secretary, with whom Ren spoke quite regularly—*too* regularly.

She gave him a brief squeeze, being careful not to mess her makeup. Her trademark waist-length blue-black hair shimmered beneath the high, overhead spotlights. "Actually," he said, drawing her to one side just as a young man with an armful of electrical cords bounced by, "I came with Bo, who, it appears, has developed sudden-onset stage fright."

The noise in Ren's head had little to do with the chaos Eve and her crew had brought to the bookstore. His instinct was to take the coward's way out, just as his ex-best friend had. "Um, Eve, have you met Sara Càrsten?" he asked, taking a step back. "She's the owner of this fine establishment. The person you're here to interview."

"Hi," Sara said. "This is my son, Brady." Brady perked up with all the activity and looked around like a turtle poking his head out of a shell. "I'm afraid my baby-sitters have all disappeared. I…um…"

"No problem," Ren said, seeing his chance to melt into the background. "I'll take care of him."

He snatched Brady out of Sara's arms before she could protest. Brady looked too surprised to cry. "Don't worry, big guy. No hard feelings. Let's play."

One quick look over his shoulder as he walked to the carpeted children's area told him both women were speechless. But Ren doubted he could count on that kind of luck for long.

SARA DECIDED if anyone asked her what it was like to be interviewed by Eve Masterson, she could sum it up in one word: *smooth*. Watching a professional as experienced and polished as Eve was like watching a surgeon at work.

Sara had no trouble answering Eve's questions, except when they turned personal. When Eve asked her something

about Brady's father, Sara deflected the query without thinking. She'd answered enough probing questions after Julia's accident, when reporters were trying to make more out of the
story than was there. "I'm a single parent," Sara said, nervously manipulating the small tube of glue Claudie had
handed her.

Eve nodded, her long black hair moving like an exotic animal. "It must be quite difficult raising your son alone while
running a business. How do you do it?"

Sara wondered if she detected a hint of condescension in
the woman's tone, but for some reason Eve's attention had
shifted toward the reading area, a pensive look crossing her
brow. "Nothing in life is easy," Sara answered. "I'm lucky because I can keep my son with me while I work, and he's exposed to something I love—books. I read to him and patrons'
children whenever I can."

Eve's eyes were the darkest brown Sara had ever seen. On
television she was beautiful; up close, China-doll perfect.
When Eve gestured toward the coffee bar, Sara spotted a very
large, glittery diamond on her finger, which jogged Sara's
memory. Something about a judge.

Eve Masterson and Judge Lawrence Bishop. Of course.

Sara's small, involuntary *peep* made Eve look at her intently.
"Let's cut, fellas. I've got plenty here," she said, reaching behind her waist to remove some kind of remote microphone.
Her tailored suit, a smart black gabardine imbued with tiny
flecks of silver, would have looked severe on anyone else.

To Sara, she said, "Thank you. That was very nice. I'm particularly impressed with your reading groups. You have that
in common with my fiancé." She glanced toward the play area
where Ren and Brady sat. "Ren started a tutorial program in
juvenile hall last year."

Her words confirmed what Sara had already guessed, making her feel all the more foolish about the steamy dream she'd had last night. Sara had tried to blame it on the *Braveheart* video she'd fallen asleep watching. Somehow her dream lover had changed from Mel Gibson into Ren Bishop.

"How well do you know Ren?" Eve asked, her reporter instincts undoubtedly making her home in on Sara's attraction to Eve's fiancé.

Sara started to set the woman straight, but a rather vivid image from her dream made Sara stutter, "We don't—he just—I…" Her cheeks turned hot.

Eve's focus moved to Ren, who sat cross-legged with Brady in his lap, their heads bent over a big, colorful book. "He looks pretty cozy with your son."

He does, doesn't he, Sara thought, flinching from the twinge in her chest. To Eve, she said candidly, "That's probably because Brady bit him. Must be a guy thing."

As if sensing their observation, Ren looked up. Oddly, his gaze went to Sara first. His smile seemed ingenuous and a little worried. Sara's heart reacted in the strangest way, making her clasp the tube of glue to her breast defensively.

Eve started toward him but was waylaid by a tall man in a turban of dreadlocks. "Sorry, Eve, but we gotta run if you want this by six," he said, taking her arm.

Eve seemed torn. With a sigh, she called to Ren, "My place? Tonight?"

He nodded solemnly.

She blew him an air kiss then dashed away. "Thank you, Sara. It was…enlightening."

Bemused, Sara watched the door close. "Enlightening?" she repeated to herself, slipping the glue stick into the pocket of her jacket. Before she could decide whether to ask Ren what his fiancée had meant, the bell over the door tinkled. Three people strolled in, trying to look nonchalant.

Only Keneesha managed to pull it off. She parked her rather large bottom on the corner of Sara's desk and said, "How'd it go?"

Bo and Claudie mumbled some kind of apology as they walked past Sara.

Sara put her hands on her hips and made a clucking sound. "Cowards," she teased. "I don't know what I'd have done if Ren hadn't entertained Brady." She shuddered in mock horror.

They stumbled over each other's excuses and apologies until Ren interrupted them. "If you're back for good, I'd like to borrow Sara a moment."

He passed Brady—who seemed totally at ease in Ren's arms—to Keneesha, then looked at Bo and asked, "Can the three of you manage the store for a few minutes?"

The seriousness of his tone made Sara's stomach turn over. "What's going on? Is something wrong?" Dire thoughts of lawsuits and legal horrors filled her head. Her panic must have shown on her face, because Bo leaned over and touched her shoulder. "It's okay, Sara. You can trust him."

That oblique endorsement puzzled her so much that Sara almost missed the fact Ren had taken her elbow and was escorting her toward the exit. When he let go to open the door, she balked. "Wait. This is crazy. I barely know you. Where are you taking me? I don't care what you do for a living— you can't just kidnap a person."

He tilted his head in a gentle, reassuring way. "I'll explain everything in a minute. I just don't want an audience."

Behind her, Sara heard Bo placating Claudie and Keneesha, who sounded poised for pursuit. "Stay calm, ladies. He won't hurt her."

With a quick glance over her shoulder, Sara made up her mind. She shoved her hands in the pockets of her jacket to keep them from trembling. "Okay," she said, walking past him. "But I'm warning you—I have pepper spray." She thrust the tube of glue against the silk fabric of her jacket pocket.

He closed the door carefully. "Really?" His brows scrunched together in a judge-like manner that pumped endorphins into Sara's system. "Can I see it?"

Her mouth went dry. "No."

"You know it's against the law to carry a concealed weapon. You'd be better off cooperating." His tone sounded teasing, but his words took her back to one of the bleakest moments of her life. The officer who'd arrested her had said the same thing, and, being young and naive, she'd believed him.

Angry beyond reason, she jerked the small tube from her pocket and waved it in his face. "There—glue. I lied. Are you satisfied? You've made your point. I was feeling intimidated, and I bolstered my confidence by pretending to be able to defend myself, which we both know is a joke since you are the long arm of the law and I'm just a person who…"

Ren's stunned look took some of the fuel out of her fire. "I was only kidding," he said in a soft, even voice. "I'm sorry I upset you."

Sara's mortification grew when she glanced behind him to the three curious faces in the storefront. Blowing out a long sigh, she shook her head. "No, I'm sorry. That was nuts. I'm a little stressed. What did you want to talk to me about?"

"Could we go to the park?" He gave her an encouraging smile. "I promise not to mug you."

She nodded, trying to smile. He probably thought she was a lunatic, but she'd been edgy ever since Claudie's suggestion that something might happen to Brady.

They didn't speak until they reached Cesar Chavez Park. "Can we sit?" he asked, pointing to an empty bench. The grass was littered with gum wrappers and cigarette butts. The quiet of the deserted inner square was outlined by the buzz-ing traffic that surrounded it.

Sara smoothed her silk skirt primly across her knees, then stiffened her spine and said, "I'd like to think you're about to tell me some long-lost relative died and left me a million bucks, but that frown tells me this isn't good news. Why don't you just get it over with? My sister used to make me take cough syrup by telling me 'What's the worst that can happen? You throw up.' So, tell me quick in case I have to barf."

The smile that tugged up the corners of his lips eased some of Sara's fear for a second, until he said, "Sara, I knew your sister."

It wasn't what she was expecting, either the words or the tone, which sounded like a confession. "You knew Julia?"

He nodded hesitantly.

"You don't seem too sure about that."

He blew out a sigh and hunched forward. "I did. And I didn't. Maybe the most diplomatic way of putting this is that I knew her in the biblical sense."

The starchy, formal words sounded ridiculous. But a sudden, piercing image of Julia and Ren together made Sara's stomach heave. Maybe she'd throw up, after all.

"I…don't understand why you're telling me this. You know she's dead, right?"

He nodded. "I just learned of her…accident. Bo has been looking for her for two years."

"Bo? What's Bo got to do with Julia? Are you working for the insurance company?" She'd dealt with a series of inves-tigators after the accident, and it wasn't an experience she cared to repeat.

He crossed his legs and leaned closer. The breeze sent a whiff of his cologne her way. An expensive, intimidating scent. Sara's breathing sped up.

"Bo's my friend," Ren said, "but he's also a private investigator. I hired him to find your sister."

"Find her? What do you mean? She lived here practically all her life."

"I know that now. Bo did a complete background check, but at the time I didn't know her name."

Questions popped into her head too fast to ask. Julia had never mentioned knowing a judge. "Why were you looking for her?"

"Primarily to make sure there weren't any surprises if I ran for public office. You know—blackmail?"

Blackmail? Julia? "Are you saying you and Julia had an affair and you were afraid Julia would use that against you? For money? Are you crazy?" Sara cried, half rising to her feet. "Julia would never have done something like that. She valued her privacy more than anything. And she and Hulger had more money than God. It's ludicrous. Why would you think it?"

He shook his head; he didn't meet her gaze. "I didn't know her. I didn't know what she was like. We spent one night together. We didn't talk much."

At least he had the grace to sound embarrassed, Sara thought, sitting back down. But that was small succor for her outrage on Julia's behalf. "Why are you telling me this? Why do I have to know if Julia had an affair? She wasn't perfect, but she was my sister and I loved her." Tears began to gather in her eyes. "She's dead. Isn't that punishment enough for her sins?"

Ren started to put out his hand to touch her, but let it drop to the bench. He swallowed and looked so serious that Sara's blood started racing, making it hard to hear his words. "There's a chance I might be Brady's father."

The words barely made it into her consciousness before she was up and running. *I have to get my baby. We have to run. As far away as possible.*

"Sara, please, wait."

"No. Go away. I don't want to hear this."

He put his hand on her shoulder. "You have to."

She shrugged it off and tried to run, but her new shoes tripped her up. She stumbled, then recovered her balance before he could help her. "I don't believe you. I don't know why you're doing this, but it's not true."

When she started off again, he dashed into her path and held out his arms like a scarecrow to keep her from going around him. "Why would I do that? Invite scandal into my life? This is a political town and I have a political job. Why would I go out of my way to make trouble for myself?"

Her gaze darted to a figure atop a sorrel horse at the far end of the park. She sometimes brought Brady to this park when the Farmer's Market was in session, just to see the mounted police. Maybe, for once, the police would be her ally. She started to hail him, but the sun's glint on the man's badge stopped her. *Fool,* she silently castigated herself. *Ren's a judge. They play for the same team.*

Drawing on strength she didn't know she possessed, Sara took a deep breath. "I don't know you. Apparently, I don't know Bo. In fact, it seems as though there's some kind of conspiracy going on here."

Ren dropped his arms. "It's not a conspiracy, Sara. After I found out about Julia's death and Brady's birth, I asked Bo to check you out. See what kind of mother you are. What kind of life Brady has."

Sara's anger surged. "And what? The two of you decided I wasn't good enough to be Brady's mother? That I'm not providing the kind of life a judge could provide? So you thought you'd just drop in and take over?"

He ran a hand through his hair, sending it tumbling across his brow. "No. Of course not. You're—"

Sara didn't let him finish. She knew all about empty promises and kind-sounding lawyers. "I don't know what you want from me, but let me tell you something. If you're after custody of Brady—a child you'd never even seen until last week, you'll have a long and difficult fight. He's *my* son. Julia gave him to me." She pushed past him, praying she could make it to the bookstore before her tears started.

CHAPTER FIVE

"SO WHAT'D HE SAY after that?" Keneesha asked.

Sara rested her elbows on her desk and cradled her throbbing head in her hands. She'd been over the whole scene a dozen times, at least, but her friends seemed incapable of grasping the idea that she might wind up losing Brady. Her baby. Yes, he was Julia's son, but Sara had been in that delivery room, too. She'd held him moments after his first cry. How could she possibly give him up to a stranger who showed up on her doorstep?

"After what?" Sara asked, drawing on all the patience she could muster.

"You asked him if you should be talking to a lawyer instead of him and he told you what?"

Sara looked at the playpen where Brady was sleeping—completely spent after missing his nap. "He said that until they did a DNA test this was just supposition. It might just be a coincidence."

Keneesha nodded with passion. "Yeah, that could be. Maybe Brady was premature."

Sara rocked back in her chair, picturing the squalling, eight-pound ten-ounce baby boy who'd peed all over the front of Hulger's surgical gown before the nurses could wrap him up. "Nope. Full term," she said, closing her eyes.

"At the moment all Bishop is asking for is a blood test, right?" Daniel asked.

"DNA. He says it's a simple procedure. No needles. You know how much Brady hates needles." Just saying Brady's name made her eyes fill with tears.

"I say we take him out," Claudie snarled, smacking a bookshelf with the heel of her hand.

Keneesha, who was perched on a plastic chair, jumped up. "I know a guy. Just got out of prison. He's a mean mother. He'd do him cheap."

Daniel stopped pacing long enough to ask, "How cheap?"

Sara surged to her feet. "Cut it out. We're not 'doing' him, no matter how cheap." Then she voiced her worst fear: "What if he *is* Brady's father?"

"Girl, don't even think it," Keneesha groaned. "Maybe this is some kind of scam. Rich people are weird—they do crazy things."

Sara didn't waste her breath arguing that they didn't know enough about Ren Bishop to gauge either his finances or his possible motives. From Daniel's quick, superficial scan of the Internet—Sara was too shaky to type—they'd learned about Ren's prison literacy program; his victory on behalf of the salmon; his appointment to the bench in the wake of his father's death. Each entry confirmed Sara's worst fear—he was for real.

The front door opened. Instinctively Sara tensed, ready to grab Brady and run. She sank back into her chair when she saw Bo walk forward, a rumpled white handkerchief extended in supplication. "Don't hurt me, please. I know I'm scum, but I have a low threshold for pain."

"Yeah, you're a man. Tell me something I don't know," Claudie snarled.

Sara looked down. She liked Bo, and it hurt to think he'd befriended her only to spy on her. When he started toward her, she spun her chair the other way. "Go away, Bo. You don't belong here."

"Yeah, Rat Boy, we exterminate rats around here," Keneesha muttered, stepping in his path.

"It was my job," he said gruffly, his voice loud enough for Sara to hear. "Sometimes I wish I'd paid more attention in college, but at the moment this is what I do. And yeah, at times it sucks. Surely you can understand that?"

Sara swiveled back around in time to see Keneesha stand aside. Bo walked straight to Sara. "I'm sorry, Sara. I mean it. I wouldn't have followed through on this if I didn't think it was the right thing to do, but maybe we went about it the wrong way. I know you don't trust me, but I want to help."

Daniel made a hooting sound. "How? Like you did by hacking confidential medical records?"

Bo frowned but his focus didn't waiver. "Sara, I tried talking Ren out of pursuing it, but he convinced me the coincidence was just too great. He did sleep with your sister, she did give birth nine months later. Can you really blame him for wanting to know?"

Sara covered her ears with her hands. If Julia had been there, she'd have laughed at the futile, childish response. Julia always told her, *You can't hide from reality, Sara girl. Mom's a drunk. Pretending it isn't so won't make her sober.*

"Human gestation is not exact," Daniel said.

Bo nodded. "That's what I told Ren, and he agreed, but you gotta admit he's in the ballpark." He looked at Claudie and said, "Not to be crude, but either she was pregnant when she went to Tahoe, or she got knocked up as soon as she went home, or one of the rubbers sprang a leak. Unless you know something I don't, those appear to be the options."

All eyes turned to Sara, who waved her hand in a gesture of futility. "Julia never talked about her sex life. Not to me, anyway."

Bo placed both hands flat on the desk and looked at Sara.

"Ren's not doing this on a whim, Sara. He's an honorable man. Responsible. He has to know one way or the other, even if it means bad publicity that might adversely affect his career."

Keneesha elbowed Bo out of the way so she could rest her butt against the desk. "So what? Are we supposed to feel sorry for him?"

"Hell, no. Although I do. I hate to think what his fiancée's going to do to him when she finds out."

Over Claudie's boisterous vote for castration, Sara asked, "He hasn't told her?"

"He wanted to talk to you first—but he's there now."

Sara wondered how the intensely focused woman who'd been in her store this afternoon would handle the news.

"They weren't actually dating when Ren…you know, but I don't think that little detail's gonna help his case," Bo added.

Keneesha snorted. "Well, he should have thought of that before he knocked her up."

Sara flinched. "We don't know that, Kee. This is exactly what Ren warned me not to do—get too far ahead of this thing. All we know for sure is that he and Brady are both Type *O,* and that's a pretty common blood type."

Daniel walked around the desk and squatted beside her chair. He put an arm around her shoulders. "We can fight this, Sara. Jenny knows a lot of lawyers. We'll find one who specializes in custody cases. Even if it turns out he is—"

Claudie pushed him away. "Don't say another word with Mr. Big Ears here."

Bo rolled his eyes. "Don't you get it? I want to help. I can, too. I've known Ren for years. I know how he thinks."

Claudie walked up to him and poked her finger at his chest. "You're a man. You think the same way. That's why we can't trust you."

Daniel hastily moved to separate them. "Hey, watch it. I'm a man."

"Couldn't prove it by me," Keneesha chimed in.

While the four argued, Sara put her head in her hands. She didn't want to think of Ren Bishop as the enemy. Even while he'd been telling her the most potentially devastating news she could imagine, he'd remained kind and gentle, almost apologetic. "I don't want to hurt you, Sara," he'd told her, when he'd caught up to her half a block from the bookstore. "I know what a great mother you are because Brady's a terrific kid. Smart. Independent. Good strong teeth." His lopsided grin—so Brady-like—had sent a shiver of fear down her back.

When she'd threatened to get a lawyer, he'd sighed and said, "I can recommend several, but I wish you'd consider getting the results from the DNA test before we call in the artillery."

Sara's antipathy toward lawyers ran just about as deep as her distrust of judges.

"What would you have me do, Sara? Walk away and pretend it didn't happen?" he'd asked. His tone made her stop and look at him. She probably shouldn't have, though, because his earnestness moved her in a way she didn't want to acknowledge.

"What if he's not your son?"

"What if he is?"

The question had echoed through her head with every pulse beat as she hurried toward the bookstore. He'd stopped her again before she could flee inside. "I have to know, Sara. There's no way I could go through life without acknowledging my son. Never being a part of his life. Never holding him, watching him grow up. I couldn't live with myself if I just walked away."

Sara knew Ren had no idea how his plea touched her heart. Even if Bo had given him every single piece of information available about her, Ren couldn't have guessed how not having a father had shaped her life. No one, not even Julia, knew how badly Sara had craved a father when she was growing up. In a way, Hank Dupertis had become a surrogate father in her teens, but that didn't make up for all the years without a dad.

Keneesha's voice brought Sara back to the present.

"If you want to help so bad," she told Bo, "then tell us where he lives. I've got some payback in mind."

Bo snagged a pen off the desk and, with a flourish, scribbled a few lines on the back of an envelope. He held it up for all to see as he read the address and phone number aloud. "It's only about a mile from here. I'll lead the way if you want. He should be home by the time we get there. But if he's not, there's a spare key under the flowerpot by the front door."

"Yeah, let's do it," Keneesha cried.

"Is this a trick? Are you telling me he doesn't have a fancy alarm system?" Claudie asked suspiciously.

"Most times he doesn't bother setting it," Bo replied. "Let's go."

Sara shook her head. "Absolutely not. No violence. I still have friends back East. Brady and I could go—"

Claudie nodded. "I'll go with you. We could leave tonight."

Bo groaned. "Don't even think it, Sara. Trust me, running away doesn't solve anything. I've met people in the FBI witness relocation program. It's a terrible way to live—always looking over your shoulder."

Sara knew he was right. This wasn't something she could run from. "I'll call the estate lawyer first thing Monday. If he won't handle it, then I'll find somebody who will. Right now, Brady and I are going home. I'm shot."

With four extra sets of hands, the transition of closing up the shop and moving Brady to his car seat went smoothly. It was only when she started to get into the car that Daniel said, "Sara, we forgot to turn on the television. We didn't get to see you on the news."

Sara's laugh sounded harsh to her ears. "That seemed kinda important for a few minutes, didn't it?"

Claudie sighed. "I doubt if Sara got much on-screen time, anyway. I have a feeling Eve Masterson wasn't too thrilled to see her boyfriend hanging out at a bookstore with a kid who has the same big blue eyes."

At the group's sudden silence, Claudie slapped her hand over her mouth and whimpered. Sara touched her shoulder. "It's okay. It's the truth." She said her goodbyes and left.

Before she'd gone three blocks, her hands were trembling on the steering wheel and tears obscured her vision. She hastily pulled over, giving in to her emotions. Fear. Anger. A sense of impending loss. "It's just not fair," she cried. Ren's resources and connections seemed limitless. How could she fight that kind of power? How could she not at least try with all her might?

Wiping her tears with her hands, she put the car in gear and stepped on the gas. Recalling Bo's directions, she turned the steering wheel sharply at the next intersection, barely acknowledging the red light.

Sara had one stop to make. She knew she'd never be able to sleep tonight without letting Ren Bishop know that where Brady was concerned, the judge was in for the fight of his life.

"IT HAPPENED BEFORE we started dating, Eve," Ren said for the third time. For some reason his infidelity, not the child's paternity, seemed to be the focus of Eve's anger. "I haven't been with another woman since we started going out, and certainly not since we got engaged. What kind of man do you think I am?"

Eve, who'd kicked off her shoes and dumped her suit jacket on the sofa the minute she'd walked into her condo, marched across the white-on-white living room like a Polynesian princess, black eyes ablaze with indignation. "I know what kind of man I *thought* you were, but now I'm not so sure. Tell me, Ren, what kind of man sleeps with a stranger in this day and age? STDs and AIDS aside, have you forgotten about Frank Gifford and the hooker? Or Bill Clinton, for that matter? It's called scandal, Ren, and you can't afford it. No one in public office can."

Ren, who'd been watching for her car from the large, arched window that afforded a view of the condominium's tastefully landscaped parking lot, lowered the mini-blinds. His private life would go on display soon enough without giving the neighbors a ringside seat. "I wasn't in public office at the time," he told her, trying to be patient. Eve was flash and sizzle; she blew up easily but didn't stay angry for long. "I'd just won the salmon verdict. You know what the climate was like—you were one of the reporters dogging me." At her indignant pout, he added, "I'd won one for the planet. I wanted to celebrate but I couldn't walk outside without half a dozen reporters in my face."

Her eyes narrowed. "Are you trying to blame your peccadillo on the media?"

"No," he cried, exasperated. "I'm explaining my mental state at the time. I went to Tahoe to get away, and maybe live it up a little."

"By having sex with a stranger."

Ren gave up trying to make her understand. He certainly didn't blame her for being mad, but he had hoped to be able to reason with her.

"So tell me again where the pretty little shopkeeper comes in? A *ménuge à trois,* perhaps?" she asked snidely.

Ren was floored by Eve's hostility toward Sara. "Sara is Julia's sister. We've never had sex," he said, perhaps a bit more loudly than was necessary. "Brady is Sara's nephew."

"She called him her son."

"Julia died—Sara's his legal guardian."

Eve turned away, but not before Ren caught the quiver of her chin, a brief glimpse of vulnerability. Eve had been adopted at birth. And while she publicly celebrated her undefined ethnic heritage, she occasionally admitted harboring doubts about her lineage.

Standing in front of her antique oriental bureau, she fiddled with a flower arrangement a moment before turning to look at him. "I saw you staring at her while I was doing the interview."

Ren walked to the bar that separated the dining area from the living room. He poured himself a second glass of Merlot and downed a big gulp. Without looking at her, he said, "I may have looked at Sara, but I didn't stare." *Liar.* In fact, he'd been mesmerized by the poise and candor she'd displayed. "I was curious. All I know about her is what Bo's been able to dig up, which isn't much. She's raising a child that could be mine—I need to know what she's like."

Eve walked over to him and put her arms around his waist. "So you say. Maybe you even believe it. But a woman senses things, Ren. There was something between the two of you. Why do you think I assumed right away that you were the father of her baby?"

Ren remained rigid. He refused to believe she'd seen anything. Besides, he wasn't interested in Sara. Except where Brady was concerned.

Her soft sigh penetrated through the cloth of his suit and shirt. He set down his glass, then put his arms around her. "I'm sorry, Eve. I never meant for any of this to happen."

The top of her head came to the middle of his chest. She didn't look up. "I know, Ren. In spite of what I said earlier, you are a good man. I'm sure you used precautions, and if that little boy is yours, it's purely by accident. But…" He felt her take a deep breath. "I have to say, the timing really sucks."

"You mean there's actually a good time for something like this to happen?"

She looked up, gave him a half smile and then walked to the sofa where she opened her briefcase. From the upper compartment she withdrew a sheet of paper. "Marcella faxed this to me today. I was hoping we'd be celebrating tonight."

"What is it?"

"My proposed itinerary for next week. She's already got two interviews scheduled—ABC and CNN. She expects the others to get interested after she stirs up a little buzz."

Ren knew how important this was. For all her outward confidence, Eve needed constant reinforcement and success to validate her self-worth.

He moved to the sofa and sat down, drawing her into the chair across from him. "You have to go to New York, Eve, and I have to stay here and take care of this."

She lifted her chin proudly, as if defying tears to come. "I'd hoped you could go with me. See a few shows. Shop. I'd even go to a museum or two if you insisted."

Her attempt at humor made him smile, but only for a second. "I can't put this off, Eve. I need to know. If Brady is my son, I'll probably have to go to court for custody. I'm sure Sara won't give him up without a fight."

Her bottom lip trembled. "Do you have any idea how damaging that will be to your career?" He lifted one shoulder carelessly, which made her scowl. "Then think about what it'll do to *my* career. There's bound to be spillage."

"'Spillage'?"

She looked at her lap. "This is going to sound terribly self-absorbed, but it's the truth. If there's bad publicity, it'll spill over on me, too, and I can't afford that right now, Ren. I'm going into these negotiations with a blemish-free life—former Junior Miss, a popular radio personality who became an award-winning television anchor, a model citizen engaged to a judge. What happens if word of this gets back to the networks?"

Ren's heart felt pinched. A prickly sensation buzzed in his sinuses. The pathos of his being dumped for a spot on *Good Morning, America* would make Bo fall down laughing.

"So, you want to call off the engagement," he said gruffly.

"No," Eve exclaimed, taking his hands. "God, no. Not yet, anyway. You said yourself this might all be a false alarm. Get the test done. Then we'll talk." She tilted her head, looking into his eyes imploringly. "Just try to keep it quiet."

Ren studied her a long moment. In his heart he knew their relationship was doomed, and it had nothing to do with Brady. Maybe they were both too self-absorbed to make it work.

Eve squeezed his hands and in a soft voice said, "We have something good here, Ren. I honestly hope things work out okay. No baby, no problem. Right?"

"Right," he said, a sour taste in his mouth. "I'll call you tomorrow."

She let go of his hands and sat back as if surprised. "You don't want to stay? I taped our six o'clock show. You could see your friend Sara."

He rose to leave. The muscles in his neck felt as though they might squeeze tight enough to pop his head off. "I'd better go. I still have to break this news to my mother."

"Oh, God," Eve said, adding a low moan of sympathy. She walked him to the door. "I don't know who to feel more sorry for, you or Babe. She isn't going to be happy. We were supposed to meet for brunch tomorrow to set a date for the wedding. I don't think we dare do that until we know if there's going to be a paternity suit."

When Ren didn't say anything, she sighed and said, "Don't

worry, honey. It'll work out. When Marcella was here she told me about her fabulous spin doctors. These guys are publicity magicians. If it turns out he is your child, I'm sure they'll find a way to make it look like you were the victim."

When she rose up on her toes to kiss him goodbye, Ren stopped her. Instead, he gently brushed her cheek with the backs of his fingers. "I'll call you tomorrow," he said and left, never looking back.

"HOW THE HECK LONG does it take to tell your girlfriend you might have a kid from an illicit affair?" Sara muttered under her breath, pounding the steering wheel with the heel of her hand.

The inanity of her question struck her after the fact and made her shake her head. She didn't know the first thing about Ren Bishop or Eve Masterson. Maybe he could persuade her it was a huge mistake that he regretted with all his heart. Maybe she loved him so much she could forgive him, and they were, at this very moment, making mad passionate love.

For some reason, the idea made her stomach heave. She knew she should go home but she'd waited too long. The bottle of warm diet soda Keneesha had left in her car, which Sara had finished half an hour earlier, was causing all sorts of discomfort in her bladder.

Squeezing her legs together, Sara sat up straighter and looked around. The neighborhood sported wide streets, gracious front yards and mature trees that bespoke a slower period when wealthy people grouped together to outdo each other face-to-face instead of on half-acre lots in the suburbs. Ren's house—by no means the most luxurious on the block—fell into what Sara believed was called the neoclassical revival period of architecture.

A spasm of discomfort made her groan. I need a bathroom, she thought, and quick. A pair of headlights brought a flash of hope. *Ren?* The car slowed, but a reflection off its bank of patrol car lights made Sara sink down in her seat—not a good position for her bladder.

When the car was gone, Sara opened the door. *If I have to choose between unlawful entry and indecent exposure, I'll take my chances with Ren.*

She tucked her purse under her arm and, with nonchalance borne of desperation, walked to the house. Two decorative coach lights illuminated the wide, covered porch. She pretended to drop her purse, spilling out Brady's crayons like Pick-Up-Stix. While kneeling to retrieve them, she peeked under the smallest flowerpot to the right of the ornately carved door. To her relief, a single brass key was, indeed, where Bo had said it would be. She snatched it up and, as casually as possible, strolled back to the car.

Brady made a few soft protests when she picked him up. But he was a sound sleeper and dropped his head back to her shoulder as she carried him up the brick walkway. The key fit. The door opened. And Sara, who'd been holding her breath expecting some kind of alarm to sound, let out a sigh of relief. "Bo was right."

With the aid of the hallway light, which was already on, Sara was able to see into the room to her left—a large, very masculine-looking office. A handsome leather tufted sofa occupied the wall closest to the door. She slipped inside and lowered Brady to the cushions. He stirred but didn't wake. Just to be safe, she whispered, "Stay right here, honey. Mommy needs to find a potty."

She dashed into the foyer and turned at the foot of the L-shaped staircase. "There has to be a guest bath down here somewhere," she muttered. She got lucky. First door to the right. A charming little room with an illuminated seashell above the porcelain basin, so she didn't have to turn on the overhead light.

She peed, flushed and washed her hands in record time. Hurrying back to the office, she had herself convinced she could return Brady to his car seat, re-hide the key and be on her way with no one the wiser. Her daydream dissolved the moment she stepped into the office and spotted an empty sofa.

"Brady?" she called, her voice betraying her panic. She turned on a bank of lights just inside the doorway, momentarily taken aback by the formal elegance of the room, with its rosewood paneling, leaded glass bow window and massive antique desk that cried money.

Sara checked behind the heavy velvet curtains and under the waist-high globe stand. "Brady, honey? We don't have time to play. Where are you, sweetheart?"

"Sara?" a puzzled-sounding voice asked.

She spun around, instantly registering the policeman at Ren's side. "Don't just stand there," she cried, torn between utter mortification and fear. "Find Brady before he breaks something."

He dumped his coat and briefcase on the sofa and motioned her to follow. At the base of the staircase, he said, "You check down here, we'll go up."

Sara's heart was in her throat as she dashed toward the back of the house. Unless a house was equipped with childproof latches, a kitchen was a dangerous playground. As she paused to flick on the light in the drab, unattractive dining room, she heard Ren tell the policeman, "He's eighteen months old, and he loves to hide."

For some reason, Ren's calm demeanor helped stave off Sara's panic, particularly when she zipped around the showy, red-and-white kitchen without encountering the toddler. She noticed a fenced-in pool with the gate standing open in the well-manicured backyard, but the sliding door to the patio was securely locked. "Brady?" she called, checking the pantry. "Where are you, sweetie?"

In the distance, she heard Ren's voice. "Sara, I found him."

Relief—with a measure of hysteria—drove her toward the sound. She grabbed the solid walnut newel at the base of the stairs and hurried toward the muffled voices on the second floor. Ren and the officer met her at the landing where the staircase turned to the right.

"Where is he?" she cried.

"Sound asleep on my bed," Ren said, subtly positioning his body to keep her from moving past. "He's okay. I covered him up."

"Did you forget to reset the alarm when you came in, ma'am?' the policeman asked her.

"A-alarm?" Sara grabbed the banister for support. "Uh…"

"It's a new unit, Officer Rivaldi," Ren said, coming to her rescue. "Sara doesn't have it down pat, yet. Half the time I forget to set it myself. We'll go over it again as soon as you leave. Judge's honor."

The cop laughed and trotted down the stairs. "Better safe than sorry. Had a burglary right down the street last month, you know."

Although Sara's instincts told her to snatch Brady and run, she sensed Ren was waiting for her to descend the staircase. Reluctantly she turned and slowly trudged downward, Ren right behind her.

When they reached the tiled floor, Ren leaned past her to shake the officer's hand. His torso bumped her shoulder, making her flinch.

"Thanks again. Sorry to have bothered you."

The man touched two fingers to the brim of his hat. "No problem. Have a good evening."

Ren walked him to the door and closed it securely. When he turned to face her, he nodded toward a discreet white box on the wall. "Alarm," he said, his voice kind and slightly amused.

Sara suddenly felt a little light-headed, and her knees started to give out. She sank down on the bottom step and covered her face with her hands. "I can't believe this happened. You must think I'm some kind of nut." She looked up, fighting tears. "I just needed to use your bathroom."

Ren, who'd hurried to her side as if fearful she might faint, burst out laughing. "My bathroom?"

She couldn't bring herself to meet his eyes as she tried to explain. "I came here to talk to you. I waited as long as I could, but you took so long and I had to go to the bathroom, then Brady…"

Taking a deep breath to stop her rambling, she pushed off from the step and lifted her chin. "Where *is* Brady? We need to go home."

Ren graciously held out his hand, indicating she should go up the stairs ahead of him. "Do you mind telling me how you got in?" he asked.

Sara watched her feet to keep him from seeing her blush. "No, I just gambled that you might hide a key under the mat out front. Lucky me, there it was," she said, unable to keep the sarcasm from her tone.

Ren's low chuckle made her stagger slightly. "A key. Hmm…next time I'll have the person who put the key there leave operating instructions for the alarm with it."

Ren was being very understanding about this fiasco. An unpleasant thought crossed Sara's mind. If he planned to use mental instability as an argument against her in the future, she was certainly giving him fuel.

At the top of the *U*-shaped landing, Sara paused, her gaze drawn to a collection of framed photographs on the wall. Unconsciously, she studied the faces, searching for familiar features—and hoping she wouldn't find any. A black-and-white snapshot in a silver frame showed a tall man and a little boy walking hand in hand down a boat dock. Except for the clothing and unfamiliar background, the shot could have been of Ren and Brady.

"Me and my dad," Ren said, noticing her interest. "Our family has a cabin up at Lake Almanor. That's up near Mt. Lassen."

Sara thought she detected a slight wistfulness in his tone. "You resemble your dad," she said.

Ren stared at the picture a moment longer. "He died about two years ago. I miss him a lot—he was a good man."

As if embarrassed suddenly, he turned sharply and led the way down the hall to the left. The double doors were open and a bedside lamp gave off a low, comforting glow. Brady's tiny body beneath an emerald-green cashmere throw barely made a bump in the king-size bed.

Ren stood to one side to let her walk past him. Sara liked the room at once. Although both masculine and functional, right down to the NordicTrack facing the balcony, the color scheme of navy, emerald and plum was warm and inviting.

"I wonder what made him come all the way up here?" Ren whispered. The intimate sound made gooseflesh cascade down Sara's neck.

"Brady loves stairs. Our house is a one-story, so anytime he has the chance he goes for the stairs." Sara walked to the bed and sat down beside her son. She brushed a stray curl from his forehead. "Naturally," she said softly, "he scares the heck out of me every time he starts climbing, but I guess he's got to learn."

Ren approached but didn't crowd her. She looked at him. He might be a judge and a lawyer, and he might hold her future in his hands, but he'd been amazingly decent about finding her in his house. She smiled.

In an instant something changed. His eyes narrowed as if

he didn't recognize her—or maybe he recognized something in her she couldn't hide. He closed the distance between them. The lamplight cast his face into relief. His eyes—Brady's eyes—looked more black than blue as they stared at her.

Hesitantly, he extended his hand, bringing the palm to her face, cupping her cheek and jaw. Sara tried to make herself move away, but there was something so warm, so nurturing in his touch that she tilted her head against his palm. The scent of warm skin mingled with a trace of cologne from his bed—a scent she'd noticed from that first evening when he'd lifted Brady from her arms.

The instant Sara sensed him moving closer, she pulled back in panic. His eyes were hooded, his lips slightly parted. Sara knew he intended to kiss her. She couldn't let that happen. She couldn't...

Ren's hand gently tilted her chin. His head lowered, lips touching hers. Not tentatively, as she expected, but squarely, as if returning to a familiar book at the exact place he'd left off. Despite her prudent mind crying otherwise, Sara closed her eyes and absorbed the feel of his soft, persuasive warmth. His fingers stroked the lobe of her ear, the side of her neck. She liked his touch, his kiss.

Where it might have led, Sara didn't dare guess. Fortunately, a ringing sound in the distance brought her back to her senses. She pulled away. "Your phone is ringing," she said, grateful to find her voice still functioning, since her mind obviously wasn't.

Ren eyed the silent cordless phone beside his bed skeptically, then tapped his forehead. "I turned off the ringer the other day." He cocked his head to listen. Below them an angry woman's voice was blaring from an answering machine. "Lawrence, are you there? Pick up the phone."

CHAPTER SIX

REN SNATCHED UP the portable receiver and walked to the glass door that opened to his private deck. *I kissed Sara.* "I'm here, Mother. Just walked in the door. Can I call you back? I'm kinda busy at the moment."

An angry huffing sound foretold Babe's frame of mind. "Don't you dare hang up on me. I want to know what's going on with your health. Good Lord, Lawrence, are you ill? How serious is it?"

Ren leaned his forehead against the cool glass. *Why? Why did I kiss her? As if this damn thing isn't complicated enough!* "Mother, I'm fine. Can we talk about this tomorrow?"

"No," Babe shrieked. "I just spoke with Eve, and she was very upset. She said we couldn't set a date for your wedding until you cleared it with your doctor. What does that mean, Lawrence?"

Ren blew out a long sigh that left a foggy mark on the glass. Behind him, he heard Sara moving about. He turned and saw her carefully folding the blanket he'd used to cover Brady. "I feel great, Mom, really. Believe me, there's nothing wrong with my health." *My mind is a little screwed up, but...* He tuned out his mother's reply when he saw Sara bend over to pick up Brady. The image caught him mid-chest, and he felt a sudden, unreasonable urge to wrap them both in his arms and beg Sara to stay.

He covered the receiver. "Wait. Please. We need to talk."

"Are you listening to me?" his mother wailed.

Ren held the phone back a few inches. "Along with all the neighbors," he told her.

The sympathetic look in Sara's eyes made him smile. A mistake. She suddenly hefted Brady to her shoulder and turned away. He followed as she walked toward the door. "Please wait."

His mother let out a cry of frustration. "Lawrence, are you listening to me? Is someone there? Is it Bo? It's Bo, isn't it. I should have known."

Ren looked to the ceiling. "No, Mother, it's not Bo. But I do have company and I have to go. I'll tell you everything tomorrow. Lunch at Fats?" he asked, naming her favorite restaurant.

"Well, all right. One o'clock. Don't be late." The moment she hung up, Ren pitched the phone toward his bed and raced after Sara. He had no idea what to say, but he needed to make amends. He knew she didn't trust him, had little reason to like him and was fearful of his motives. What that unplanned, unprovoked kiss was all about, he didn't have a clue, but he had to make her understand he wasn't some sort of lunatic who made a habit of lusting after women he barely knew. Jeez, first her sister, now Sara.

You are an idiot, Bishop, he silently groaned.

SARA REPOSITIONED BRADY against her shoulder before starting down the stairs. She'd stayed in the bedroom as long as she could, but the shrill sound of his mother's voice—just the tone and pitch were enough to produce an unpleasant sensation in her gut—had made her snatch up Brady.

Sara's mother had died the summer after Sara graduated from high school. Audra Carsten had been a dynamic personality, even when she was reduced to tugging around oxygen.

Sara remembered her as the kind of mother who could be loving and concerned one moment, raging and cruel the next—depending on her level of intoxication. Angry voices brought back memories Sara went out of her way to avoid.

When Ren had noticed her leaving, he'd quickly moved from the window and mouthed *Wait.*

Focusing on his lips had been even more unnerving than the sound of his mother's anger. *He kissed me. I let him kiss me. What was I thinking? I should never have come here in the first place,* she told herself. She thought she heard Ren set a date to meet his mother, and a part of her heart felt sorry for him.

As she began to descend the stairs, Brady shifted restlessly, knocking her slightly off balance. She grabbed the railing with her free hand, but her hip collided with the newel. She let out a soft "Ouch."

"Why don't you let me carry him down for you," Ren said, coming up behind her.

She shook her head. "I can do it. I carry him all day long."

Centering Brady's weight as much as possible, she slowly and carefully descended. The arm that supported the bulk of his weight was quivering by the time she reached the black-and-white marble squares of the foyer.

Ren hovered like a mother hen the whole way down, making Sara more nervous than she already was. He let out a big sigh when they reached the foyer. "I'll walk you to the car, but let me get a flashlight first. Those paving stones out front are tricky at night."

Sara was independent but not foolish. "Okay."

While she waited by the front door, she studied the green-and-red lights of the alarm. "Fink," she muttered, just as she heard the *clip* of Ren's shoes on the floor.

He waved the flashlight triumphantly, then leaned past her to open the door. "Whoa, that breeze turned cold. Do you want to borrow a jacket?" His nearness and smell made her heart flip-flop.

Sara shook her head, desperate to put as much distance between her and Ren Bishop as possible. Drawing on Brady's warmth, she hurried to the car, grateful for the beam of light Ren kept trained ahead of her. She maneuvered Brady into his car seat, then pulled his soft, much-loved blanket from his backpack. She tucked it around him and kissed his forehead. His breath, warm and sweet, smelling faintly of bubblegum—his favorite toothpaste flavor—brought tears to her eyes. She loved being his mother. It would kill her to lose him. She had to make Ren Bishop understand that.

Taking a deep breath, she straightened and turned to face her enemy—the man whose kiss had opened doors inside her she hadn't known existed. No matter how wonderful it had felt, she wasn't about to let it happen again.

"I came here for a reason," she said, drawing strength from her fear. "My friends and I are prepared to fight to the death—I hope it won't come to that, but you need to know how I feel about this."

A gust of wind zipped under her skirt, making her shiver.

"You're cold. Let's go inside," he said.

She shook her head. "No. I'm exhausted. I have to go home, but I want to tell you something first," she said stubbornly.

He placed the flashlight between his knees and shrugged out of his suit jacket, then draped it over Sara's shoulders. Its warmth and subtle scent enveloped her. The gallantry of the gesture touched her.

"Thank you," she said in a small voice, hoping her emotions weren't broadcast on her face.

"I apologize for making you wait. When my mother gets going, sometimes it's best just to let her rant. I think that's why she doesn't have high blood pressure."

"And you do," Sara said softly, covertly rolling her shoulders against the silky lining of the coat.

He cocked his head to one side. "How do you know that?"

"I saw the prescription on your bedside table. A friend of mine used to take the same thing. You know, it's not safe to leave pills sitting out with children around."

"I didn't know Brady was going to be around, but I'll be sure to keep them in the medicine cabinet from now on. I don't actually take them," he added.

She blinked. "You just keep them there for appearance?"

His quick smile made her inch back. He was just too darn handsome for someone as vulnerable as she was at the moment. "Hypertension runs in my family. My blood pressure was a little high after my father passed away."

Sara, who witnessed her own mother's painful death, wanted to reach out to touch his forearm, but she kept her hands in her pockets and waited for him to speak again.

Ren was silent for a moment, then in a low serious voice he said, "Sara, about what happened upstairs. I apologize. It was unprofessional and…not very smart, given what we'll be dealing with in the future. Do you think we can put it behind us?"

Even though Sara agreed with him, perversely, his apology struck her as too lawyer-like. "Is that how it happened with my sister?" she said without thinking. "Just a quick kiss, then *wham, bam,* you're in bed?"

He stepped back as if slapped. In the light from the street lamp she saw a stark, judicial mask settle over his features. The narrow squint of his eyes reminded her of Brady's reaction when scolded. On a toddler it was cute; on Ren Bishop it was intimidating.

Instead of scurrying to her car, Sara screwed up her courage and said, "That is, if anything actually happened between you. I only have your word that you even met her. And until you prove otherwise, I won't agree to a paternity test. Period. *That's* what I came to tell you."

His face changed, but Sara couldn't tell what he was thinking. She thought she read disappointment, not anger.

"I can get you an affidavit from a hotel clerk who saw us at the lodge, and I can subpoena the hotel's records."

Court words. Lawyer-speak. Sara's old antipathy surged. "Can you find a witness who saw you make love to her? Someone from the room next door who will testify that she called out your name on climax?" She snorted facetiously. "You probably could—I've heard money's even better for the memory than ginkgo biloba."

Her anger obviously took him by surprise, but he didn't back down. "No, I can't. All you have is my word."

"And because you're a judge, I'm supposed to believe you. I'm supposed to listen to what you say and hear what's in your heart and make a decision that might affect the rest of your life, right?"

He nodded slowly.

"Then I guess that makes me a judge." She tapped her chest and lifted her chin. "And I'm sorry, Mr. Bishop, but I don't believe you. Your evidence is flimsy, your key witness is dead, and, frankly, I'm not convinced you're truly repentant enough to be a productive member of society, let alone a father."

His mouth gaped in amazement. "What?"

Sara's eyes filled with tears and she blinked fiercely. On the rare moments when memories of her trial and judgment decree flashed through her mind, she usually fought them down. Bile rose in her throat. She hated everything about the judicial system, but she'd learned a great deal from her brush with the law. She knew she could use the court system to drag this out for months, probably years. It would cost a fortune, but she'd sacrifice her business, her house—whatever it took—to keep Brady.

She shrugged off his jacket and passed it to him. "I have to go. You can expect to hear from my lawyer next week."

Suddenly drained by her memories and all that had happened tonight, she took a step, but misjudged the distance to the gutter and fell against the fender of her car.

"Sara, you're in no condition to drive. You're exhausted, emotionally spent and you probably haven't eaten all day, have you?"

Sara couldn't recall eating anything after finishing off Brady's toast at breakfast. Her head did feel a bit out of focus. The idea of her forty-minute commute sounded daunting.

"Let me call you a cab."

"I live in Rancho Carmel."

He nodded. "I know."

She felt a twist in her stomach. "That's right. You had me investigated."

He drove a hand through his hair. "Sara, I explained about that. Please, let me get you a cab. For Brady's sake."

She looked at her son curled up so peacefully in his car seat. She wouldn't let her pride put him in danger. "Okay. Call a cab."

He passed his coat back to her, saying, "Why don't you pull your car into my driveway, while I make the call. It'll be safer than leaving it parked on the street."

Sara stared at her nine-year-old wagon a moment. Julia and Hulger both had driven leased cars—always brand-new. The estate lawyer didn't seem to think Sara needed a newer car, and Sara hadn't bothered arguing the point.

Expelling a long sigh, she shrugged on Ren's coat, then climbed into her car and pulled into the space beside his Lexus. A motion detector's bank of floodlights momentarily blinded her, but she was grateful for the illumination when she dug through the mess on the floor of the back seat to find the par-aphernalia she'd need in the morning. She stuffed all she could fit in her backpack, then carefully unhooked Brady's car seat.

Ren met her before she'd made it two steps. "Let me," he said, taking the awkward plastic contraption from her hand. His fingers were warm; hers felt like Popsicles. "It'll be a few minutes. Some game is letting out and all the taxis are tied up."

Instead of leading the way to the curb, he headed for the front porch. He'd donned a vintage fisherman-type cardigan that made her think of John Kennedy, Jr.

"I put down a blanket and made you some cocoa," he told her.

"Cocoa? You had time to make cocoa?"

"Just some instant stuff I zapped in the microwave."

She chose the far end of the blanket. Her legs were numb from the chilly breeze, and she fought to keep from shivering. Once Ren had set down the car seat at her feet, he reached behind them to pick up a steaming mug. Sara latched on to its warmth with a murmur of thanks. Its sweetness and heat seduced her. She in-haled deeply. The first sip reached all the way to her toes.

They sat in surprisingly comfortable silence. "Are you being nice to me because you're hoping I'll change my mind?"

"Sounds like a lawyer kind of thing, huh?" His tone held a note of humor.

"Yes, actually."

He flinched as if dodging a bullet. "You don't like lawyers, do you?" He held up a hand. "Don't answer. It was a rhetor-ical question. But in answer to your first question, yes, I do hope you'll change your mind."

"I—"

He didn't let her finish. "Because if you do, we might be able to avoid dragging in a whole fleet of very expensive law-yers." He grinned. "I mean, since you don't like them."

The cocoa loosened her up enough to ask, "How?"

"Simple. Do the test. If I'm not Brady's father, then the whole thing's over. I fade away like a bad dream. Of course, I'd be happy to reimburse you for any expenses you incur during this ordeal, the cost of the doctor, the mileage, time off work…"

His spiel was exactly what she'd expect from a lawyer.

"And if you are…" She couldn't bring herself to finish.

He took a deep breath and let it out slowly. "Then, naturally, I'd want to be a part of his life." Gently, he added, "I imagine that would mean some kind of joint-custody arrangement."

The words hurt her ears. She set her cup aside and pulled the lapels of his jacket around her neck as if she could just shut out the sound. It was a childish gesture, she knew.

"Sara, please, think about it," he pleaded. "I've seen what happens when a child becomes a negotiable point of contention in a courtroom. Only the lawyers come out ahead. I'm asking to add to the quality of Brady's life, not take away from it."

Sara couldn't think about that right now. His tone was very persuasive, but that was to be expected—he was a lawyer. He'd had her investigated. He probably knew just what to say to sway her. He couldn't be trusted—she had to remember that.

Fortunately, a pair of car lights broke the long dark expanse in front of them. The car slowed and turned into the driveway.

Saved by the cab, she thought minutes later, taking a deep breath of stale air. A country-and-western station played on the radio. After securing Brady's seat, Ren had shoved a wad of bills at the driver with instructions to return for her the next morning. Sara didn't meet his gaze when he told her goodbye. Instead, she muttered a weak "Thank you," then wrapped her arms around the hard plastic shell of Brady's car seat and closed her eyes.

REN WATCHED until the taillights were out of sight, then he walked to the porch and picked up Sara's mug and the blanket. His jacket was draped over one arm. He'd argued that Sara should wear it home, but she'd insisted the taxi was heated and she would be fine.

"Stubborn woman," he muttered softly.

"Talking to yourself these days, old man?" a voice asked.

Ren almost pitched his entire load into the bushes as his instincts prepared him for battle. Only the familiar chuckle that accompanied the droll accent saved him the embarrassment. "That does it, Lester. You're fired. Go hound some other client."

Bo followed Ren up the steps like a puppy. "Can I have cocoa, too?"

Ren stopped mid-stride. "How long have you been here?"

His tone must have made an impression, because Bo, who was dressed like a cat burglar complete with black stocking cap, paused and looked at his watch. "Four minutes, thirty-eight seconds."

"I meant, how much of our conversation did you hear?"

Bo looked him square in the eyes. "None. I was walking up when the taxi arrived. I parked half a block away when I saw Sara's car in the drive."

Ren relaxed. He proceeded into the house, pausing to drape his jacket over the banister. "Why are you here?" he asked, when Bo followed him into the kitchen.

"Thought I'd see if Eve left any skin on your hide." He opened the refrigerator and withdrew a can of flavored tea. After a couple of healthy guzzles, he burped.

No wonder Eve found his manners so appalling, Ren thought, putting away the box of instant cocoa.

"So, is Eve bootin' your ass or what?"

Ren walked to the far end of the counter and selected a bot-tle of brandy from his liquor cabinet. He poured a small amount into a snifter. "Let's go to the den. I'm weary, my friend. Very weary."

Before Ren settled into the chair behind his desk, he punched the message retrieval button on his answering ma-chine, out of habit. The first message was a cheery reminder from his dentist of an upcoming appointment. The second was his mother's voice. He erased both.

"Babe sounds healthy," Bo said, dropping to sprawl on the couch.

Ren took a long sip of his brandy, savoring the smoky, ro-bust bite as it went down, then he rocked back, kicking his feet on top of the desk. He was tempted to call Sara to make sure she got home okay.

"Do we have Sara's home number?"

"Why do you want to know? Did I mention I'm changing sides in this battle? I'm gonna work for Sara from now on."

Ren ignored the threat. "I just want to make sure she got home safely."

"You seem kind of interested in her—beyond just the cus-tody thing. I thought she wasn't pretty enough for you."

Ren pictured the moment before he had kissed her. Sara's lips had trembled—whether from fear or anticipation he didn't know. Her eyes had been luminous, her cheeks flushed. Pretty? Not even close. More like phenomenal. "I would ap-preciate it if you forgot I ever said that."

Bo regarded him shrewdly. "It'll cost you."

"Are you blackmailing me?"

"Wouldn't that be against the law?" Bo asked innocently.

"Yes."

"Then no, Your Honor, I'm not. I'm just suggesting that a pie might, on occasion—shall we say, once a week—find its way from your unworthy and unappreciative kitchen to my very worthy, very appreciative kitchen."

Ren wasn't in the mood to laugh, but he chuckled, anyway. "I would have thought a cookbook man like yourself could bake his own pies."

It was Bo's turn to frown. "Don't call me that. Sara's a soft touch compared to Claudie and Keneesha."

Ren shook his head. He ran his fingernails along the faint bristle of new growth on his chin. "I think it's safe to say that as far as the females of our acquaintance are concerned, neither one of us could get elected dog catcher."

Bo nodded. "Not even dog-poop catcher."

Ren laughed and Bo joined him. When his friend rose to leave, Ren told him, "Your first payment of hush money is in the fridge. Take it with you."

Bo grinned and said, "Thanks. By the way, Sara's number's in the book. See ya' around, pal. Don't hang anybody I wouldn't hang." With that he disappeared.

Ren listened carefully. He heard the suction of the refrigerator door, but after that only silence. He started to snap off the light, then reached into the lower cabinet and withdrew the phone book. He found the number and wrote it on a Post-it note. With the little yellow flag attached to his finger, he reset the exterior alarm, turned off the lights and walked upstairs.

I won't call, he decided. She's fine. They're fine.

He prepared for bed, doing the yoga and meditation that gave him an edge over hypertension. The biofeedback techniques he'd learned told him his blood pressure was within the acceptable range.

When he walked to his bed, Ren spotted the slight indentation in the covers where Brady had slept. He ran his fingers over the spot, then pulled back the spread and crawled into bed. When he reached over to turn off his lamp, his gaze landed on the little yellow note. He snapped off the light. *I'm not calling. She's probably already asleep.*

He rolled onto his stomach. As he scrunched his pillow into a ball, his hand encountered something hard. Raising up on his elbows he clicked the light back on. His phone.

SARA SPIT AND RINSED, zombie-like. The forty-minute snooze she'd had in the taxi had helped take the edge off her fatigue, but she still felt shell-shocked. The driver had been helpful and had insisted on carrying Brady to her door. He had even waited until she was inside with the lights on before backing out of the drive.

Brady, bless his heart, went right back to sleep after she changed his diaper and put on his pajamas. She'd rocked him for a few minutes—more for her peace of mind than his—although even that simple gesture almost brought her to tears. How often would she be able to rock her little boy if Ren Bishop turned out to be Brady's father?

After wiping her mouth with a towel, she looked in the mirror. The eye makeup Claudie had insisted she wear for the camera had left dark smudges under her eyes. In the glow of the overhead lights, Sara thought she looked half dead. Surely that's what she'd be if she lost Brady.

The jingle of the telephone made her jump. Probably Daniel, she thought, dashing across the cold tile to the plush carpet. She vaulted into bed and drew up the covers. "Hello?"

"Sara, it's Ren. Did I wake you?"

A lump formed in her throat. "N-no."

"I just wanted to make you sure you got home safely."

His voice did weird things to her equilibrium. She felt small and vulnerable around him, and that wasn't a very smart way to feel if he were about to become her enemy. "I'm fine. Just exhausted. You were right, though."

"I was?" He sounded surprised to hear her say anything positive. "About what?"

"The cab. I was in no condition to drive. I slept the whole way home," she admitted.

He was silent a moment. She could picture him smiling. He had such a warm smile…for a judge. "Good," he said. "I'm glad I could help since I was at fault for causing you…" His voice trailed off as if he didn't want to bring up a sore subject. "Will you be able to go back to sleep now?"

Sara smiled. One good thing she'd retained from her military experience was the ability to sleep on command. "Yes."

"Good."

"What about you?"

Sara wondered if his pause meant he was surprised by her question. "I doubt it. Fortunately, my golf partner loves it when I'm not at my best."

Sara smiled. He was teasing. She could tell by the softening of his tone.

The pause between them lengthened. "Would it be all right if I stopped by the bookstore tomorrow, Sara? Maybe if you got to know me, you might—"

Sara interrupted. "No. I mean, no, don't bother stopping by. I won't be there. I'm opening up, but Claudie and Keneesha are taking over in the afternoon so I can meet with a contractor. My eaves need painting."

"Why do you live so far out?" he asked. "That commute must get old."

Sara looked at the cathedral ceiling above her bed. Spiders were spinning condo-webs.

"I wasn't thinking too clearly right after the funerals. It seemed logical that Brady should stay in an environment he knew, so I gave up my apartment and moved in. But you're right, the commute can be pretty awful. Fortunately, I go in a little later than the white-collar commuters."

She snuggled down, for some reason reluctant to break off the conversation. "How'd you manage to find such a convenient location?"

His low chuckle made her shiver. "I was born."

"I beg your pardon?"

"I grew up in this house. My parents lived here until Dad passed away. Then Mother moved into a condo on the golf course and offered me this place."

"Must be nice," Sara said.

His sigh caught her by surprise. "Actually, it was a tough choice. I was in the process of restoring a 1906 Victorian in Folsom—a true money pit, but I loved it."

"So why did you move?"

"Mother pointed out that this place fit all three real estate criteria—location, location, location." There was a pause. "If you met my mother, you'd understand. She should have been a lobbyist."

Sara's grin faded when Ren continued, "I've been thinking about what you asked me—about how I became involved with your sister. Would you like me to tell you what happened? I guarantee you'll be under no obligation to believe me."

Sara's heart moved into her throat. "I'll listen."

"Okay—"

She heard him draw a breath. She closed her eyes and focused on his voice.

"I truly can't explain why it happened. Believe me, nothing like this had ever happened before. All I know is I was running away from my life at the time. I figured fresh air and fast skiing would help me find some perspective. Then on the very first trip up the hill, I found myself sitting next to the most beautiful woman I'd ever met."

Julia was good at catching men's attention, Sara thought, smiling.

"We flirted. I was flattered."

Sara made a snorting sound.

"No, I mean it. I'm no Don Juan. I've dated very few women in my life, actually. I attended an all-male high school. The girl I dated in college broke my heart when she chose medicine over me. Law school was all-consuming, then I went to work for a government agency that frowned on frat-ernization among colleagues."

"You're engaged to a very beautiful woman," Sara felt obliged to point out.

"I wasn't when I met your sister. I'd met Eve that January, but we hadn't been out on a date." He sighed. "Anyway, Julia and I skied together all day. She was great—bold, a little crazy. I was utterly infatuated. I invited her to dinner. She said, 'Let's order room service.' When I woke up in the morning she was gone. Not a note, not a clue. All I knew was her first name—Jewel."

Sara frowned. "Our mother sometimes called her that. 'My little Jewel.' I thought Julia hated that name."

Ren blew out a breath. "Maybe that's why she used it. If she went there intending to have a fling, she might not have liked herself very much at that moment. I really can't say. To me, she seemed very up, spontaneous, poised. Totally in con-trol. It was always her call."

"Nobody made Julia do anything she didn't want to do."

"Why do *you* think she did it—went to Tahoe that week-end alone?"

His subtle phrasing disarmed her; she forgot her fear of saying something that might be used against her in court. "I don't remember that exact weekend, but I know she was rest-less. She pretended to be happy living the life of a wealthy doctor's wife, but she really missed her job, her friends, the sense of accomplishment she got from nursing."

"Maybe she got tired of pretending," he suggested.

"Maybe," she agreed. "Too bad we'll never know."

Ren ended the conversation a few minutes later, telling her she needed to rest.

Sara hung up feeling oddly torn. She could have liked this man under normal circumstances. She could certainly understand how her sister might have been attracted to him.

Tears filled her eyes as she rolled on her side and pulled her pillow to her belly. "Did I fail you, Julia?" she softly cried. "Were you so lonely, so sad, you turned to a stranger for consolation? Or did you sleep with him for another reason—to get pregnant?"

CHAPTER SEVEN

"AHOY, MATES, come aboard," Bo hailed, employing a hearty pirate voice that made Brady dig his fingernails into Sara's bare thigh. She took his hand to reassure him and also to lead him safely across the metal dock to the end berth where Bo's houseboat was moored. "Happy Memorial Day," he called, waving a Brady-size flag.

"Hi, Bo, thanks for inviting us," Sara called back, hoping to ease her son's trepidation. On the drive to the Delta, Brady had jabbered nonstop about boats, but now seemed frozen in either terror or wonder—Sara wasn't sure which.

"Glad you could make it. How's my little fishin' buddy?"

Brady ducked his head behind Sara's leg, almost knocking her off balance. Bo gallantly cleared the short distance between them and relieved her of her overstuffed backpack. "So, tell me again why the Cowardly Hooker, I mean Claudie, isn't with you," Bo asked, ushering them aboard the boxy-looking vessel.

Sara had never seen a houseboat up close—with horizontal vinyl siding and metal awnings, it resembled a mobile home on pontoons. She looked around, taking in the small harbor outlined by banks of dense, bushy trees, and counted a dozen vessels, from rowboat size to canopy-topped residences like Bo's.

"Claudie said to tell you she had to wash her hair," Sara

said, her nostrils crinkling at the fishy scent in the warm, humid air. "I told her she could do better than that, so she said to say it was cramps. Take your pick."

As Bo led the way to an exterior patio at the rear of the houseboat, Sara's free hand clamped tight to the waist-high metal railing that encircled the vessel. The decorative upright columns seemed too far apart to keep Brady from the water. *This might have been a mistake.*

After plunking her bag down atop a round picnic table covered in a cheerful geranium-print tablecloth, Bo scratched his head. His wrinkled Hawaiian-print shirt topped baggy cargo shorts. His feet were bare except for dime-store thongs. "Humph. I'll tell you whose butt I'm gonna kick on Wednesday night."

"She charges extra for that, you know," Sara quipped, smiling when his mouth dropped open.

"Never underestimate the quiet, demure type," he muttered, as if filing away an important fact.

She herded Brady away from the exterior corridor. "Actually, Claudie's trying hard to turn her life around, Bo. She's taking an online study course to help her pass the GED, and Sundays and holidays are the best days to study."

Bo looked unconvinced. "Why lie about that?"

"She doesn't want anyone to know, in case she fails. This is pretty shaky ground for her. Someone went to a lot of trouble convincing Claudie she was dumb, and when you're taught that as a child, it's hard to make yourself believe otherwise."

Bo nodded sagely. "I'm glad she's climbing out of the pit. Maybe I'll go a little easier on her." He frowned. "Naw, that would just make her mad. Anyway, Brady's here and you're here—that's what counts, right?"

He squatted low and held up a high five for Brady, who studied the hand as if it were an interesting piece of art. Bo sighed. "We'll work on your good ol' boy camaraderie, but first we gotta get you a life jacket, bud. Only way I'll have a moment's peace."

She still felt a little uncomfortable socializing with the person who has investigated her, but Bo had stopped by the bookstore several times in the past week to convince her of his sincerity. He'd even volunteered to help her scrape paint next weekend.

And when Sara needed a favor from Ren—to hold off trying to get a court order for the DNA test until Hulger's estate lawyer returned from his two-week vacation—she'd used Bo as an intermediary. He'd returned her call saying Ren would wait, if she'd promise to reconsider doing the test without a court order.

Sara vacillated between standing her ground at any cost and giving in to the inevitable, but Daniel and Keneesha adamantly opposed any concession. "Only a fool would believe a political player like Ren Bishop," Daniel had told her. "His fiancée is going to be the next Jane Pauley. Do you think she's going to stick around Sacramento just so you can help raise that little boy?" He'd read in a gossip column about Eve Masterson's reputed talks with the networks.

Bo's offer of a relaxing day on the water seemed like just the break she needed.

After giving a quick tour of his home, Bo showed Sara to the room where she and Brady could change clothes. "Don't forget the sunscreen," he warned, pulling the door closed behind him.

A short time later, Brady—bright and pudgy in his coast-guard-approved life vest—worshipfully held a small plastic fishing rod in his hand. "Let's catch dinner, pal," Bo said, leading the way to a fishing platform attached to the rear of the houseboat.

Sara—frosty mug of beer in hand—watched them from a lawn chair. Her heartstrings twanged. Brady not only responded to this kind of male camaraderie, he gravitated toward it like a moon. It was odd, Sara thought, how in a few short days she'd come to see something was missing in both their lives—when they had seemed pretty complete before.

Sara leaned her head back and closed her eyes.

"Where's Ren today?" she asked, despite her best intentions to the contrary. Sara hadn't seen him since that Friday night when he'd called her a cab, although she'd spoken to him several times on the phone.

"Some political fund-raising bash. Very posh," Bo told her. When he named the host of the event, Sara choked on her beer. Only the wealthiest, most influential of Sacramento's upper echelon. "He said he might stop by later. If that's okay with you."

Sara shrugged as if it didn't matter one way or another. But, her stomach jumped.

"I wasn't sure how you'd feel about him coming here," Bo said, looking at her. "Claudie's kinda backed off from hating him so much, but Keneesha's still ready to hire a hit man."

Sara nodded. "She's like a mother bear protecting her cubs—me and Brady. I've warned Ren to take precautions—bodyguards, bulletproof vest, whatever," she joked.

"I'm sure that went over big."

"Actually, he burst out laughing. I guess he doesn't consider an angry hooker a big threat."

Bo looked up and grinned. "I doubt if Kee's even a blip on his radar screen compared to Babe and Eve—now, those two have fire power."

Sara wanted to ask about Ren's fiancée, but managed to fight the temptation. Instead, she watched as Bo helped Brady bait his hook and cast his line into the water. Its bright red-

and-white plastic bobber fell close enough to the platform for Brady to cheer triumphantly.

Sara savored the moment. In the distance, jet skis and powerboats raced on the river's main thoroughfare—the noise a mere mosquito buzz in her ears. The sun made her drowsy; her eyes closed.

"You haven't heard from Ren's mother, have you?" Bo asked.

Something about his tone made her stomach clench. She sat up straighter. "Should I have? Ren said she was less than thrilled about the news—but who could blame her? Why? Is something wrong?"

As if sensing her disquiet, Bo frowned. "Babe Bishop is a battle-ax—I mean, ship. I can't see her letting this thing go without a skirmish."

"What could she do?"

"Make trouble between you and Ren."

"You make it sound like we have a relationship. We're just opposing sides in a custody battle. I'd expect Babe to be in Ren's corner."

Bo ruffled Brady's curls. "It's too damn—I mean darn—bad you two can't work this out without going to court. I'm not saying this for Ren's benefit, but I've been thinking about it from Brady's point of view, and I think he'd want to know the truth—I know I would. After that, if Ren is his daddy, then you could work out what's fair for the three of you."

"What about Eve? As Ren's fiancée, wouldn't she have a say?"

Bo's broad shoulders rose and fell. "Frankly, I think Eve's a long shot at this point, but that's just my opinion."

Sara would have asked what he meant, but Brady's sudden cry of joy made her lunge for her camera to record her son's first catch.

Although it was a long way from a keeper, Bo made a big

deal about the wonderful prize, then he solemnly explained how to release the fish back into the water. Brady wavered, his bottom lip quivering, but after some coaxing leaned over the water and let it go. Sara watched for several heart-stopping seconds until the fish got a second wind and sped away. Brady cheered, ran to her and gave her a big hug.

When Sara looked at Bo, she was surprised at the tender look on his face. For a man who usually kept his emotions hidden, he couldn't conceal how he felt about children. Before she could ask why he wasn't married, though, Bo said, "Who wants to water-ski?"

A GLANCE AT THE SPEEDOMETER made Ren ease his foot off the gas. He purposely relaxed his fingers on the steering wheel and filled his lungs with a deep, calming breath. His stomach still churned from the mixture of political rhetoric, rich food and poisoned glances courtesy of his mother and fiancée. Babe had been outraged that he planned to cut out early from the lavish affair he'd paid royally to attend, but Ren didn't care. The only place he wanted to be at the moment was on Bo's houseboat.

He exited the freeway, thankful for the twenty or so miles of country highway that would give him time to decompress after the rarefied atmosphere he'd just left. Although he and Eve had put on a good front, he was sure he'd seen a few raised brows, no doubt a result of the gossip column revelation that Eve was up for a network job.

Ren, too, wondered where he stood with his fiancée, but her frantic schedule since her return from New York had inhibited any face-to-face discussion. His one chance to see her alone at dinner the previous evening had been sabotaged by her pager.

"Sorry, honey," she'd told him, gathering up her purse and

cell phone. "I know we were supposed to talk, but I'll see you at the fund-raiser tomorrow. I took the night off, so maybe we can go to my place afterwards."

When he'd mentioned Bo's fish fry, Eve's eyes had narrowed angrily. "Naturally Bo takes precedence over our plans for the future."

"It's not Bo. Sara is going to be there, and she's bringing Brady. I've been keeping my distance to give Sara time to think, but I want her to get to know me, so she'll see I'm not some kind of ogre just out to steal her kid."

"Sara," she'd hissed, pettishly. "The woman you've never made love to but whose child you covet."

Ren, who'd already spent a week dealing with his mother's chastisement, had answered with a sigh. "This has more to do with Brady than Sara, but she's his guardian. I have to go through her to get him."

Eve had leaned close and said, "I talked to Marcella about this when I was in New York, and she said the child's actually not such a bad idea. If it turns out he is your son, then you won't need me to take time out of my career to give birth. Right away, I mean. I'd like to have a child of my own some day, but not anytime soon. I have too much to accomplish career-wise."

After she'd left, Ren had digested her words instead of dinner. He'd even contemplated going to her place so they could try to work things out. He and Eve had good history together—but he couldn't help wondering if they had a future.

Ultimately, he'd chosen to go home instead, where he'd surfed the Internet, learning about paternity issues and DNA testing kits. He learned that no DNA test devised could prove with one-hundred-percent accuracy if a man was a child's father, but it could prove with a 99.6-percent accuracy rate if he wasn't.

Ren glanced down and adjusted his speed once more. The

profusion of trees and advent of levees told him he was getting close. Biofeedback told him his heartbeat was speeding up, but it didn't worry him. He was looking forward to seeing Brady and Sara.

He'd talked with her several times by phone but hadn't seen her or Brady since that Friday night when he kissed her. He'd stopped by her bookstore the day after the disastrous lunch with his mother. As Sara had told him, Claudie was in the store on her own. Ren had hoped to use the opportunity to mend a few fences with Sara's friends, but it proved a bigger challenge than he'd imagined.

As he drove down the winding country road, he pictured the exchange.

"Let's get one thing straight," Claudie had said, plunking a cup of coffee in front of him. "I don't trust you and I don't like you."

She'd paced back and forth behind the coffee bar agitatedly, then stopped across from him and added, "You mighta scared me into shuttin' up when I was workin' the streets, but I been done with that for a couple of months, so you can't do nothing to me. I know it's against the law to threaten a judge, but you better believe, if you do anything to hurt Sara, I'll…"

Ren had saved her the trouble of naming a torture. "I have no intention of doing anything to hurt Sara."

"Taking away her baby don't hurt?" she'd shouted. Resuming her pacing, she'd orated with all the power and passion of a senator. "What is it with you men? Maybe you think you know about being a mother because you had one, but it ain't the same for men as it is for women. Nature planned it that way—she gave us more hormones and a bigger heart. You could never know what it's like to lose a baby."

Ren had felt castigated by the young woman's words.

"You're right. I don't know what Sara is feeling. I only know what I've felt ever since I first learned about Brady. Wonder. Hope. Anticipation. Like I might have won the lottery but I'm waiting for that last number to appear. It's scary and exciting at the same time."

She'd studied him a long time before saying, with a sigh, "Why can't you just go away?"

"Because *if*—and that's the big word here—*if* I'm Brady's father, then he deserves me as much as I deserve him." Ren had had to blink against the sudden moisture that filled his eyes. "This doesn't have to be a bad thing, Claudie. I know I can add to his life. I have money put away that could pay for his college education. I could teach him yoga—show him how to golf, how to ski." Her sudden frown had made him bite his tongue. "Maybe not skiing."

Her lips had flattened as if trying not to smile, and Ren had decided to leave while he was slightly ahead.

Before he could reach the door, Claudie had called, "Sara called a few minutes ago. She said the car fairy had washed, waxed and vacuumed out the inside of her car while it was parked at your house."

Ren had shrugged nonchalantly. "Imagine that."

"She sounded happy. Real happy," Claudie had added, her tone remarkably free of rancor.

He'd smiled, gratified to know his small act of kindness meant that much to Sara, but it also made him realize how alone she was and what a heavy burden she carried.

Three gaudy flags, weathered almost beyond recognition, alerted Ren to the location of Bo's dockside residence. Ren liked to give his friend a hard time about his floating hovel, but in truth Ren envied Bo. Ren's house was too big and austere; despite his renovations, it was still a long way from his dream home. Bo's little home was cozy and personal.

Ren parked, grabbed his gym bag from the seat and hurried toward the houseboat. A quick scan told him Bo and his guests were out on the water in the speedboat, so Ren stripped off the layers of the outside world, pulled on a pair of navy swim trunks, then dashed to Bo's fishing platform and dove into the water.

"Ren." He heard a voice call as soon as he surfaced. A sleek ski boat—Bo's pride and joy—trolled toward him. Bo killed the inboard engine, and the boat coasted to within an arm's length. Ren grabbed the chrome railing at the rear of the boat and hauled himself aboard, shaking the water from his hair. Brady squealed with laughter.

Sara handed him a towel, which he accepted with a smile. The appreciative look in her eyes surprised him and warmed him. She liked his body.

"So how was your snooty party?" Bo asked, once Ren was sitting down. He gave the throttle a nudge and the boat surged forward, heading for the main channel.

"Predictably elegant, lavish and boring," he said, smiling at Brady who was hanging over the side, his hand trailing in the water. Sara, Ren noticed, had a firm grip on the child's life vest. "The only halfway entertaining part was when Mandy Hightower's boyfriend stumbled over Edith Sherwood's walker and sent a table full of crab puffs airborne. I caught one in midair," Ren said, winking at Sara.

He helped himself to a beer from Bo's cooler. The speedboat was one of the newer models that offered wraparound seating. Sara and Brady were directly across from Ren; her bare feet were almost touching his.

"Did Eve accept her award on behalf of all the little people she had to step on—I mean over?" Bo asked.

Ren shrugged, his attention fixed on the way Sara's hair glistened in the sunlight. "I don't know. I left before that."

Bo choked on the soda he held to his lips. "You left? Holy sh—Sheryl Crow, I bet Babe liked that."

Ren's focus was drawn to the way Sara's slim body filled out her swimsuit. Swigging his beer, he moved to the copilot's seat beside Bo. "I lucked out. Neither Babe nor Eve is speaking to me. So I have no idea how they feel."

Bo gave a hoot, then looked over his shoulder and called, "Hang on tight, Sara, I'm gonna open her up."

Sara pulled Brady back and settled him on her lap. Now Ren could appreciate the way her swimsuit displayed her curves. He realized, suddenly, that he liked her body, too.

"WOULD IT HAVE HURT HER to act a little curious, Bo? My God, we're talking a possible grandchild—her own flesh and blood. All she cared about was how I've jeopardized my future. 'What will this mean to your judgeship?' she kept asking. My political viability."

Ren's voice penetrated the houseboat's thin walls to the room where Sara was trying to get Brady to nap. After their exciting ride in the speedboat—with Ren and Bo taking turns water-skiing—Sara had sensed Brady's fatigue. Naturally the little boy didn't want to miss a minute of fun with his big friends, but she'd finally calmed him by lying down beside him. She'd been on the verge of dozing herself, when Ren's voice had seeped into her consciousness.

"She asked me why I couldn't have a normal middle-age breakdown like other men. 'Buy a sports car,' she said. 'Get your ear pierced like Harrison Ford.'"

"Did she ask for names?" Bo asked.

Sara's breath caught in her throat.

"Of course. I'm sure she thought if I'd dallied with someone famous, she could make that work in my favor."

Bo snorted. "You didn't tell her about Sara, did you?"

"God, no. Sara has enough on her plate without dealing with Babe."

His tone made Sara shiver. She'd heard enough. She rose, walked to the adjoining bathroom and splashed water on her face.

Her head throbbed from too much sun. She found some aspirin in her purse and took two, then closed her eyes and leaned forward to rest her forehead on the cool mirror. Too much sun, too much fun, too much Ren, she thought, picturing the incredible jackknife dive he'd made into the water—clean and elegant like an Olympian. As she'd deduced from their encounter the previous Friday, Ren Bishop was built with broad shoulders, narrow waist and long, well-muscled legs.

I have to stop thinking of him, she told herself. *Just remember that he has his own agenda and I have mine. Julia left Brady to me—he's my responsibility. Period.*

"Where's Bo?" Sara said a short while later, opening the screen door to the rear patio area. She'd changed out of her swimsuit into shorts, T-shirt and sandals.

Ren was alone, sprawled in a chaise longue. He started, and she realized she'd awakened him.

"Oh, sorry I woke you."

He hid a yawn behind his hand. "No problem. Bo ran to the store. I was just relaxing. That's the problem with a desk job. If you play too hard on the weekend, you pay for it all week."

"You ski well. Jumping wakes—pretty impressive."

He'd put on a gray tank top over his swimsuit. He shrugged one shoulder. "I like the water. How come you didn't try it?"

Sara walked to the railing and looked at Bo's speedboat moored a few feet away. *Julia died in a boat like that.* "My brother-in-law tried to teach me, but I just couldn't get it. Maybe I'm dyslexic when it comes to skiing. Hulger wouldn't give up—'round and 'round he'd go trying to get me up. But

I couldn't do it. After a while I just quit going out with them. When Brady was born, I had the perfect excuse—baby-sitter."

Ren was silent a long time. "Did it bother you to be in the boat today? It hadn't occurred to me…"

She turned to face him. "I had a great time. Brady was ecstatic. He loves the water, and I haven't made much of an effort to take him swimming or anything. There are a couple of lakes at Rancho Carmel and a nice big pool, but there never seems to be enough time to do everything."

Sara bit her lip. Maybe it wasn't a good idea admitting her shortcomings as a parent to the person who wanted to be Brady's other parent.

"He doesn't strike me as deprived," Ren said, smiling warmly. "He's inquisitive, spontaneous, fearless, willful, kind… He really is a great kid, Sara."

She couldn't believe how good his praise made her feel. She smiled back. "Well, just don't let me forget to wake him. If he sleeps too long he'll be a bear to get to bed tonight."

"Brady?" he said with staged disbelief.

"He's going to be two in November. He's a little boy. Need I say more?"

Ren's chuckle strummed a chord deep inside her. She flattened her hand against her tummy, trying to place it.

"Are you hungry?" Ren asked, leaning forward to push a basket of chips her way. "Bo's picking up steaks. He said the only good-size fish they caught was Brady's, and you made them put it back."

Sara laughed. She held up her hand, spreading her index finger and thumb about four inches apart to show him the size of the fish. His throaty chuckle made Sara think of rich chocolate sauce. Decadent.

Still smiling, she walked to the chaise adjacent to his and sat down. She nibbled on a chip and stared at the play of shadows on the water. "Ren, I didn't mean to eavesdrop, but I overheard you talking with Bo about your mother. Maybe she's right to worry about what effect this could have on your career."

He inhaled deeply, then sighed. "To tell you the truth, Sara, my career is not *my* career. I've heard people say you should wait a year after the loss of a loved one to make big, encompassing changes in your life. My dad died, and a month later I was up for appointment to his seat. I don't really remember ever making a conscious decision that this is what I wanted to do with my life."

Sara was intrigued. She'd assumed every lawyer wanted to be a judge. "What about the money? The power?"

He sat up and faced her, his feet on the floor between them. "Superior Court judges in California earn 120,000 a year— 10,000 a month. That's not chicken feed, but—" he looked her squarely in the eye "—I learned the fine art of investing from my father. It got to be kind of a competitive game between us—to see whose companies did best. I like to win at games. So frankly, I don't need the money."

Sara stared at him, mute. Her budget was so bare bones that some months she didn't think there'd be anything left over.

He went on. "As for the power…some people might enjoy holding a person's life in their hands—I don't. Sometimes I don't know whether or not I've made the right decision. I'm just thankful there's an appellate court that can correct my mistakes if I've made any."

His intensity made Sara's heart expand in her chest.

"My father didn't become a judge until he was fifty-nine years old. I'm forty-two. Maybe if I had another seventeen years of experience…"

Sara felt oddly moved by his revelation. "What would you do if you weren't a judge?" she asked.

Ren rose and walked to the railing where she'd been standing. The sun was beginning to set, and his face was shaded. Just as well, Sara thought. *I can't look in his eyes without remembering our kiss.*

"I used to think about teaching. I do a little tutoring a couple of nights a week at the jail. It feels good when a person connects with what you're teaching him."

"What would your fiancée think about your changing professions?" Sara asked.

Before Ren could answer, Bo's noisy arrival signaled an end to their intimate talk. Sara told herself she was only asking because of what it might mean to Brady, but a part of her knew she was curious for other reasons. Foolish reasons.

BO TOSSED A MATCH on the pile of charcoal, then jumped back. The minute he'd walked in he'd felt something just as combustible between Ren and Sara—even if they pretended otherwise. He shouldn't have been surprised—things had been brewing all afternoon. Overly casual stares. Contrived accidental touches.

He'd debated about getting involved or minding his own business the whole time he was shopping. Basically, except for giving Ren a hard time about Eve—who wasn't a bad person, just not the right person for Ren—Bo stayed out of people's romances. But this was different. Sara was an innocent; she wouldn't last a minute in a Bishop sea—not with Babe and Eve circling.

"Sara, shouldn't you wake Brady? Ren promised to help him fish some more."

Sara bolted toward the bedroom, and Ren followed Bo into the kitchen.

"Something bothering you?" Ren asked.

"Yeah, there is. You said you were coming by today so Sara could get to know you better. I want to know how much better."

Ren's eyes narrowed. "I like her. Is that a crime?"

"Depends on who's the judge."

Ren gave him a steely stare, then turned away to catch Brady who barreled past like a runaway pumpkin.

"Whoa, kiddo, slow down you'll scare the fish." He picked up the little boy and smiled. Both sets of midnight-blue eyes flashed with joy, and Bo felt himself chagrined with envy.

Ren hiked Brady to his hip, then gave Bo a stern look and muttered, "Stay out of this, Bo."

A minute later Sara emerged from the bedroom and joined Bo at the counter. He started to hand her a tomato, but stopped. She looked at him questioningly. Her nose was a little sunburned, her hair windblown. She looked sixteen. He wanted to warn her not to get involved with Ren, to arm herself in any way possible against a possible attack from Babe, and to prepare herself for Ren's inevitable victory.

Instead, he asked, "What kind of salad dressing does the kid like?"

"When Bo would come home with me for holidays—Thanksgiving, Christmas, Easter—he and Dad would take off and disappear for hours. Drove my mother crazy."

"Now, you can't pin that one on me," Bo argued. "Babe has always been crazy. Larry was just too nice to point it out, and she's got you pussy-whipped."

"Baloney."

"Gentlemen," Sara interjected, thoroughly regretting her innocent question that had somehow turned best friends into antagonists. "Whose turn is it to push?"

After dinner, they'd walked to a nearby playground, where the three adults took turns entertaining Brady. Bo took over swing duty from Sara.

"Sorry," he mumbled under his breath.

Sara sat down on the empty swing beside Brady's and watched the little boy's face light up with joy as Bo cautiously pushed him. "So," she said carefully, "the bottom line is you were roommates in college, you spent holidays together—Bo partied, and Ren was the dignified one."

A pair of hands touched her waist, making her jump. "Pretty close," Ren said softly, gently giving her a push. "After graduation, Bo stopped drinking, joined the police department and eventually became a PI. I went to law school."

Sara lifted her feet and closed her eyes, reveling in the unexpected sensations.

"And Ren continued to be his dignified self—except for one small indiscretion, which is how we all came to be here tonight."

Sara, caught up in the dual pleasure of Ren's touch and gliding upward, let Bo's comment drift past her. She used her legs to pump higher, anticipating the solid warmth of Ren's hands against the small of her back when she returned to earth.

"What about you, Sara?" Bo asked. "Who was your best friend growing up?"

Maybe the freedom of near flight made her answer with uncharacteristic candor. "Julia." The name seemed to float on the air, as if Sara had conjured up her presence. "My father died when I was three, and my mother had a problem with alcohol, so mostly it was Julia who took care of me. She was part mother, part best friend."

On her next upward arc, Sara leaned back to view the world upside down. "We fought like you guys—ongoing arguments over nothing, but we always made up. I knew I could count on her for anything, and she knew I'd always be here for her. I don't know if that made us better sisters or better friends, but we were both."

The breeze kicked up, and Sara realized it was nearly dark.

"Bombs away," she called, jumping into the air. "It's getting late, Brady boy. We have to go. Tomorrow's a workday."

Ren and Bo took turns giving Brady piggyback rides. Sara knew from the tenor of Brady's shrieks of laughter that she was going to be in for a difficult time getting him to leave. Her head began to ache just picturing the long drive home with a crying, whining child in a car seat.

"Sara, what if I offered to drive you home?" Ren said, startling her with his empathic abilities.

"My car's here."

"Bo could pick you up in the morning and have Claudie run him home later. I have an early morning docket, or I'd do it."

She looked at Bo, who seemed less than thrilled by the idea. "It's really not necessary," she said, sorry she couldn't put more force behind her words.

"I know, but you had wine with dinner and it's a long, unfamiliar drive. What do you think, Bo?"

Bo looked at Sara intently. She was certain he intended to say no.

For some reason he said, "Okay. Whatever."

CHAPTER EIGHT

"THAT'S ALL WRONG, lamebrain. If you put that strap there, where does this one go?" one voice snarled.

"Get out of my face," the other growled. "How can I see when you're hogging all the space?"

Sara took Brady's hand to lead him away from the Lexus, half expecting it to blow up from the tempers brewing in the back seat. Once Bo had agreed to Ren's suggestion that he drive her and Brady home, Sara had assumed it would be a simple matter of transferring Brady's safety seat to Ren's car, then they'd be on their way. Apparently, she'd underestimated the potent mixture of male ego and technology.

Brady pulled on her arm, whining to help the men. The little boy had reached his limit even without the undercurrents of tension between Ren and Bo. "What, love?" she asked, trying to calm him with her touch. "No, you can't help them. They're having enough trouble as it is."

He pushed her hands away and flung himself to the ground, sobbing as though his world were coming to an end. "Brady," Sara soothed, squatting beside him. "We're leaving in just a minute." That promise seemed to upset him even more, although she couldn't understand a syllable of his weepy diatribe.

Sara sensed a presence at her side and looked up to see Ren, his concern obvious even given the fading light. "Can I help?"

She nodded. "He doesn't get like this often, but he's exhausted. Just pick him up and let's get him strapped in the car seat. Is it in?"

"I hope so." He lowered himself to one knee, focusing on Brady, who'd rolled onto his back and was kicking his feet against the dusty concrete floor of the parking lot. Eyes squeezed shut, his face almost apoplectic, his tantrum raged. Sara would have been mortified by this public behavior under normal circumstances, but for some reason—maybe Ren's calmness—she simply watched as Ren picked up her screaming child. Walking beside them, she tugged off Brady's heavy shoes to keep him from inflicting bodily harm.

Ren tried cajoling, but the child was beyond words. When they neared the car where Bo stood holding open the rear door, Brady tried to fling himself out of Ren's arms toward Bo, but Ren held fast. Sara chose not to watch the actual wrestling into the car seat. Instead, she gave Bo a quick hug and thanked him for the wonderful day, then slid into the passenger seat of the elegant car.

A moment later Ren joined her behind the wheel. The noise from the back seat filled the air, but Ren flashed a thumbs-up and started the car. They'd only gone half a mile before Sara groaned, "That's it. I can't take it anymore."

She unbuckled her seat belt.

"He's going to run out of steam eventually," Ren said, his voice full of concern.

"I'm afraid he'll make himself sick before that happens," she told him. "I think I can get him to calm down now that the car is moving. I have to try."

She climbed over the seat as gracefully as possible, careful to avoid touching Ren. She already regretted her decision to ride home with him—his proximity reminded her of his kiss…and the countless erotic dreams it had spawned.

"Brady, my sweet, remember your fish? Your big fish? Where do you think he is right this minute?"

Her singsong voice seemed to reach him. He stopped crying and looked at her, although his huffing little sniffles continued like a broken train. "I bet he's home with his mama under the water. I bet he's telling her about the nice boy he met today. The nice boy who let him go."

Brady's bottom lip shot out, and he looked ready to cry again, so Sara hurriedly added, "You're such a good boy, Brady. I love you. Someday when you're bigger you'll be swimming in the river and that fish—he'll be bigger, too—will look up at you and tell his buddies, 'Hey, guys, that's my friend, Brady.'"

The nonsense made Brady smile. She took a moistened towel packet from the backpack and wiped the streaks of dirt, tears and ketchup from his face. "Should we sing Ren our night-night song?"

Brady suddenly looked up, as if remembering the other adult in the car. He waved to Ren, who apparently caught the motion in the rearview mirror and waved back. "How'ya doing, Brady? Time to sleep?"

Brady responded by asking if Ren was going to sleep at their house so the two of them could play in the morning. Sara felt herself blush.

Fortunately, very few people aside from Sara could understand Brady. "He wanted to know if you'd read him a bedtime story," she ad-libbed.

"Sure, big guy. Anything you want."

Yawning, Brady reached out and took Sara's hand. "Mommy sing."

Sara laid her cheek against the soft padding of his seat. In a low, soothing voice, she softly sang the lullaby Brady liked best. He popped his thumb in his mouth and closed his eyes. Sara closed her eyes, too, intending to rest them just a second or two.

"Sara, wake up." Ren's voice was gentle. "I need your authorization to get in."

Sara sat up, startled by the bright lights outside the car. She realized in an instant where she was—the back seat of the Lexus, parked at the Rancho Carmel security gate. "Oh, my gosh, I slept all the way. Oh…" she groaned.

The rear passenger window slithered down. "Don't worry about it. We're here now, so check us in." His tone was kind, almost amused.

She swallowed her embarrassment and leaned out the window to wave at Clark, the night guard. He handed Ren a visitor's pass, and Ren pulled ahead.

"So, where to?"

She directed him to her house. At night, the rambling, angular building didn't look quite as hideous as it did by day. As soon as he was parked in the driveway, Sara scrambled out and dashed to the door to unlock it and turn on lights. Before she could return for Brady, Ren was there, child in arms. "Lead the way," he said.

Brady's nursery was the one room in the house Sara liked. She flipped on the light switch and pointed to the crib nestled in an alcove replete with skylight.

"Leave him on his back. I need to change his diaper and put on his jammies," she said, taking both from a built-in dresser.

"Won't he wake up?" Ren asked, his low whisper sending crazy messages up her spine.

"I doubt it. He was wiped out."

"So were you," Ren said softly, moving aside to give her space.

His closeness made her nervous. "I know, but I still can't believe I zonked out like that. How rude! I'm so embarrassed."

"Don't be. You needed the rest. I'm glad I was there." He

moved away a step. "Besides, I'd had a pretty hectic day my-self. The drive gave me time to think."

Sara didn't ask about what. As she changed Brady, Ren walked around the spacious room. "Great room," he said, studying the mural on the walls. "Who did the paintings?"

"Julia found a struggling young artist from Sac State. She lived here for six months while going to school. It's Julia's design."

Ren whistled under his breath. "Your sister was very tal-ented."

"Yes," Sara whispered back. "But her true talent was nursing."

She kissed Brady and turned him on his side, tucking his stuffed elephant beside him.

Sara motioned Ren to follow. "How about a cup of coffee? It's decaf." At his nod, she led the way to the kitchen. A vast, humorless room, its steel-and-chrome motif resembled the control panel of a space capsule.

"Wow, can this thing get us to Mars?" Ren asked, looking around.

Sara laughed. "Amazing, isn't it? State-of-the-art every-thing. Hulger always bought the best."

Ren walked to the wall of glass at the far side of the break-fast nook, where Sara and Brady ate all their meals. He cupped his hands on either side of his head and looked outside. When he looked back, his face remained impassive, but Sara knew what he was thinking.

"Big, huh?"

"Did it come with a zebra and giraffes?"

Sara burst out laughing. She didn't stop until Ren touched her shoulder. "Sorry," she said, wiping the corners of her eyes. "Most people say things like, 'Were all those rocks here or did you bring them in?'"

She lowered her voice. "Do you know what? Hulger did have the rocks moved in. They cost a fortune. Julia almost divorced him over it."

When the coffee was ready she handed him a cup and directed him to what Hulger had called his "Valhalla."

"Oh," Ren said, lifting his chin to take in the massive fireplace of rock and mortar. "That's some fireplace."

Sara sat down on one of the leather couches, arranging a multicolored throw so her legs weren't touching the white leather. She disliked the feel of the cold leather against her skin.

Ren, who was also wearing shorts, didn't seem affected by the modernist leather-and-chrome sling he chose to sit in. "This décor doesn't suit you," he said, sipping his coffee.

Sara smiled at his diplomacy. "I know. None of the furnishings are mine. I was living in a three-room apartment before I moved in here. My stuff is stored in one corner of the garage." She pictured the small pile of boxes and half-dozen antiques she'd been carefully acquiring—none of which would have jibed with Hulger's taste.

"You don't have to live here, do you?"

She took a deep breath. "I often think about moving, but it's complicated. Like I told you, I moved in because I thought this would be less stressful for Brady." She shook her head remembering those hectic, heartbreaking weeks after Julia's death. "It was pure chaos after the accident. I had two funerals to plan…Hulger's parents came from Denmark. You can't imagine how crazy it was."

Sara could tell by his frown that he wanted to ask her something. She took a guess. "You're wondering if I heard any of the speculation about the accident, aren't you?" His brow crinkled as he nodded. "People will always talk, Ren. Even at the memorial service I heard someone say Hulger drove the boat into a rock on purpose, but that isn't true."

"You sound pretty sure."

"For one thing, the inquest ruled it an accident, but above that, I knew Hulger. He was selfish, brash, impulsive and temperamental, but, above all, proud. He would never have given Julia the satisfaction of getting to him." She massaged the muscle at the base of her neck. "Maybe that doesn't make sense to you, but it does to me. Hulger was a very vocal, demonstrative person—he could rant and rave like a two-year old, but within seconds of blowing up he'd be smiling, acting the congenial host. That was one of the things that drove Julia crazy."

"So you think he might have been caught up in the heat of the moment and missed seeing the rock, but that he didn't purposely aim for it," Ren said, keeping his gaze on her face.

"Exactly. He worshiped Julia, and he loved this stupid house. Plus, he was very good at his job. He had a great future ahead of him. I know he'd never have committed suicide. Never."

"What kind of father was he?"

Sara took a drink of coffee; it tasted bitter. She rose. "I'm going to freshen this up. How 'bout you?"

He shook his head. The look on his face told her he knew she was avoiding his question.

"I'll be right back." She'd never particularly cared for her brother-in-law, but she didn't think it prudent to speak of his shortcomings to Ren. Maybe Hulger's petty jealousy—even toward his baby son—could be used against her in court.

Plus, it didn't help matters that she was feeling more and more attracted to Ren as a man. Her friends would be horrified if they knew she felt drawn to him—his kindness, his flaws and especially his touch. Sara hated to admit it, but she liked Ren Bishop.

REN ROSE AND WALKED around the vastly unattractive room. What a horrible house! Poor Sara, he thought. The more he learned of her sister's life, the easier it was to picture Julia escaping to Tahoe for a weekend of fun and games. The man who had designed this room was looking to impress people, not enjoy life.

He paused before a painting. Ren recognized the artist's scrawl but not the work. The unframed canvas of grays and browns sported a diagonal dissecting streak of red.

"Hulger paid a fortune for that painting," Sara said, joining him.

"Hulger was an idiot," Ren said shortly.

"Actually, the estate lawyer had that piece appraised and it's tripled in value. I asked him if we could sell it so I could use the money to finish the yard, but he said he'd prefer to see the estate stay intact."

"He's an idiot, too."

She laughed, and he had the urge to kiss her. "I should probably get going."

She nodded. "It was a busy day. I haven't had so much fun in a long time, and I know Brady will be talking about it for days."

Ren still hadn't figured out how anyone could understand anything that came out of Brady's mouth. His doubt must have shown on his face, because Sara said, "He does speak English, Ren—it just comes out so fast nobody can understand him but me. It's normal. Trust me."

"I do. You really handled him well in the car. I'd have just let him cry."

"That would have been okay, too. I'm probably too softhearted. Keneesha says I spoil him, but it breaks my heart when he's upset."

"It must be tough to be both the caregiver and the disciplinarian." He'd meant to sound supportive, but he could tell by the way Sara's chin came up that she interpreted his words as condescending. He decided to change the subject. "How long were Julia and Hulger married?"

"Four or five years, I think. I can't remember. They dated several years before that. Julia had been a nurse at the hospital where he worked. She always said people accused her of marrying for money, when in truth Hulger probably married her to avoid deportation."

"Really?"

She lifted her shoulders. "Who knows? I never asked."

"Bo said people at the marina claimed they fought a lot."

"That's true," Sara said, looking down. Her toes curled against her leather thongs. "But it wasn't all bad. They had fun, too. They traveled all over the world. They threw lavish parties—he was a terrific dancer, and Julia loved to party."

"Had they been trying for long to have children before Brady was born?"

She let out a breath. "I think so, but I can't say for sure. Julia was intensely private about some things. She was a complex person, and she hated anyone to second-guess her decisions. She prided herself on being in control at all times." Sara tilted her head and gave him a serious look. "You know, it occurred to me earlier when Bo was describing your mother that she sounds a lot like Julia—no-nonsense, forward action, perhaps a little self-absorbed."

Ren couldn't picture the slightest resemblance between the woman he knew as Jewel and his mother. "Hmm…" he said, trying to sound agreeable.

"In fact," Sara said, looking introspective, "now that I think about it, your fiancée is that kind of person, too, isn't she?"

Ren took a step back, surprised by her question. "Are you suggesting a pattern here?" he asked, trying to be amusing.

She shook her head, giving a harsh, unhappy little laugh. "No, I'm the last person who should be giving advice about dating. I…"

She looked at him, and Ren could tell she was remembering something painful. He ached to pull her into his arms and comfort her, but he'd already made the mistake of kissing her; he wasn't foolish enough to compound it.

He said good-night and walked to his car, conscious of her gaze following him. As he pulled away, the porch light blinked off, removing the single dab of cheerfulness from the hulking fortress.

SPEEDING DOWN Highway 16 toward town, Ren pushed a preset button on the built-in car phone and listened to the remote ring. There was no answer at the houseboat. "That's weird. Where'd he go?" Ren mumbled. He punched a different button. *Maybe he has his cell phone on him,* he thought.

After four rings, a voice said, "Yeah?"

"Hi. Where are you?"

"None of your business."

Ren wasn't put off by his friend's bluntness. "I tried the house and you didn't answer."

"I'm talking to you now, aren't I?"

"Listen, after you drop off Sara tomorrow, would you come to my office? I want you to look into the trust that controls Julia's estate. There's no reason Sara should have to live in that godawful house. Have you seen it?"

There was a pause, and Ren heard Bo murmur something to another person. Ren realized he must have intruded on a personal moment. "Are you with somebody?" he asked.

"Yeah, as a matter of fact, I am."

"Oh. Sorry. I just wanted to get this settled. Do you want to call me back later? I'm on my way to Eve's right now."

Bo made a muffled comment to whomever was with him, then asked, "You're calling from your car?"

"Yes, I'm taking the back way to Eve's."

There was another pause that made Ren think he'd lost the connection. He was about to hit Redial, when Bo said, "Listen, buddy, I should warn you. Eve called my house looking for you, and Claudie said she called here—at the bookstore, too."

Ren's mouth fell open. "You're at the bookstore?"

The connection started to crackle. "Yeah," Bo returned testily. "Wanna make something of it?"

Ren grinned at his friend's contentious tone. "No. Not at all. I know what a big reader you've become." Snickering, he added, "Give my regards to Claudie." But the line went dead.

Ren wasn't sure what to make of Bo's interest in the young woman. Granted, she'd given up working the street when Sara hired her to work at the bookstore, but that didn't mean she was right for Bo. Ren shook his head. He had more pressing matters to think about, namely what was he going to say to Eve.

He wasn't surprised to see the lights on in his fiancée's apartment. She was a night owl. He parked and hurried up the steps to her door. She opened it before he could knock.

"Hi," he said, stepping into the foyer. "I heard you were looking for me." His shin encountered a large black suitcase. "Going somewhere?"

"Yes," Eve said shortly. She was dressed in workout clothes: black leggings and a jade-green sports bra that left her midriff exposed. Her feet were bare. Her hair was twisted into a knot atop her head.

He stuck his hands in the pockets of his Dockers and waited. He'd learned to respect Eve's sense of drama—whatever kind of scene this was, it was going to happen her way.

"Ren, I'm taking the job in New York."

"Is there a reason why you're going so soon?"

Her black eyes flashed in anger. "Damn right. When you chose that woman and her brat over me, I knew then and there our relationship was over."

Ren frowned. "I told you I was going to Bo's."

"Yes, but I didn't know you couldn't even wait long enough to see me receive my award. If I mean that little to you, if my feelings are so far down on your list of priorities…"

Ren stepped toward her. "I'm sorry, Eve. I didn't realize it was that big of a deal. You get those kinds of awards all the time. What's one more?"

Tears clustered in her eyes, and she turned away. "Nothing to you, obviously, but it meant something to me. And it meant something to the people who came up to me later asking where you'd gone and why you weren't there to congratulate me."

Ren grimaced. "I should have stayed until after the ceremony. I apologize."

Eve turned around slowly. "It doesn't matter now. I'm leaving in the morning."

Ren started to walk past her to the living room. "Can't we talk about this?"

She placed her small, perfectly manicured hand on his arm. "Why subject ourselves to the ordeal? It won't change anything. You know this is the way it has to be."

Ren's heart felt heavy in his chest. A rash of wonderful memories—Eve on Valentine's Day wearing strategically placed construction-paper hearts; the two of them making love on the beach in Maui; their Sunday mornings together sharing bagels and the *New York Times*—chased across his vision, momentarily blinding him.

"Are you sure this is what you want?" he asked, covering her hand with his. "I'm sorry I hurt you today, but there's nothing going on between Sara and me. Unless that DNA test proves I'm Brady's father, I won't have any reason to ever see her again."

Eve pulled her hand back and walked to the door. "I'm sure you believe that, Ren, but I don't. I know you. Probably better than you know yourself. She's your escape, your get-out-of-jail-free card."

Ren shook his head. "What does that mean? I'm not trying to escape from anything. You're the one who's leaving."

"But you left first. Why else have sex with a stranger? Why go to such desperate lengths to prove you're the father of somebody else's child? Why else would you give up on a wonderful relationship that could take you right to the top?"

"Maybe I don't need my relationships to take me anywhere, Eve. Maybe I like where I'm at."

She made a scoffing sound. "If you liked where you're at, you never would have gone looking for Miss Bookstore. A lawyer could have handled any responsibility you feel toward her child, but you hired Super-Snoop to track her down. You're involved with her, Ren, whether you want to admit it or not." She took a breath. "I have an early flight tomorrow."

Stunned by Eve's slicing summary of his motivations, Ren moved cautiously back into the foyer. He stepped around her suitcase. "What about all your stuff?" He made a sweeping motion with his hand.

"The movers come Thursday." She lifted her chin proudly. "Marcella got me a full relocation package, great benefits and stock options. It's everything I ever wanted—career-wise."

Ren heard a softening in her tone. She was hurting, too. He moved to her and put his arms around her, drawing her close. Bending low, he pressed a kiss to the top of her head. He breathed in her scent—exotic and spicy.

"I'm proud of you, Eve. You're living your dream. I'm sorry I can't be a part of it anymore."

He felt her shoulders shake, and she clasped him tight. "Me, too," she whispered softly.

After a minute she broke away and took a deep breath. "I have a lot of packing to do."

He started toward the door.

"I already called your mother and told her goodbye. She seemed pretty upset. You might want to call her when you get home."

Ren flinched. "Maybe."

"Oh," Eve said. "I almost forgot this." She held up her left hand and started to pull off the diamond ring he'd given her.

Ren clasped her hand in his and shook his head. "It's your ring, Eve. You picked it out. You said it was a brilliant stone for a brilliant future. That hasn't changed."

She blinked rapidly and raised up on her toes to kiss him. "I love you, Ren Bishop. You're a good man, and you've been a good friend to me. I'll really miss you."

"I'll miss you, too." He hugged her once more, then left.

Just as he reached the curb he heard her door open. Eve walked to the top of the stoop and called out, "I hope you get your son, Ren. Don't give up trying. Sara won't be able to hold out forever."

He smiled and called back, "How do you know?"

"Because you're you."

CHAPTER NINE

KEEPING HER EYES CLOSED, Sara held on to the pictures in her mind, reluctant to reenter the real world. *Another Ren dream,* she thought, savoring the breathless passion that lingered in her memory. She'd given up trying to control her subconscious—refused to feel guilty about something she had no control over. Besides, these dreams were a very nice part of her day.

"Up and at it, sex fiend," she muttered under her breath. "This is Saturday. Bo's coming to help prep the gutters."

As she started to move, Sara realized she felt thoroughly rested, such a rare sensation that she barely recognized it. She glanced at her alarm clock and saw a flashing number twelve. Power failure, she thought—not an uncommon occurrence in the country. Did I oversleep?

Not bothering with a robe, she sprinted down the hallway to check the clock in the kitchen. As she passed Brady's room, she glanced in. Her heart stopped at the sight of his empty crib. "Brady?" she cried, clutching the door frame.

A movement just to the side of her line of vision made her jump back; the doorknob collided with her lower back, making her cry out. A large form started to rise from the floor in the vicinity of Brady's frog-shaped toy box.

"Good morning," the creature said, straightening to its full height. "Did we wake you?"

Sara's heart seemed to jump sideways. Pinpricks flooded her fingers and perspiration tingled under her arms. "Ren," she croaked.

Brady, who was draped over Ren's left shoulder in some kind of wrestling move, waved from his upside-down position. "Hi, Mommy. Ren here."

Sara tried to smile back but wasn't sure she could do it without crying. Her initial fear had robbed her of any equilibrium. Her knees felt wobbly.

"Did I scare you?" Ren asked, his concern obvious. "Bo and I were scraping the eaves outside the window, and Brady saw me. I figured you were still asleep, so I used the key you gave Bo and let myself in. I thought I'd keep him entertained until you woke up."

Ren bent low and set Brady on the floor. The boy dashed to Sara, who pulled him into a tight hug. Over Brady's shoulder she looked at Ren, who was wearing broken-in jeans and a loose denim shirt speckled with brown paint.

"You're scraping my eaves? Why?"

His gaze shifted downward. "It has its rewards."

Sara looked down and realized she was wearing her oldest nightie. She felt herself blush. "Stay here, honey. I'll be right back."

"Can I make some coffee?" Ren called after her, his voice rich with amusement. "The hired help is threatening to walk."

"Sure. Of course. Whatever."

When she entered the kitchen a few minutes later, it was to the smell of coffee brewing. Brady was sitting in his high chair, banana smeared in his hair and brows.

"He's not real neat, is he," Ren said, humor masking any criticism.

"Were you, at this age?"

"Actually, I was considered a holy terror until I was four."

Sara took a carton of milk from the refrigerator. "Really?" she said wryly. "What happened at four?"

He didn't answer right away, then said, "My older sister drowned. Everything changed after that, including me."

His tone was flat. He wasn't looking for sympathy, just stating a fact—but Sara's heart ached for him just the same. "How terrible! I'm so sorry for your family's loss."

The toast popped up, and he dutifully applied butter. "Her name was Sandra, but everybody called her Sunny," he said, handing Brady a toasted triangle. "Dad always said that described her personality, too—bright, smart, happy. She was the perfect one actually."

Sara couldn't stop herself. She reached out and touched his arm where bare skin was exposed below the turned-back cuff of his shirt. "And after she was gone, you became perfect to take her place."

He looked at her, his face composed. "It wasn't a conscious decision—I was only four. But things changed. There was sadness and tension in our home that wasn't there before. I'm sure it affected me."

She squeezed his arm. "Only if you were human."

He smiled, but his eyes had a faraway look. "My father quit his job at the district attorney's office to stay home and take care of me. Mother was pretty shook up—it took her a long time to…" He didn't complete the thought.

Babe never fully recovered from the loss, Sara guessed. "Grief and guilt go hand in hand," she said. "Hulger's parents were in Denmark at the time of the accident, but they blamed themselves, just the same."

He moved to the opposite counter and poured two mugs of coffee. He added sugar to one and set it aside. "It happened at our family's cabin at Lake Almanor. My uncle Frank and his family were there, too. His twin daughters were Sunny's age. The men were fishing from the shore, the girls playing in the water out front of the cabin."

He took a drink of coffee. Sara gave Brady his milk in a spill-proof cup and sat down at the table. "How did it happen?"

"The three girls were messing around with a raft they'd made out of driftwood. Sunny dove underneath the raft to fix something. Apparently she got tangled in a rope. By the time the other girls figured out she was in trouble, it was too late."

"Where were you?" Sara asked, forcing herself to swallow a bite of toast.

His sad, strangled laugh broke her heart. "I was being a brat, and Mother was trying to get me to lie down for a nap."

"Surely nobody blamed you for what happened?"

"No. But the loss of a child affects everyone." He picked up the mug of sugared coffee. "I'd better get this out to Bo before he goes on strike."

Sara leaned back. *Why did he tell me that?* Was he looking for sympathy, or was he trying to tell her he'd understand how she'd feel if he tried to take Brady from her? She suspected the latter, and it touched her deeply. She could fall in love with a man that sensitive.

"HEY, MAN, TAKE IT EASY. You're gonna scrape a hole in that downspout," Bo said, looking down at Ren from his vantage point on the ladder.

Ren glanced up. Frustration made him growl, "I'd like to strangle the person who originally primed this piece of shit."

"Are you sure that's who you're mad at?"

Ren rocked back on his haunches. "Who else would I be mad at?"

Bo wore his Raiders cap backwards. Brown paint chips made his hair and skin appear diseased. Ren was certain he didn't look any better. Talk about a detestable job! What had seemed a gallant gesture had turned into the job from hell.

"Maybe *mad* is the wrong word. How about *frustrated?*"

Ren sighed. He was frustrated—in more ways than one. The more time he spent with Brady, the more anxious he became to prove the little boy was his son. The more time he spent around Sara—especially when she showed up wearing a gossamer nightgown—the more... He put the thought aside and growled, "I'm fine. I'm still a little pissed about the way that estate lawyer blew Sara off, but she told me she has an appointment with the jerk next week, so maybe we can get the ball rolling—one way or the other."

He looked up at his friend. "By the way, what's going on with you and Claudie? You never mentioned your evening visit to the bookstore."

The ladder skidded to the left. Bo cursed fluently. "Nothing. She called the boat to tell me that Eve was looking for you. Why she felt the need to warn you, I haven't a clue, but she sounded kinda down, so I went over. We talked. I went home. End of story." He glared at Ren, challenging him to say more.

"Are you boys fighting again?" an amused voice interrupted. "Maybe you need naps, too."

Ren looked over his shoulder to find Sara standing a few feet away, hands on her hips, a smile on her lips. In frayed shorts and a baggy gray T-shirt, she looked fresh and appealing.

"I just got Brady down. How about a break? Sandwiches and iced tea on the patio."

They followed her to the rear of the house, where a plate of fruit and thick sandwiches on French rolls awaited on a picnic table shaded by a large green umbrella.

"I hope you're hungry, Ren," Sara said, smiling.

He smiled back.

"Would you prefer cola, Bo?" she asked, dropping her gaze from Ren's.

"That would be great, if you have it."

"No problem." She pivoted on one heel and dashed to the house.

Bo made a gagging sound. "What?" Ren asked.

"She's falling for you, big time."

Ren's heart did a little spin. "Do you think so?"

"I'm gonna barf."

"Why?" Ren asked, exasperated.

"It hasn't even been a week since you and Eve broke up, and you're already hitting—" He wasn't able to complete the thought because Sara returned.

"You and Eve broke up? Really?"

Ren heard the concern in her tone. "Yes. She took a job in New York. Her dream job. I'm truly happy for her," Ren said, trying for a casual note.

Sara handed Bo his can of soda, then sat down woodenly. "Wow."

Ren wished he had a clue what she was thinking.

"Why are you here?" she asked suddenly. "Shouldn't you be more upset or something?"

"He's taking out his anguish on your eaves," Bo said, his tone amused. He grabbed Ren's hand and held it out for her to see. "Look at those blisters."

"Oh, my gosh!" she exclaimed, frowning. "They're starting to bleed. I'll get the first-aid kit."

She disappeared into the house.

"Cretin," Ren said, noting Bo's satisfied smirk.

Bo took a sandwich off the plate. "It was your idea to come here today."

A few minutes later, Sara returned out of breath. "I hate this house. Any time you want something, it's like running a marathon." She drew her chair close to Ren's and took his hand in hers. With a frown on her brow and bottom lip clamped between her teeth, she tenderly cleaned the raw-looking blisters on his fingers and palm with a cotton ball soaked in peroxide.

Ren tried to inhale her scent, but his nostrils crinkled from the odor of the astringent. Bending lower, he tried again. Fresh air and mustard. When she glanced up, he spotted a dab at the corner of her lips. He also had a clear view down the neckline of her shirt. No bra. Perfect, compact breasts that made his throat constrict and other parts of his anatomy swell.

Forcing himself to look away, Ren glanced at Bo, whose knowing smirk made Ren glower.

"You could try magnets," Sara said, pulling an adhesive strip out of the first-aid box. "Keneesha said she tried them on a burn once, and they worked great."

"I'll be fine," Ren said, hoping that was true. He was lusting after a woman who probably shouldn't even be talking to him. Surely her asshole lawyer had told her that.

She finished her task, then scooted back, looking from Ren to Bo. "That does it. You're both fired."

Ren, who'd just downed a gulp of tea, sputtered, "I beg your pardon?"

She ran a hand impatiently through her hair. "This is a stupid job. An endless job. It's too much for three people. I should have known that."

Ren pulled out a chair at the table and pointed to it. "Sit down. Have a drink. It won't look quite so daunting after you eat something," he promised, although he knew she was right. The entire house needed work, and neither he nor Bo was a carpenter.

"You shouldn't have to pay for any of this out of pocket,

Sara," Bo said. "The house is part of your sister's estate. Let the estate pay for the repairs."

She sighed. "It's so frustrating dealing with the attorney who handles this case. He never returns my calls. He was a friend of Hulger's, and I don't think he ever liked Julia. I know he doesn't like me." She frowned. "Someone from his office called me at work yesterday to change my appointment—again. When I told him it was urgent, do you know what he said?"

Bo shook his head.

Ren tried to stop her from saying more, but she blurted out, "He said to stall Ren, so they could do a little investigating. He made it sound like I should ask for a healthy sum up front—something about *quid pro quo,* then worry about the custody battle later."

Ren exchanged a look with Bo.

Bo said, "I smell a feeding frenzy."

Ren nodded. He didn't know the attorney but obviously the man had heard the Bishop name and saw dollar signs—and the opportunity for a little legal extortion.

Bo chewed for a minute, then said, "You know, Sara, I have a friend who's a remodeling contractor. He's good, reliable and cost-effective. He owes me a favor. Want me to give him a call?"

Sara's face lit up. "I'd love it, but…I'm not sure I can afford it. The painter's bid will take most of my savings." She looked down as if embarrassed to be discussing her finances.

"I could pay for it," Ren said. Seeing her frown, he added, "If you take your lawyer's advice, I'll be paying up front just to have you *consider* letting Brady take the DNA test. This way, the money would directly benefit you and Brady, not the estate."

Sara sat back, looking dumbfounded. She turned to Bo, who nodded. "Sounds like a good deal to me."

She took a deep breath and slowly let it out, then stuck out her hand. "You don't have to pay. I should have agreed to the test before. It's the right thing to do." Her eyes filled with moisture. "It always was. I was just afraid of losing him."

Ren's mouth dropped open. "No. That's not what I meant. You don't have to decide right now. Talk to your lawyer—"

She interrupted. "He's not my lawyer. He doesn't care what happens to Brady or me as long as the estate looks good on paper. I don't care what he says."

A pain sliced open Ren's heart. "I promise you that you won't be sorry. You'll never lose Brady. And I *am* going to pay for the painting."

She ducked her head and put on a false smile. "If you could save me from the Rancho Carmel lynch mob…"

She rose abruptly and dashed into the house. Ren looked at Bo. "Wow, I didn't see that coming."

Bo nodded. "Gutsy lady. I know I don't have to ask this, but you will treat her fair, right?"

"You know I will," Ren snapped. The two glared at each other in silence until Sara returned—the portable phone in her hand.

"It's Claudie," she said. "There's something wrong with the espresso machine, and she thought you might be able to help, Bo."

Bo put the phone to his ear. His look of surprise changed to a smile as he listened. "Jiggle it a little harder," he said. "That worked for me the other night."

Sara let out a small giggle, and Ren grinned as he saw Bo's face flood with color.

Bo rose and turned his back. "Listen, we're winding things up here, so I'll stop by on my way home. Okay?"

Sara looked at Ren questioningly. He answered her with a shrug.

Bo mumbled something else, then passed the phone to

Sara, who listened for a minute before saying, "I'm sorry. I wish I'd known. I'll be down as soon as Brady wakes up from his nap."

She pushed a button on the receiver and placed the phone on the table. "Keneesha didn't come in this morning. She sent a kid over to tell Claudie she wasn't feeling good. She's been like this for over a week, but won't see a doctor. Claudie thinks it might be diabetes. We're really worried about her."

Ren suddenly felt a little sheepish about his off-hand attitude toward her friends. "Would she go to a doctor if you and Claudie took her?" he asked. "There's a clinic near the hospital that deals with non-emergencies."

Sara sighed. "Maybe, but I don't want to expose Brady to any germs if I don't absolutely have to. Maybe I—"

Ren didn't let her finish. "Diabetes can be life-threatening. It's not something you treat lightly. Bo and I could look after Brady and the bookstore this afternoon, while you and Claudie take Keneesha to the doctor."

Sara seemed stunned, as did Bo.

Even Ren wasn't really sure why he'd made the offer. A part of him wanted to do something for Sara after she'd agreed to the DNA test. Another part didn't want to spend a long afternoon in an empty house.

REN'S GOOD MOOD was put to the test the minute he walked into the bookstore.

"Sara told me about the deal," Claudie said, meeting him before he took a step inside. "I don't like it. You may not be the scum I thought you were, but I ain't completely convinced you're not up to something. Just don't forget—I'm here, and I'm watching you."

Ren politely replied, "Good afternoon, Claudie. Beautiful weather we're having, isn't it?"

She snorted and backed up a step so he could walk past her to the coffee bar. He noticed a hand-inscribed sign on the brass espresso machine that read, Out Of Survice. The misspelled word touched his heart. He glanced over his shoulder. "The jiggling didn't work, huh?"

Her usually impassive face turned red. "I gotta get something out back. Don't steal nothin'."

He watched her stride confidently away, noting her outfit—jeans and a white Henley buttoned to the throat. Quite a change from the woman he'd first met that night in the bar with Bo. He speculated about what—or possibly who—had inspired the transformation.

His musings ended when a door opened at the rear of the store, and Sara walked in with Brady. The little boy's arms were filled with stuffed animals, which he dropped the instant he saw Ren. With a howling cry of joy, Brady raced across the room.

Ren dropped to one knee and opened up his arms to catch him. "Hi, big guy. Did you have a nice nap?"

Brady began chattering away. Ren was beginning to be able to catch a few recognizable words. He listened closely, but saw the amused look Sara gave Claudie.

"We should hurry, Claudie, before Kee changes her mind. She wasn't wild about this idea, but I begged. Do you want us to wait until Bo comes?" Sara asked Ren.

Feeling confident, Ren shook his head. "How hard can it be?"

An hour later, when Bo sashayed in, Ren was looking for blood. "You dirty rotten coward," he cried. "I can't believe you did that."

Bo blinked with mock innocence. "Did what? I fell asleep. So, sue me."

"We had a rush, for Christ's sake. Nine customers, and Brady!" he exclaimed. "I don't know how Sara does it."

"Hey, this wasn't my idea," Bo challenged.

"I helped you scrape paint."

"Well, now we're even. I'm here, aren't I?"

"Yes, but you're too late. The rush is over, and Brady's settled down with a book." He gave Bo a steely look. "You owe me, Lester. Tonight. You baby-sit while I take Sara out to dinner."

"Maybe I have a hot date tonight. Did you think about that?" Bo asked.

"Does Claudie know?"

Bo turned away and headed to the coffee bar. "Okay. I'll do it." He twirled a small screwdriver and asked, "Isn't it a little premature to celebrate? You haven't even taken the test."

Ren's stomach turned over. He'd ordered the test kit online when he'd gone home to change. With express delivery, it would arrive Monday. Then, it would be a four-to-six week wait. A lot could happen in that time.

"This isn't about celebrating. It's about spending quality time with the woman who might be the aunt of my child."

Bo looked up from his work. "Might not be, too."

Ren didn't want to consider that possibility. Fortunately, the jingle of the bell over the door offered him a diversion.

SARA CLOSED HER EYES and took a deep breath, then added a spritz of cologne. *A date.* She was going out to dinner with Ren Bishop.

In the distance she could hear Bo and Brady jabbering about something. She'd already prepared a self-rising pizza for the two of them. Nerves and awkward embarrassment kept her from lingering in the kitchen, so she'd hurried back to her room to fuss with her dress.

She turned sideways to study her image in the cheval mirror. The twisted silk fabric was sculpted in a baby-doll style that made her legs look longer than they were. The low-heeled sandals helped, too.

"Sara?" Bo called from the hallway.

"I'm dressed. Come on in."

Brady tumbled in, tripping over his feet. He sprawled face-first on the carpet, but before Sara could go to him, he bounced back to his feet, laughing.

"Man, the ability to do that would have come in handy in my drinkin' days," Bo said, chuckling.

Brady crawled up on her bed and started bouncing. "Hey, monkey, that's a no-no," Sara said, reaching for him. He bounced away in glee.

Bo chased him down amid shrieks of feigned terror.

Sara withdrew a light sweater from the drawer and turned to look at the two "boys" wrestling on her bed. "I know somebody who's going to sleep like a rock tonight."

Bo sat up looking winded. "Yeah, me."

He tilted his head and gave Sara a thorough look. "Very nice."

"I haven't been on a date in so long, I'll probably try eating my soup with a salad fork."

Brady tackled Bo from behind. Bo leaned forward, drawing the child over his head but catching him before he hit the floor. "Let's go eat, wild man. Pizza?"

"Pissa," Brady exclaimed and dashed away.

Sara stopped Bo from following. "I probably shouldn't be doing this, but I couldn't resist the chance to play grown-up. Sometimes, I think my mind is turning into two-year-old mush."

Bo clapped his big hand on her shoulder in a supportive manner. "Go out. Have fun. Forget about the rest and don't worry about Brady. I'm no wimp like Ren. I can take it."

Wimp? She'd have asked for an explanation, but the door-bell took away her breath. She was going out on a date. A real live date.

"Wow!" Ren said, handing her a lush bouquet.

"Thank you!" she exclaimed. "They're beautiful. Look, Brady, pretty flowers."

Brady grabbed the hem of her dress and yanked hard, trying to reach the flowers. Ren gently removed the material from the little fist, then picked him up. Together they leaned toward the roses. "They smell nice, don't they? But women are like flowers, Brady—they don't appreciate it when you grab them. You need to treat flowers and girls very gently."

His serious tone seemed to make an impression, because Brady sniffed but didn't touch. "That was pretty sexist," Bo muttered. "I could never get away with that."

Sara laughed. "You guys are really something."

Ren seemed oddly shaken by her happy reception. He looked at Bo and said, "Can you handle the flowers, too? I don't want to miss our reservation."

Bo accepted the bouquet with a curtsy.

Giggling, Sara kissed his cheek, then knelt to hug Brady. "You be good for Bo. I love you."

Brady waved from the door, as Sara and Ren pulled away. Sara looked over her shoulder, feeling a trifle let down. "I expected that to be more traumatic. I've never left him at night before."

Ren glanced at her but didn't reply. She made small talk on the drive to the restaurant, but it seemed oddly one-sided.

Once seated at a table overlooking the river, she asked Ren, "Is something wrong?"

There was a pause before he spoke. "Bo said something to me earlier about this being a celebration…because you'd agreed to the test." His eyes were dark with emotion. "That's not what this is. I…I don't want you to think I'm trivializing your feelings, your fears. I asked you out because I'm attracted to you and I like spending time with you," he said somberly.

Sara couldn't repress the smile that bubbled up from her heart. "Ren, I had my doubts about this, too, but Claudie helped me put it in perspective."

"She did?"

"She said, 'A free dinner's a free dinner. Go for it.'"

He seemed momentarily nonplussed, then laughed. "She gave me some advice, too," he said, his lips twitching in mischief.

The look was so Brady, Sara's heart almost stopped.

He leaned forward as if to impart a secret. "She said, 'No kissing, no touching and, above all, no oysters.'"

Now Sara was also laughing. "Good. I don't like oysters. I don't know what I'd do if you made me eat them."

He studied her for a moment, then said, "You're far more beautiful than I realized."

Her pulse quickened. "I am?"

He nodded. "Yes, and normally that wouldn't be a problem. But I just figured out I'm very attracted to you—and that *is* a problem."

Her heart fluttered wildly at the word *attracted.* "Because of the paternity issue."

"No, actually. Because of me."

"I don't understand."

He sighed. "As Bo would so eloquently put it—my social life sucks. Eve called off our engagement less than a week ago, and here I am drooling over you. Don't you think that's just a little emotionally immature?"

Sara perked up as if someone had given her a shot of adrenaline. "You're far too sophisticated to drool, Ren. But I appreciate the compliment."

"You do? You're not appalled?"

She grinned and made her brows waggle suggestively. "Actually, I'm flattered. I haven't had time for a lot of dates, so this one is kind of special. It doesn't have to be anything more than that."

Ren seemed surprised by her candor. "You never cease to surprise me," he said.

"Give it time. You haven't known me very long." She opened the menu, aware of his gaze on her. "What's good here? I've seen this place from the road."

"I haven't been here in a long time, but I understand the food's great. I think I'll have the pasta primavera."

When the waiter returned, she ordered the steak and shrimp, and Ren ordered a bottle of wine.

"How'd it go at the clinic today?" he asked, after the waiter had left.

Sara focused on buttering a piece of sourdough bread. It was one thing to talk flirtatiously, quite another to pull it off. She decided it would be best if she treated Ren as she did Bo—like a big brother.

"Kee was a wreck. Claudie gave her a hard time to keep her focused."

"Big stretch there," he said drolly.

Sara took a sip of water. "Claudie isn't as brave as she acts. When the technician put a needle in Kee's arm to get a blood sample, she almost lost it. She once told me she saw a girl OD on heroin. That might be why she's trying so hard to turn her life around."

The wine arrived. Ren tasted it, then nodded his approval. When both glasses were filled, he lifted his glass to hers and smiled. "To good company."

Sara took a sip. Buttery and delicious.

"Bo told me Claudie's working on her high-school equivalency exam. That's a good start."

Before she could reply, an older couple stopped at their table. The man's silver hair added to his aura of power and wealth. He shook Ren's hand. "Lawrence, good to see you. Your mother tells me you're thinking of running for office in the near future. I'm glad to hear it."

"Actually," Ren said, "politics is Babe's forte, not mine. I tried to convince her to run for office, but at the time, Senator, your seat was the only one up for vote."

The man guffawed, then looked at Sara. She thought she read speculation and curiosity as Ren introduced her. "Sara owns a bookstore. We share an interest in literacy," he told them. Under his breath, he added, "Among other things."

The older couple asked a few questions about mutual acquaintances, then wished them a good evening and left. Ren looked at Sara over the rim of his glass. "What?" he asked, cocking his head.

"Nothing. It's just…they didn't seem overly surprised to see you with someone other than Eve."

He shrugged. "Yesterday's news. And, frankly, I doubt if our breakup was a big surprise to anyone other than my mother."

Before Sara could say anything, the waiter arrived with their meals. He added a bit more wine to both glasses, then tactfully disappeared. Ren lifted his glass, "To new beginnings."

Sara touched her glass to his, but found it hard to swallow over the lump in her throat. Fortunately, Ren steered the conversation to more light-hearted subjects, and Sara relaxed. Between his dry wit and the best meal she could ever remember eating, the evening flew by.

On her front porch later, she found herself wishing Claudie hadn't been quite so specific about what *not* to do.

"I had a great time. Thanks," she said, meaning it.

Ren kept his distance. "So did I. Maybe we could—" His words were cut short by Bo, who stumbled outside like a just-released hostage.

"You're back," he cried. "Thank God."

Sara frowned. "What happened?"

"You didn't tell me he likes to hide, but I only lost him twice," he boasted.

"Lost him?" Ren repeated, his tone tense.

"Hey, it's a big house, and he's fast. But Claudie called, and when I told her what happened, she suggested I tie a bell around his ankle."

"Like a cow?" Ren snarled.

Bo bristled. "I'd like to see you do any better."

Laughing, Sara stepped between them. "Thank you for baby-sitting, Bo. I'm sure the bell delighted Brady. Claudie and I put little bells on his shoes when he first started walking, because he'd take off in a blink. I should have warned you."

He gave Ren a smug look, then told Sara, "Actually, I had a pretty good time, but he wore me out. I'm taking off, if that's okay with you."

She gave him a friendly hug. Then Bo and Ren exchanged nonverbal grunts that made her repress a giggle.

Once the Mazda disappeared into the night, Sara took a deep breath and looked at Ren. He was studying her face for some reason. "Thank you for the wonderful meal and great company," she said, pleased by how calm she sounded. Memories of that first kiss were never far from her mind—a teasing hint that made her crave more. "I felt like a real grown-up."

Ren took a step closer. "A grown-up? Was that ever in doubt?"

Sara's breath caught in her throat. "All the time. Right now I feel like a teenager on her first date."

"Really?" He smiled wolfishly, his fingertip tracing the scalloped trim at her shoulder. "In that dress you look young enough to get me in trouble."

Leaning down, he narrowed the gap between them. Sara's heartbeat sped up; her lips parted on their own accord. *Kiss me.*

But at the last second he veered slightly, his lips brushing her cheek. "I have a feeling where Claudie's concerned it wouldn't take much to get me in trouble. I should leave while I'm still ahead."

Sara dropped her chin to keep her disappointment from showing. "I'll tell her you were a perfect gentleman," she said softly.

Ren didn't move. When Sara looked up, she saw something that took her breath away. Desire.

"Good night, Sara," he said, his voice low and husky. "I'll call you tomorrow. Sleep well." When he turned and walked away, Sara thought she heard him add, "Lord knows *I* won't."

CHAPTER TEN

REN STOPPED PACING the moment Rafael Justis poked his head around the door between their offices, his brows knit with concern. "Are you okay?" he asked.

"Fine," Ren said, and to prove he meant it, he walked to his desk and sat down. The young man didn't look thoroughly convinced, but he backed out and closed the door.

With a weighty sigh, he pulled his calendar into his line of vision. Six weeks…the results of the DNA test wouldn't be back for at least six weeks. It wasn't a lifetime, but it sure felt like one.

All parties had met at Armory's office earlier that morning. Sara hadn't wasted any time living up to her part of the bargain. "If it's as easy as you say it is, we can stop by on our way to the bookstore," she'd told Ren on the phone last night. He was certain he detected a nervous tremble in her voice, but she didn't hesitate when he suggested meeting at his attorney's.

"He's old school, Sara, a friend of my father's. He wants to oversee everything to ensure there are no problems farther down the road," he'd explained.

She didn't quibble. "Tomorrow morning at nine? We'll be there."

When Ren called Armory at home to confirm this morning's meeting, the older man had expressed curiosity about

why Sara had agreed to the test. "You're not in any way co-
ercing her or taking advantage of her circumstances, are you?"

Ren smiled, pleased that Armory had the strength of character to care about Sara's welfare, too. "I'm paying to have
her eaves scraped," he said.

"I beg your pardon? That's not some kind of kinky body
surgery, is it?"

Ren was well acquainted with Armory's sense of humor, so
he'd let the question slide. "I'm helping her finish some repairs
that should have been done long ago through the estate. As a matter of fact, I'd like you to check up on the lawyer handling those
matters. I'll give you the details when I see you tomorrow."

The actual test had gone smoothly. Both Sara and Brady
seemed to relax, thanks to Armory's gentle charm and obvious goodwill. His grandfatherly white hair had thoroughly en-
tranced Brady, and Ren's heart had clutched for a moment as
he wished his own father were there.

To get the ball rolling, Ren began by reading the instructions aloud. Brady had been intrigued for about one minute,
then wanted off his mother's lap.

"It can't be all that complicated," Armory said, pulling his
chair out into the middle of the room adjacent to Ren's and
Sara's. "You've got some extra stick-things there. Let's all do
one, so Brady can see how easy it is. If you don't mind, young
lady, I'll do yours," he said to Sara.

She giggled when the swab touched her inner cheek, and
Brady immediately wanted in on the action. "Me?"

"Why don't you try Ren, Brady?" Sara suggested. "Be
very gentle, sweetie. You don't want to hurt him."

Ren added extra sound effects that made Brady chortle.
"Me?" he asked.

"Okay. Your turn. Open wide." Just to be safe, Ren collected two samples from Brady, then two from himself.

Armory produced four lollipops. "Sugarless," he told Sara with a wink.

And that had been the end of it. Armory had assured Ren that he would have the samples sent by courier to the company that afternoon.

Flawless. Simple. It was just a matter of waiting, Ren thought now, penciling out the weeks on his calendar. Could he wait that long? What choice did he have?

"Sir?" Rafael asked, opening the door. "You wanted to finish up the defense witnesses before lunch."

Ren rose and reached for his judge's robe. "I know. Would you please do me a favor? Call Sara Carsten at No Page Unturned and ask her to meet me in Capitol Park by the Vietnam Veterans Memorial. Twelve-thirty."

SARA HUNG UP THE PHONE—for once grateful the store wasn't busy. Her stomach felt queasy. The test this morning had been painless and she'd liked Ren's attorney, but she hadn't slept well the night before, thanks to her talk with Daniel. His concern about the test had made her begin to second-guess her decision. Was her attraction to Ren getting in the way of common sense?

"Are you sure you can trust Ren Bishop?" Daniel asked. "I'm not saying he's a low-life bum like Jeff, but he could be using you for his own purposes."

Daniel's words had haunted her sleep. Could Ren be believed, or did he plan to take Brady away from her once his paternity was established? What would keep him from seeking sole custody if he was Brady's biological father? Even Julia's wishes would take second place to that kind of leverage, wouldn't they?

Sara rubbed her temple, cocking her head to listen for Brady's quiet chatter in the story area. One of her regular customers had popped in a few minutes earlier, asking Sara to keep an eye on her little girl while she ran to the bank. Brady and the little girl had spent five minutes staring at each other before finally deciding it was safe to engage in play. Sara had felt saddened, realizing how much Brady needed to be around children his own age and how rarely the opportunity arose.

Then Ren's clerk had called, shaking her even further. The procedure that morning had gone smoothly—almost too smoothly. Why did Ren want to see her? Was something wrong?

The bell over the door tinkled, making Sara start. Her tension eased a bit when she saw Keneesha and Claudie enter. "Hello, ladies," she called. "Aren't you looking chipper today, Kee. That medicine must be working."

"I not only look good, I feel good," her friend replied, helping herself to a cup of coffee from the air pot. Instead of her usual sweet roll, however, she took a banana from the bowl and carried her snack to Sara's desk. "See this. I'm watching what I eat. Natural sugars from fruit are better for you than refined sugars."

Sara blinked. "Wow. You've been reading all that literature the doctor sent home, haven't you?"

Keneesha gave her a sober look. "A visiting nurse came to see me this morning. She told me if I didn't take care of myself I could wind up losing a leg or going blind."

Claudie joined them. "There's an image. How much money do you think a one-legged, blind hooker could make on the street?"

The blunt question made Sara cringe, but Keneesha and Claudie looked at each other and burst out laughing. Sara shook her head. "You guys are bad."

"Not for long," Keneesha said.

Sara could tell by her serious tone that something was up. She waited for the woman to continue.

"I called back home last night. My mama lives in Georgia. She's got my kid."

"You have a child?" Sara asked, astounded by the news. "And you never told me?"

"A boy. He's fourteen. I haven't seen him since he was three. My mama told me if I left, he was as good as dead to me, so I tried to pretend he was." She was quiet a minute, then said, "Mama says he's doin' real good. Plays sports in school. She told me I could come home if I wanted to."

"So when ya leavin'?" Claudie asked, her face stony.

Keneesha gave her a look that said she understood her friend's attitude. "It'll take me a couple of weeks to get all my shi—stuff together. I gotta get my blood sugar level and my medication stable, too."

"You're moving to Georgia?" Sara exclaimed. "Really?"

Keneesha nodded. "My mama's got diabetes, too. I figure we can watch out after each other. And being around Brady so much has made me kind of miss my kid."

Impulsively, Sara hugged her friend, tears coming to her eyes. "I will really miss you, but I think it's wonderful you're reuniting with your family. How can I help? Do you need boxes? There are a million out back."

Planning Keneesha's move helped take Sara's mind off her upcoming talk with Ren, but Claudie seemed to sense something was amiss. When they walked into the storeroom, she asked, "So what's going on with the judge? How was the big date?"

Sara sat down on a wobbly stool. "The date was fabulous. Beautiful restaurant. Wonderful food. Ren was a perfect gentleman. He even brought me flowers."

Claudie didn't look impressed.

Sara took a breath, then said, "We did the DNA test this morning."

"Bo told me." Claudie shrugged. "It was gonna happen, anyway. Are you sorry you did it?"

"No, but Daniel's worried that Ren is only being nice to me because of some ulterior motive."

"Like what?"

"Like he wants to lull me into a false sense of security so he can get close to Brady, then sue for sole custody." Sara couldn't stop her voice from squeaking as she spoke.

"Sounds like something a lawyer would do," Claudie said under her breath.

"Ren's clerk called a little while ago and said Ren wanted to see me at the park at twelve-thirty."

Claudie scratched her chin thoughtfully. "I haven't quite figured the guy out. My gut says he's dangerous, but so far he's been okay. I think I should go with you. Kee's ready to kiss the ground he walks on for insisting we take her to the clinic, so she wouldn't be much help if he tries something shady."

"Good idea," Sara said, feeling a little less troubled.

Claudie, who was neither naive nor gullible, had killer instincts when it came to men. She'd help Sara guard against her unreliable response to Ren Bishop's sex appeal.

REN SHIFTED against the wooden slats of the bench. At an adjacent bench, a homeless man slept curled in a tight ball as if trying to ward off society. Ren could sympathize with him. All morning he had been bombarded—defense lawyers, prosecutors, the District Attorney, his mother.

Somehow Babe had managed to weasel Sara's name out of Eve, and now seemed convinced Sara was a shakedown artist trying to extort money from him to support her child. Exasperated, Ren told Babe she was wrong. If anything, just the opposite was true: he was trying to extort shared custody from Sara.

He'd managed to hang up without blowing up, but his patience with his mother's interference in his life was diminishing.

"Ren!" a gleeful voice cried.

Ren looked up to see Brady racing toward him. A prickly sensation attacked his sinuses, and he swallowed against the emotion that constricted his heart. If anyone had told him a child could affect him this way so quickly, he'd have laughed out loud. Actually, the strength of the bond he felt for Brady helped convince Ren of their biological connection.

He sank to one knee, and when Brady hurled himself into his open arms, Ren hugged him fiercely. "Hi, big guy, how's it going?"

Brady returned the hug, then squirmed to be free. "'Quiddels,'" he said, pointing toward a skinny creature with a moth-eaten tail.

Ren released him, and the boy took off, chasing the animal, which raced up a tree and then scolded raucously.

"Hi," Sara said, walking up to Ren.

Something's up, Ren thought, rising. If they were at a different place in their relationship, he'd take her in his arms to reassure her that whatever the problem, they could handle it together. But they were a long way from that point, which was probably why she'd brought along reinforcements.

"Hi, Sara. Hello, Claudie."

Claudie acknowledged him with a nod, then set about putting out their picnic lunch. She unfurled a blanket in the shade of a leafy buckeye tree and withdrew a soft-sided cooler from the stroller.

"I brought an extra peanut-butter-and-jelly sandwich, if you're hungry," Sara told him.

Ren knew he wouldn't be able to relax until he'd gotten his proposition out of the way. "Maybe we should talk first," he said, nodding toward the park bench.

She exchanged looks with Claudie, then walked to the bench. Her tan cotton slacks showed grape jelly smudges that almost matched her lavender pullover. A pair of dark glasses held her hair off her face. Her eyes looked worried.

He didn't know how to begin.

Sara watched his face intently as if sensing his nervousness. Claudie broke the silence by calling Brady to come eat his sandwich. Ren watched the boy swerve from his pursuit of another squirrel and run to the blanket. Brady dropped flat, wiggling in protest when Claudie wiped his hands and face with a cloth she produced from a plastic bag.

"I really appreciate what you did today," Ren started. "I just wish there were some way to expedite matters. Six weeks is a long time to wait." He scooted forward to face Sara. His heart pounded in his chest. "But I have a suggestion for the interim that I'd like you to consider. I thought about it all day yesterday. I realize it may sound a little radical, but…"

Her eyes widened. "What?"

"I'd like you and Brady to move in with me. Into my house, I mean. It's a big house—five bedrooms, four baths. I have a housekeeper who comes twice a week."

Sara appeared dumbfounded, as if that were the last thing in the world she expected to hear him say.

"If you think about it, it makes sense…in a way. My place is closer to town. You wouldn't have that long commute. And you mentioned at dinner you were thinking about selling Hulger's house. This way a Realtor could show it without your having to worry about keeping it spotless."

Sara looked at Claudie, who suddenly shot to her feet and stomped over to the bench. "Are you freakin' nuts or what?" Claudie shouted at Ren.

"Claudie," Sara said reprovingly. Ren followed her gaze

to Brady, who sat cross-legged on the blanket, watching with big eyes.

"Well, excuse me, but that's the lamest proposition I've ever heard. He must think you're stupid, Sara. That's all some family court judge would need to decide in his favor if he wanted to press for custody."

Ren watched Sara's expression turn anguished. Inwardly he groaned, cursing himself for being so stupid, cursing Claudie for being so smart.

"That was never my intention."

"Yeah, right. Then why suggest it? Out of the goodness of your heart?"

Oh, his heart was involved, but Ren couldn't claim altruistic motives. Purely selfish was more like it, since this arrangement would give him a chance to be around the child he was coming to adore and the woman he desired.

"It seemed like a practical solution. Sara hates her house, and it's a long, unpleasant commute."

Claudie snorted. "If she wants to move, she doesn't need your help."

Ren recognized the truth in her words. His perfect scenario was flawed, seriously flawed. "You're right," he said quietly.

He rose, hoping to salvage some pride. He looked at Sara and said, "It seemed like a good idea at the time." He gave her an apologetic smile and started to leave.

"Nooo," a voice cried.

Ren glanced over his shoulder and saw Brady scramble to his feet and charge after him. Sara caught the little boy in her arms. She fought his struggles, then comforted him when he started to cry. Over Brady's sobbing shoulder, she looked at Ren. He was too far away to read her eyes, but he thought he saw tears. He cursed himself for causing her more anguish. *Damn.* He turned away and kept walking.

SARA AND CLAUDIE didn't speak the whole way back to the store. Both seemed to share some kind of emotional ennui. Sara still felt stunned by Ren's offer. Why would a man like Ren Bishop open his home to a stranger? Could he really be trying to compromise Sara's custody? Somehow Claudie's explanation seemed too cold-blooded for a person as kind and generous as Ren.

It was with a sense of relief that she greeted Bo when she found him arguing with Keneesha above an atlas. "This boy ain't never been to Georgia, but he thinks he knows the quickest way to go."

"It was just a suggestion," Bo said testily.

"Bo, I need your help," Sara said quietly.

He turned to her. "What happened?"

Claudie extracted a grumpy Brady from the stroller and passed him to Sara. "You rock. I'll tell him all about it," she said.

Sara nodded and moved to the rocking chair a short distance away. Once seated, she closed her eyes and listened to the retelling of Ren's strange offer. She couldn't help picturing the look of pain on his face when he heard Claudie's accusation.

"What do you think he had in mind?" Sara asked in a low voice. She could tell by Brady's breathing that he was almost asleep.

Bo paced back and forth a few steps. "I know Ren is lonely—who wouldn't be, living in that big house? And things were never really all that great with him and Eve. They hung out and went through the motions more because it was expected of them than because they really loved each other. I knew that from the beginning. But this is kinda scary."

"You mean, he was for real?" Claudie asked, her tone shocked. "He wasn't just using Sara to get hold of Brady?"

Bo gave her a stony look. "Ren wouldn't do that. He may be a forty-year-old guy who's starting to think life is passing him by, but he's not cruel and calculating. If he asked Sara to move in with him, it's because he wanted her and Brady around."

Before Sara could ask about the risk to her custody claim if she did consider Ren's offer, the bookstore bell chimed. All watched as an older woman stepped inside, then paused to look around. When she zeroed in on the group huddled around Sara's desk, Bo groaned, "Uh-oh."

Sara's stomach rose and fell. Instinctively she tightened her hold on Brady, who was deadweight in her arms.

"I wish to speak with Sara Carstairs," the woman said, her voice strong and cultured.

Sara recognized the voice from Ren's answering machine. *Ren's mother.*

Sara rocked forward and stood. "I'm Sara *Carsten,*" she said, emphasizing her last name. "If you'll give me a moment…" She bent down to place Brady in his playpen. She positioned one of his stuffed animals beside him, then rose and turned to face Ren's mother.

"You must be Mrs. Bishop," she said. Stepping forward, she put out her hand.

Babe took Sara's offered hand with discernible reluctance; she shook hands using two fingers and her thumb.

"These are my friends," Sara said. She started to introduce them, but Babe made a dismissive motion with her hand.

"Yes, I know Bo. Haven't you got work to do somewhere?" she asked, giving him a steely look.

"Oh, yes, most definitely. See you later, Sara." *Sorry,* he mouthed before hurrying away.

"Coward," Claudie whispered.

Mrs. Bishop gave her a quelling look that caused Claudie to edge closer to Keneesha. "I wish to speak with you alone," Babe demanded.

Sara walked to her desk, but motioned for Keneesha to stay sitting. "I'd prefer my friends to stay."

Babe's lips narrowed. She gave Sara a chilly look. If she weren't so cold, Sara thought, she'd be beautiful. Several inches shorter than Sara, Babe Bishop carried herself like a queen. Her exquisite suit of light pink wool dramatized her slim, athletic figure.

"Very well, if you insist," Babe said disapprovingly.

Reaching into the large leather purse she carried, Babe produced a plain manila file folder and laid it on Sara's desk. The cover flipped open, revealing a glossy photograph obviously torn from a men's magazine. The idea of Ren's mother toting that around almost made Sara laugh—until she zeroed in on the face in the photo.

"Julia?"

Sara grabbed the thick dossier.

"You didn't know your sister posed for *Playboy* magazine?" Babe asked, her tone showing surprise.

Sara shook her head, blood pounding in her temples. *When? Why didn't she tell me?* In the photo, Julia—in thigh-high white stockings and with a nurse's cap tilted at a rakish angle—posed beside a gurney. Her temptress smile was one Sara had seen her use many times when teasing men.

"She lost her job at the hospital because of it," Babe said.

Sara vaguely recalled some kind of fracas around the time of her own trouble with the law. Julia had downplayed her firing as political nonsense, and consequently Sara hadn't given it much thought.

"She wasn't unemployed long, however," Babe added, her

tone steeped in innuendo. "Her future husband hired her. A short time later, she married the boss. I believe they call that 'job security.'"

Sara scanned the report from Babe's private investigators. She noticed neither Ren's nor Bo's name appeared in the report, so she reckoned Babe had acquired it independently.

"Why did you do this?" Sara asked.

"My son has a big heart. He doesn't see things in black and white, but I do. Right now, he's only thinking about doing the right thing for the child—but somebody has to look to the future. If the boy is going to be a Bishop, we have to know everything there is about his mother so we can be prepared."

"Prepared for what?"

"When a person enters the political arena, the press has been known to dig. It's best to know in advance what they'll find so one can put the proper spin on it."

Sara had no problem picturing the spin they'd put on Julia—a tramp who posed in the nude seducing a judge, then hiding his child from him. Sara looked at Brady, sleeping so peacefully, and knew she'd do anything to keep him from having to hear those kinds of lies about his mother.

"What do you want from me?" Sara asked.

Babe seemed momentarily taken aback by Sara's frankness. "I want the same thing my son wants."

Sara looked at Claudie, who slowly shook her head, warning Sara not to do anything impulsive. Sara shrugged as if to say, *What choice do I have?*

Turning to Babe, Sara said, "An hour ago, your son asked me for something that I feared would compromise my claim for custody if this went to court. I told him no. I'll change my answer to yes if you agree to destroy this file—" she dropped the folder to the desk "—and give me your word that Brady will never be exposed to its contents. My sister was a good person. She may have made mistakes in her life, but she loved her son with all her heart, and I won't have him believing any differently."

Babe gestured dismissively again. "I can't speak for the press but I can't imagine any of this will come up as long as the child is under Lawrence's protection."

Protection. The word, which sounded so feudal, continued to skip through Sara's brain long after Babe left. Ren might be able to protect Brady from the past, but who would protect Sara from falling in love with a man whose main goal was acquiring a son? Or was it already too late?

Sara knew if she were honest she'd have to admit that Ren's offer initially thrilled her, for no other reason than that it would give her a chance to spend more time with him. But Ren wasn't looking for a girlfriend—he just ended a relationship, and Sara had heard enough rebound horror stories from other women. *Unfortunately,* Sara thought, *that doesn't mean I can keep my heart from going crazy whenever he looks at me.*

"Whatcha thinkin', Sara J?" Keneesha asked.

Sinking back into the rocking chair, Sara regarded her friends and sighed. She couldn't tell them the truth. "I was thinking, 'So this is what it's like when you sell your soul to the devil.'"

Claudie snickered. "A witch is more like it."

Sara groaned. It was one thing to make a pact with the devil but quite another to see it through. "Well, right or wrong, it looks like we're going to need more boxes."

BO SHADOWED REN from the courthouse. It wasn't hard since Ren seemed oblivious to the world around him. In the dozen or so blocks to his house, he'd only just missed running over a dog, then sat through a green light until another driver angrily leaned on the horn.

When they reached Ren's house, Bo waited a few minutes before entering through the back door, which his friend had failed to lock. Apparently lost in thought, Ren stood at the base of the stairs. Bo grabbed his elbow from behind, and with a twist of his wrist slammed Ren up against the wall. An *oof* of air left Ren's lungs, and he drew his arms up defensively, crying, "Jesus, Bo. What the hell are you doing?"

"Beating the shit out of you," Bo snarled, needing to release the tension that had been building ever since Babe Bishop had showed up at the bookstore. Not only did Ren's mother always manage to make Bo feel eight years old and worthless, but the more Bo stewed over Babe's attitude, the more upset he became about Ren's outrageous proposition. Like mother, like son—always trying to control other people's lives.

"Could you at least tell me why?" Ren asked, moving slightly out of the line of fire. His briefcase clattered to the tile floor.

"Why'd you ask Sara to move in with you?"

Ren didn't seem surprised that Bo knew of his suggestion. His shoulders slumped in defeat, and he sank downward, his shoes making a hissing sound against the tile. "Because I'm an idiot, okay?"

Bo folded his arms across his chest. "That's a start."

Ren dropped his head in his hands. "I think I'm in love with her, Bo. I know it's crazy and I shouldn't be feeling this way."

"So this moving-in thing wasn't some ploy to get leverage in a custody suit?"

Ren groaned. "That's what she thinks, isn't it. Claudie pounced on that, but I didn't think Sara would believe it. Does she hate me?"

Before Bo could answer, the doorbell chimed.

"Did you order a pizza to go with my beating?" Ren asked sarcastically as he got to his feet. He yanked open the door without checking the peephole.

"Sara," he croaked.

Bo hurried into the foyer. His mouth dropped open at the sight of Sara, Brady and Claudie standing on the stoop. A diaper bag, two oversize totes and one small old-fashioned suitcase rested between them.

Sara stepped inside. Claudie, who held Brady's hand, crowded behind her.

"All right," Sara said, glancing first at Bo, then back at Ren. "This is the way it is. I cut a deal with your mother this afternoon. Has she talked to you?"

Ren shook his head. "Not since this morning. I told her to stay out of this. What did she do to you?"

"We can go into that later. The bottom line is I've agreed to move in here."

"My *mother* asked you to move in with me?"

"Not exactly. In return for her destroying some very mean-spirited information about Julia—" She looked at Bo, her eyes narrowing. "Did you know Julia posed for a magazine?"

He gulped. "Yes."

"Did you know?" she asked Ren.

He nodded. "It was in Bo's report. It didn't seem like a big deal to me."

Some of the stiffness went out of her posture. Claudie coughed, and Sara went on. "Anyway, your mother agreed to destroy the file if I did whatever you wanted. You asked us to move in with you, so here we are. I don't think this is exactly what she meant, but this is what she's getting."

Bo almost choked on his howl of laugher. "I bet the old bat shits green when she finds out," he said, ignoring Ren's brusque shove.

Sara frowned. "But there's one condition," she said, her tone formidable.

Bo sobered. He glanced at Ren, who seemed to be holding his breath.

"What kind of condition?" Ren asked.

"Claudie moves in, too. This is purely a business arrangement. We're here until the DNA test results come back and we know whether or not you're Brady's father. If you are, I want your word we'll work out a fair and equitable joint-custody arrangement. If you're not Brady's father, I should have my house sold by then, and Brady and Claudie and I can find a place closer to work. Agreed?"

Ren didn't hesitate. "Yes."

"I'll start bringing in your stuff," Bo said, scooting past Claudie, who gave him an evil look. He hurried to the Toyota wagon. With his back to the house, he didn't care who saw his grin. Who but Sara could have turned the tables so neatly on Babe Bishop? he thought.

The poetry of it almost made him weep with laughter.

CHAPTER ELEVEN

SARA SHIFTED BRADY to her left hip and walked through the dining room to the kitchen. She'd been through every room the previous evening moving breakable objects out of Brady's reach. Overall, Sara liked the house, but she didn't care for the dining room, which struck her as gloomy and ostentatious. Ren said it was next on his remodeling list.

Her hand was poised to push open the door, when Sara caught the sound of voices—angry voices. She started to turn around, but Brady yodeled, "'Nana"—the word for his favorite fruit.

The door swung inward, and Ren looked at them. "Good morning," he said. "Come in."

Sara cautiously stepped into the sunny kitchen. Dressed in baggy sweatpants and a tank top that showed a dark trail from jogging, it was apparent from the screwdriver in Ren's hand that he'd been in the process of assembling Brady's high chair when an unexpected guest had arrived.

His mother stood beside the counter, arms folded across her chest. Her three-piece ivory slack outfit made Sara regret throwing on yesterday's shorts and T-shirt.

"Sit down. I'll have this together in half a minute," Ren said, squatting beside the pieces of molded plastic. "Mother, you remember Sara, the woman you tried to blackmail."

Babe sputtered. "I did nothing of the sort. Did she tell you that?"

Sara clutched Brady tighter. The little boy stared at Babe with big eyes. Sara figured he was either drawn to her impressive gold necklace or fascinated by her bristling outrage.

Screwing up her courage, she stepped forward. "I told him the truth, Mrs. Bishop. That you had photos of Julia that you threatened to use if I didn't cooperate. Moving here was your son's idea, not mine."

Babe seemed to shrink slightly, although her chin remained high. "It's not as though I planned to give those photographs to the press—they could damage Lawrence's reputation as well, since he was associated with her."

Ren shot to his feet. "Her name was Julia, Mother. She was a beautiful, exciting, dynamic woman. I wasn't associated with her. I made love to her, and I don't regret it—especially not if the DNA test proves I'm Brady's father. This child—" he stepped beside Sara and put his hand on Brady's head "—is a blessing. He's already brought more light and happiness into my life in a few short weeks than I can remember feeling in a long, long time."

Babe started to speak, but Ren added, "I want those pictures, Mother. In fact, I want your entire file on Sara, Brady and Julia. We'll have a little bonfire tonight and toast marshmallows."

His mother, who was staring at Brady, turned abruptly to pick her purse off the counter. "If that's the way you feel about it. I was only trying to help."

She left without saying goodbye, and Sara doubted Babe would be around much during the next six weeks.

"Well, that was fun," Ren said dryly. "I always like to start my day with a little family drama."

Sara tried not to laugh, but the relief she felt was too great. She tickled Brady under his arm, and he giggled, too, until he spotted a familiar yellow fruit. "'Nana," he cried triumphantly.

Sara peeled the banana and sat down on one of the stools, positioning Brady on her lap. "Thanks," she said softly.

Ren tightened the last of the screws, then turned the chair upright. "For putting this together? No problem. Having familiar stuff around will make everything a little less confusing for Brady. Don't you think?"

Sara nodded. "Yes. But I meant thank you for defending Julia."

Ren held out his arms to Brady, who went without hesitation. He carried him to the high chair, then helped Brady wiggle his chubby little legs through the opening. Once Ren had secured the strap around Brady's waist, he looked at Sara. "My mother is a complex person. I'm sure she has my best interests in mind. The only problem is, we don't always agree on what those are."

"Is this going to cause problems between you? Maybe I shouldn't have—"

He didn't let her finish the thought. "I made it clear to Mother before you came in that you and Brady and Claudie are off-limits to her. She's welcome here anytime as long as she's prepared to treat you civilly."

Sara didn't say anything. She knew all about difficult mothers, and only hoped he wouldn't have to cope with long-term repercussions after she and Brady were gone.

"Believe me, Sara, I know my mother. She's a born politician. Give her a little time, and she'll find a way to blame this on someone else, but I guarantee it won't be you or Brady." He grinned. "I think Armory's her new target. She's mad because he left her out of the loop."

Sara smiled. She didn't believe him, but his joking helped ease some of the weight on her shoulders.

"How'd you sleep?" Ren asked, walking to the counter where the coffeepot sat.

"I slept fine," she lied. Despite an exhaustion so complete she'd expected to sink into oblivion, Sara had tossed and turned, rehashing her decision. She kept asking herself if her true reason for giving in had more to do with the attraction she felt toward Ren than her need to protect Julia's memory.

When she looked at Ren, she found him staring at her. His facial expression remained neutral, but the look in his eyes set her heart racing.

"Coffee?" he asked.

He poured her a cup and carried it to her. Sitting on the high stool, she was just about eye level with him. He smelled of maleness and fresh air. Was it that or the aroma of the coffee that made her mouth water? She could easily reach out and touch his chest, where a few errant dark hairs curled above the neckline of his tank top.

"*O*'s, Mommy," Brady hollered, breaking the spell. "*O*'s."

Ren set the cup on the table and spun around. "*O*-what?"

Sara moved past him in search of the box of cereal she'd brought from home the night before. "Cheerios," she explained, retrieving it from a lower cabinet.

Ren took a carton of milk from the refrigerator and was reaching for a bowl, when Sara told him, "Brady likes his cereal dry. I pile it right on the tray—one less bowl to wash. Let me find his spill-proof cup."

"It's in the dishwasher," Ren said, opening the appliance door. He pulled out the cup and wiped it with a towel before handing it to Sara. "Dry cereal? Why dry cereal?"

"Tell Ren why you like your cereal dry, Brady," she said, pouring milk into the *Lion King* mug.

Brady chewed a bite of banana, then said in Brady-talk, "It goes *crunch-crunch* on my teeth better."

Ren's face screwed up in concentration. "He likes crunchy peanut butter?" he asked Sara.

She laughed. "Pretty close. You're getting better at understanding him." She set the mug in front of Brady. "He said he likes it crunching on his teeth."

"Oh."

"Brady knows his teeth are very important. That's why he drinks milk and brushes after every meal. Right Brady?"

Brady looked at Ren and gave him a toothy grin, complete with half-eaten cereal.

The swinging door opened inward, and Claudie walked hesitantly into the room. Ren did a double-take at seeing her with hair sticking up and no makeup. Sara thought Claudie looked about twelve in her baggy boxer shorts and wrinkled T-shirt.

"Can I use the pool?" she asked in a shy voice.

Ren reached for the key, which he'd placed on the top shelf of the brass baker's rack the night before. They'd all shared pizza on the patio last night after Bo and Sara had returned from a second run to her house. Brady had headed straight for the pool—a move that had alarmed Ren despite the presence of a fence. After some searching, he'd managed to locate a padlock and key. He hadn't returned to his cold pizza until the lock was safely on the gate, the key hanging where only adults could reach it.

"My mother fought long and hard to keep this pool from being built," he'd told them. "In the end, my dad twisted her arm by convincing her it would be good for his heart. But she insisted on the tallest, safest fence on the market. I've been lax about locking the gate because I was the only one using it, but from now on, we use the lock."

Handing the key to Claudie, he said, "There are beach towels in the cabana. You can swim, can't you?"

She gave him a black look. "I once lived six blocks from Lake Michigan. I can swim." She exited through the sunroom's sliding glass door, pulling the screen closed behind her.

The morning breeze filtered into the room. Mature trees and well-groomed bushes kept the yard shady and cool. Sara moved to the window and watched her friend execute a clean dive into the water.

"I want you to know I appreciate your doing this, Sara," Ren said.

Sara looked over her shoulder. "It was probably a mistake."

He didn't dispute that but said, "I'll do my best to make sure you don't regret it. If I can help you get your house on the market or anything else, just let me know."

He is a good man, Sara thought. *It's not his fault I'm falling in love with him.*

"I'm going to run upstairs and take a shower," he said, swallowing a last gulp of coffee. "When I get back down, I'll fix you and Claudie breakfast."

"You don't have to do that."

He flashed a smile that made Sara's heart stop. "I know, but I want to. This is our first morning together. I'd like to do something special. I make a great omelette. Wait'n see." He gave her a nod, fluffed Brady's curls on his way past, and then disappeared out the swinging door.

Sara was idly squishing *Cheerios* with her thumb, when Claudie returned a short while later. Wrapped in a huge yellow towel, she padded barefoot to the coffeepot and poured herself a cup. "Where's the judge?"

"Showering, but when he returns he's going to fix us a big, beautiful breakfast."

Claudie's brows shot up. "Cool." She studied her friend. "My room is as pretty as one of those bed-and-breakfast places you see in fancy travel magazines. I slept like a princess last night, Sara. How 'bout you?"

Sara looked at her. "You know that story about the Princess and the Pea?"

Claudie nodded.

"The pea was under my mattress."

Claudie, who seldom touched anyone other than Brady in a casual manner, walked to where Sara was sitting and placed her hand on Sara's shoulder. "Don't keep beating yourself up about this, Sara. You're doing the best you can. Remember? That's what you always tell me."

Sara swallowed the lump in her throat.

"Besides," Claudie continued, "it's like I told you last night. If Brady is the judge's kid, you'll have firsthand knowledge of how he lives so it'll be easier for you to share custody. Most women who give up their babies never know if they're being treated good or not."

Sara heard something very telling in Claudie's tone but didn't pry. "You're right," she said. "Getting an ulcer over this isn't going to help matters. Besides, I still have to deal with that damn estate lawyer. I wonder what he'll say when I tell him I moved out and want to sell the house."

Ren walked in at that moment. Sara had no idea a man could shower and dress so rapidly, but except for damp curls where usually there were tidy waves frozen in place by mousse, Ren looked ready for the courtroom. He moved about the kitchen with economic motions honed by practice.

"I'd offer to help, but somehow I think I'd only be in your way," Sara told him.

"You can man the toaster, if you want to help," he said. "Claudie, you're in charge of juice. There should be orange and cranberry in the fridge."

The three worked in harmony to the background chatter of Brady, who, growing restless, began spinning Cheerios across his tray like hockey pucks. A dozen or so casualties fell to the floor. Sara planned to release him from his chair as soon as she finished buttering toast, but Ren beat her to it. Ignoring the threat to his spotless gray flannel suit, he jerked the tray free, dumped it in the sink and hoisted Brady into his arms.

"You look ready for some fresh air, young man," he said, carrying Brady to the door. He nudged the screen open with his foot and set him down outside. "Go see if there are any squirrels in the yard."

"'Quiddels?" Brady asked brightly. With that, he shot away.

Sara saw the look on Ren's face as the little boy raced about, enjoying his new world. It was the same expression that might have sent her to her knees last night if she hadn't already been kneeling beside the huge tub. Her room and Brady's were connected by a spacious blue-and-white tiled bath, and she'd been dodging Brady's happy splashes when she'd looked up to find Ren watching the scene. His face had seemed poignantly expressive, as if he were glimpsing something painfully dear to his heart.

After the bath, Sara had dressed Brady in his summer-weight jammies and an overnight diaper. She had been thinking about which book to read him, when Ren poked his head in the doorway. She motioned him over and arbitrarily grabbed one of the books she'd brought from home.

"Would you read him a story?" she asked. "I want to check on Claudie."

Although surprised, he'd risen to the occasion by snuggling Brady on his lap in the chintz-covered armchair and plunging into a rousing rendition of "The Three Little Pigs." Sara had watched from the doorway. Ren's obvious joy at Brady's pleasure touched her deeply.

Now she felt Claudie looking at her. Embarrassed, she asked Ren, "Will he be safe outside alone?" Her tone sounded stiff and overprotective.

"I think so. I'll call the gardener later to make sure none of the plants are poisonous," Ren told her.

Sara shook her head. "Brady doesn't eat plants. I meant, will he be safe from getting out or wandering away? I couldn't let him out alone at Hulger's house."

"Yeah, a mountain lion might have come down and got him," Claudie teased.

"Well, we do have a neighborhood cat that digs up the flower beds, but I don't think he's ever attacked anyone," Ren said lightly. He glanced outside before returning to his egg preparations. After a minute, he said to Sara, "I overheard what you said to Claudie about your house when I came in. I'd like to suggest either Armory or I go with you when you talk to the estate lawyer. I don't like the way the man's been treating you. Would that be okay?"

"Are you kidding? It would be great. He intimidates the heck out of me."

"That's because you've never seen him naked," Claudie said.

Both Sara and Ren turned to look at her. She blinked co-quettishly, causing Ren to burst out laughing. "Remind me never to get on your bad side, Claudie," he said, chuckling as he slid a steaming omelette on a plate and carried it to the table. "*Bon appétit,*" he said. "Sara, you're next."

Sara took the plate of toast to the table, then sat down on the stool opposite Claudie. A girl could get used to this, she thought dreamily, until a sober voice in her head reminded her this arrangement was only temporary.

After serving Sara, Ren rinsed the pan and bowl and placed them on a wooden rack beside the sink, then walked to the little white box near the door to the garage. "Let's go over this one more time," he said, and proceeded to point out the mechanics of the alarm system. He'd explained the whole thing the night before when he'd issued Sara and Claudie house keys. "I've left a note on my desk for Revelda, in case you leave before she gets here. She's terrific—you'll like her, and she will go nuts over Brady." He picked up a well-used leather briefcase from beside the counter and started to leave. "Well, have a good day. I'll see you tonight."

"Wait," Sara said. "Aren't you eating breakfast?"

"Already did. I'm an early riser. Sorry to run. If you need to reach me, get a message to my clerk, Rafael Justis. 'Bye."

The door closed, and Sara cocked her head to listen for the sound of Ren's car starting. When she was sure he was gone, she dropped her chin in her palm and sighed. "This is very strange."

Claudie nodded sagely. "We're not in Kansas anymore, are we?"

"Nope," Sara said, taking another bite of the most delicious omelette she'd ever eaten. "I'm not even sure we're still in California."

REN'S MIND RACED as he dashed up the steps to the third floor of the courthouse. He couldn't quite believe how things had worked out. Sara and Brady were living under his roof—and he had Babe to thank for it. The improbability of that fact made him grin.

He flashed back to his conversation with his mother prior to Sara showing up. Babe had been mortified to learn that her machinations had resulted in Sara and Brady moving in with him. "That's preposterous!" she'd stewed. "That was never my intention."

Ren hadn't cut her any slack. "I'm sure it wasn't, but they're here, along with Sara's friend Claudine. And as long as they are my guests, Mother, I expect you to treat them with respect. This is a complicated matter. Until we have proof that Brady is my son—"

"You just have to look at him to know, Lawrence," Babe had interrupted. "He has the Bishop eyes."

Ren hadn't been able to prevent the little surge of hope that followed her words. "Blue eyes are a dime a dozen, Mother. We need biological proof, and that won't be back for another six weeks."

"I understand that, which is why I have not allowed myself to regard him as my grandson. But why do they have to stay *here?*"

"Because I want Brady to get to know me, and I want Sara to feel comfortable with my parenting skills if it turns out I'll be sharing custody with her—which will only happen if Brady's my son. If he isn't, then you and I are to blame for turning Sara's life upside down, and we'll be lucky if she doesn't sue us."

As he passed through the outer office area, Ren paused at his clerk's desk. "I know I'm late, but could I have a few moments of your time?"

An idea had blossomed during the drive to work—given the short distance, it wasn't fully formed, but Ren hoped Rafael could help shape it. Ren had met Rafael's wife on several occasions and he knew the couple had two small children. He figured Rafael would be the perfect resource.

As Ren hung up his suit coat and adjusted his tie, Rafael entered the room, walking to the desk. "What's up? You seem pretty energized."

"I am. I had a great run this morning. Plus, I have some guests staying at my house. That's what I wanted to talk to you about. Sara Carsten and her eighteen-month-old son are staying with me for a few weeks. I think Brady—that's Sara's little boy—might benefit from mixing with other children. How did you and Daria decide on which day-care center to use?"

Rafael, who seldom showed surprise at anything that happened within the hall of justice, was slow to answer. "Constancia is six now. She's in first grade. Paulo's four—he goes to a Montessori preschool. It's a very nice place, but it doesn't take toddlers. The kids have to be potty trained."

"Is there any place in this area that takes babies?"

"I think Bright Stars does, but I'll check with Daria. She researched all the local day-care providers and preschool programs for a paper she did recently. Her major is early childhood education."

Ren fastened his robe and took the sheaf of papers Rafael handed him. "Thanks. Tell her I'd really appreciate the help."

Ren sensed the other man's curiosity. "If she could give me a couple of names this morning, I might try to visit them during the lunch break."

"No problem."

Once Ren sat down behind his raised dais, he drew on years of practice and his law school training to stay focused for the next three hours.

When his hour and a half lunch break arrived, Ren visited the first of four facilities on Daria Justis's list: Bright Stars. According to Daria's synopsis, the place offered something called "layered structuring" with emphasis on Montessori teaching aids. The director greeted him at the door.

"I'm so pleased you're considering us, Judge Bishop. Won't Mrs. Bishop be joining you?"

Ren hadn't been expecting the question. His pulse spiked. "Not today. I'm doing the preliminary legwork," he said, realizing how public his and Sara's living arrangements would become if they enrolled Brady in day care. Maybe he'd be smarter to wait until they had a formal custody arrangement.

He almost turned around, but the director, an enthusiastic woman with a beaming smile, took his arm and led him into the facility, which had been converted from a home built in the same era as Ren's. The high, cove ceilings and big windows gave the rooms a light and airy feeling. Squeals of laughter and children's voices made Ren smile. Before he left, Ren had acquired a new best friend—a toddler named Michael who melted Ren's heart with his slightly crossed eyes and thick glasses.

He gave the boy a hug before leaving. On the outer stoop, Ren asked the director about the child. "He's from a single-parent home. His mother works in the Building. He's very bright and loving but craves male attention. He latches on to every adult male who comes to visit. You should have seen him with the firefighters who gave us our annual fire-safety talk. You'd have thought they were gods."

Ren found he didn't have time to visit the second address on his list, but he liked Bright Stars. If Sara liked the place— and the idea of putting Brady into day care—he planned to offer to pay for Brady to attend the morning program a couple of days a week.

A quick stop at the hardware store nearly made him late for court.

"Sir, do you mind me asking? Does this day-care thing have anything to do with Mr. Lester's inquiry?" Rafael asked, as they hurried toward Ren's courtroom.

"What inquiry?"

"He called right after you left and said to ask you if he could officially close your missing persons case? He said he's tying up loose ends because he has a new case starting and may be out of town for the next few weeks."

"Damn," Ren muttered. Not only would Ren miss his friend on a personal level, he'd come to rely on Bo as a sort of mediator. Ren knew Sara liked and trusted Bo and valued his opinion. And Claudie seemed less hostile to Ren when Bo was around. Although he and Claudie bickered like siblings, Ren knew Bo liked the young woman and was hoping she'd make the transition to a better life.

"Please call him back and ask him to come by after work. I need to talk to him." Ren saw Rafael make a note on his pad. He decided the young man deserved to know some of what was going on. "In answer to your question, yes, this all pertains to the search I hired Bo to conduct. He found that the woman in question was killed in an accident last summer, leaving behind a young child. Sara is the boy's legal guardian. They're living at my house until she can find suitable housing closer to town."

If Rafael was shocked, he didn't show it. "My sister and her husband just moved into one of those new town houses on the other side of the river. I could get her some information if you want."

Ren didn't, but he nodded. "Thank you. That would be nice. Don't forget about Bo. I need to see him today."

BO DIDN'T WANT to talk to Ren. He'd vacillated all night about the wisdom of Sara's move. When she'd showed up on Ren's doorstep, Bo had worried his friend might stroke out, but with that inborn Bishop poise, Ren had handled the whole transition with grace. He'd sent Bo and Sara back to Sara's for another load of belongings, while he and Claudie and Brady disassembled the double bed in what would serve as Brady's room.

Sara had been in a somber mood during the drive, but Bo did his best to buoy her spirits by congratulating her on her amazing coup. "You are my new hero," he'd told her. "For some reason Babe Bishop has my number. You saw how she acted at the bookstore. I can't explain it, but she gives me that haughty look of hers and my blood turns to water. When we were in college, Ren would drag me home for the holidays because my family lived on the East Coast. I'd try real hard to be on my best behavior, but Babe seemed to consider me a bad influence on her son."

"How about Ren's father?"

"Larry? He was a peach. Everybody adored him. So easy-going and likable. Once in a while he and I would slip away to go boating on the river. I think that's when I decided I'd one day live on a houseboat. Larry loved the water and he made me appreciate its serenity." Picturing that particular time in his life—when most days were spent recuperating from a hangover—Bo couldn't help marveling at Larry's insight and kindness.

"Ren is a lot like his dad. Thank God. I'd have killed him years ago if he was like Babe. She's sort of a female version of *my* dad, which explains why I haven't been home in ten years. Those kind of people need a little comeuppance now and then. So my hat's off to you, Sara."

Sara had groaned and sunk lower in the passenger seat of her station wagon, which Bo was driving. "You don't understand, Bo. I think I overreacted. Julia used to tell me, 'Act, don't react. You'll live to regret it.' I have a feeling I'm definitely going to regret this move."

"I disagree, Sara. I think this is a good first step—a transition. Ren can provide a sort of way station for you and Brady until you get your bearings."

"That makes it sound as though I'm using Ren," she'd said, and Bo had sensed her true feelings toward Ren. She, of course, didn't know Ren had admitted to Bo his love for her. If Sara felt the same for Ren, things might either work out great or blow up something fierce. That was why Bo distrusted love. He'd had a few romantic attachments over the years, but had always managed to keep them friendly. The one time the word *love* had entered the picture, things had immediately gone sour. No, Bo Lester didn't have much faith in love.

Now, stifling a sigh, he knocked on Ren's door.

"Come in, Bo."

Bo shuffled in. He walked to the window, not meeting Ren's eyes.

"Rafael told me you might be out of town for a few weeks. Is that true?"

Bo shrugged. "A guy from Security West called me this morning. They're hardwiring some new condos in Placerville. They need a supervisor."

"I thought you'd given up that side of the business."

"The money's good."

"I'll match it if you stay."

Surprised by the offer, Bo turned. He rested his shoulder against the window and studied his friend. "Why? I've done everything you asked. I found Julia. I hooked you up with Sara. The rest is up to your DNA guys. What do you need me for?"

Ren made a few squiggles on a piece of paper. "I'm so far over my head here, I don't know which end is up." He looked at Bo. "I really care for Sara, and I know she feels a certain attraction toward me, but this is all moving too fast." He held up his hand when Bo started to point out the speed of the situation could be attributed to Ren. "I know, I'm to blame for that fact. But the bottom line is, I'm afraid I'll blow it."

"And you think I can help?"

"Yes. Sara likes you and trusts your advice."

Bo's hackles started to rise. "What are you suggesting I do? Manipulate her?"

"Of course not. I'd just like you to be around to help make sure things go smoothly. Sara has Claudie for the same reason."

Bo snickered softly. "I thought Claudie was a chaperone. Do you need two chaperones, Mr. Stud Muffin?"

Ren shot him a dark look. "I'm talking moral support."

To his surprise, Bo found himself sympathetic to Ren's cause. He pushed off from the window and walked to the door. "I'll stick around for a couple of weeks, but no more baby-sitting. Not alone, anyway. Brady's too damn fast for an old man like me." He paused, his hand on the doorknob. "If you tell anyone I said that, however, I will amputate your left nut." With that, he left.

At his car, Bo paused. He'd never admit it, but in a way he envied Ren. Brady was a great kid, and Bo had lied when he'd said he wouldn't baby-sit. He didn't blame Ren for wanting to make sure things went smoothly—a lot was riding on what happened in the next few weeks.

SARA WAS STARTING TO THINK about locking up the store, when Ren walked in the front door. The sight of him made her heart shift gears.

"Hi. What are you doing here?" she asked, hoping she didn't sound as giddy as she felt.

"I know I should have called first," he said, bending low to pick up Brady, who'd hurled himself at Ren's kneecaps. "But I was hoping I might persuade you and Brady to have dinner with me. I thought I heard Claudie tell Bo last night that she was planning to study at the library tonight, and this way you could ride home with me and she could have your car."

"That's incredibly thoughtful."

He lifted Brady up and nuzzled his belly, making the toddler shriek. "Not altogether altruistic, though. I have no idea what's available in the refrigerator, and I don't want to go to the grocery store." He set Brady down and gave her a serious look. "Plus, I want to talk to you about a few things."

Sara gulped. If she'd somehow convinced herself today that she and Ren would be able to cruise along like two vessels occupying the same waters without bumping into each other, she knew now she'd deluded herself. Ren seemed to have every intention of staying connected to her and Brady. What that meant exactly, she didn't know.

"Okay. I'll go tell Claudie—she's in the reading area. Here are my car keys," she said, taking the key ring from her desk drawer. "Would you mind transferring the car seat?"

A grin popped up on Ren's face. "Don't have to. I bought a new car seat today and had it installed. I figured it was a heck of a lot easier than switching yours back and forth."

Sara swallowed. Either he was very confident of the results of the DNA test or…Sara wasn't sure what other explanation might exist.

She waited until they were seated in the noisy, family-friendly atmosphere of a local Italian restaurant to ask. "The car seat is very nice, Ren. Top of the line. Wasn't it a bit extravagant for a couple of weeks? What if the test comes back negative?"

He rolled his shoulders. "It cost a hundred and forty-five dollars. That may seem wasteful for a month's use, but I value my time, and the time it takes to transfer yours back and forth seemed like a bigger waste to me."

He pulled two bread sticks from a tall glass container in the center of the table and handed one to Brady, who waved it like a wand. "As long as we're on the subject, I'd like to suggest another way to spend some of my money." His words were light, but something about his tone struck her as serious.

"How?"

"I'd like to pay for Brady to spend two or three mornings a week in a preschool. I looked at one today." He produced a slim promotional flyer from his jacket pocket. "I have the names of three others from my clerk's wife."

Sara studied the glossy paper. She was amazed that this would even cross Ren's mind. It was as if he'd read her thoughts. She'd wanted to place Brady in some kind of day-care situation so he could be around other kids his age, but she hadn't been able to afford it.

She looked up and found him watching her. "This is very generous of you."

His face lit up. "Are you okay with it? You're not upset that I didn't consult you first? It was sort of spontaneous. I thought about it on the way to work. Brady looked kind of lonely out back without any playmates, and I figured it might be hard for you to arrange day care when you're alone at the shop all day."

She swallowed against the lump in her throat. "I'm fine with it. If you like this place, we could take Brady there and see what he thinks."

"Terrific. Maybe during lunch tomorrow." He turned to Brady in his high chair and ruffled his curly locks. "What do you think, big guy? Want to go to school?"

This time Sara missed Brady's reply—her heart was pounding too loudly. But Ren nodded and laughed as if understanding every word. Sara tried to take a mental picture of the moment, hoping to keep the image in her head forever. This might be the closest she'd come to a traditional family setting, and it was so beautiful it almost broke her heart.

CHAPTER TWELVE

SARA KEPT ONE EAR on the sounds coming from Brady's room as she answered the phone beside her bed. Since Ren had departed for the golf course only twenty minutes earlier, she didn't expect him to be calling—everyone knew his aversion to cellular phones. Hesitantly, she put the receiver to her ear, hoping the caller wasn't Ren's mother.

"Hello," Sara answered tentatively.

"Sara? This is Janice Andrews. Am I calling too early?"

Janice was the real estate agent handling her house. "It's never too early in the home of a toddler," Sara assured her. "Have you heard anything?" Janice had shown the house to a couple from Texas on Thursday.

"Yes. Are you sitting down? They called last night with an offer—a good, solid offer, Sara. Cash."

Sara couldn't believe it. The house had been on the market for three weeks, and while a dozen prospective buyers had toured it, all expressed concern over the amount of landscaping left to complete. "Really? They'll take it as is?"

"Yes. It turns out the wife is into exotic animals, and she plans to make a habitat for her pets. I didn't dare ask what kind. Let the neighbors deal with that."

Sara grinned, picturing the look on Mary Gaines's face if an emu or llama showed up next door. "That's amazing, Janice. I'm thrilled. When do they want it?"

"The sooner the better. I've got their deposit money in hand. Do you want me to run over with the paperwork? I could be there in an hour—I have to return a few calls first. Trust me, Sara, it's everything you hoped for."

Although Sara would have liked to have Ren present, she agreed to meet the woman at ten-thirty. She hung up the phone and sat down on her bed.

"If that was supposed to be good news, I sure don't want to see how you take bad," Claudie said, entering Sara's room through the bathroom that connected to Brady's room. She balanced a stack of folded clothes on one arm. This was Claudie's week for laundry.

When she and Sara had first moved into Ren's house, they'd agreed to divide up certain chores. Revelda did the general sweeping, dusting and vacuuming downstairs, and she cleaned Ren's room. Sara and Claudie looked after their rooms and Brady's. Laundry was a shared task—one that Ren had asked to be included in, as well.

Claudie set a neatly folded column of clothing on Sara's dresser. A pair of white Jockey shorts fell off the pile and dropped to the floor. Picking them up, Claudie grinned. "Nothing like dirty clothes to put everybody on the same level. He may be the judge, but I fold his shorts."

"Laundry—the great equalizer," Sara said, smiling.

To Sara's amazement, Claudie and Ren had developed a playful kind of repartee that Sara envied. With Sara, Ren was always thoughtful and considerate, but somewhat circumspect. With Claudie, he allowed himself to cut loose a little.

"That was Janice. She sold the house."

"You're kidding! That's fantastic."

Selling Hulger's house had proved to be a valuable learning experience for Sara. Ren had accompanied her to the appointment with the estate lawyer. Sara had expected the meeting to be confrontational. To her surprise the man had been understanding, even supportive, when she informed him of her desire to sell the property.

"Wise move," he'd said. "I thought the house was a bit un-wieldy for a woman alone."

"I don't think it would have been much easier for a man," Sara had returned.

"Of course not. I didn't mean it that way. I only meant—"

Ren had cut him off by laying a business card on his desk. "My lawyer's number. He's going to help Sara with some other legal matters, and I'd appreciate it if you'd send copies of the trust history to him."

"Are you suggesting some impropriety?"

"Not at all. I'm just curious why Sara has had to fight for every nickel she needed to care for Brady. I agree that it's important to save for the future, but not at the expense of the present."

Sara had never seen Ren pull rank before. Later, when she described the episode to Bo, he'd told her, "You think that was something, you should see him take on bad cops. Ren doesn't tolerate ineptitude."

"How long 'til escrow closes?" Claudie asked, bringing Sara back to the present.

"I don't know, but Janice said it was a cash deal."

"Cash? What is he? A drug czar? Maybe he's in a witness relocation program."

Sara shrugged. "All I know is they're from Texas and they have four kids. The youngest is an infant, and the wife fell in love with Brady's room."

At the sound of his name, Brady dashed into the room, his arms stuffed with toys. He dropped the load in a patch of sun-light on the floor, and began to play.

"I guess this means we should start house-hunting, huh?" Claudie asked, her tone subdued.

A flutter of trepidation danced in Sara's chest. "I guess so." She glanced at the calendar by her bed—it was already July 8. The results of the DNA test could be back any day, and she hadn't managed to make herself take a single step toward the future. Instead, she allowed the simple pleasures of living—volunteering at Brady's day care, running the book drive, spending time with Ren—to keep her from planning ahead.

"Maybe Monday," she said, trying to sound upbeat. Changing the subject, she asked, "Did Ren say what time our reservations were for tonight?" She walked to Brady and knelt beside him, picking up one of the new trucks Ren had given him.

Claudie ground her bare toes in the thick carpet. "Are you sure about this? I told Ren it's not necessary."

Sara looked up, smiling. She knew Claudie was both pleased and unnerved by Ren's reaction to the news she'd passed her equivalency test. He'd immediately called Bo and set up a dinner date. "Don't be so modest. This is a terrific accomplishment, Claudie. We are definitely going to celebrate."

"But the Stockton Club is the most exclusive place in town. And I doubt if Brady will like it there."

Sara tousled her son's hair. "You may not believe this, but Mrs. Bishop is coming over to stay with Brady."

"What?" Claudie croaked. "Are you okay with that?"

Sara sighed. "I was a little hesitant at first. But Ren says his mother is looking forward to getting to know Brady. I think she's beginning to believe he might be her grandson. Now, it's just me she doesn't approve of."

"Wow, Brady! Grandma Mean-Lady's coming," Claudie said. "She'll probably serve you boiled bat tongues and lizard innards for dinner. Yum, yum."

Fighting a smile, Sara scolded her. "You shouldn't tease him like that, Claudie. He comprehends more than you and

Bo give him credit for. Just because you can't understand everything Brady says doesn't mean he can't understand you."

Claudie gave Brady a long, serious look. "Really?"

Sara nodded. "Just the other day Brady told Ren that Uncle Bo and Aunt Claudie were getting married."

"What?" Claudie shrieked.

Sara tried not to smile. "Well, not in so many words. But Ren was sure that's what he meant." Actually, Brady, who seemed to prefer things grouped together rather than alone, used his favorite expression, "bofagator"—which Sara interpreted to mean "both together"—to describe his adopted aunt and uncle. Ren took that to mean Brady thought Bo and Claudie should get married so he could stay with them at Bo's houseboat more often.

Claudie stared at Brady as though he'd just grown horns. "Good God. He's not really that smart, is he?"

Sara hid her grin with her hand. "All I'm saying is, you'd better start thinking of him as a miniature adult, not a puppy."

Brady picked up on the word *puppy* and started barking like the neighbor's dog.

Claudie dropped to her knees and charged forward, growling. Brady's shrieks of laughter made Sara cover her ears. He jumped on Claudie's back, demanding a horsy ride. The play continued until Claudie collapsed. "You're too much, Brady boy." She pulled him into a hug. "But I love you."

Sara's eyes filled with tears. She'd never heard Claudie use those words about anyone or anything.

Claudie stood up and walked to the door. "Ren told me he made the reservations for seven, so I thought I'd open up this morning. Then you and Brady can come down after his nap. Angela's coming in to help with inventory."

Angela was Claudie's new recruit—a skinny, pimple-faced girl whom Claudie was trying to keep from a life on the streets. She hadn't been in the market for a job and didn't seem to appreciate Claudie's interference, but somehow Claudie had persuaded her to give the bookstore a chance.

"Is it okay if Bo picks you up after work?" Claudie asked. "I need to use the car to run a few errands."

Sometimes Sara couldn't help but marvel at the changes she'd witnessed in her friend over the past month. She didn't know if the impetus had been Claudie's scholastic achievement or the fact that she felt—and was—needed by Sara. The respect Bo and Ren gave her might have helped, too, Sara thought.

"Fine. I have to take Brady to his playgroup at ten, then meet with Janice. Later, I want to run a box of books over to the jail."

"Will that give you enough time for Brady's nap?" Claudie asked. "We don't want him grumpy for Grandma you-know-who."

Sara laughed and shook her head. "Ren will be back around noon. He's going to stay with Brady."

Claudie confirmed the last of their convoluted child-care and social arrangements, then left.

Sara put away her clean clothes and finished straightening up her bedroom. She loved her room. At the thought of leaving this place, a small sound of pain escaped from her lips.

Brady looked at her curiously.

She smiled to reassure him. "Which is the new truck Ren gave you, Brady?" she asked, motioning him to come to her. "Is it red? Show me the red one."

He studied the pile a moment, then snatched a bright red fire truck from the jumble and carried it to her.

Sara clapped and gave him a big hug. Claudie wasn't the only one benefiting from all the attention. Between Ren and Bo, as well as the teachers at Bright Stars, Brady was blooming. There was no denying that Ren Bishop had made a huge difference to the lives of Sara and her extended family. So why did she feel so miserable?

Absentmindedly accepting the toys Brady brought her, Sara sat on her bed and thought about her relationship with Ren. In the four weeks they'd been living under the same roof, he'd done absolutely nothing untoward or improper. He treated her with respect, yet, there was something—a heat, a tension—between them that she sensed but couldn't define.

She knew Ren felt it, too, but any time she caught him looking at her with what might be longing or desire, he turned away. Whenever they accidentally touched, Sara felt sparks reverberate through her body, but Ren would merely apologize and put more space between them.

Sara hadn't forgotten their kiss, but apparently Ren had. Sighing, she blinked back tears, silently admitting the futility of her feelings. How could she expect Ren to lust after her when he'd made love to Julia? Sara knew Ren liked her, respected her, but he didn't feel that same gut-wrenching passion that made Sara listen for his footsteps at night. That made her sneak into his room early each morning to watch him from the window as he did laps in the pool.

Sara wasn't sure she could last another two weeks, but the alternative was just as harrowing. The cliche—caught between a rock and a hard place—came to mind. How could she stay? Worse, how could she leave?

"SO, HOW DO YOU PLAY this game, anyway?" Bo asked, examining a golf ball as if it might hold a clue.

Ren, who was in the process of squaring his stance in front of the first tee, looked up and frowned. "You took golf in college, Bo. I know. I lent you my clubs."

"Oh, yeah, I forgot," Bo lied. He hadn't set up this golf date to knock around little white balls. He was a man with a mission.

He waited until Ren started the downward stroke of his swing, then said, "It's time to shit or get off the pot."

The club made a dull *thunk* when it connected with the ball; a large hunk of grass flew up, too. Ren glared at him. "There is a certain etiquette to follow, Lester. Don't talk when someone is swinging."

"Oh, I thought that only applied in baseball."

Ren stuffed his club back in the bag, then moved aside.

Bo wiped his hands on his checkered double-knit pants—the most audacious he'd been able to find—and approached the finely manicured tee. "I meant it, though," he said, squinting down the fairway as though he gave a hoot.

"Meant what?"

"You've got to do something. You're killing her."

"Who?"

"Who do you think?"

Bo swung the club and felt the wooden head connect squarely with the ball. The ball arched into the air and flew straight down the green turf. "Wow. I think they call that beginner's luck."

Shoulder-to-shoulder the two men walked down the fairway. Ren didn't look at Bo when he said, "You're wrong. Sara's doing great. Brady loves his school. Claudie's a success story. Everybody's fine."

Bo knew by Ren's tone that he didn't believe what he was saying, even though it was all fact. Everyone *was* doing great—except the two lead players, who were miserable.

Ren stalked to his ball, grabbed a club and walloped it with enough force for Bo to hear the swishing sound as the club sliced through the air. Bo watched the ball streak along the outer edge of the fairway, then drop into the rough. "Tough break," he said unsympathetically.

Ren gave him a black look and marched away. They met up again at the first putting green. "I didn't mean you were killing her on purpose," Bo said, a second before Ren's putter connected with the ball. The ball hugged the cup for a heartbeat before arcing away to stop four feet from the hole.

Ren's epithet made Bo snicker.

"I'm not killing her," Ren shouted.

The words seemed to echo in the still morning air. Ren closed his eyes and lifted his face to the sky. "Great," he muttered. "If the paternity issue doesn't screw up my reelection, a murder scandal will."

Bo putted his ball into the cup, then walked to Ren's side. He patted his friend's shoulder consolingly. "It's not like you love this job, anyway."

"How would you know?"

Bo shrugged. "I watch people, Ren. It's what I do. And I've watched you for twenty years. I know you took the judgeship for the same reason you went to law school—because it was expected of you. But you don't love it. I'm not saying you're not good at it, but it's not your thing."

Ren looked at him with a blank kind of astonishment.

"What?" Bo asked. "Did you think I was just some illiterate gumshoe?"

Ren didn't respond. He finished his putt, then packed away his equipment. "Let's go get some breakfast. We can talk there."

"What about the rest of the game? It's starting to come back to me. I must not have been bombed that entire semester."

THE COFFEE SHOP Bo picked out was not the kind of place Ren or any of his golf buddies would frequent, which probably was why Bo chose it, Ren thought, pulling into the parking lot behind the Mazda. Ren sent Bo in to pick out a table, while he used the phone.

Sara answered; her voice made an automatic smile spring to his lips. He loved the sound of it.

"Hi. It's me. Bo and I cut our game short. We're grabbing a quick cup of coffee, then I'm coming home. Do you need me to pick up anything?"

"Um…no, not that I can think of. What will your mother want for dinner? I was planning hot dogs for Brady."

"Perfect. She loves hot dogs," Ren said, grinning at his blatant lie.

"Okay." She didn't sound as though she believed him. "Oh, and guess what? Janice just called—she said the house is sold."

Ren's heart jumped skittishly. "Really? That's great news."

Sara hesitated a moment before agreeing with him. "She's going to come over in a little while with the proposal. If you're here, maybe you could look it over for me. I hate to ask, but…"

Ren bit off a curse. Didn't she know he'd do anything for her? Why did she always sound so apologetic when she asked for a favor?

"No problem. I should be there in twenty minutes. I'd better run. See you soon."

Sliding onto the booth's cracked, red plastic cushion, Ren saw Bo look at him appraisingly.

The waitress delivered two coffees. "Menus?" she asked.

"No, thank you, we can't stay," Ren said.

"We can't? Why not?" Bo asked, when she walked away.

"Sara sold the house. She wants me there when the Realtor brings the paperwork."

Bo added a packet of sugar to his mug. "Hey, that's good news. Did she sound happy?"

Ren thought a moment. "Sorta."

"'Sorta.' What does that tell you, Ren? A woman sells the biggest white elephant ever built and she's just sorta happy? What is wrong with that picture?"

"I didn't get all the details. Maybe it's not a good offer."

"Bullshit. Janice is a mercenary. She wouldn't bring in a shabby offer. I'm telling you Sara is miserable. She's sinking fast, bud."

"You make her sound like the goddamn *Titanic*."

Bo sat back, giving Ren a look his friend knew all too well. With a muffled curse, Ren gave up. He knew Bo was right. Worrying about Sara kept Ren from sleeping at night. He pushed his coffee cup away and said, "What am I supposed to do? I've tried everything I can think of. I know she's happy about Brady's school and she was jumping for joy over Claudie's exam—but you're right. Something's missing."

"Like the sparkle in her eyes," Bo said, sitting forward again. "God, I miss that little glint of humor whenever she'd look around and see one of us standing there. I haven't seen that in weeks."

"I know," Ren said. "I tried gifts. I made her go to that day spa. We've taken Brady to the zoo and the wild animal park and Discovery Zone. He's been doing great in his swim lessons, and I know she's thrilled with that. He loves school and he's getting along well with the other kids—"

Bo shook his head. "Brady's not the problem."

"And Claudie is doing fantastic. Ever since Sara made her assistant manager at the bookstore, you'd swear she's a different person."

"It's not Claudie."

"Babe hasn't—"

"Ren, it's you."

Ren exhaled as if Bo had hit him in the gut. He ran his hand through his hair impatiently. "I've tried to keep my distance, Bo. God, it's been killing me, too. You should see her in the morning when we're downstairs alone. She likes to get up when she hears me come in from doing my laps. There's something so fresh, so innocent about her. Damn."

Bo was silent a minute, then he said, "Have you talked to Sara about your feelings?"

"Hell, no. Do you want to see her head for the hills? Christ, Bo, it can't be easy living in the same house with the man who slept with your sister and could be your nephew's father. I don't know why she doesn't hate me."

"I don't either, but you know she likes you. Maybe she likes you as much as you like her." Bo made a sound of disgust. "Did I just say that? Maybe I need to go back to high school."

Ren frowned. "I don't know what to think, but I agree that things can't go on like they are. I was planning on talking to her tomorrow—we've got Claudie's party tonight, but maybe we can grab a few minutes alone once Janice leaves."

Ren reached in his pocket for his wallet, but Bo said, "Get out of here. Go home to Sara. Try not to blow it, okay?"

REN THOUGHT ABOUT BO's words all the way home. As he pulled into the driveway, he noted the late-model Suburban with the real estate logo on the door parked in front of the house. He left his clubs in the trunk and hurried inside.

Sara and Janice were in his office, sitting on the sofa with a stack of papers between them. Instead of going to his desk, Ren sat down on the other side of Sara. She seemed startled by his proximity but didn't edge away. "You got here fast," she said. "We barely sat down."

"Time is money in the real estate business. How's everything, Janice? What have you got for Sara?"

The actual paperwork was a snap. Janice, a true professional, seemed perfectly comfortable walking Sara through all the steps, answering her questions with courtesy and understanding. The offer was sound, better than he'd thought possible.

Later, as he and Sara walked Janice to the door, he said, "I'm very impressed, Janice. That was not an easy house to market. You certainly earned your commission."

"Thanks, again," Sara called to Janice from the step. She watched until the Suburban was out of sight, obviously reluctant to go inside with Ren.

Screwing up his courage, he held the door open and said, "Sara, could we talk?"

She faced him, a grim look on her face. "I have to pick Brady up from his play group in fifteen minutes."

"This won't take long."

She walked inside and waited for a signal from Ren. He led the way to the back patio. He knew one of her favorite places was the gazebo. In fact, he'd added thick pads upholstered in a rich forest-green print just for her. He sat down on one side of the octagon; she sat opposite him.

She wore a simple cotton shorts set of peachy orange. Her newly acquired tan made her arms and legs look sleek and sexy. The sun had lightened her hair several shades to a warm honey color. Ren longed to reach out and pull her into his arms.

"Sara, I…" The lawyer in him had a whole speech prepared, but in the end it was the man who blurted out, "I love you."

Sara frowned as if trying to decipher a foreign word. "How do you mean that? The same way you love Brady and Bo and Claudie?"

"I don't love Claudie. She's a pain in the butt. I like her, and I respect how she's turned her life around, but I don't—" Ren shook his head to get back on track. Her question had thrown him. But he realized it was valid. "You're right. I love my friends and family. A lot. Especially Brady. But those feelings have nothing to do with the way I feel about you."

"They don't?"

Ren tapped his forehead with his fist. "I'm really bad at

this. I guess I don't know how to explain love because I've never been in love before."

"Eve…"

He shook his head. "Eve and I seemed liked a good idea at the time. That's it." He sat forward, closer to her. Sara didn't draw back, but she seemed wary. "Sara, I know you're not happy here. I've tried to make everything as easy as possible because I wanted to give you time to get to know me. I hoped that maybe, if I was lucky, you'd start to feel about me the way I feel about you."

He reached out and took her hand in both of his. "I know it's a little crazy to think two people thrown together the way we were could actually fall in love, but that's what happened—for me, anyway."

Her hand trembled but she didn't pull it back. She looked at him, searching his eyes. "Are you saying you want to—" The color in her cheeks deepened.

"You have no idea how hard it's been for me to resist you."

"*You've* been trying to resist *me?*" she whispered.

She sounded so dumbfounded that Ren moved back, knowing that the best way to avoid blowing this was to take it slowly and deliberately. "Sara, I'm crazy about you. About your smell. Your smile. The way you look in your swimming suit. I fantasize about the way you'll look out of your swimming suit."

Her blush deepened.

"You're sexiest in the morning when you're all sleepy-eyed, standing there with a cup of coffee, waiting for me when I get out of the pool. No, wait, I've changed my mind. You're even sexier when you've just tucked Brady in bed and you stand beside his door with your eyes closed listening to him. I can't tell you how many times I've thought about scooping you into my arms and carrying you to my bed."

"That's sexy?" she asked, tilting her head dubiously.

"To me it is. Because I know the energy and soul you put into raising that little boy, and I love you for it."

Sara sat forward, and Ren saw tears glisten in her eyes. "Do you mean *love* love? Not just I'm-Brady's-mother love?"

Ren reached out and cupped her jaw in his palm. "I mean forever, long-after-Brady-is-grown-and-gone love. Just you and me, Sara. The whole nine yards, as Bo would say."

She squeezed her eyes tight and moved back. She drew her knees to her chest and wrapped her arms around them. "Ren, I love you, too, but I can't make love to you."

Ren's heart soared, then crashed. "Why not?"

She wouldn't look at him. "I couldn't stand to see the look of disappointment on your face."

"What are you talking about?" Ren asked, although deep inside he knew.

"I could never live up to my sister's image. Even when she was alive, I barely fit in her shadow. You've had two years to build and shape your memories of a sexual goddess, and trust me, I'm not like that. I don't even know how to pretend to be like that."

Her confession ripped his heart out. Moving very cautiously, he slid along the gazebo seat until he was beside her. He wiped a tear that seemed poised to drop to her cheek. "I kissed you once, remember?" She nodded. "At the time I thought it was a mistake. I thought it would complicate things between us." He lowered his head and kissed her cheek, the corner of her eye, the bridge of her nose. "Maybe my mistake was in stopping."

She tilted her head to meet his lips.

SARA CLOSED HER EYES and slipped into the magical world Ren provided. His lips were warm and sweet, a hypnotic blend, gentle and demanding. When his tongue entered her mouth, a spike of passion ripped through her midsection. On their own, her arms went around his shoulders.

Ren gently pushed her knees away so he could move closer. Without the impediment he pulled her to him; her bosom flattened against his chest. Sara wondered if he could feel her heart pounding. He slipped his hand beneath her top and made room between them to cup her breast. The warmth of his touch spread to every part of her body.

He pulled back and looked into her eyes. "Sara, you have beauty so rare, so perfect, no one can compare to you. You said yourself, sex without love doesn't really count, whether it's good sex or bad sex—it's only sex."

He's right. Sara realized in that instant Ren wouldn't be thinking of Julia when he made love with her.

She smiled. "Should we go to my room? Or yours?"

His grin made her heart flip. "How 'bout the Hyatt?"

"Do they have baby-sitters?" The word barely left her lips before she pushed him back and jumped to her feet. "Oh, my God! I forgot about Brady."

"Hell!" Ren exclaimed. "So did I. Go get your purse. I'll meet you at the car."

Like an Indy driver, Ren raced to the house where two harried mothers were waiting patiently at the door for parents to show up and claim their children. Ren apologized profusely, while Sara rounded up a very wired Brady.

In the car, they shared simultaneous sighs, then looked at each other, grinning. Sara couldn't name a time when her heart had felt more filled with joy.

"We're postponed till tonight, right?" he asked, reaching out to claim her hand.

"What about Claudie's party?"

"After the party." He smiled at her with a wicked gleam

in his eye. "Don't worry—I promise I won't ask you to skip dessert."

She brought his hand to her cheek. Just the scent of his skin made her heart happy. "I read something once about strategically placed whipped cream," she teased. "Maybe we could make our own dessert."

His low groan made her laugh.

"Did we decide where?" he asked, glancing over his shoulder at Brady.

Sara thought a moment, picturing the kind of love that belonged in a home filled with family, children and friends. "Your room."

CHAPTER THIRTEEN

"SO? WHAT DO YOU THINK'S going on?" Bo asked Claudie once they were sitting beneath the shade of the gazebo. "Is this little celebration tonight going to involve more than your personal achievement? Maybe we're going to see a little high-scoring by Judge Bishop, too, huh?"

He'd recognized a change in Sara the minute he walked in the bookstore to pick her up. His gut instinct told him it was good, but he didn't ask, choosing instead to observe.

"I don't know," Claudie said. She wore a simple, canary-yellow linen dress that gave her a young Audrey Hepburn look. "They both seem a little weird. Ren was humming when he carried out the garbage. When I asked him what was going down, he hugged me." She frowned. "What about Sara? What'd she say on the way home?"

"She said they had a long talk." He snickered. "I think perhaps there was less talk and more touch."

Claudie's eyes opened wide. "Seriously? It's about time."

"Ren and I did a little golfing this morning, and, I told him to shit or get off the pot."

Claudie made a gagging sound. "That's romantic."

"Humph. It worked. When I called him at noon, he said things were clicking. I got the impression progress had been made."

Claudie looked skeptical. "I hope so. For a while there, I

was afraid I was going to have to be the one to kick him in the butt." She crossed her legs.

Bo noticed, as he had on several occasions, the shapely quality of her limbs. Claudie and Bo had spent a lot of time together thanks to Brady. This wasn't the first time Bo regretted an obvious lack of interest on her part—a friendly camaraderie seemed to be the extent of their relationship.

"Do you think he'll propose?"

Bo pictured the look on Sara's face when he'd entered the store. She'd been wearing a denim skirt and a T-shirt with the slogan I Read For The Love Of It. Bo thought she looked as radiant as an angel atop a Christmas tree. But when he mentioned the sale of her house and the changes it would bring, some of that glow had dimmed. "Maybe, but I think whatever's going down is still in the early stage."

Claudie frowned. "I don't know. It's been like a pot ready to boil around here lately. So I wish he'd hurry up. Maybe even tonight."

"Nah. Ren likes to take things slow and conservative."

"Wanna bet?"

Bo couldn't resist the challenge in her eyes. "You're on." He looked at her sternly. "But there's one condition. No interference. Tonight we're just out celebrating your scholastic triumph—no matchmaking, okay?" he said. "If it's the real thing, it'll happen on its own."

Claudie stared at him a moment, then threw her head and laughed. "God, Lester, that sounded positively poetic. You'd better be careful or someone might mistake you for a real human being instead of a redneck hillbilly."

He gave her his most ferocious squint. "How'd you like to wear that pretty little dress swimming?"

With a shriek of fake terror she bolted from the gazebo. Smiling, Bo followed.

SARA HAD JUST PUT the finishing touches on her eye makeup, when she heard the sound of the doorbell. "Can somebody get that?" she hollered.

"I'm still working on Brady," Ren called back, followed by a high-pitched shriek and Ren's muffled "Come back here, you little sneak."

Sara had returned home from the store to find Ren up to his elbows in bubble bath, trying to wash Brady's hair. So sweet was the image that she'd watched in silence longer than she was able to afford to do. Then, realizing she was running late, she'd grabbed her clothes and dashed to Ren's bathroom. Although pressed for time, Ren's big marble shower evoked an exhilarating fantasy—just the scent of his soap was enough to make her wish the festivities were already over.

Would they make love tonight? Sara was pretty sure the answer was yes, and the thought made her jittery with anticipation, queasy with apprehension. She had no idea how she was going to get through dinner. It had been tough enough dodging Bo's and Claudie's questions earlier.

"What am I—an open book?" she'd asked aloud after Claudie's barrage of questions that afternoon. Julia had always said Sara was too easy to read. *"You give away all your secrets every time you smile,"* she'd once said. Sara feared that was true. Somehow she'd managed to keep her feelings about Ren a secret, but it had been difficult.

All that's changed now, Sara thought as she started down the hallway. Ren and I are going to be together. A nagging voice reminded her that she didn't know exactly what that meant—but he had used the *L* word. She was almost to Brady's door, when a flash of movement made her pause.

Shrieking with delight, a naked Brady dodged Ren's outstretched hands. "Come back here, you little streaker. I could put you in jail for indecent exposure," Ren teased.

The doorbell chimed again, making Sara tear her eyes from the scene. He said he loves me, she thought, slowly descending each step. *God, what if it's true? What if he meant it—really meant it? Could we make a family here in this beautiful home? Maybe give Brady a baby brother or sister someday?*

Her speculation ended the moment the front door opened and a familiar head popped into sight. "Is anybody home?" Babe Bishop asked, stepping into the foyer.

Sara gulped. Even dressed in a wonderful black Yves Saint Laurent sheath—her splurge at the consignment shop down the block from the bookstore—Sara felt inferior. To her amazement, today Babe wore sporty knee-length shorts and a loose top in a post-holiday red, white and blue pattern. Sara had never seen her dressed so casually.

"Sorry, Mrs. Bishop. Ren's upstairs with Brady, and I just finished getting ready," Sara said, closing the door behind her. Babe's expensive-smelling perfume reminded Sara she'd forgotten to put on cologne. "Come in. We really appreciate your helping out like this."

"You're welcome."

Sara looked at Babe more closely. For some reason the older woman seemed subdued, a little sad even. "Are you all right? Are you sure this isn't too big an imposition?"

Babe straightened haughtily. "I managed to survive Lawrence, I'm sure I can handle Brady."

"Of course. I didn't mean to imply you couldn't. I just thought you seem a bit…down."

Babe stepped back as though the observation had somehow undermined her control. Her chin rose in a standard Babe Bishop gesture, but her gaze went to the top of the stairs. Sara looked, too. No one was there. All she could see was the collage of family photos.

In a halting voice, Babe said, "Today's the anniversary of my daughter's death."

Sara's heart sunk. Ren hadn't mentioned that fact. He rarely spoke of his sister, and Sara had never pressed for details of the accident.

"Oh, no," Sara cried. "I'm so sorry. We'll cancel. You don't have to do this."

"Nonsense. It was almost forty years ago. I sometimes feel a little blue, but it'll pass. I'm fine."

Sara took a step back. "Would you care for a glass of wine?" she asked, wishing Ren would appear.

"Yes. Chardonnay, please. Lawrence usually keeps a bottle chilled for me."

"I think there's some in the refrigerator," Sara said. She walked toward the kitchen, conscious of Babe following her.

They were halfway through the dining room, when Sara heard Babe gasp. She looked over her shoulder and saw Babe standing frozen in the middle of the room, looking around in shock. Ren had hired the same contractor who'd made the repairs on Sara's house to renovate his dining room. A crew had begun stripping the walls and cabinets on Monday. The chandelier was gone—six black holes for the new recessed can fixtures made the ceiling resemble a domino. Babe's table and chairs were stored in the garage.

"Didn't Ren tell you he was remodeling?" Sara asked gently.

"He might have mentioned it, but I didn't think…" Babe walked to the wall where the windows, now relieved of their heavy venetian blinds, displayed a panoramic view of the backyard. She ran her fingers over one of the few strips of embossed wallpaper that remained. At its edge was a remnant of an earlier wall covering—pale blue, the color of a summer sky. "This was Sunny's favorite room. She would come home after school and do her homework at the dining room table."

Babe looked out the window. "We used to have a big concrete birdbath right there—" she said, pointing.

Sara could almost picture it nestled among the thick ferns and philodendrons.

"She loved to watch the birds play and splash," Babe went on. "She was such an animal person. I always imagined she'd grow up to be a veterinarian." A bemused look crossed her face. "I wonder what ever became of that fountain."

Sara had no answer. Her heart ached for the loss Babe Bishop had endured. Quietly she slipped into the kitchen and poured a glass of wine. Hurrying back, she handed the glass to Babe, as if her offering might in some way ease the pain. Ren's mother accepted it without looking at Sara, her attention focused on Bo and Claudie, who were walking across the lawn from the direction of the gazebo. They were obviously laughing and joking with each other.

"She's come a long way toward changing her life, hasn't she?" Babe asked.

"Some might say a quantum leap," Sara said. "I had good news from my friend Keneesha, too. She's back in Georgia." Keneesha's e-mail message yesterday said her health was stable and she'd reconciled with her son, who was teaching her how to work the computer. Sara couldn't have been happier for her.

"Nobody chooses the low road," Sara said quietly. "Sometimes you just find yourself there."

Babe turned to look at her.

"When you get off-track, you sometimes need a helping hand to get back on course." Screwing up her courage, she said to Babe, "After you showed me that picture of Julia, I spent a lot of time thinking about why she would have done that—it wasn't like her at all. You have to understand," Sara continued forcefully, "Julia was a very private person. With good reason. When she was twelve, our mother's boyfriend tried to molest her. He'd been living with us for over a year, and he was very sneaky about 'accidentally' catching Julia in her underwear, leaving pornography around for her to see, and touching her even though she tried to avoid him—" Her voice cracked. "Anyway, the point is, Julia *never* would have posed for that picture without a very compelling reason."

Babe remained silent.

Taking a deep breath to regain her composure, Sara said, "I think she did it to help me."

"How do you mean?" Babe asked.

Sara knew what she was about to say would probably drop her even lower in Babe's opinion, but she didn't care. "My mother died shortly after I graduated from high school. She was only forty-nine."

Sara sighed, trying to picture herself at the time—barely eighteen, scared spitless and all alone, except for Julia. "I was working at the bookstore but I didn't feel as though my life was going anywhere. Julia was dating a guy who was stationed at Travis—he made the Air Force sound exciting and glamorous. So one day I enlisted."

Babe didn't show any sign of surprise, so Sara guessed this part of her history had shown up on her background check. "At first it felt like I could make a life for myself in the military—the structure was something I'd always craved. But I was young and naive, and I made a couple of bad choices. I might have gone to jail if Julia hadn't come to my rescue. She hired a lawyer to defend me."

"I thought the Air Force had to provide you with a lawyer," Babe said.

"They did, but Julia said that wasn't good enough. She wanted the best person money could buy. She wired me the money to pay him—he wasn't cheap. She never told me where the money came from, but I think I've now figured it out." Sara bit down on her lip.

In the kitchen, Bo and Claudie's banter seeped from the backyard through the door. Babe took a sip of wine, then cocked her head as if in thought. "Lawrence has always picked up strays. One Christmas I bought him a purebred puppy—a Cardigan Welsh corgi. I wrapped up a photograph of the breed because the dog was too young to leave its mother—but do you know what Lawrence did?"

Sara shook her head even though Babe didn't seem to be addressing her directly.

"He said, 'Thank you, Mother,' then ran to the garage where he'd been hiding the most ragtag looking mutt on the face of the earth. He told me that since I was willing to let him have a puppy, he'd prefer the one he'd found, instead."

Momentarily, her smile seemed tinged with pride, but when she looked back at Sara, Babe's face was blank. A loud crash in the adjoining room made her flinch. "Bo is another example."

"I suppose you think Brady and I are, as well," Sara said softly.

Babe sighed heavily. "I have nothing against you, Sara. I think you've done a fine job with Brady—he's a delight. But Lawrence has a promising future in politics ahead of him. Thanks to a few high-profile cases, he's become noticed. There's been talk of a possible Senate race. A scandal would destroy all that."

Nothing more was said, because at that moment Ren walked in carrying Brady, a bright, clean bundle of smiles. "Hello, Mother, I thought I heard your voice." He looked at

Sara, but she felt too exposed, too vulnerable to meet his eyes. Instead, she put on an artificial smile and held out her arms to Brady. He dove for her.

"Whoa, kiddo, take it easy," Ren cautioned. "Your mommy looks beautiful. We don't want to mess with perfection."

Sara hugged her son fiercely, inhaling his just-bathed smell. Tears clustered in her eyes. Maybe the best thing she could do for Ren's future was disappear, but she knew he'd never let Brady go unless the test came back negative—and in her heart, Sara knew that wasn't likely. These past weeks had confirmed what Sara had feared from the start—Ren and Brady were two peas in a pod, so alike at times that Sara marveled at them.

Nope, if it came down to doing the honorable thing, she knew it would fall to her to leave.

She looked up and saw Ren watching her, his brow knit with concern. She took a deep breath and put on a pretend smile. Any serious decisions would have to wait until after Claudie's celebration.

REN TOOK A SIP of wine, his gaze following the two women as they headed for the rest room. Peripherally he caught the admiring glances of other men. Two beautiful women. One he admired, the other he loved more than words could express.

"What's wrong with Sara?" Bo asked in a low, serious voice. "I thought you said things were working out between you."

"They were—this morning. What'd she tell you?"

"Nothing, but I thought she looked happy. She seemed a little worried about what would happen after the house deal closed… But something's not right. I get the feeling she's faking the smiles for Claudie's sake. What about you?"

Ren slumped back. He'd barely noticed the opulent surroundings that both Sara and Claudie had gushed about. The

Stockton Club was fabled for its elegance and exclusivity—
only recently had it even started granting memberships to
women—but Ren could have been dining at a hamburger
joint for all he cared. "I agree. I was giving Brady a bath when
she got home. I haven't had a chance to talk to her alone." *Or
touch her.* "If you didn't say anything to her, then it had to ·
be Babe."

Bo cursed under his breath. "Claudie and I were goofing
around outside. We should have been there when Babe arrived."

Ren straightened. He and Sara had shared more than a kiss
this morning—they'd connected. "I should never have let her
go to work, but she insisted she needed to run some books by
the jail and relieve Claudie."

"Shall we cut this short?" Bo asked, alerting Ren by his
nod that the women were returning.

"I don't want to hurt Claudie's feelings."

Bo made a funny face. "I don't think she'd care if you play
your cards right. Follow my lead."

Bo rose and motioned for Ren to stand. "Claudie, you are
much too beautiful to waste on all these rich old farts. You
need to go dancing. Ren's going to take us home to get my
wheels, then I'm taking you out on the town."

"Really?" she asked, obviously surprised by the change
in plans.

Ren pretended to be offended. "Who are you calling old?
I'd dance you under the table, but I know Sara's anxious to
check up on my mother and Brady. Right?" he asked.

She nodded. "I don't want to be a wet blanket, but I
wouldn't mind making sure Brady didn't decide to disappear
on her. What about dessert, Claudie?"

Claudie shifted her gaze from Bo to Sara. Her smile was
both real and infectious. "This was the most wonderful meal
of my life, and I ate so much I don't think I'll ever have to eat

again. I'm ready for some exercise." She grinned wickedly and said, "Just don't get any ideas, Lester. A graduate like my-self has to be careful of her reputation." Her tone was so "Babe" that they all laughed.

Ren paid the bill, and they left. On the way home, Ren handed a small, wrapped gift to Claudie, who was sitting in the back of the car with Bo. "This is just a little something to help commemorate the day, Claudie. I'm proud of you."

Sara shifted to look over the seat. In the lights from the dash, Ren could see her bare knee and smooth calf on the seat beside him. The muted glow gave her an ephemeral appear-ance—like a magical sprite that might disappear without warning. Silently, he prayed they'd be able to recapture the passion they'd shared earlier.

"Oh, Ren, it's wonderful," Claudie exclaimed, leaning for-ward to show Sara the opal pendant on a gold chain.

"It's a fire opal," Ren said. "It reminded me of you—lovely and resilient."

While Bo helped Claudie fasten the necklace, Ren glanced at Sara. There were tears in her eyes. She reached out and touched his face, a gentle, loving caress. "That was incredi-bly kind," she whispered.

He turned his face to kiss her hand. "You are incredibly beautiful."

She pulled back, moving closer to the door.

What did you say to her, Mother? Ren's disquiet intensi-fied when he pulled into his driveway and spotted a burgundy Cadillac parked behind his mother's Lincoln.

"Whose car is that?" Sara asked.

"Armory's."

"I wonder what he's doing here. I hope nothing's wrong."

His rich meal rumbled in his gut. Ren wasn't sure he wanted to find out. He didn't bother to put the car away. Instead, when Bo got out, Ren handed him the keys. "Here. I don't trust your heap."

Bo tossed the keys in the air. "Cool. Are you ready, Miss Graduate?"

Claudie looked at Sara. "It's getting chilly. I think I'll grab a sweater."

"I'll wait for you in the kitchen," Bo said.

Sara spun around. "You can't possibly be hungry."

"I always have room for Revelda's pie."

She rolled her eyes and laughed. "You and Brady."

Together, the group entered the house. Ren ushered Sara ahead of him through the dining room, saying, "Shall we go see what kind of damage Brady managed to do to Babe's self-confidence?" She put on a nice smile, but Ren could tell Sara wasn't looking forward to seeing his mother.

He found Babe and Armory in his office, drinking coffee on the sofa. "Hello, Armory. You remember Sara."

Armory, looking dapper in lightweight slacks and open-collar golf shirt, rose and put out his hand. "Hello, Sara, good to see you again."

"He's brought us the lab results, Lawrence," Babe said.

Armory pointed to a courier's box sitting on Ren's desk. Ren was grateful to see it was unopened.

"They delivered on a Saturday?" Sara exclaimed.

"We paid extra for express delivery," Armory said.

"When he called to tell you it was here, Lawrence, I told him to bring it over directly. No use waiting," Babe said.

Ren reached for Sara's hand and pulled her closer to him. He sensed she wanted to run away. "That was nice of you, Armory, but it could have waited until morning—I'm sure you have better things to do with your time on a Saturday night."

"Well, aren't you going to open it?" Babe asked, standing.

Ren looked at Sara. "Yes. As soon as we're alone."

"What?" his mother croaked. "Alone? The whole point of having Armory here is so you can plan your strategy. Surely you know everything you do from this point on will come under scrutiny."

Ren looked at her sharply. "Mother, thank you for watching Brady tonight. I assume he's in bed—you don't have him tied up someplace do you?" he asked, injecting a bit of humor to soften the frustration he felt at her interference.

He caught Sara's tiny choke of a laugh.

Babe wasn't amused. "Of course, he's in bed. He was a perfect angel. But I didn't drag Armory all the way over here, just so I could leave before you open that."

"I'm afraid that's exactly what's going to happen. The contents of that box concern Sara's future and mine, and we'd like to be able to go over it in private."

Babe looked shocked and angry. She turned toward Armory as if to make him do something. He shrugged sheepishly, then extended a hand to Ren. "Give me a call if you need anything."

Armory's defection seemed to enrage Babe. She grabbed the older man's arm to keep him from leaving. "Armory, talk to him. Lawrence Bishop, do you have any idea what you're doing?"

"Yes, Mother, I think so."

"How you handle this matter will affect your future for the rest of your life."

He squeezed Sara's hand. When she looked up at him, he smiled. "I certainly hope so."

"Lawrence, you and Armory should be discussing a strategy for custody. If that little boy is yours—"

"Mother," he said sharply, "I told you five weeks ago to stay out of this. Sara and I will handle it. Why is that so hard for you to accept?"

She glanced at Sara. Her tone softened some when she said, "Sara is a very nice person, Lawrence, but I think she'd be the first to agree that, given her background, she'd be more of a liability than an asset to your career."

Ren's mouth dropped open. "I can't believe you said that. Where in the hell do you get off acting like some kind of upper-class matron? Good God, Mother, your father was a farmer."

Babe stiffened. "I was referring to her criminal past."

Ren groaned. He didn't know how Babe learned those details, since they hadn't been part of her investigator's report. "She was a kid. She made a mistake. The only reason I don't have a record is Granddad Bishop pulled a few strings."

At Sara's puzzled looked, he said, "When I was thirteen, a couple of my friends and I broke into a neighbor's house and stole some booze. On the way out, one of the guys pocketed a bunch of old coins that were sitting on the bar—they turned out to be valuable collector's items. The next morning, the guy with the coins confessed to his mother, who called my grandfather."

Babe looked appalled. "That is not the kind of thing that would come out of the woodwork to affect your campaign, but Sara's record—"

Ren interrupted her. "What campaign? My reelection? Mother, you know most judges run unopposed. I think it's a little premature to worry—"

She broke in, crying. "Your senatorial prospects!"

Ren took a deep breath, struggling for patience. Out of the corner of his eye, he saw Armory move into the shadows. "Mother, we've been over this many times, although you seem to conveniently tune out my feelings on the matter. I have no senatorial prospects, and if I did I would sell them to the lowest bidder. I can't think of anything I'd like less than to be in politics. My current job is more political than I'm comfortable with."

Babe's face drained of color, and Ren felt Sara flinch as if she wanted to reach out to comfort the older woman. "But you—"

"No, Mother. *You.* You're the one who's interested in politics. You're the one who loves the game playing and the power. I don't want anything to do with it. And if it turns out that Brady is my son and someone has a problem with Sara's past, then they can have my judgeship, too. It wouldn't be worth it to me."

"You can't mean that," Babe whispered, her eyes wide with fear.

He ran his free hand through his hair. "Mother, I took this job to make you happy. I knew how upset you were when Dad died. His career was the foundation of your life, and I knew it was important to you to have those political connections. But this was never *my* dream."

Babe looked wobbly as if her legs couldn't support her any longer, and Armory hurried to her side, helping her back to the couch.

Reluctantly, Ren let go of Sara's hand. He pulled the armchair close to the couch and sat down facing his mother. "I know what day this is, Mother. I know it's hard for you. It's hard for me, too. I remember it clear as a bell."

She shook her head. "You can't remember that far back. You were only four."

"Four-and-a-half." When Sara's hand touched his shoulder, he took it. "I can still picture it. The minute I woke up from my nap I knew something was wrong. Becky and Jane were crying. Aunt Elaine and Uncle Frank were talking in low voices. When I asked where you were, Frank said you'd gone in the ambulance with Sunny. I knew ambulances meant hospitals. Hospitals were where you went if you were sick." Ren didn't know for sure how much of his memory was real, how much conjecture, but he had a very clear picture of sitting on the step waiting for his mother to return.

"It was almost dark when Dad brought you home. You were crying. I'd never seen you cry before—it scared me. When I reached for you, you pushed my hand away at first, then dropped to your knees and pulled me into your arms. You told me Sunny was gone and I was all you had left."

Babe hunched forward, her face in her hands.

"I've tried to be the person you needed me to be, Mother, but I can't do it anymore. I need to be my own person." Gently, he touched her shoulder. Her body seemed small and frail. She'd aged more than he'd realized, more than she let the outside world know. His heart ached, knowing this would hurt her, but deep inside he knew both Sunny and his father would have understood.

"What does that mean?" she asked in a small voice.

"It means I need for you to go home so Sara and I can talk."

She lifted her chin. "You're my son, Lawrence. I care about what happens to you."

"I know. But I'm forty-two years old, Mother. I think it's time you admitted I can think for myself." He smiled conciliatorily. "I haven't done too badly so far, have I?"

Her eyes narrowed as if weighing his question.

"Granted, I should have bought Intel when I had the chance, but other than that…"

Her face softened, her lips turning up slightly. After wiping her tears with a lacy handkerchief she'd had in her pocket, Babe rose. Ren walked her to the door.

"Armory," Ren said, motioning his old friend to him, "would you please drive Mother home? We'll get her car over to the condo later."

He gave his mother a hug. "Good night, mother. I love you

and I hope you can trust me to do what's right—after all, I am a judge."

Her left brow lifted dryly as she took Armory's proffered arm. Her ladylike snort seemed to sum up her opinion of both his wit and wisdom.

With a sigh, Ren closed the door. As he returned to the office he glanced toward the kitchen, but since he didn't hear any sound, he assumed Bo and Claudie had taken off as soon as the fireworks started.

He hesitated at the threshold of his office. Sara was standing beside his desk, one hand hovering above the courier box as if trying to muster the courage to touch it.

His heart constricted in apprehension. This was their moment of truth. Never had Ren felt more empathy for what a defendant must feel awaiting his verdict. What was in that box would determine Ren's fate: life or an emptiness as hollow as death.

CHAPTER FOURTEEN

SARA'S FINGERS SKIMMED over the cardboard box, but she couldn't make herself pick up the package that would most certainly alter the shape of her future. Turning, she moved to the sofa and sat down, her legs as insubstantial as the craft dough she'd made that morning for Brady.

Her heart pounded in her chest from the turbulent emotions she'd witnessed and felt on Ren's behalf. If she closed her eyes, she could vividly picture him as a child, waiting on the stoop for his mother to return from the hospital.

Poor Ren, she thought, her heart aching for the little boy who loved his mother so much. Babe had manipulated—maybe unintentionally—many of Ren's life decisions, and Ren had every right to resent her for it. But he didn't.

"Tell me what you're thinking," Ren said, plopping down beside her as if drained. He reached for her hand and squeezed it. "That must have been very uncomfortable for you. I'm sorry if my mother hurt you when she said that about your past."

"She was acting in your best interests. I'd probably do the same thing—only I doubt if Brady would be that understanding." She sighed. "I don't think I ever realized what a weighty responsibility the role of parenting is. I don't know if I'm cut out for it."

His smile—so kind and endearing—brought her close to tears.

"As a judge, I see a couple of problems with your theory. Number one, it's too late to back out—you already are a mother. And number two, you're a wonderful mother. Brady will never resent you."

Sara pulled her hand free of his and sat forward. Nervously gnawing on a cuticle, she focused on the courier box. "If those test results prove you're Brady's father, then you'll be the one who decides how much say I have in his life. If you're his father, Ren, you really don't need me in the picture." She felt him jerk and quickly went on before he could say something he might later regret. "I mean, you'd have no legal obligation to me other than as Brady's aunt, and I promise you I won't fight for custody. I know I said I would, but that was before I found out what a great dad you are. He loves you, Ren, and I wouldn't want to come between the two of you."

Sara had tried to keep her tone level and unemotional, so Ren's low oath took her by surprise. He vaulted to his feet and turned to face her. He seemed incensed.

"Did you say I wouldn't need you?" he repeated, his voice shaking with anger. "Do you mean if that test proves I'm Brady's biological father, it somehow negates your connection to him? Your love? Everything you've done for him?"

"I just don't want you to feel obligated to make a place for me in your life."

Swearing under his breath, he threw up his hands. "God Almighty, Sara, don't you know what you are? Who you are?"

She shook her head, feeling as lost and frightened as she had on those nights when her mother hadn't come home, and the only thing standing between her and the big scary world was her twelve-year-old sister.

Without warning, he reached out and pulled her to him, saying fiercely, "Sara Carsten, you *are* Brady's mother." He clasped her shoulders and set her back so she could look in his eyes. "It doesn't matter that you didn't give birth to him. You've been there for him every step of the way, and when he's forty-two and his life is a mess, you'll still be there for him."

Fighting tears, she tried to smile. "Yeah, and he'll probably blame me for it, just like you do your mom."

Ren shook his head. His tone softened. "Even if Babe is to blame for some of my choices, that doesn't mean I don't love her. She's my mother. She's haughty and pretentious and can be extremely shallow at times, but she's also loyal, softhearted and brave—like you."

A little sound slipped from Sara's lips. "If your life's a mess, Ren, it's probably because of us. If we hadn't—"

He cut her off with a small shake. "Don't say it. Don't even think it. I don't know what I can say to make you believe me, but until you and Brady came along, I didn't have a life, Sara. I existed. Period. I had to run away to steal a glimpse of life."

He lowered his head and said softly, "Weren't you listening this morning? Or didn't you believe me?"

Sara's breath caught in her throat. "I want to believe you, but maybe this isn't the best thing for—"

He didn't let her finish. His lips crushed against hers; his arms wrapped around her as if he'd never let her go. This kiss was different. Urgent. A bit desperate—as if he feared rejection and was as unsure of her love as she was of his. The idea radiated inward, connecting with a part of her hidden in a dark abyss. *He needs me as much as I need him.*

She pulled back. Searching his eyes for confirmation, she said, "This *is* the real thing, isn't it?"

His blue eyes lit with joy—the identical look Brady gave her when he hugged her each morning. It was a look Sara couldn't imagine not seeing every day for the rest of her life.

She cupped his jaw and tenderly kissed his lips. "I love you, too, Ren Bishop."

He crushed her to him again, giving her a taste of the passion she no longer feared. In fact, she welcomed it. "Aren't we going to your room?" she asked, when he trailed a string of scintillating kisses down her neck.

Her question seemed to bring him back to reality, because he locked his fingers at the small of her back and sighed. "I hope so, but we still have to deal with that box," he said somberly.

With obvious reluctance, he let her go and walked to the desk. He picked it up, ripped open the tear strip and dumped a sheaf of papers—held together by a large, black metal clip—to the desk. He set the empty box to one side and was reaching for the papers, when Sara cried out, "Wait."

Her pulse raced and a creepy sensation made her shiver. "Do we have to do this now? Couldn't it wait until tomorrow?" Trying to express her fears without making him think she questioned his feelings, she asked, haltingly, "I'm not saying it will, but what if it changes things?"

He placed both hands flat on the desk and gave her what Claudie called his "judge look." "It *will* change things, Sara. Hell, a part of me wants to chuck this in the fireplace and grab a match, but we can't do that. This is Brady's future, too. He deserves to know the truth." He placed the neatly stacked papers to one side. "But before we look, I have to ask you something."

Sara stepped forward. "What?"

He drew her to his side and took both her hands in his. "Will you marry me?"

She heard the words and comprehended their meaning on one level, but couldn't make sense of them on another. "Marry you?"

He kissed her fingers. "Marry me. Be my wife, the mother of our son." He emphasized the word *our.* When Sara questioned him with a look, he said, "I don't need to see the results to know he's my child. In my heart I know I could never love him more than I already do, but if the test says that biologically he isn't, then he'll be mine when I marry you. If the test says he is, then we did the right thing, because either way you are his mother and that will never change."

Sara's throat was too constricted to speak so she nodded her chin. "I love you," she whispered.

"Is that a yes?" he asked, brushing aside her tears.

She nodded eagerly.

"I'm sorry," he said formally. "You'll have to speak up for the record."

Laughing, she threw her arms around his neck and cried, "Yes, Your Honor. Definitely, yes."

He clutched her tightly, then gallantly scooped her up as nimbly as he would have Brady. "I believe I'll need proof of that before I can pass judgment," he teased, heading for the stairs.

"What about the test results?" she cried.

"Later. They're not going anywhere, but we are. Upstairs. Now."

Heart soaring, Sara allowed herself to experiment. She used her tongue to trace the outline of his ear, provocatively exploring every nook and cranny. His step faltered halfway up the staircase.

"Jesus, Sara," Ren said, his tone laughing, "watch where you put that thing. You might kill us both."

Emboldened, she whispered, "Speaking of putting things in certain places, I'm a little out of practice. You may have to refresh my memory about what goes where."

Ren froze one step shy of the top. His look was dumbstruck, then he put back his head and laughed. "Oh, Sara, you are the answer to my prayers, and I'm going to spend the rest of my life proving how thankful I am."

Sara felt herself blush, but she didn't contradict him because she knew the same was true for her.

BO CAREFULLY EASED OPEN the closet door. The coat closet wouldn't have been his first choice for reconnaissance duty, but it happened to be where he and Claudie were standing when the proverbial shit hit the fan. Afraid Babe might spot them, he'd hustled Claudie inside and partially closed the door, leaving ample width for air—and conversation—to enter.

Bo might have felt guilty about eavesdropping if the results had been different, but from what he'd gleaned, things were working out right for his friends—and he couldn't be happier. He poked his head out, checking to make sure the coast was clear.

Claudie shoved him from behind. "Move it, garlic breath," she muttered, shouldering past him. "You had to order scampi, didn't you?"

"How was I supposed to know?" he grumbled. He brushed some lint from his jacket sleeve. "I was just gonna congratulate you on being a good sport, and you have to turn into a whiner."

Her eyes narrowed. "I'll show you whining."

A door closed upstairs, and Bo forgot about arguing with Claudie. Ren had finally connected all the dots. Once in one of his beer-hazed moments, Bo had expounded to his best friend the Bo Lester Theory of Life. *"Life is like a connect-the-dots puzzle. You're given this big formless maze when you're born, and it's up to you to make a picture, connecting all the right dots."* Ren had laughed and said that at the rate he was going, he'd wind up with someone else's picture.

Bo bet Ren would change his tune after tonight.

Claudie snapped her fingers in front of his face to bring him back to the present. "That reminds me. We had a bet. I told you he'd propose, and you said he wasn't that spontaneous. Read 'em and weep, Cookbook Man. Time to pay up."

Bo looked at her. "We didn't shake on it."

"Are you going to welsh? I should have known."

Frowning, he grabbed her hand and led the way to Ren's office. "I didn't say I wouldn't. But technically, it wasn't a real bet. Next time, you should make sure you follow protocol."

He saw her trying to keep the grin from her face. If he weren't so happy for Ren, he'd have let that grin get to him. "Just sit down and shut up," he ordered with mock severity.

She settled one hip on the corner of Ren's desk, while Bo walked around and sat down. "Close the doors. This is humiliating enough without disturbing Ren and Sara."

She did so, then quickly returned to her pose, a perfect place from which to watch him make a fool of himself.

"I can't remember the number," he lied, pretending to concentrate on the telephone keypad.

With a sigh of disgust, she leaned over and grabbed the phone, punched out a series of numbers, then handed him the unit. "It's ringing."

Bo rocked back. For a person who valued anonymity above all else, this was torture—which undoubtedly was why she'd selected it as his payment.

When a female voice came on the line, Bo swallowed, then told her what he wanted. There was a slight pause, and then she gave him his cue. He nodded at Claudie, who quickly dashed to the stereo and hit a button, keeping the volume low.

"Now, fellow poetry freaks, we have Bo from Sacramento on the line," a voice said over the airwaves. "Bo is going to share with us a poem he wrote. I get the feeling this is the first time for Bo, so be gentle with him, fellow writers, poets and songsmiths. Remember your first time—a combination of agony and ecstasy."

Bo rolled his eyes. She had the agony part right.

"Go ahead, Bo. You said your poem doesn't have a title,

but maybe one will come out of the open-line critique session that follows. Go ahead. Let's hear your poem."

Critique session? Not if I slit my wrists first. He gave Claudie the blackest look he could muster, ruing the night on his boat when he rocked Brady to sleep by reciting one of the stupid poems he'd written. Claudie had immediately pounced on his weakness, but to his surprise had claimed to like it and had wanted to hear more.

He cleared his suddenly parched throat, then closed his eyes and recited words he'd never before shared with a single soul.

"White cranes guard the secret palace—a
reed haven where children of the river live.
Old men with no allegiance to life—lost souls made invisible
by their need, stumble along slippery banks
searching for escape from a world that doesn't fit right.
The river children know the evicted ones are not the enemy.
Screaming metal fins churn the water, dripping blue poison—
Toys of smiling ones with bright teeth and oil-slick skin.
Fear them, children, for your home is but a playground to those
who see only a domain to dominate.
Alert, white cranes. Alert. Forewarn the babies,
the minnows,
the polliwogs.
Children of the river, hide."

He opened his eyes. The first thing he saw was Claudie, sitting frozen, her mouth open. What shook him most was the tears in her eyes. He didn't wait for the DJ's comments. He hung up the phone and jumped up to turn off the radio, blocking out what sounded like a very positive response.

"That was really beautiful, Bo," Claudie said softly. "I'm sorry I made you do it on the radio like that. You should submit it somewhere and have it published."

Bo snorted. "You're just surprised because you didn't think I had it in me. Trust me, it's not great poetry. In fact, it's not poetry. It's just words."

"Words that make sense, Bo. Good words."

He sat back down, pleased by her praise despite himself. He idly fiddled with the stack of papers before him, until it dawned on him what it was. He casually scooted the stack closer and arched his neck to study the writing on it.

"Bo," Claudie scolded. "That's private. Leave it alone."

His curiosity was tempted. "But don't you want to know?"

"No."

She had the grace to blush over her lie.

"Yes, you do," he said, turning it around. "Damn, it's upside down." Using Ren's pen, he wiggled it under one corner and flipped the stack over. "Wow! How'd that happen?"

"Bo, stop it. I'll tell."

He gave her his most shit-ass grin. "Who? I don't think Ren and Sara would appreciate it if you bothered them just now."

She scowled, "But…"

He used the pen to nudge a few pages back until he found one that looked promising. Leaning closer he scanned the words, zeroing in on what he was looking for. He read it twice, then let out a long, low sigh. "Well, I'll be damned. Those condoms didn't fail, after all."

Claudie let out a *yip* of surprise and raced around the desk to lean over his shoulder. "Show me where it says that. I don't believe you."

Bo pointed to the paragraph in question. He knew the minute she confirmed his analysis of the words. She fell back, tears in her eyes. "Oh, my God, I can't believe it. Ren's not Brady's daddy."

Bo spun the chair around and stared at her until she met his gaze. "Let's be very clear about this. Ren may not be Brady's biological father, but he is definitely that little boy's daddy."

A bleak look flitted across her face and disappeared. She took a breath, then smiled. "You're right. It takes more than genes to make a father."

Bo rewarded her with a grin, then jumped to his feet. "Okay. Now that we've got that settled, let's go dancing. We have a lot to celebrate."

REN DREW IN A DEEP BREATH, savoring the fragrance that was uniquely Sara. Curled in the curve of his body, a perfect *C*, she slept as peacefully as Brady did. Lately, Ren had known many a sleepless night that found him leaning on Brady's crib, memorizing his features, watching his eyelids move, his lips pursed in some dreamed response. Ren's heart would fill to the brim, then find room for more images too wonderful to pass up. He'd never imagined one heart could hold so much love and still have room for more—the kind he'd shared with Sara just hours before.

If he closed his eyes and tried to picture the process of their lovemaking, the nuance and texture and taste, his brain became overwhelmed from the sheer joy of remembering. Making love with Sara was like learning to dream in a new language—none of the old words fit. *Wonderful. Perfect. Sensual. Exciting.* All fell short of describing the actual sensations, the giggles, the moans. His only fear was that his face muscles might never go back to normal, since all he could do was grin.

Sara sighed and stretched, bumping his chin with her hand. She started slightly as if suddenly realizing she was lying naked beside him. He waited to see how she would react.

"Umm," she purred, arching back to press more closely against him, "you feel wonderful. Is this heaven?"

"I think so," he whispered, nuzzling her neck. "Only one thing could make it any better."

She caught his implication and a sexy chuckle hummed in her throat. "Hold that thought. I want to check on Brady."

Ren vaulted out of bed and walked to his closet. He pulled out two robes and carried one to her. The moonlight streaming through his windows cast her body in a silver glow almost surreal in perfection. "You are the most beautiful woman I've ever known," he told her, holding the robe for her. When she turned to slip her arms in the sleeves, he reeled her in to his body and closed his arms around her.

She snuggled against him. "You don't have to say that," she said softly. "I love you, anyway. I know I'm not beautiful. I look like a librarian. Always have. My mother told me that when I was ten." She shrugged. "Maybe that's why I like books so much."

Stricken by the memory of his words coming back to haunt him, he turned her around to face him and sternly scolded her. "Sara, you are everything that's beautiful to me—mother, friend, lover. Are we clear on that?"

She began to execute a smart salute, but her hand got lost in the sleeve of the robe. Laughing, she raised up on her toes and kissed him. "I'll try to remember that. Now, let's go check on our little boy."

Ren pulled on his robe and followed her down the hall. The grandfather clock in the hallway read half-past midnight. If Claudie had returned she was already asleep, because her room was dark. Brady's door was partially open and a Winnie-the-Pooh night-light glowed festively near his closet. The blinds on the window let in enough moonlight for them to see without turning on any other lights.

Together they hunched over the crib. "He's a gift beyond all gifts, isn't he?" Sara whispered.

"Then I'm doubly blessed."

She chucked softly. "Try telling that to your mother."

"I will. We will. Tomorrow." When he felt her shrink away, he clapped his arm across her shoulders and squeezed. "Don't worry. Once Babe realizes you're going to be a Bishop—and believe me, that is part of her mind-set, not mine—if you want to keep your last name, hyphenate, whatever, I don't care as long as we're married—she'll take on anyone in your defense."

Sara didn't look convinced.

"Remember on the way home tonight you told Bo and Claudie about my old dog, Freckles?"

"The mutt you preferred over your mother's fancy pure-bred puppy."

"Freckles was not a mutt. She was a fine dog of indiscriminate parentage. She was a good friend and an excellent watchdog. And Babe came to adore her. When I went away to college, Freckles and mother became very close. It broke Babe's heart when she died. My point is, no one could ever say anything bad about Freckles because once she became a member of the family, she was no longer a mutt—she was a Bishop."

Sara's grin made him want to drag her back to bed. "Freckles Bishop. That has a nice ring to it. But if your mother doesn't mind, I think I like Sara Bishop better."

His heart jumped, but Ren wasn't worried about his blood pressure. His heart was whole, healthy and incredibly happy. He knew for a fact that love was the best medicine in the world.

He drew Sara into his arms and kissed her. "I love you, Sara. Thank you for making my world complete."

She kissed him back with an ardor he'd come to recognize as pure Sara. "You're what I've been looking for all my life, Ren. I'd almost given up hope, but believe it or not, Claudie inspired me to keep believing in love."

"Claudie?"

She nodded. "Even at her lowest moments when she was flat broke and out of work and men hurt her and she didn't have a dram of self-respect left, she'd come to the bookstore and take Brady in the corner and read him a book. Somehow he seemed to sense her need, because no matter how hyper he was, he'd wind down and sit on her lap as if absorbing every word she read. I'd look at them and know that love exists all around us—we just have to let ourselves be more like children. We have to open ourselves up to it."

Turning, they looked at Brady again. "He really was the key, wasn't he," Ren said, marveling at the miracle of ever connecting with this wonderful woman and her child. *His* child. He thought about the papers on his desk, but shoved the image away.

As if sensing his thoughts, Sara asked, "Shall we get it out of the way?"

Ren pulled her close. "You and Brady are mine. That's all I need to know—all anyone ever needs to know."

He kissed her but sensed the slightest hesitation, and he knew it wasn't that simple. They needed to deal with the results so they could get on with the business of living. He led the way to the study.

His heart was beating faster than normal, but Ren felt confident of the results. He sat down at his desk; Sara stood behind him, bending down to scan the cover sheet. He adjusted the desk lamp and flipped past the documentation garbage to the result sheet.

The result was there in black and white: Negative.

Sara's gasp told him she read the word at the same time. "Does this mean Hulger was his father?"

Ren shook his head. When he found his voice, he said, "No. It means Julia and Hulger gave birth to our son. And when Brady's older, we'll share him with them—but for now, he's all ours."

Sara turned the chair to make room to climb into his lap. She wrapped her arms around his neck and held him tight. "You are going to be the best father in the world."

Ren squeezed his eyes tight against the disappointment, the shock. He'd been so sure. "I love him so much," he said, his voice catching on a sob.

"I know. I feel the same way. Sometimes I can't believe I didn't give birth to him."

They held each for a long time, then Ren said, "If it's okay with you, I'll put the file in the safe. Brady will have it if he ever needs it, but this doesn't change how I feel about him. And if Hulger's parents have no objections, I'd like to adopt him after we're married."

"You are a remarkable man, and I love you," Sara said, her eyes shining.

She took his hand and led the way back upstairs. They paused in the doorway of Brady's room. Brady let out a small grunt and rolled to his side. Searching in his sleep, he found his elephant and his fingers closed around the creature's trunk. He hauled the dilapidated beast to him and sighed with complete satisfaction.

"That's his 'funt.' Julia bought it for him that first Christmas when he was only a month-and-a-half old. He loved it from the start." The memory seemed to sadden her, and her expression made him draw her close.

"I'm sorry Julia died, Sara—for Brady's sake and yours. We'll make sure Brady knows the good memories. My father used to say the way to keep Sunny alive was by talking about her. He said, 'I plan to make her the first one I look up when I get to heaven, so I have to keep her close by.' Picturing them together was the one thing that made his death tolerable."

Sara hugged him. "I love you for the man you are and the man you'll help Brady to be, but right this moment I'm in need of the man you were an hour ago."

She slipped her hands between the gap in his robe and pressed up against his naked body.

"Sara," he half choked.

"I'm sorry, but I like making love with you and I'm ready to try something new."

He hugged her tight and kissed her breathless. "No problem, but let's go back to our room. I've heard other parents complain about never having private time. We're going to make the most of ours. Starting right this minute."

CHAPTER FIFTEEN

Four months later

REN TOOK A LAST GLANCE at the election results, then closed his laptop and stretched back in his chair, kicking his feet up on his desk. He couldn't recall the last time he'd spent an election night at home. The sight of his loafers made him smile—one of the perks of being a professor was the casual dress. Another was having the holidays off, and he was looking forward to the upcoming Thanksgiving break with joyful anticipation.

He closed his eyes and breathed a deep, satisfied sigh. Being married to Sara these last three months was a fulfillment that touched every aspect of his life. Her support had enabled him to do what he'd secretly dreamed of doing—teach law. At times he missed the judiciary, but he loved the challenge of inspiring students to look beyond grades to the people, the soul and the character of law.

"Honey, would you bring up that last load of clothes when you come?" Sara called from upstairs.

"You bet," he hollered back. He sat up and took a pen from his desk drawer. *Upstairs laundry room,* he wrote on a notepad. First thing in the morning he'd call Rich, the contractor who had transformed his parents' house into his and Sara's home. It was silly to make Sara cart clothes back and forth upstairs—especially now.

Claudie's old room would be perfect, he thought.

Ren started to get up, but sat back down when the phone rang. "Hello."

"Hey, Ren, it's me. Any more calls from you-know-who?"

"Not since Sunday. What about you? Any leads?"

"Not enough to amount to a hill of beans."

Bo had been as perplexed as everyone else had when Claudie suddenly disappeared. Sara had been frantic until Claudie left a message on the answering machine informing them she was on some sort of self-imposed mission.

"I gotta set something right, Sara," Claudie had said. "Tell the Cookbook Man I can handle this myself. It's a family thing, and I don't need him butting in. That's why I took off like I did."

In typical Claudie fashion, she'd added, "Don't worry, Sara, I'll be back in a week or so. Give Brady a kiss for me and tell the girls at One Wish House I'm sorry about abandoning them like this, but they'll understand. Sometimes you get a chance to prevent history from repeating itself and you just gotta take it." With that, she'd hung up, leaving Bo with very few clues to follow.

Now Bo's angry sputtering made Ren sigh. "How one skinny, little ex-hooker can disappear like that is beyond me! I've had my staff working overtime and they're flat-out pissed. So am I."

Ren knew bluster when he heard it. Bo was hurting. "She said she'd be back soon," Ren said. "Maybe you ought to just let her do this on her own."

Bo snorted. "Once I find her, we'll discuss that possibility. Dammit," he added, half under his breath, "I thought we had something going."

Ren grimaced at the pain and frustration he heard in his friend's voice. "You'll find her, Bo. You're the best."

The sigh that came over the line seemed very unlike Bo.

"What's the problem, Lester? Are you getting soft? Can't handle the challenge?"

Bo growled. "Oh, I'm gonna find her and when I do…"

A loud *honk* obscured Bo's words. "Where are you calling from?" Ren asked.

"My car. I thought I'd run by One Wish House and see if I can shake loose a few lips. Those women are as secretive as Claudie."

Bo paused for a second, then added, "I'm thinking about flying to New York."

"Why? Do you think Claudie's there?"

"No. I think she's somewhere in the Midwest, but that's just a hunch at this point. I'm hoping my cousin, Matt, can fine-tune the search. He used to work for the NYPD. Now, he's doing computer tracking for the FBI, and he owes me a favor."

New York. Ren frowned, recalling Eve's last letter. "I don't suppose you'd have time to see Eve while you're there, would you? Sara called her office yesterday, and they told her Eve didn't work there anymore."

"Knowing Eve, she probably found something bigger and better," Bo said.

"Bigger than network news?" Ren asked doubtfully. "Sara said the last time she talked to her, Eve had complained about picking up some kind of flu bug on that trip to Panama. You know Sara; she thinks something terrible has happened to her."

There was a slight pause. "I doubt if Eve would be all that thrilled to hear from me. We've never been bosom buddies, you know."

Ren snickered. "That's an understatement, but if you have a chance I'm sure a voice from home would be welcome."

There was another pause, then Bo said, "I'll let you know

once I hook up with my cousin. If Matt's as good as my aunt says he is, I might not be there very long." A barely audible "Thank God" followed.

Bo's connection started to fade, so they cut the conversation short. Ren replaced the receiver with a sigh then went to retrieve the basket of freshly laundered clothes.

Aside from Claudie's disappearance, things were going fabulously. Ren hoped Bo could solve this case fast. The worry wasn't good for Sara, and he knew Claudie's absence was felt at One Wish House, her halfway house for prostitutes. When he'd first offered Claudie the use of his old Victorian for the project, she'd been reluctant to accept. But Sara and, remarkably, Babe had convinced her to give it a try.

Ren could never have predicted his mother's support of Claudie's efforts, but he credited Brady with having a mellowing effect on his grandmother. Ever since the honeymoon, when Babe and Claudie took care of Brady while Ren and Sara explored New Zealand, Ren's mother had shown a remarkable transformation. She laughed more, joined them on family outings and even volunteered at Brady's day care twice a week.

After climbing the stairs, he walked to Brady's door and looked inside the room. Sara lay on Brady's bed reading aloud from the book *I'll Love You Forever.* Brady, who would turn two on Sunday, lay beside her, his head pressed against the side of her rounded belly. With solemn concentration he drove a toy car up the incline.

Ren made up his mind not to mention Bo's call until morning. Knowing Sara, she would spend the whole night racking her brain for clues, and the doctor had advised additional rest. "Twins mean double prenatal care," he'd admonished.

Ren was thrilled at the thought of two babies. The news had created quite a stir among the Unturned Gentlemen's reading club, since it fouled up the odds in the betting pool, but at least it eased competition between Bo and Claudie for "god-person" rights.

Sara motioned Ren to join them. He set down the laundry basket and walked to the bed, then tousled his son's hair and leaned over to kiss his wife. Ren couldn't gaze upon her beautiful, glowing face without marveling at his initial blindness. *How could I have called her plain?* he wondered with chagrin.

"Cooties," Brady said, hiding his face.

"I'll cootie you," Ren said, tickling Brady under the arms.

Sara scooted out of the way of the wrestling match that ensued, laughing when Ren playfully tumbled to the floor, carrying Brady with him. She didn't try to stop it—every moment Ren and Brady spent in play was a cherished gift. She knew those moments would be harder to come by once the babies came.

She ran a hand over her belly, smiling with pure contentment. Marriage was everything she'd ever dreamed it could be—a true joining of spirit and soul. On those rare quiet afternoons at the bookstore when Brady was in school, and Claudie was campaigning to get young girls off the streets, Sara would ponder the quirks of fate. If Julia hadn't gone to Tahoe, Sara might never have met Ren. Why she went remained a mystery, but Sara liked to think her sister would be pleased with how things had worked out.

Sara glanced at the framed photograph sitting atop Brady's bureau—Hulger and Julia beaming with pride at Brady's christening. As a wedding gift, Ren had taken Sara and Brady to Denmark to visit Hulger's parents. Sara doubted that Brady understood how Grandmother and Grandfather Hovant fit into his life, but his gregarious nature seemed to give the older couple tremendous pleasure. Although Sara had worried that Hulger's parents might object to Ren adopting Brady, they'd warmly welcomed Ren into their home and had thanked Sara for keeping Hovant as Brady's middle name.

Brady Hovant Bishop. Smiling at her sister's image, Sara silently whispered, *You always said the right middle name would come along.*

"Help," Ren cried, when Brady tackled him. "You're reading the wrong book, Sara. You need *Where The Wild Things Are.*"

"Brady, love, time for bed." She closed her book and rose, feeling awkward and clumsy. By the time she'd put away the book and returned to his bed, Ren had Brady calmed down and tucked in.

Watching Ren kiss his son good-night, she blinked back tears. So alike, so handsome. In unison they looked at her—matching blue eyes, alive with humor, charm and goodness.

Perhaps not genetically identical, she thought, smiling back, but what does science know of love?

BACK IN KANSAS

CHAPTER ONE

CLAUDINE ST. JAMES knew the value of a dollar, or rather a twenty-dollar bill. That was how much she'd made the first time she'd sold her body.

"I'll give you eight-fifty for it and not a penny more," she said, keeping her voice as stern as possible. Inside, a rare feeling of frivolity made it hard to keep a straight face.

The old man behind the counter of the Wyoming thrift-store-cum-gas-station gave her a squinty look from his single watery eye—the other was concealed behind a hard plastic cup taped to his face with old-fashioned white tape, the kind that left black tracks behind when you pulled it off.

"Are you trying to snooker me, little girl?" he asked, his voice warbling as if he'd been silent too long.

At five-five, Claudie was used to being called "little," but she was nobody's "girl."

"No," she said, drawing her shoulders back. "The tag says twenty. It might be worth ten. Don't know. Don't care, because, frankly, I don't happen to need it that bad. If you want to get rid of it, then I'll give you eight. If not, keep it." She'd had twenty-seven years to perfect her poker face, and no old man with only one good eye would ever see past it.

He hefted the object in question into the dim light of his storefront window. Claudie assumed a pose of careless nonchalance and looked over the old man's shoulder through the coating of grime that almost obscured the four old-fashioned gas pumps out front.

Sara would kill me if I let the bookstore window get that dirty, she thought.

Claudie winced as an image of Sara Bishop—her friend and the owner of the Sacramento bookstore that Claudie managed—popped into her head. Claudie hadn't talked to Sara in almost a week. She and Ren, her husband of three months, had left early last Friday for their cabin at Lake Almanor; Claudie's impulsive decision to embark on this self-imposed mission hadn't come until later that day when her Internet search turned up a ghost from her past.

Knowing Sara would be worried about her, Claudie had phoned the Bishop home Sunday evening from her motel in Wendover, Utah, but could only leave a message since no one answered.

I hope everything's okay, Claudie thought, poking at various pieces of dust-covered junk while the man debated. *I hope they didn't get caught in that storm that was following me.* A burning sensation in the pit of her stomach made her frown. For a person who'd been on her own since seventeen, Claudie wasn't used to worrying about other people, or vice versa.

"Oh, all right," the man grumbled. He pitched the book to the counter as if to get it out of his limited sight as quickly as possible. "But you said eight-fifty the first time. Not eight. No way I'd be letting it go for eight."

Claudie bit down on the smile that tried to worm its way to her lips. She jammed her hand into the front pocket of her jeans and withdrew the exact amount, a five, three ones and two quarters. She'd been saving the quarters to call Sara but figured it was worth the sacrifice for an original copy of Mark Twain's *Pudd'nhead Wilson.* Ren, a collector of rare and old books, would keel over when he opened it at Christmas.

Claudie swept the prize into her voluminous purse and hurried to her car. Humming under her breath, she slipped behind the wheel of her 1986 Toyota wagon and pulled on her sunglasses. The car, which had belonged to Sara for most of its hundred thousand miles, was the first possession of any worth Claudie had ever owned. Except for some transmission trouble in Wendover, which had wasted two long days and cost her three hundred bucks, the car was running like a dream.

"Okay, baby, let's hit the road," she said aloud, easing the car into gear. As she waited for the streetlight to change, she glanced appraisingly at the sky. Horizon-to-horizon blue. Yesterday's brief, tumultuous storm, which had stranded her in western Wyoming overnight, might have seemed a figment of her imagination if not for a few residual snowdrifts.

The miniblizzard had reminded Claudie of Maya's ominous forecast prior to Claudie's departure. Maya, the newest resident of One Wish House—the halfway house for ex-prostitutes that Claudie had helped establish—had pulled Claudie aside to whisper, "You can't trust November. One minute it's nice, the next you're buried alive in snow. The weather can be more brutal than a man."

Claudie had shrugged off the dire prediction. It wasn't like she had a choice. Her baby sister would turn seventeen next month. Seventeen. A grim number that had marked a turning point in Claudie's life. The point when life had gone from bad to worse. She wasn't about to let the same thing happen to Sherry. Claudie only hoped she hadn't left it too late.

No, her trip couldn't wait—which is exactly what she planned to tell Bo. That is, if he was still speaking to her.

ROBERT BOWEN LESTER, JR., or Bo, as he preferred, slammed down the receiver with gusto. "Who the hell came up with automated answering systems?" he muttered under his breath.

His secretary, Karen Kriegen, a sixtyish German with the build of a sumo wrestler and the voice of a porn star, appeared in the doorway of his office. "You break the phone—I'm going home."

Bo knew she was only half kidding and he gave her a look of contrition. "Sorry, Mrs. K. By the time I got to the fifteenth option, I'd forgot what I was calling about."

She made a tsking sound and shook her head. "Where's that happy-go-lucky P.I. I used to work for? I think I liked him better before he fell in love."

"L-lo-ve?" he sputtered. "Believe me, Mrs. K., that's the last emotion on my list where Claudie St. James is concerned."

A ladylike snort filtered past the partially closed door. Karen and the other four members of his staff apparently had put their own interpretation on his impassioned search for Claudie. *They're wrong,* he adamantly insisted, swiveling his chair to face the floor-to-ceiling window at the far end of his office. The tinted glass afforded a pleasant view of the building's Andalusian square, but Bo's mind was not on his surroundings. He'd been plagued by harrowing thoughts of what-if… ever since learning Claudie disappeared.

"She's not here," the Asian girl had told him Friday night when he'd knocked on the door of One Wish House. Bo had cut his Vegas trip short—ostensibly because he'd been bored. In reality, he'd missed Claudie. And he'd been worried about her, too. She'd seemed preoccupied and distant for over a week. "She's gone off on a mission, and you are best to leave this alone," the woman had added, her voice steeped with portent.

She'd have shut the door of the old Victorian house in his face if not for Bo's cop-trained reflexes. "Claudie's gone? Where? She didn't mention anything about a trip when I talked to her last night." But she had seemed tense and distracted—maybe a little down, which was another reason he'd cut his trip short.

"It is not for me to say," Maya—Bo was certain that was the woman's name—had replied. She spoke with a spooky singsong intonation that made him uneasy. "Her wounds are deep and painful. There is much healing to do." For some reason her speech sent a bolt of fear through Bo.

Before he could ask anything else, a tall black woman had appeared in the doorway to add her two cents. "Get lost, asshole. If Claudie wanted you to know where she was, she'da called you. But she didn't, so guess what? You're f—"

Bo hadn't waited around to hear the rest of Rochell's colorful diatribe. He'd dashed to his car and started calling people. First, Sara, Claudie's best friend. *"Hello, you've reached the Bishops. Please leave us a message…"* Bo ended the call with a curse and tried Ren's cell phone but wasn't surprised when a voice told him the number was not in service. Ren seldom turned the damn thing on.

Next, Bo had tried the bookstore. "She came by about four and asked if she could have the week off," Daniel Pagannini, the comanager told him. "I kinda assumed she was joining you in Vegas. Next Monday is a holiday, and she was due for a vacation. Why? Is there a problem?"

Bo's gut said, yes. With anyone else, he might have shrugged it off, but not with Claudie. People like her weren't generally impetuous. They'd learned the hard way that unplanned risks often left you exposed and vulnerable. It had taken Bo months to win her trust—at least he'd thought she trusted him, but apparently he'd been deluding himself. She hadn't even bothered to tell him goodbye.

A staged cough brought Bo back to the present. He spun his chair to find Ren Bishop standing in the doorway.

"Don't shoot," an amused voice said. "My wife's pregnant with twins."

Bo's body gave a little shudder as the wasted adrenaline dissipated in his veins. "Dammit, Bishop, haven't I told you not to sneak up on me?"

"I knocked," Ren Bishop said, moving into the room. He looked around, his expression appreciative. "Nice digs. Beats the hell out of the spare bedroom of your houseboat."

"I moved here in September, you jerk. Is this the first time you've been to my office?"

Ren shrugged carelessly. "Have you been to mine on campus, yet?"

Bo rocked back in his chair and kicked his feet up on his desk. Ren had recently switched from dispensing the law to teaching it. "Point taken. Have a seat. Any word from Claudie?"

"No, she didn't tell Sara where she was going, either. To me that says she didn't want to worry the two people she cares most about."

Bo snorted. "Some way of showing it."

Ren walked to the window, checking out the view. "At the moment, Sara's more worried about you than Claudie. Mrs. Kriegen told her you haven't left this place since Saturday."

"Mrs. K. exaggerates. Besides, I got a shower and a closet full of clothes here. The couch makes into a bed and there's a pizzeria next door. Maybe I'll sell the boat and move here permanently."

Ren returned to the tufted leather sofa and sat down. Bo

could see the depth of his concern. "I know you're worried about her. We're all—"

"Screw worried," Bo snapped. "I'm just plain pissed now. I thought we were past that I-don't-need-anyone-and-no-body-needs-me stage. She has a life here, Ren. Responsibilities. A job." He swallowed to keep from saying, "A relationship."

"I'm sure she took all that into account before she left," Ren said equitably. "Claudie's not what I'd call impetuous. This must have been darned important."

Bo shook his head. "Too important to share with the people who care about her?"

Ren sighed and lifted his shoulders in resignation.

Bo regretted his outburst. Mrs. K. was right—this really wasn't like him. "By the way," he said in a more equitable tone, "I know Daniel's managing the bookstore while Claudie's away, but I forgot to ask when I talked to you last night. Who's running One Wish House while she's gone?"

Ren looked up, a bemused expression on his face. "Believe it or not, my mother volunteered. Apparently, Claudie called her late Friday afternoon and said she had a family emergency and asked if Babe would keep an eye on the place until she returned."

"She called Babe but not me," Bo said, not caring how bitter he sounded.

Ren sighed. "Like I told you on the phone, this must be something she thinks she has to do on her own. You're the same way, Lester. Jeez, getting personal information out of you is like pulling teeth. How long did we know each other before I ever met your family? I probably never would have met Matt if he hadn't come to visit you." He waited a second then asked, "Are you still going to New York?"

Bo studied his fingernails—being a judge had given Ren

an unfair advantage when it came to reading people's faces. Bo didn't want to reveal how hopeless this case looked. "I don't know. I left a message on Matt's machine, but it's not like we have a lot to go on. I don't even know her real name."

Ren rose. "Here," he said, taking a piece of paper from the inside pocket of his lightweight blazer. "Maybe this will help. Sara found this drawing in Brady's backpack."

"What information could your four-year-old son possibly have?"

"Apparently Claudie was doodling when she baby-sat Brady last week," Ren told him.

Bo took the rumpled paper. He switched on his desk lamp and held it under the light. Claudie had apparently been teaching Brady the alphabet. Beside letters were names. "Do you recognize any of these names?" Bo asked, working to keep his voice even. Just the sight of Claudie's carefully crafted penmanship made a funny ache blossom behind his breastbone.

"Nope. But Brady told Sara they were the names of Claudie's brothers and sisters. He said the two with the sad faces beneath them died."

Bo sat up straighter. "You're kidding. She never mentioned any family." He scanned the names again. "My God, she has two brothers and two sisters still alive, and I've never heard of them. That woman makes a clam look chatty."

Ren shrugged. "That's our Claudie." He turned away but stopped. "By the way, Sara thinks she once heard Claudie say something about growing up near one of the Great Lakes."

Bo groaned. "Terrific! That narrows down the search to the upper third of the country."

"Why don't you come home with me, Bo? Sara's fixing lunch. Maybe we could do some brainstorming."

Bo shook his head. "Thanks, but I'm gonna run over to the

bookstore. Claudie told Daniel she'd e-mail him if she got a chance." He couldn't stop himself from adding, bitterly, "I have an e-mail address, too, you know."

Ren squeezed Bo's shoulder. "She's a big girl, Bo. She can take care of herself." He stopped at the threshold and looked back. "Let me know if you decide to go to New York, okay? We still haven't been able to reach Eve. Weird, huh?"

Bo didn't have the energy to care about whatever troubles might be facing Eve Masterson, Ren's former fiancée. She'd chosen her course—a shot at network news, complete with all the fame, glamour and salary that went with it. If anyone could take care of herself it was Eve. Claudie, on the other hand, was as defenseless as a baby chick.

True, Claudie had survived for years in the emotionally desolate world of prostitution. But that was the old Claudie. The hooker. The new Claudie had her GED and was signed up for her first semester of college next spring. The new Claudie was fragile, vulnerable. Bo knew this on a gut level. And his gut was telling him to find her before something or someone could hurt her again.

He studied Claudie's sketch a minute longer. Wedged between *Wesley* and *Valery* was a word he'd overlooked. A name. A surname. "Anders."

This might be the break he needed. Bo buzzed his secretary. "Mrs. K., try my cousin again, please. And see if you can get me on a flight to New York. Tonight."

AS HER CAR joined the easterly flow of traffic on Interstate 80, Claudie heaved a sigh and let her thoughts drift to Bo— where they seemed content to stay way too much of the time.

"Bo's head over heels crazy about you, Claudie," Sara had said last Tuesday as they'd relaxed on the bench of the BART train during their ride back from San Francisco. An array of fancy bags—trophies from their shopping expedition—encircled their aching feet.

"If he is, then he's just plain crazy, Sara. I'm not the girl next door, you know."

"He knows who you are, Claudie," Sara had protested. "He's seen you turn your life around these past seven months and he knows how hard you've worked to help other women get off the street."

Sara's praise had a way of making Claudie squirm—it felt good but somehow undeserved. "I'm no saint, Sara. I'm not the kind of person who deserves a happy ending. Life just doesn't work that way for people like me."

Sara's eyes had filled with tears. "You are so wrong about that, Claudie. And if you think Bo believes that then you don't know Bo."

Their conversation had been interrupted by the train's arrival at the Pleasanton station where Sara's Explorer was parked, but Sara's words had stayed with Claudie during the drive home. Claudie did know Bo. He was a kind, decent man who'd always treated her with respect.

He'd never judged her or questioned her about her years on the streets. The more she came to know him—they were often thrown together thanks to Ren and Sara's situation—the better she liked him. But that was as far as their relationship should go. They needed to keep things superficial.

Friendly. Bo was a friend. Period.

So maybe you're hoping your friend will come looking for you, a little voice said.

"No," she said aloud, startling herself by the volume of her denial. "I can do this myself. If I'd have wanted his help, all I had to do was ask."

But that would have meant telling him about her past. That was nobody's business but hers—and Garret Anders's.

A sign announcing a truck stop caught her eye and Claudie impulsively took the exit. The clock on the dash read: three-thirty. She was less than twenty miles from Cheyenne. Her brother probably had a job, which meant Claudie would have to time her arrival. She knew she could call first, but she wanted to surprise him. Perhaps just to see if he still recognized her. She was curious herself—was there any of the old Claudie left to see?

She parked near a bank of phones and got out of the car. The wind sliced through her sweatshirt, but the clean, brisk air felt exhilarating. She sat down at a picnic table partially sheltered from the wind and mentally catalogued all that she'd left behind to undertake this quest.

First and foremost: One Wish House.

Back in July when Ren first suggested using his partially renovated Victorian home in Folsom, California, as a halfway house for prostitutes, Claudie had laughed in disbelief. But somehow the project had become a reality.

The name had come from her friend, Keneesha, a former prostitute who'd turned her life around and was now living in Georgia, raising the son she'd abandoned years earlier. "When I was hookin', I can't tell you the number of times I'd find myself thinking, 'If I could have one wish, I'd ask to start over,'" Kee had said when she'd returned for Sara's wedding.

The home's current residents ranged in age from nineteen to thirty-three. While linked to various bureaucratic agencies, the halfway house was a volunteer residence program.

Claudie feared her absence might undermine all she'd worked so hard to create.

"You know what people are going to think, right?" Davina had fretted as she watched Claudie pack. "They're going to think you abandoned us or something."

"It's dangerous out there, Claudie," the world-weary Maya had added. "I've been across this country more than once—bad things can happen. And this is a terrible time of year to travel. Storms. Snow this high," she'd said raising to her tiptoes to hold her hand above her head.

"*Sí*," Davina had concurred, "you shouldn't do this alone. Meester Bo would go. I know he would. He likes you."

A foul epithet had introduced Rochell's opinion. "She don't need a man to do this. She got off the street on her own, didn't she? Why do you always act like men are the answer?"

"Bo's at a gadget fair in Vegas until Monday," Claudie had interjected. "This can't wait. I'll call him from the road and let him know I'm okay. Besides, we're just friends, you know."

Sally Rae, a willowy blonde and youngest member of the group, made a snorting sound. "Yeah, right, like we believe that."

Claudie had grabbed her jacket from her closet and faced the group. "Hey, this isn't a best-case scenario, but I've got to go, and you all know why. Babe Bishop's going to check in on things from time to time."

Their simultaneous groans summed up their feelings about that topic. Claudie flinched. "Sorry, but she's on the board of directors. If you need any help, call Sara."

Davina, the most spontaneous of the group, surged forward, clasping Claudie in a hug. "Don't worry. We will be okay, Claudie. And I will pray for you and your little sister."

The women walked Claudie to the door. A sober stillness hung in the foyer as she opened the door. Beyond the porch, a steady drizzle fell, cold and uninviting. Claudie feared she might not make it over Donner Pass without chains. She'd debated about waiting until morning to head out, but the weather report showed a big storm approaching from the northwest.

Maya spoke softly. "You are a warrior on a quest, Claudie." Her obsidian eyes had seemed capable of viewing the core of Claudie's heart. "Find the truth and it will release the pain you keep locked away."

A warrior on a quest, Claudie silently repeated, gazing across the windswept vista. *Bo would love that one, wouldn't he?*

Guilt made her grimace, but she closed her mind to Bo's image. She couldn't think about him right now. She had to stay focused.

She rose and started toward her car, but detoured at the bank of phones. She counted her remaining coins—only enough for one call. *If I call Sara, she could give Bo a message.*

Coward, a voice whispered. A cowardly warrior on a foolish quest. *Yep, that about sums things up,* she thought, shaking her head to keep the wind-induced tears at bay.

BREATHLESS FROM her run to catch the phone, Sara croaked, "Hello."

The voice on the other end triggered a flood of emotion. "Claudie! Thank God you're okay. Tell me you're okay."

"I'm fine, Sara J. Don't get all worked up. That can't be good for the babies."

An immediate sense of relief made Sara's knees weak. She sat down on a stool and caught sight of the notepad and pen Bo had left beside every phone in the house. *Notes. Bo said I'm supposed to concentrate and take notes. Impressions. Background noises.* "Where are you? Why'd you leave without telling me? You are coming back, right?" Sara asked, picking up the pen. It was hard to be a sleuth and talk at the same time.

Claudie's small laugh sounded sort of lonely and sad. "I'm a bad penny, remember? I keep turning up."

Sara's eyes misted over. "You'd better come back soon. Brady's missing you, and Bo's going nuts."

"Bo's one of the reasons I left without telling anyone. You know Super Snoop—he'd have his nose in this up to his eyebrows. I have to do this on my own, Sara."

"But we're your friends, Claudie. Can't we help? That's what friends do."

"Between keeping up with Brady and getting ready for the new babies, you've got your hands full at the moment, remember?" Her friend was obviously not going to reveal much, so Sara tried to focus on the noises coming through the line.

She hastily jotted down "Trucks? Freeway? Interstate?" Sara decided to gamble. "Does this have anything to do with your family?"

In the moment of stunned silence that followed, Sara heard a tinny voice give the call letters of a radio station. She wrote them down. "How do you know that?" Claudie asked, her voice tense.

"You left a piece of paper in Brady's backpack. There were names. Brady said they were your brothers and sisters."

Claudie blew out a breath. "I keep forgetting how smart that little guy is." Sara added the notation: *She misses Brady...and us.* "Well, all I'm gonna say about it right now is that I'm trying to find my half brother. Hopefully Yancy can put me in touch with the rest of the bunch. A regular old-home week," she said her voice sounding less than pleased by the prospect.

Sara added a few quick notes to her list. "That sounds wonderful. I'm happy you're reuniting with your family."

Claudie's chuckle didn't sound encouraging. "I haven't seen any of these people since I left home ten years ago. I doubt they're going to be thrilled to see me, but that's just tough. This is something I gotta do. Period."

An Important Message from the Editors

Dear Reader,

Because you've chosen to read one of our fine romance novels, we'd like to say "thank you"! And, as a special way to thank you, we're offering you two more of the books you love so well, and a surprise gift to send you — absolutely FREE!

Please enjoy them with our compliments...

Pam Powers

Peel off Seal and Place Inside

FREE GIFT

How to validate your Editor's
"Thank You"
FREE GIFT

1. Peel off gift seal from front cover. Place it in space provided at right. This automatically entitles you to receive 2 FREE BOOKS and a fabulous mystery gift.

2. Send back this card and you'll get 2 brand-new *Romance* novels. These books have a cover price of $5.99 or more each in the U.S. and $6.99 or more each in Canada, but they are yours to keep absolutely free.

3. There's no catch. You're under no obligation to buy anything. We charge nothing—ZERO—for your first shipment. And you don't have to make any minimum number of purchases—not even one!

4. The fact is, thousands of readers enjoy receiving their books by mail from The Reader Service. They enjoy the convenience of home delivery...they like getting the best new novels at discount prices BEFORE they're available in stores... and they love their Heart to Heart subscriber newsletter featuring author news, special book offers, book reviews and much more!

5. We hope that after receiving your free books you'll want to remain a subscriber. But the choice is yours— to continue or cancel, any time at all! So why not take us up on our invitation, with no risk of any kind. You'll be glad you did!

GET A *Free* MYSTERY GIFT...

SURPRISE MYSTERY GIFT COULD BE YOURS **FREE** AS A SPECIAL "THANK YOU" FROM THE EDITORS

THE EDITOR'S "THANK YOU" FREE GIFTS INCLUDE:

▶ Two BRAND-NEW Romance Novels

▶ An exciting surprise gift

YES! I have placed my Editor's "thank you" Free Gifts seal in the space provided at right. Please send me 2 FREE books, and my FREE Mystery Gift. I understand that I am under no obligation to purchase anything further, as explained on the back and opposite page.

PLACE
FREE GIFTS
SEAL
HERE

▶ DETACH AND MAIL CARD TODAY! ▶

193 MDL D37Q   393 MDL D37R

FIRST NAME	LAST NAME

ADDRESS

APT.#	CITY

STATE/PROV.	ZIP/POSTAL CODE

Thank You!

The Reader Service — Here's How It Works:

Accepting your 2 free books and gift places you under no obligation to buy anything. You may keep the books and gift and return the shipping statement marked "cancel." If you do not cancel, about a month later we'll send you 3 additional books and bill you just $4.99 each in the U.S., or $5.49 each in Canada, plus 25¢ shipping & handling per book and applicable taxes if any.* That's the complete price and — compared to cover prices starting from $5.99 each in the U.S. and $6.99 each in Canada — it's quite a bargain! You may cancel at any time, but if you choose to continue, every month we'll send you 3 more books, which you may either purchase at the discount price or return to us and cancel your subscription.

*Terms and prices subject to change without notice. Sales tax applicable in N.Y. Canadian residents will be charged applicable provincial taxes and GST.

. Sara recognized the determination in her friend's voice. "I know you, Claudie. You'll do whatever you set out to do. I just wish we could help. We're family, too, aren't we?"

"You're my California family, Sara, and I know you want to help, but this is the past. My past. Believe me, it isn't pretty. And I don't want my future godchildren exposed to any of it."

Sara swallowed loudly. "Then Bo. Couldn't he help?"

"No," Claudie responded. "This is something I ran away from a long time ago, and if I learned anything from you and Ren it's that the past has a way of catching up with you. I have to deal with it. I can't sit by in my safe little world and let Garret ruin another girl's life."

"Who…?" Sara tried to ask, but her question was interrupted by a mechanical voice asking for more money.

"My stepfather, that's who," Claudie snapped. A second later, she sighed, as if regretting her disclosure. "I'm outta change, Sara J. Gotta go. I'll call again soon. Tell Brady I haven't forgotten his birthday. I'm going to send him something. And tell Bo he can yell at me all he wants when I get back. Bye."

The line went dead and Sara replaced the receiver. She walked into Ren's office and turned on the computer. Within minutes she was online; seconds later she'd found a page dedicated to the call signs of radio stations. She pushed the button to access the other phone line and hit the speed-dial number of Bo's office. As soon as he picked up, she said, "Hi, it's me. I think she's in Wyoming."

CHAPTER TWO

KNOCKING ON the door of her brother's house turned out to be harder than Claudie expected. Her heart pounded in her chest as she forced herself to take a deep breath. The raw Wyoming wind penetrated through her Sacramento Kings sweatshirt making her shiver. The November sun was already sinking below a stratum of thin, horizontal clouds—eye-catching ribbons of tangerine and magenta.

The hollow tinny sound her knocking produced didn't seem substantial enough to magnify past the wooden inner door. She looked for a doorbell but found a piece of frayed duct tape over an empty hole.

Her hand was poised to rap again when she heard a loud, hollow thump. A moment later the inner door opened with a swoosh. A tall, trim man in a worn plaid shirt greeted her with a curious, "Yeah? What can I do for you?"

The lanky auburn hair was familiar even if the long handsome face wasn't.

Claudie swallowed. "Yancy?" she asked in a small voice.

He bent down slightly and put his face closer to the screen. "Do I know you?"

"It's Claudie," she said, suddenly realizing her wind-combed, Meg Ryan hairdo probably bore little resemblance to the girl with long dark hair that he'd last known.

He stepped back as if someone had yanked him by the collar. His mouth dropped open and he shook his head. "My *sister* Claudie? Really?"

Claudie's heart galloped against her ribs. She'd visualized this moment a dozen times. She just hadn't expected to feel so...tearful. "Yeah, it's me."

Yancy stepped forward again, this time fumbling with the latch on the metal screen door. "Well, I'll be... It's been ten years, ain't it? Good Lord, I'd never have recognized you. Come on in."

Gratified to find her legs still worked, she stepped over the threshold and moved in enough for him to close the door. Once inside, she was struck by conflicting odors: overly pungent male cologne and the too-sweet stench of chlorine. He must have noticed her nose crinkling. "We're bleaching the toilets," he said apologetically. "We all had the flu since Sunday, but everybody's better today."

Claudie smiled—not sure what to say. Yancy seemed just as tentative. His big, coarse-looking hands made start and stop motions as if he wanted to hug her but wasn't sure how to do it. Finally, he indicated the room to her right. "Let's go sit down. This is just too weird. I can't believe it. Zach and me were sure you'd died or something."

Claudie picked her way past an assortment of shoes, toys and old newspapers, which Yancy apologized for with another reference to their recent illness. The couch was a plush navy sectional adorned with a dozen throw pillows in a rainbow of hues. She nudged aside a plump square of sunshine yellow and sat down.

"I've been living in California. Sacramento, mostly," she said.

"Really? I been through there. I used to drive long hauls but I've been with a cement company the last six years. Closer to home. Wife likes it that way." He lowered himself to a dusty piano bench across from her. Behind him sat an electric keyboard enveloped in an opaque plastic cover.

"You're married," Claudie said, looking around. A brass frame on the end table held an eight-by-ten photo of a woman with long blond hair and two young boys, one dark, one light. "Is that your family?"

"One of 'em," Yancy said, making a wry face. "My first wife, Becca, lives in Denver with our daughter Darcy—she'll be seven in January."

"Wow," Claudie exclaimed, mentally doing the math. Yancy was two and a half years her junior. "You started young."

"Yeah, you think you know everything when you're seventeen. Hell, I didn't even know enough to use a rubber. Becca was six months along when we got married. It was a mistake from the start."

Claudie nodded as if she understood.

"You married?" he asked.

"No."

He opened his mouth as if to speak but just then a small child burst through the front door then slammed it resoundingly. Yancy poked out one long arm and grabbed the boy before he could escape.

"Slow down, Pika. Your Aunt Claudie's here to visit. Say hi."

The child, who looked a year or two older than Brady, squirmed like a fish on a line. "Hi," he said, not making eye contact. From what Claudie could see, he was the spitting image of his father at that age—wavy auburn hair, all legs and arms.

Yancy let him go and the boy dashed down the hallway.

"What did you say his name is?"

"Pika. As in Pike's Peak. Renee says that's where he was conceived when we were on a camping trip. Hell if I know. I was probably stoned or drunk."

Claudie kept her expression blank. She'd known plenty of men who wanted sex when they were stoned or drunk. If she'd been the dishonest type, she could have ripped them off when they passed out. But she wasn't a thief.

"Who?" a woman's voice asked in the distance. "Yancy, is someone here?" she called out a moment later.

"Yeah, Renee, my sister's here." Yancy shook his head once more as if the idea still boggled his mind.

A shuffling sound preceded Renee's arrival. Curious, Claudie sat forward. The woman who appeared in the doorway looked far different from her photograph. Her bleached locks hung limp beside her long sallow face. Her pale skin was blotchy and a large cold sore festered at the corner of her lip.

Dressed in baggy red sweatpants, heelless mules and a paint-splattered Mickey Mouse T-shirt, she attempted to fix up her hair and clothes but gave up with a sigh, "Oh, hell," she grumbled, extending her hand. "I'm Renee."

Claudie rose and shook her hand. "Claudie."

Renee's chin turned abruptly toward her husband. "*That* one?"

Claudie's hackles rose until Yancy said, "Yep, my long-lost sister who ran away from home when she was sixteen."

"Seventeen," Claudie corrected. "I was sixteen when Mom died, but my birthday's May 7, and I didn't leave home 'til the fifth of June."

He nodded. "That's right. We were still in school, which was how come Val's teacher offered to take her in."

Renee motioned for Yancy to move over so she could sit down beside him. Claudie sat back down, uneasily. She hadn't talked about that time in her life for ten years, and she wasn't sure she wanted to do so with a stranger present.

"How long have you been married?" she asked, stalling.

Renee shrugged. "Four years next week. Pika was six

months old when we tied the knot. We'da done it sooner, but his divorce from the Barbie doll wasn't final."

Yancy's grimace told Claudie his ex-wife was a sore spot in his current marriage.

"And you have a second son," Claudie said, nodding toward the photo.

"Laramie. He's three. He's over at his grandma's—my mom's house. She lives across the alley. He still ain't feelin' too good."

"Oh." Claudie looked at her brother. "They're pretty close together, aren't they? Like you and Zach."

Yancy frowned. "Yeah, but that's all we're having. Two, not ten. I already went in and had the operation just to make sure there weren't any *accidents*."

Startled by his vehement response, Claudie glanced at Renee. Her scowl said this was another sore subject.

"Renee wanted to try again for a girl, but like my pal Andy says the first rule about holes is, if you're in one, stop digging."

Renee snorted then looked at Claudie. "Like Andy knows shit from shinola—he's single. You got kids?"

Claudie pictured Sara's adopted son, Brady. At times he felt like her child. At times she wished he were her child. She shook her head. "No."

Yancy made an understanding sound. "Not surprised. With Mom sick so much toward the end, you were practically raising the rest of us." To Renee, he said, "Claudie had to drop out of school after Mom passed away to stay home and take care of our little sister, Sherry."

Claudie looked down at the floor. Sweet darling Sherry hadn't been the problem. If Garret hadn't started drinking…

She put the thought aside when Yancy asked, "So, Sis, what brings you to Cheyenne?"

Claudie swallowed. "I ran across your name on the Internet. I couldn't find anything on Zach or Val, so I thought I'd get a hold of you and see what you know."

He nodded. "Searching for your roots, huh? A guy I work with's big on that genealogy crap." He shrugged. "Not me. Past's behind us—right where I like it."

A year ago Claudie would have agreed with him whole-heartedly.

"So you're online, huh?" Renee asked. "We're talking about getting a computer. I have one at work, but our boss is like Mr. Scrooge—if he thought you were using his toys for anything but work he'd fire you."

"We have several computers at the bookstore where I work," Claudie said, picturing the new office space Sara and Ren had created at the rear of the bookstore—one cubicle for Daniel, one for her.

"You work in a bookstore?" Yancy asked, obviously surprised.

"Part-time. I manage a halfway house, too." She'd told a watered-down version of her story so many times, it almost sounded like someone else's life. Here, she thought, uneasily, is someone who knew the truth.

"You mean like for ex-cons?" Yancy exclaimed. "How weird! You know Zach's gonna be getting out of jail in another year or so. Maybe he could go to your place."

It was Claudie's turn to sputter. "Zach's in jail?"

"South Dakota State Penitentiary. Vehicular manslaughter. Drove his rig into a car one night when he was drunk. Killed two people."

Claudie grimaced. A part of her wasn't surprised to learn that her brother's life had turned into a nightmare. As the eldest son he'd borne the brunt of his father's demands. He'd also been the most devastated by their younger brother Wesley's death.

"I didn't know that. How long ago?" she asked.

Yancy looked at Renee. "Four, maybe five years ago. We write each other once 'n a while."

Renee snorted. "Like once a year if you're lucky."

He gave her a black look, and she stood up. "Listen," she said to Claudie, "I'd like to stay and chat, but I gotta finish up before Mom brings Laramie home. And, don't forget, Yance, you promised to take Pika to the video store if he cleaned up the dog shit," she told her husband.

"Did he do it?" Yancy asked.

"He said he did. Go look for yourself." With that she turned away, but stopped and said, "It was nice meeting you, Claudie. I'm sorry we can't offer you a place to stay tonight, but, believe me, you don't want to catch what we just got over, and Laramie might still be contagious."

Claudie hadn't thought about her plans for the night, but she definitely didn't want to catch the flu. "Thanks, but I need to push on anyway. I've got a lot of stops to make."

After his wife was gone, Yancy heaved a sigh. "Families are such fun."

He'd meant it as a joke, but Claudie shook her head. "Not ours."

He flinched. "Are you gonna bring all that stuff back up? 'Cause I don't want to hear it, Claudie. What's done is done, you can't take it back."

She cocked her head. "What do you mean I can't take it back? Do you think I lied about what happened?"

He shrugged. "The old man said you did. He claimed you just wanted to get out of staying home with Sherry. He tol' the police you were mad 'cause he made you miss the prom or something."

A fury so deep and massive it nearly choked her made Claudie leap to her feet. "That bastard. That lying scumbag.

He raped me, Yancy. He was supposed to go to jail. Miss Murray promised he'd go to jail if I told the police what happened."

Yancy drew back. "Well, I don't know about any of that. Once the police came and took us all away, me 'n' Zach never got to go home. We saw Dad a couple'a more times at the courthouse, but the judge said it was apparent Dad couldn't handle us. The judge said me 'n Zach needed more discipline and structure than we were getting at home, so he sent us to a group home in Emporia."

Claudie saw a hooded look descend over his face. "It sucked big time. The food was bad, the beds stunk. Only good part was we were together most of the time. Zach learned to work on engines and they helped him find a job with a trucking company when he turned eighteen. I was supposed to stick around another year, but I split when Zach did. We went to Omaha."

"What'd you do there?"

"Zach drove truck. I was a dishwasher mostly, but then I met Becca. Her dad owned the company Zach was working for."

"How'd you wind up here?"

He shrugged. "Long story. Could we save it for later? You kinda caught us at a bad time—what with the family being sick and all."

She got the hint. "Look, Yancy, I came here for a reason. I think Garret—" she couldn't bring herself to use the word Dad "—might do to Sherry what he did to me. I want to go back there and make sure it doesn't happen."

Yancy looked stunned. "You came all this way 'cause…" he slowly inhaled. "He really did it, huh?"

A fist clenched in her stomach. "Did you think I'd lie about something like that?"

He shrugged. "Zach said maybe you got knocked up by

Darren Blains and just stirred things up so you could get away without anybody noticing."

Claudie frowned. "Darren and I did it a few times, but I wasn't pregnant—no way was I going to wind up like Mom. But I didn't lie about Garret. It happened the day he lost his job. He came home drunk and…" She squeezed her eyes closed, blocking images that skittered about on the edge of her consciousness.

When she looked at Yancy he was doubled over, hands folded between his knees. "Shit." He was quiet a minute then asked, "Was it just the once?"

Claudie fought to keep her expression even. "Yes. Does that make it all right?"

He flinched visibly. After a long pause, he let out a sigh. "What do you want from me?"

"I'm going back and I want you to come along."

He snorted. "Yeah, right. Just drop everything and head back to Kansas because you're afraid the old man might be playing hide the salami with Sherry, huh? How do you even know he's still alive? I ain't heard from him since we left. Maybe he's dead."

Claudie open the purse at her feet and withdrew three sheets of paper folded in half. "He's not that old, Yancy. Fifty-one or two. I found his Web page on the Internet. That's what made me come looking for you."

She handed Yancy the papers. Even seeing her stepfather's image produced a sick feeling.

Yancy read for a minute. "He's a preacher? I thought he was Catholic. Remember all that church stuff we had to do up 'til Mom got sick?"

Claudie remembered—it was one of the reasons she hadn't stepped inside a church in ten years. "I don't know how he got to be a preacher but it's him."

Yancy flipped to the second page. "He's on radio?"

Claudie nodded. "Makes sense if you think about it. He always was a salesman. Mom used to say he could sell sand to Arabs. Now he's peddling God."

She rose and walked to her brother's side. When he turned to the third page she pointed out a paragraph she'd highlighted in yellow. "See. It mentions his teenage daughter named Sherry."

Yancy grunted.

"So? Will you go with me?"

He paused as if considering her request, but in the end his answer was the one Claudie expected. "I can't, Claudie. I got a wife 'n' two kids, an ex-wife and child support, a mortgage and two car payments. I leave 'n' the whole damn thing goes to hell. Just being home sick the last two days means I gotta pull weekend overtime to break even."

Claudie swallowed her disappointment. When he handed her the papers, she carefully folded them and picked up her purse. "Could you at least put me in touch with Zach and Valery? Maybe they can help me. I don't like the idea of going in there cold." A lesson she'd learned from watching Bo at work.

He scratched his head. "Zach ain't hard to find. The prison's in Sioux Falls, and he won't be going anywhere for a while." He rose. "You gotta call ahead to make sure your name is on his visitor list. Yours probably ain't, but they might make an exception since you come so far. I got the number of the prison around here somewhere."

He disappeared into the room across the hall but returned a few seconds later. "Here," he said, passing her a scrap of paper. "I don't have a clue about Val. She changed her name when she got adopted, but I can't remember what that teacher's name was." He sighed. "Ask Zach. I think he said he got a Christmas card from her last year."

Claudie left without telling her sister-in-law good-bye or meeting her youngest nephew. She gave her brother a hug—the first in ten years, but somehow it didn't produce that warm, fuzzy feeling greeting cards always talk about. As she walked to her car, she sighed, surprised by the deflated feeling that engulfed her.

What the hell did you expect? she asked herself severely once she was sitting behind the wheel.

Suddenly, out of the blue, she felt the need to talk to Bo. He'd understand, she thought starting the car. Impulsively, she pulled into the first gas station she found. Its lighted telephone booth stood on the side of the building.

After three rings a familiar voice requested the caller to leave a message or try Bo's cellular number. Taking a deep breath, she said, "Hi. It's me. I'm sure as hell glad you're not there to get this call—you'd just yell at me and I'd end up hanging up on you." She smiled, knowing it was the truth. "I'm just calling to let you know I'm doing fine. You know me—the Energizer Bunny—I keep going and going."

She shook her head at the inanity of her dialogue. "Listen, I'll make this quick. I don't expect you to understand, but I'm doing something I need to do and I didn't tell you because I thought you'd freak. Sara probably told you by now I'm tracking down my long-lost family." She tried to keep her tone light. "I just saw brother number two and now I'm on my way to see number one. Apparently there's no big rush—he won't be going anywhere for the next three to five," she said dryly.

She could picture the look on Bo's face when he heard this message. He'd be mad…and hurt. "Well," she said, trying to keep her tone from betraying how much she missed him, "I'll call you later. Bye."

BO PLAYED the recording a third time. According to the machine's log, he'd only missed her call by ten minutes. He glanced at his watch. Less than an hour until his flight.

Karen Kriegen walked in—a sheaf of papers in her outstretched hand. "Here's the latest on those names," she said. "Looks promising."

Bo took the inch-thick stack and shoved it in his briefcase without looking at it. "I'll go through it on the plane. Anything from Matt, yet?"

"Not yet. I'll give him your flight information if he calls before I leave for the night. If he doesn't call, I'll make sure the switchboard has the details."

"Great. Thanks. The less time I have to spend in New York the better," Bo said, suppressing a shudder. He wouldn't have made the trip at all if he wasn't banking on his cousin's help. Matt, who was four years younger than Bo, was a cop. But he'd been injured on the job and relegated to a desk job. He was also apparently doing some kind of computer tracking for the FBI. If anyone had access to the information Bo needed, it would be Matt.

Bo flipped open his answering machine and pocketed the recording of Claudie's voice. He told himself Matt might be able to use it to help track her whereabouts, but in all honesty Bo had decided their best bet would be to figure out where she was going, not try to guess where she was at the moment. "Do we have any more tapes for this thing?" he asked, nodding at the empty machine.

Karen nodded tolerantly. "Go. I'll take care of it."

He gave her a grateful smile then turned to leave.

Bo was halfway across the parking lot when he bumped into Ren and Sara. Sara's face, already a little puffy with pregnancy, was flushed from hurrying.

"Hey, Sara, if you don't slow down you're going to have those kids in three months instead of six."

"My doctor said walking is good for me," she told him breathlessly.

"Walking. Not wind sprints." He looped his arm around Sara's shoulders. "What are you guys doing here? I'm on my way to the airport."

Sara squeezed him briefly. "I know. Ren said you were going to New York. That's why we came by. I wanted to give you this." Bo had to trot to keep up with her. He took the folded piece of paper she passed him.

"More drawings?" Bo asked, stopping to look it over.

"No," Sara said. "I just remembered something I thought might be important. When I was helping Claudie study for the GED, we got in an argument over the capital of Kansas. I didn't believe it was Topeka. She was right. She said she'd lived on a farm about twenty miles north of there. I thought she was kidding. I mean, can you picture Claudie as a Kansas farm girl?"

Ren added, "When Sara told me that, it triggered something. Last week, Claudie asked me about the statute of limitations on rape. I told her it would depend on the state, and she said, 'How 'bout Kansas?'"

"You think she was raped?" Bo asked, his voice catching.

Sara nodded. "It's possible. She mentioned her stepfather the last time she called. Something about not letting him ruin another girl."

"What's this?" Bo asked, fingering a yellow Post-it note adorned with a florid scrawl.

"That's Babe's theory. She's home with Brady."

Bo's heartbeat quickened as he scanned the note. "Revenge? She thinks Claudie may be on her way to Kansas to kill the guy who molested her?"

Ren grimaced. "I told Mother I thought that was a bit extreme, but you know Babe."

"Bo, you've got to find her." Sara's voice broke.

"I will, Sara," Bo said, touching her shoulder supportively. "But I don't believe Babe's theory." He added the paper to his briefcase. "Listen, you guys, I gotta run. Don't worry, Sara. I'll make sure nothing bad happens. I promise."

With a wave, he left his friends behind. Impatient now to begin the search, Bo started his car and pulled into traffic. Ren and Sara's news had brought additional worries he didn't need. If his researchers had been more confident in their theory, he'd have skipped New York and gone straight to Kansas, but Bo believed in being prepared. He wanted to learn as much as he could about Claudie's past before thrusting himself into the middle of something he didn't understand.

Accelerating, the Mazda joined the cars headed north on I-5. If all went as planned, he'd be in New York shortly after midnight. And, if his cousin was as proficient at the computer as his mother claimed, Bo might beat Claudie to Kansas.

If that's where she's going, he reminded himself.

MATTHEW ROSS kicked the door closed behind him. The dim glow from the night-light he'd left burning in the guest bath was just enough for him to negotiate the narrow hallway with his arms wrapped around two full bags of groceries. Ashley was coming for the weekend, and he'd stocked up on all her favorites—Goldfish crackers, apples, toaster waffles with honey—not syrup—and praline fudge ripple ice cream. Ashley was easy to please; her mother, on the other hand, made the Middle East peace talks look like a negotiator's dream job.

He carefully lowered the bags to the counter in his kitchenette then dug past the four-pack of toilet paper to reach the freezer bag. The nightmare of New York City traffic never ceased to amaze him. Even though he'd grown up in New Jersey, and, as a cop with the NYPD he'd learned to deal with the decaying infrastructure and moronic drivers, the state of the roads seemed to be getting worse by the day.

Or you're just getting too damn old to take it, he told himself.

Once the ice cream was safely stored in the freezer section of his small refrigerator he took his time putting things away. As he leaned down to stow the box of crackers he noticed the number two in red on his answering machine. He checked his pager first, but saw no new messages so figured the calls were personal, not work-related.

He cracked open a Heineken before lowering himself to the stool where he kept a pen and paper handy.

"Yo, Cuz, this is Bo," the first message began.

Matt almost choked on his swallow of beer. He hadn't spoken with his cousin, Bo Lester, in ages. As he listened to the message his surprise intensified. A woman. Missing. A friend. Something told Matt the mystery woman was more than a friend.

He scribbled down the time and flight number of his cousin's plane. Sure, he'd meet the plane and provide a bed— or rather, a couch for a couple of nights. Matt's guest room with its four-poster bed and down comforter was still at his ex-wife's house—along with his daughter and the better part of his life.

"Matthew," the second message started, causing Matt's beer to curdle in his stomach, "Ashley won't be able to make it this weekend after all. I know this is your regular weekend but something wonderful came up that she couldn't resist. She feels terrible about this and will call you later to explain." There was a pause and Matt could picture the troubled look on his ex-wife's face—she never could lie without frowning in a way that made a crease between her eyebrows. That giveaway point had been what alerted him to her affair. "Please try not to blow this out of proportion, Matt. You can have her next weekend, which technically is our weekend, but I'm prepared to be flexible if you are. This is about Ashley's happiness, not her parents' schedules."

Matt gripped his beer bottle, willing himself not to smash it against the wall. Sonya knew just how to manipulate his emotions. She knew how much he loved his daughter, and she constantly used Ashley's state of mind as a weapon against him.

"Call when you get this message so I can explain about the dressage school. Bye."

Matt polished off his beer with a long gulp then tossed the bottle in the garbage. It wasn't as satisfying, but it beat the hell out of cleaning up broken glass—he'd learned that one the hard way. A glance at his watch told him he might as well head to the airport. There were plenty of bars there, and since Bo was a reformed drinker, he could play designated driver.

CLAUDIE SAT in the middle of the bed, her legs crossed Indian fashion. She'd changed into sweats and heavy socks the minute she got to her room. Beside her lay the road map, and she studied it as she sipped on the frappe she'd picked up at the pizza place down the street. Her motel wasn't much to look at, but the price was right.

She'd opted to stay in Cheyenne rather than drive any farther. For one thing, she didn't know where she was going— South Dakota or Kansas? Her decision would depend on Zach—or rather, whether or not she could get in to see him.

I'll worry about that tomorrow, Claudie told herself. Tonight, she planned a long soak in the tub. The tension of meeting Yancy and the long hours in the car had given her a

stiff neck. What she wouldn't have given to have Bo there—
Bo with the great hands.

She closed her eyes and pictured him. Not tall and start-
lingly handsome like Ren, Bo's looks kind of sneaked up on
you when you weren't looking. Strong and compact, he em-
anated power when he chose to or slipped into obscurity
when it suited him. His wardrobe was a joke, but Claudie
knew he dressed to fit an image he had of himself—nondescript. What he didn't realize was, he was anything but.

Rolling her chin to stretch her tired muscles, she imagined
him massaging her neck. It had taken months of patience on
his part before she let him so much as hold her hand. The massaging part had come two weeks ago after a game of tag with
Brady when she slipped on the wet grass and wound up
sprawled flat on her back.

"Do you need a doctor?" Bo had asked, kneeling beside
her, concern written all over his face.

Brady had draped himself over Bo's shoulder, his small
face pinched with fear. "Claudie hurt?"

"I'm fine, silly boys," she said, but when she tried to sit
up, a twinge of pain shot from her hip to her neck.

Bo's sharp eyes caught her flinch, and he moved closer,
placing one hand on her shoulder to keep her from moving.
"Brady boy, run get your mama. Okay?"

The lad shot off toward the house. Claudie had groaned
more from the fuss than the pain. "Now, hush, sweetheart,"
he said, situating himself squarely at her back so he could
place both hands on her neck. "Let me check this out."

Claudie hadn't been able to keep herself from reacting.
Not that his touch felt bad—in fact, it was wonderful—but
she wasn't used to such intimate contact. His fingers froze in
place until she let out the breath she'd been holding.

"Does this hurt?" he'd asked, his voice low, just inches from her ear.

The roar of blood racing through her veins had made it impossible to speak. She'd tried to shake her head, but his hands kept her chin still. "Don't move. Just relax. Close your eyes and feel my fingers. If I hit anything sensitive, yell."

Yell? Good grief. Everything you touch is sensitive. If I open my mouth, the entire neighborhood's going to hear me.

The whole episode couldn't have lasted more than two or three minutes, but it changed Claudie's life. She went from hating touch to craving it. Maybe this urge to protect her sister wasn't the only reason she'd taken off so impulsively. Maybe she was afraid she couldn't trust herself around Bo anymore. When she was with him, she wanted things she couldn't have—like a relationship, a boyfriend-girlfriend relationship. But that meant sex. And for Claudie, sex was commerce and she was out of that business for good.

Jumping off the bed, Claudie walked to the bathroom to draw her tub. She turned on both handles full blast then set out her washcloth and shampoo. She paused before the small, old-fashioned sink and mirror. She eyed her image critically. Nothing fabulous, but not bad. Maybe a little older around the eyes than she'd have liked, but nowhere near as wasted as some of the working girls she'd known.

Over the din of the water, she repeated the vow she'd taken last January when she made up her mind to change her life. Her lips formed the words with reverence: "No sex. No cigarettes. No drugs. No excuses."

She was finally beginning to like Claudie St. James, and she wouldn't give that up for anything or anyone. Even Bo.

CHAPTER THREE

BO TUNED OUT the droning voice of the flight attendant tell-ing the passengers to wait until the plane came to a complete stop to unfasten their seat belts. He closed his eyes and tried to focus on his objective, not his fatigue. Normally, while on a job, he could go for days with a bare minimum of food and sleep, but for some reason, Claudie's leaving seemed to rob him of his ability to concentrate. He kept imagining her in bad places.

"We can go now," his seatmate, a white-haired woman who'd snored softly most of the way, told him.

Apologizing, Bo rose, leaving his laptop computer on the seat. He wrangled his carry-on bag from the overhead com-partment then removed the woman's overstuffed paisley tote as well.

She rewarded him with a smile. "I wouldn't worry if I were you," she said, cryptically, "your girl will come around in time."

He leaned forward. "I beg your pardon?"

Her powdered flesh crinkled in a road map of wrinkles. "Your gal," she repeated, as if he had a hearing problem. "She'll come around." Her watery eyes twinkled from the overhead light. "I peeked at your computer board when you were in the toilet," she said, motioning toward his laptop.

"Oh," he said, marveling at his sloppiness. He'd walked off and left his laptop open? Jeez, he was slipping.

He picked up the lightweight machine and stuffed it in his briefcase. As he reached for his carry-on bag, the woman said, "You must love her a lot to follow after her like this. At first, I was thinking you might be one of those stalkers I'm always reading about, but I can tell you've got a good heart."

Bo couldn't decide whether to be angry or amused. She seemed harmless so he asked, "How can you tell?"

Her elfin grin made him smile back. "I'm old. You know these things when you get to be my age."

Bo courteously moved to one side to allow her to pass ahead of him. She patted his arm and told him, "That's very kind, but you'd best run along and find her. She won't wait forever, you know."

Bo chuckled then bowed slightly and hurried up the aisle and out the door. He put the woman's remarks out of his mind as he scanned the terminal for his cousin. No tall, broad-shouldered guy with wavy black hair in sight.

"Where are you, Cuz?" Bo muttered as he walked along the corridor, picking his way through throngs of incoming passengers.

"Bo," a voice called.

Bo stopped and looked around. A familiar face peered at him between some artificial greenery. Bo wound his way through a maze of tall stools. The place differed little from the dozens he'd visited in airports around the country—only the colorful logos of the city's sport team changed.

"Hey, man, how ya' doin'?" Matt asked, not bothering to stand.

Bo sat opposite him and ordered a Pepsi from a waitress who drifted past. "Still not drinking, huh? Good for you," Matt noted, his speech slightly slurred.

"How long have you been here, Matt?"

Matt pushed back the sleeve of his leather bomber jacket

to look at his watch. He blinked, finally closing one eye to gain the focus he needed. "A few hours and twenty-two minutes. Give or take."

Bo paid for his soda with a five then hastily gulped half of it. "Hand over your keys, Cuz. I hope you still live in the same place 'cause I'm not sure I trust you to give me directions."

Matt drew himself up offended. "I may be intoxicated but I'm not decapitated."

"Thank God," Bo said, helping his cousin to rise. "I was worried about that."

The long trek to the parking lot seemed to help clear Matt's head to some degree. Bo thought Matt's limp seemed more pronounced than it had the last time they were together, but he didn't say anything. He wanted to ask about his cousin's recovery and physical therapy but decided to hold off until morning. He knew how sensitive Matt was about the injury that had nearly claimed his life.

Matt handed Bo the keys to his Jeep Cherokee without protest. Once they'd exited the parking lot, Bo asked, "So what's this about? You've never been what I'd call a big drinker."

Matt slumped down as far as the seat belt would permit. He kept his face aimed toward the passenger window. "Your basic drowning of sorrows, I guess. Turn off the antennae and go blank—booze helps."

Bo understood. In his youth, alcohol had been his drug of choice. By the time he was sixteen he'd lost count of the number of times he'd puked his guts out. Bo counted himself lucky that more exotic drugs hadn't been readily available or he might have fried his brain before Larry Bishop and his son came along to help him find sobriety.

"It's a little late in life to become an alcoholic, bud. I really wouldn't recommend trying—it just prolongs the agony of whatever it is you're trying to escape from."

Matt didn't respond.

"Is it the divorce?" Bo caught Matt's negative motion but his long sad sigh said otherwise. "What's it been? A year?"

"Almost two," Matt muttered. "Sonya and Alan have been married a year."

Bo nodded. "How's Ashley?"

"Great—considering her parents are immature jerks who fight for every spare second of her time," Matt said bitterly. "That's what set me off tonight. This was my weekend to have her but Sonya called at the last minute to say Ashley had been invited to a dressage sleep-over."

Bo frowned. "I thought dressage had something to do with horses."

"It does. That's Ashley's new passion. It goes with her age, I guess. She and a couple of friends are sleeping at the dressage school."

"Isn't that an expensive hobby?" Bo asked, knowing it was none of his business.

Matt's sigh sounded heartfelt. "Money isn't a big problem when your stepfather is the nose-man of the stars."

"I take it you're referring to plastic surgery, not cocaine."

"Dr. Al," Matt said, snorting with disgust. "Don't get me started." He sat up a little straighter. "Want to tell me what you're doing here? Isn't New York the last place on earth you want to be? You heard about your old man, right? He moved in with his mistress a month or so ago."

Bo's stomach gripped what was left of his airplane food and punched it toward his throat. He swallowed the taste of bile. "Yeah, I got the lowdown when I spoke to my mother."

"How's Aunt Ruth taking it?"

Bo shrugged, grateful the traffic wasn't as constipated as usual. He pictured his mother at Ren and Sara's wedding last August—his father had claimed a prior commitment. Short and a little pudgy, Ruth Lester never seemed to change. She'd worn her salt-and-pepper hair in the same style—a chin-length pageboy—for twenty years. "She sounds more resigned than hurt," Bo said truthfully. "I got the impression she finds his behavior a bit silly but not all that surprising given his age and gender."

Matt seemed to swallow a laugh. "That Ruth is one cool lady. My mother would have my dad's balls embalmed and strung on a necklace."

Bo smiled. He hadn't planned to see either of his parents this trip, but a nagging sense of guilt made him wonder if his mother was truly as blasé about the news as she'd sounded. Maybe he'd find some time tomorrow to look in on her at work.

Following Matt's pointers, Bo pulled the Jeep into a parking garage three blocks from Matt's apartment building. "How much does this set you back a month?" he asked, curious.

Matt groaned. "Enough to send my daughter to Harvard. I'm seriously considering moving. Maybe Sacramento," he said, flippantly. "Got a job for me, Cuz?"

Bo had never heard such a defeated tone in his cousin's voice. Matt was the proverbial golden boy—the person to emulate. Handsome, smart, top student, heroic cop. He was four years younger than Bo—which would make him 36 years old. What happened? Bo wanted to ask, but he knew that would have to wait for the morning, too.

CLAUDIE TOOK her time admiring the chiseled faces of the Mount Rushmore National Monument. When she'd called the prison early that morning, she'd been told her name would have to be added to Zach's visitor list before she'd be allowed to see him. Her disappointment must have traveled through the phone line because the control-room guard told her they would try to expedite the process. She was told to show up Saturday at twelve-thirty and they would let her know.

Since Claudie had never traveled as a tourist, she decided to make the most of this opportunity, starting with the Black Hills of South Dakota. She'd headed north out of Cheyenne and soon found herself in some of the prettiest country she'd ever seen.

She'd stopped for breakfast in a cute little town called Custer, then paid a remarkable fee to see a hole in a hillside, which if you squinted was starting to take on the shape of Crazy Horse. The project truly was a labor of love, and she hadn't regretted the expenditure once she learned the whole story behind the mammoth undertaking. After Rushmore, she planned to hit a few tourist spots around Rapid City, ending her afternoon with a tour of the Badlands. Tonight, she planned to stay at a place called Wall Drug, then on Friday she'd complete her trip across the state to Sioux Falls.

As Claudie leaned forward for a better view, an older woman accidentally jostled her elbow. "Oh, dear, I'm so sorry," she said.

"That's okay," Claudie said, slightly embarrassed by the way she'd jumped back. *Old habits,* she thought, moving away to take a seat at a small bench. She watched the woman interact with a man, presumably her husband. The couple were taking turns snapping pictures of each other with the four faces in the background. Without really intending to, Claudie rose and approached them. "Would you like me to take one of the two of you together?" she asked.

The woman let out a small of squeal of delight. "That would be great. This is our fortieth anniversary. We were married in The Little Chapel in the Woods," she said, apparently assuming Claudie was familiar with the place.

"Congratulations," Claudie said.

The husband put his arm around his wife's shoulder and hugged her close. He was a distinguished-looking man with a kind face. Claudie snapped two photos then handed the camera back to the man. "Thank you, miss," he said with a pleasant smile. "Do you have a camera? We could return the favor."

Startled by the question, Claudie realized she'd never owned a camera, and aside from the photos of Sara's wedding, she had very few pictures of herself. "No, I don't, but that's a good idea. I saw one of those disposables for sale in the gift shop. I think I'll buy one."

He nodded and smiled, as if pleased to have contributed to her trip. "Well, we'll be drifting around here for another hour or so. If you want to find us, we'd be happy to do the honors."

She hurried to the shop and made the purchase before she could change her mind. *Maybe if they turn out, I'll give one to Brady,* she told herself. *And Bo.*

BO AWOKE to the smell of coffee. Grudgingly he opened one eye. Sunlight streamed through the room's single window, highlighting spots of rust on the ornate bars. "Why does a cop have bars on the windows?" he asked, sensing his cousin's presence in the adjacent kitchen.

"Ex-cop," a disembodied voice returned.

"Is that official?" Bo asked, sitting up.

There hadn't been much chitchat once they'd reached the apartment last night. Matt's eyes had been at half-mast. He'd handed Bo a set of sheets and a blanket and pointed to the couch. "It folds out or you can sleep on it that way. It's not bad," he'd said. "I slept on it for a full year before Sonya kicked me out."

His cousin entered the room carrying two steaming mugs. "With sugar, right?" Matt asked. "Mom always called you Mr. Sweet Tooth."

Bo took the cup, inhaling the aroma. "Yep, and your sister always called me Mr. Sweet Spot. I bet Aunt Irene didn't know that." Chuckling, he asked, "How is Deborah, anyway? Last I heard she was married to a banker and had a dozen kids."

"Jack's a stockbroker and they have four kids, two are adopted. Deb's great. Is there something about this 'Sweet Spot' name I should know?"

Bo laughed at his cousin's suspicious look. "You ought to be ashamed of those incestuous thoughts. Deborah used to tickle me until I'd cry. At the time she was bigger than me, but I bet I could take her now."

Matt visibly relaxed. "Do you want something to eat? I bought Cheerios…for Ashley."

Bo planted his feet on the floor and rose, stretching. "What time is it?"

"A quarter after eleven," Matt said sheepishly. "I guess neither of us thought about setting an alarm."

Bo experienced a momentary jolt of panic, but took a deep breath and let it out. "No biggie. You're gonna crack this case wide-open in a matter of minutes, right?"

Matt started to roll his eyes, but flinched and put his hand to his head. "Just as soon as my head goes back to its normal size." He rubbed the crease between his brows. "Now I remember why I don't drink."

Bo gave him a conciliatory pat on the shoulder. "Hangovers suck. I haven't missed them at all." He carried his cup to the window and looked outside. The weather actually seemed halfway decent. "Anyway, as soon as you're up to it, I'd like to get cracking on this. Did you get my fax?"

"I just found it," Matt said, stretching his neck as if he were the one who'd slept on the sofa. In a baggy, NYPD T-shirt and faded gray sweatpants and bare feet he looked like a grown-up version of the kid Bo used to tease on those rare occasions when Ruth had taken him to visit her brother's family.

Estranged from her family for most of Bo's childhood, Ruth had reestablished contact with her brother after their father's death when Bo was eleven. Relations between the siblings remained tentative at best, but the two sisters-in-law became friends.

"So tell me what's going on with you and the force," Bo said.

Matt rose and walked to the window. He was silent a minute. "They've tried to be diplomatic and make a place for me the best they can, but what do you do with an eleven-year veteran with a gimpy knee? They loved the FBI gig because then they didn't have to see me every day, but that's just temporary." He looked over his shoulder. "I doubt if they're looking forward to my return any more than I am."

Bo yanked on his canvas slacks and tucked in his undershirt. He'd shower and change as soon as he had an itinerary in place. "Listen, I know our circumstances weren't the same, but I went through my own kind of burnout in the force, and, believe me, I've never regretted going out on my own."

Matt looked interested, but Bo could almost hear the cautionary words of advice barking in the back of his cousin's head. "I know I don't have child support payments and I'm sure the cost of living hasn't gone down since the last time I lived in this burg, but you do have options, Matt. You asked me last night if I was looking for employees, and the answer is no. But I would consider taking on a partner. You could handle everything east of the Mississippi, and I'll keep my side of the continent."

"No problem," Matt guffawed. "Half a country is more than enough for me."

Bo withdrew a map from the inside pocket of his ancient winter topcoat. "Consider this a test case. You help me find Claudie, and we talk business."

Matt turned away, but not before Bo caught the spark of interest in his eyes. "I'm a desk jockey now, Bo." He pointed to his knee. "I'm not too hot in the hundred-yard dash any more."

Bo spread the finely detailed map on the table. "Trust me, Cuz, neither am I. This job is ten percent physical, ninety percent mental. I'll hustle jobs, you handle the computer and we'll hire some young jock to take care of the rest."

Matt laughed outright. "You're just as whacked out as ever."

"Yeah, and you're just as uptight. You remind me of Ren. Thank God Sara came along and loosened him up."

Matt shook his head. "I still can't get over the fact he was engaged to Eve Masterson, and called it off to marry someone else." He walked across the room to join Bo at the dinette. "Who in their right mind gives up a chance to sleep with the hottest woman on network news?"

Stifling a sigh, Bo picked up his briefcase. He focused on the tumbler locks. "Listen. For your information, Eve's a decent enough person, but she was all wrong for Ren. If they'd gotten married, they wouldn't have lasted a year. Sara's like a Broadway musical where Ren's concerned. Eve was intermission. But, now that you mention it, Ren wanted me to check up on Eve while I'm in town. Sara's worried about her."

Matt's face scrunched up in confusion. "Sara, the wife, is worried about Eve, the ex-girlfriend?"

Bo nodded. "You'd understand if you knew Sara."

Matt took a sip of coffee. "Eve hasn't been on the air for

a couple of weeks, you know. I heard a rumor she jumped networks. Word has it there's a guy involved."

Bo shrugged. "Personally, I can't picture her putting anyone above her career, but who knows? Remind me to call her later, will ya? But, first, let's get cracking on finding Claudie. Time is of the essence, as my father would say."

"Particularly *now*," Matt said with a snicker. "Keeping a twenty-something girlfriend happy can't be easy for a man in his sixties."

Bo grimaced. He slammed his pen flat and leaned over the map. "Here's where my crew thinks she was born. Maybe you'll have better luck pulling up the hard facts. I'll give you what we know, or think we know, and you tell me where we go from that."

Matt joined him at the table, his shoulder a few inches from Bo's. "Okay. I'll do it—on one condition. I get to call Eve. Who knows, maybe I'll get lucky."

Bo looked him straight in the eye. "No problem, but might I remind you, you have limited bargaining power here? You're working off an old debt, remember?"

Bo bit down on his inner cheek as the color rose in his cousin's face. "Bite me, Lester."

"After you, Ross."

The two men looked at each other a minute then chuckled simultaneously. Matt's quick temper was a trait Bo remembered well as were Matt's grit and determination—characteristics Bo hoped would serve them well on the task ahead.

MATT STUDIED the highlighted notations on the map, his brain vaguely listening to the sound of the water running in the shower. Thanks to his hangover, it had taken him all of Thursday and part of this morning to construct a viable profile of the woman called Claudine St. James, from her birth in 1973 at the St. James School for Unwed Mothers, where her birth certificate read Claudine Yvonne Smith—to the present.

The fundamentals of Matt's computer program were neither new nor revolutionary, but the interactive format was user friendly and fast. Normally, a project this complex might take two or three days to finish, but Matt had worked nonstop to complete the analysis. This way Bo could get going, and Matt wouldn't have to miss Ashley's school play tonight.

Bo, whose antsy energy just about drove Matt up the wall, spent his time on a weak attempt at locating Eve Masterson but came up empty-handed. "You can run this program on Eve after I leave," Bo had told him. "If it's as good as you say, you should be able to tell me where she lives and what she had for dinner last night, right?"

Matt had laughed. "You make me sound like Big Brother." Sadly, the program did have invasive connotations if used improperly, which is why he couldn't market it for "big bucks," as his ex-wife had suggested.

As he highlighted certain events in Claudie's life—a shot record admitting her to kindergarten, the 1981 record of death for Timothy John Anders, age one day—Matt's mind flashed back to his cousin's earlier comment. *Payback,* Matt thought. This little job would eradicate a twenty-year debt of gratitude.

He tried to picture himself at sixteen—junior varsity jock, pimples, shiny new driver's license. His only goal at the time was to get laid, and in his mind the way to accomplish that was by taking Sharon Jensen to the prom. Unfortunately, he didn't have the money to rent a tux and buy the tickets, let alone purchase a corsage.

A moment of foolishness—plus one unguarded cash box filled with the weekend's basketball game receipts—might have screwed up his life for good if not for Bo. Matt silently groaned picturing the hubbub over Bo's arrest for vandalism after he broke a window to get inside the building to return the money. The charge was reduced to malicious mischief once Bo's dad had been called, but it still meant five months of community service.

"So," Bo said, walking into the room, a towel tucked about his waist, "are we set, then? You're sure her ultimate destination is eastern Kansas, but you see stops in Wyoming, South Dakota and Minnesota to connect with her siblings."

"Hey, I'm not a soothsayer and I don't want a midnight phone call from you if I'm wrong. You saw how this was done—facts and percentages, not smoke and mirrors. At the moment, with all things considered, this is where your best odds are."

Bo yanked on jockey shorts and a pair of socks, then slipped on a hideous shirt of greens and gold. "Good Lord," Matt sputtered, "where do you shop? Dumpsters?"

Bo grinned. "No, but I've heard you find some good stuff there. This is a disguise."

"As what? A wino? Hell, I know street people who wouldn't be caught dead in that shirt."

Bo laughed, obviously not put out by his cousin's criticism. "You sound just like Claudie. Maybe I'll let her start picking out my clothes once I convince her to marry me."

Matt rocked back, surprised. "Marriage? She's an ex-hooker, Bo. God, to think about all the—"

Bo reached out and grabbed Matt's shirt right below the neckline. "Don't say it."

Matt swallowed. "Baggage," he managed to choke out. "I started to say I hate to think about all the emotional baggage a person's got to carry around after a job like that." Bo's fingers opened. "Probably right up with cops, don't you imagine?"

Bo looked him straight in the eyes and nodded. "Yeah, you're probably right."

CLAUDIE SHOPPED for her motel with care born of frugality. She found a clean-looking place not far from the mausole-umlike prison perched on a bluff above the Sioux River. The motel manager was a friendly woman with three very loud miniature poodles. The dogs—Mitzy, Fritzy and Poo—cried when Claudie took her room key and started to leave.

"Now, just you hush," the manager told them as Claudie closed the door. "She'll be back here in the morning for her Danish so you can talk to her then."

Claudie shook her head. She'd never owned a dog or cat and she couldn't remember her family ever having pets. Maybe that was something she'd ask Zach when she saw him, she told herself, unlocking the door of her room. *If I see him.*

Claudie hated to think what she'd do if they didn't let her see her brother. Her finances weren't limitless and, although she had a credit card, she hated to use it.

After unpacking a fresh sweater and clean pair of jeans to wear the next day, she decided to go for a walk.

"Excuse me, ma'am," Claudie said, poking her head inside the door of the office. "Is there a grocery store nearby?"

A cacophony of barking almost drowned out the woman's reply. "Sure is. Right down the street about four blocks. Can't miss it," the manager called out brightly, then added more gruffly, "No, Mitzy you can't go along. I promised you a walk later, but only if you're patient."

Claudie closed the door softly. The autumn twilight felt soothing, even with a bite of winter in the air. The long drive eastward from Wall had gone surprisingly fast thanks to a book on tape that she'd found on sale. The story—a romance—had touched her.

Whistling softly under her breath, Claudie thought about Bo. There was no denying it—she missed her Cookbook Man, which is what she and Keneesha had first named him when they saw him skulking in the cookbook section of Sara's bookstore. She wondered where he was at that moment. *Is he thinking about me?*

As she entered the small, well-lit grocery store, she spotted a pay phone just inside the door. Maybe they call this homesickness, she thought, veering toward the phone. She tried Bo's number but received a busy single. Too impatient to wait and try again, she dialed Sara's number.

Ren answered.

"Hi, Ren. It's me. Is Sara home?"

"No, darn it, and is she going to be mad that she missed you," Ren said, his voice as cheerful and positive as usual.

"Aren't you supposed to be teaching?" Claudie asked.

"My class was canceled. They're painting our building. I'm sitting here grading papers. So, how's everything going with you? We've been worried about you."

"I'm fine. The car's running great. I saw one of my brothers. The other one's in jail…I might get to see him tomorrow." Claudie almost clapped her hand over her mouth, surprised by the amount of personal information she'd just shared.

"Really? Anything I can do to help?"

Claudie had actually considered calling Ren when it sounded like she might have to wait to get visiting privileges but nixed the idea since that would mean broadcasting her location to Bo. "I don't think so. The staff sounded pretty cool on the phone. I'll call you if they give me any grief tomorrow."

Ren was silent a second. "Monday's the Veteran's Day holiday, you know. Sara wanted to use the long weekend to take

Brady to Disneyland for his birthday, but I talked her into going to Half Moon Bay instead. We're leaving in the morning." He sounded almost apologetic.

He was a good man, and Claudie knew Sara had never been happier. She envied them their closeness.

"That ought to be fun. Brady will love the ocean."

"Yeah, we'll probably spend the whole day poking around in tidal pools. I wish you were going with us, but I guess you're doing what you need to do." He hesitated as if he were going to give her some advice, but said instead, "We'll have the cell phone with us if you need anything."

Claudie appreciated the concession because everyone knew how much Ren hated cellular phones. "Thanks, but I'll be fine. Don't worry about me. Have you heard how things are going at One Wish House?"

Ren's soft chortle seemed positive. "Pretty good, I think. Sara was there this morning with Babe. One of the residents…let me see…Maya? Is she Korean?"

"Uh-huh."

"Maya talked them into planning a fund-raiser."

Claudie almost dropped the phone. She'd been praying the place wouldn't fall apart without her; she certainly hadn't expected it to thrive. "What kind of fund-raiser?"

"A dim sum cook-off or something. Sara could tell you more about it. I think it's a ploy to keep the girls from missing you." His voice went a shade deeper. "We all do, you know. Brady's been so lonely. First, you disappear then Bo."

Claudie had to swallow a funny lump in her throat. "Bo? Where's he? He was due back from Vegas on Monday."

There was a pause. "Umm…he was here, but then he left again. He's…ah…in New York, actually."

"What's he doing in New York?"

Ren cleared his throat. "I…uh, that is we, Sara and me,

asked him to find out what's happened to Eve. She kinda fell off the face of the earth."

Claudie remembered Sara mentioning something about not being able to reach Eve, but some quality in Ren's tone made her skeptical. She let it go. "Well, I'd better run. Tell Sara I called and give Brady a big kiss for me. I bought him a dinosaur from the Badlands and two T-shirts—one has a picture of a jackalope on it."

"A what?"

"It's what you get when you cross a jackrabbit with an antelope."

Ren's laugh made her even more homesick. "I hate to tell you this, Claudie, but you sound like a real *tourist*."

"Yep, that's me," she said, fighting to keep from embarrassing herself. "Hey, Ren, it's been good talking to you. If you hear from Bo, tell him I said hi. I hope everything's okay with Eve. Gotta go. Bye."

Claudie hung up, swallowing against the lump in her throat. She grabbed a cart and mindlessly pushed it up and down the rows of the store. "Where are you Bo?" she whispered under her breath.

Looking for me?

She knew the answer. The real question was, what would she do if he found her? Or rather, *when* he found her.

CHAPTER FOUR

THE PENITENTIARY frightened her, and despite the overheated air within the building, she felt chilled to her bones. Waiting for Zach to be admitted to the visitation room, Claudie kept her chin down and concentrated on keeping her lunch in her stomach. Furtively she wiped a bead of sweat from her upper lip then tucked her hands under her butt, tuning out the disharmonious chatter of other inmates and their visitors.

"Claudie?" a voice croaked.

Her chin shot up to see a bald stranger staring at her.

"My God," he softly cried. "It is you. I couldn't believe it when they told me you were coming. Claudie."

Tears filled her eyes, but she blinked them back. She wasn't some weepy little girl. She was tough. Strong. "Zach," she whispered, choking on emotions she hadn't expected to feel. Her arms lifted automatically, but she let them fall to her sides, recalling the warning about appropriate behavior between residents and visitors.

Zach walked to her, a crooked little catch in his step. Yancy's parting words to her had been about Zach's injury. "He messed up his hip pretty bad in the accident," he'd called to her as she walked to her car. "Still has a lot of pain."

Her gaze was as jumpy as her heart—skittering over the deep creases in his face and the somberness in his eyes that made him look old beyond his years. He eased into an empty chair and after an awkward hesitation took both of her hands in his. Hand-holding was allowed. As was a kiss hello and goodbye. She leaned forward shyly and kissed him lightly on the cheek.

"What are you doing here, Claudie? God, you look terrific. I'd have known you anywhere," Zach said with conviction. His voice—deep and kind of scratchy-sounding—was as unfamiliar as his face.

"Really?" She searched his eyes for a trace of the boy she'd known and loved. "Yancy nearly keeled over when I showed up at his door. He said you thought I was dead."

One side of his mouth twitched. Claudie remembered his smile, slow and deliberate when it came—which wasn't often. "Nah. You're tough. And smart—the smartest of us all. I knew you'd land on your feet."

Claudie let out a harsh laugh that made the others in the room turn her way. Softly she said, "On my back, you mean." At his puzzled look she added, "I was a hooker, Zach. Off and on for years. I'd try other jobs—waitressing, I was a clerk in a convenience store for a while, an usher at a wrestling arena and I even parked cars, but somehow I'd always end up working some corner."

He let out a low epithet.

Claudie shrugged. "But that's all behind me, now. I finally passed the GED, and I've got a great job—two actually. I help run a bookstore and I manage a halfway house for prostitutes."

The gladness that filled his eyes made her heart soar. "You can't know how good that makes me feel, Claudie girl. It's like seeing a light at the end of a long, black tunnel. Maybe some of that glow will come my way after I get out of this place."

They talked until Claudie's voice sounded as parched and

scratchy as Zach's. She told him about Ren and Sara and Brady, the girls at One Wish House, her interest in old books, her trip so far.

"What about a guy? No boyfriend?" he asked, zeroing in on the part she'd purposely left out.

"There's a guy. A friend. I think he'd like to be more than a friend, but that won't happen." She sighed softly. "I guess I'm not made for that kind of thing."

Zach's wiry brows bunched together. "We sure ended up with some big holes in our souls, didn't we?"

Claudie nodded, understanding him completely.

"Know what I don't get?" he asked. She shook her head. "I attend a bunch of self-help groups in here—AA, NA, a Christian ministry. I see guys who really had it tough growing up—I mean bad. We had it really good compared to them."

Claudie's heart twisted peculiarly. "Garret…"

He didn't let her finish. "I don't mean after Mom died. I mean when Dad was working regular and on the road most of the time. Mom was good to us. She'd read us books, and we'd take picnics to the park. Hell, even when the old man was around we had some fun sometimes. Remember our trip to Pipestone? We saw that play about Hiawatha."

Claudie frowned, trying to remember. "Sorta."

Zach closed his eyes and sighed. "Things weren't all bad—at least not while Mom was alive." He turned his face away. "I think things started going downhill after Timmy was born, and then Wesley…"

She squeezed his fingers. "It was an accident, Zach. Whoever heard of a kid choking on a balloon? Cripes, we all used to chew them like gum."

Claudie always figured Wesley's death hit Zach the hardest because it had happened on his ninth birthday. A party with four or five little boys raising Cain. Everyone too busy to notice Wesley's distress until he dropped flat, blue in the face. By the time the fire truck got there, he was gone.

To distract him, she asked, "Zach, did we ever have a pet?"

He looked upward as if searching his memories. "We had bunnies once. Remember? I found a nest of rabbits and Mom helped us feed them with a doll bottle." His smile held a look of nostalgia. "It was your doll bottle, so you said that meant you got to name them."

She shook her head, dubiously. "Bunnies?"

He nodded. "How could you forget Elizabeth?"

Flopsy, Mopsy, Cottontail and Elizabeth. She closed her eyes and pictured herself holding a tiny gray bunny in the palm of her hand. Its heart beat so fast she worried it might explode. "I do remember," she said. "Garret came home that night and told me Elizabeth was the stupidest name for a rabbit he'd ever heard."

Zach's smile faded. "He was always hardest on you."

Claudie took a deep breath and straightened her shoulders. "I'm going back to Kansas, Zach. I'm not going to let Garret ruin Sherry's life, too. I'd have gone sooner, but I wasn't ready to face him. I only hope I'm not too late."

Zach didn't try to talk her out of it. Before she left he gave her Valery's address and telephone number, which he had memorized. "She's the manager of a video store. Her stepfolks own two or three in the area. She sent me a flier a few months ago announcing their latest grand opening." His expression turned humorous. "She sent along a picture of herself with her new fancy car. Quite the success story."

Claudie thought she detected a facetious note but let it go. With any luck Val would have enough clout to take off a few days so they could go to Kansas together. As she prepared to leave, Claudie asked, "How much longer do you have?"

"Hard to say. I've got a parole hearing in February." He didn't sound overly optimistic.

"Would it help if I wrote a letter on your behalf? My best friend's husband used to be a judge. Maybe Ren would write something, too."

He squeezed her hand. "I'm doing okay, Claudie. Really. I'm sober. I work with a Christian outreach group in here, and I feel as if I'm making a difference. Like I said, there are a lot of guys who are a whole lot worse off than me."

She leaned over and kissed him goodbye. "I'll write."

"I'll be here." He smiled, and for the first time looked like himself.

BO REPEATED the address of the prison to Matt. "1600 North Drive." The fact that its street address was the same as that of the White House amused him.

"I heard you the first time," Matt grumbled, steering the rental car along one of Sioux Falls's quiet, tree-lined streets.

It hadn't been easy convincing Matt to accompany him to South Dakota. The lure of a partnership seemed to be the only incentive that worked. Fortunately, Bo wasn't above resorting to bribery. Especially after talking to his mother Friday evening.

"Our mothers seem to think you're suffering from depression," Bo said, hoping his mother and his aunt were exaggerating.

"Yeah, I know," Matt snorted. "Poor sad Matt. First the divorce. Then the awful accident." He shook his head. "My mother calls me daily and Aunt Ruth weekly. They're a sort of intervention tag team."

Bo liked his Aunt Irene, who was a charge nurse at St. Mary's. A no-nonsense woman with a wry view of the world. If she was worried about her son, things had to be worse than

Matt let on. And, Bo thought sheepishly, I've been too wrapped up in my problems to give Matt's much thought.

When he'd mentioned the possible partnership idea to his mother, she'd suggested he start by taking Matt with him. His cousin hadn't been overly excited, but Bo was glad for the company.

"Left or right, Mr. Navigator?" Matt asked grouchily. Spending the night on the floor of the airport after a blizzard left them—and a couple of thousand other travelers—stranded hadn't helped either man's temperament.

"Left," Bo gambled noticing the map on his lap was upside down.

A minute later, Matt put on the blinker and turned into the drive leading to the prison.

"Jeez," Bo exclaimed, craning his neck for a better look at the two-story gray stone fortress. "This place looks old."

Matt nosed the car into a parking place. "The information I got off the Internet said it was constructed as a territorial prison in 1881—eight years before South Dakota became a state."

"Wow."

The two men got out of the car and walked toward the imposing stone structure. Even though he told himself it was foolish to get his hopes up, Bo couldn't help scanning the parking lot for a Toyota wagon with California plates. He'd hoped she might stick around to see her brother on Sunday, too.

"Do you think he'll talk to us?" Bo asked.

"You," Matt corrected. "I'll wait in the lobby."

Bo's admittance was expedited by a phone call from Ren. Even a *former* judge had connections. Matt's FBI credentials didn't hurt matters. As Bo waited for Zachary Anders to join him, he debated about how to handle the meeting. He couldn't help wondering if Claudie had mentioned him when she spoke to her brother the day before.

"They said you want to see me," a husky voice said, making Bo look up sharply.

A small, wiry man with a shaved head and stooped shoulders looked back at him. At first Bo thought he must have the wrong person because Zachary was two years younger than Claudie. Instead of twenty-five, this man looked fifty. But as he studied the haggard face Bo began to detect a hint of Claudie in the eyes. He put out his hand. "Bo Lester. I'm a private investigator, but this isn't work. It's personal. I'm trying to catch up with your sister."

"Claudie," Zach said softly.

Bo nodded. "I know you spoke with her yesterday. I'd have been here sooner, but I got caught in a blizzard in New York."

"I thought you were from California."

He knows who I am. "I went to New York to get my cousin's help locating her. She left without telling anyone where she was going."

Zach's face took on a shuttered look. "Musta had her reasons."

Bo sighed. "The reason is she's stubborn, secretive and ornery as a moose." Zach's mouth twitched as if in agreement.

"She's been on her own a long time," he said loyally.

"I know that. She's also strong, brave and resourceful. And, in all honesty, she probably doesn't need my help, but I'm worried about her and I want to be there when…" He didn't finish what he was going to say. What if Claudie hadn't filled Zach in?

"When she takes on our daddy," Zach finished.

Bo nodded.

Zach was silent a moment, studying Bo. When he spoke, he said, "Tell me why you care what happens to her."

A lump the size of Manhattan formed in Bo's throat. He had to swallow twice before he could say, "Because I love her."

MATT STARED OUT a window at the prison grounds. Autumn had passed, but winter hadn't quite settled in, he decided, noting the crusty patches of grimy snow beneath a knee-high hedge. The grass was a mottled blend of browns and greens. He'd never been to the Midwest and doubted if November was the optimum month to visit, but somehow he'd let Bo talk him into making this trip.

"You don't need me," he'd argued while his cousin stubbornly made the travel arrangements.

"Yes, I do. I know I'm superhuman in certain departments but I haven't figured out how to clone myself so I can be in two places at one time. The weather looks like crap out there. If our plane gets canceled and we miss Claudie in Sioux Falls, then we have a fifty-fifty chance she'll try to find her sister or go straight to Kansas."

Matt tried logic—after all, they knew her ultimate destination so all Bo had to do was go to Kansas and wait, but logic didn't work on people who were in love—and it was crystal clear to Matt *that* was Bo's problem.

Sighing, he walked to the door and exited the building. The bite of the wind felt good on his face and he turned into it, closing his eyes against the sting. *Love.* He and Sonya had been in love once but that died the instant he realized she was having an affair.

"Let's move it and groove it, Cuz."

Matt spun around to find Bo standing less than two feet away. *Damn that man could move softly!*

Bo started toward the car.

"Where to?" Matt asked, following.

"The airport."

Matt had to hustle to catch up with his cousin. "You're giving up?"

"Of course not. We're splitting up. I'm going east. You're going south." He flashed Matt a smug look. "Told you so."

If Matt weren't thirty-six, he would have stuck out his tongue; instead, he flipped him off. Bo laughed outright. "Come on. Let's hustle. I sure as hell don't want to miss her at Valery's."

BO SETTLED BACK in the seat of the chartered airplane—a six-passenger Cessna that his pilot had planned to "take out for a little spin this morning, anyway." Bo was the only passenger. The pilot's wife, who was sitting in the copilot's seat, had told him with a definite gleam in her eye that Shokapee—his destination—was just a stone's throw from some really serious shopping.

The twenty-minute flight would put him less than a stone's throw from Claudie's sister's house.

Bo was glad to have a few minutes to collect his thoughts. Matt was not the most cheerful of traveling companions. Bo guessed he had a right to be sour—life had been pretty perverse lately. Bo's thoughts turned to Claudie's brother. Life hadn't been easy for him either but he'd seemed philosophical about it.

"I figure I'm in here for a reason...and it don't necessarily have to do with paying for my crime," Zach had told him. "Nothing I do will ever bring those people back. I was on a downward slide and, unfortunately, I took two other souls with me."

Zach's unexpected candor had taken Bo by surprise. "I gotta admit, I didn't think you'd give me the time of day," he'd told him.

"I wouldn't if Claudie hadn't given me the okay."

Bo's mouth had dropped open. "She what?"

Zach had smiled. "Not in so many words, you understand. But I know my sister, and I know how she feels about you—even if she won't admit it." His eyes had narrowed and he'd added sternly, "But she's been hurt a lot. Our father just had it in for her. Nothing she did was ever good enough for him. One time she brought home a report card with all A's and B's on it and he called her a kiss-ass teacher's pet. She just couldn't win. And there was other shit...." His voice had softened to almost a whisper. "So you'd better not hurt her or I will personally beat the crap out of you when I get out of here."

Sighing, Bo arched his neck against the high-backed seat and took a deep breath. He glanced at the muted squares of color below him punctuated with rivers and gray-looking lakes, but his mind was on Claudie. He had every intention of taking it slow and easy once he made sure she was okay. But first, he had to catch up with her. He'd expressed his fear about missing her at Valery's, but Zach had laughed.

"You don't know Val," he'd said. "Mom always said Val was born late and at the rate she was going she'd be late for her own funeral. Don't worry. Claudie will still be there."

THE SUNLIGHT streaming through the breakfast nook window was almost enough to calm Claudie's nerves. It hadn't taken long after reconnecting with Valery for Claudie to recall the long list of her sister's annoying habits that had always driven her crazy. At the top of the page was her glacierlike start-and-stop pace.

Val had insisted on fixing a fancy breakfast to prepare Claudie for her journey, but it was now almost noon and Claudie's stomach had been growling for hours.

"This is so much fun," Val said, poking through a drawer for something. "I couldn't believe it when I looked up from my desk last night and there you were. Wow. It was eerie. You look just like I remember Mom…except her hair was brown. Like mine."

Claudie studied her half sister as she puttered about the homey, cluttered kitchen. Val, who'd recently turned twenty-two, favored the Anders side of the family—short and dark with broad shoulders, narrow hips and delicate wrists and ankles. She carried an unhealthy spare tire around her middle but otherwise was quite attractive. Her curly auburn hair framed her face in a feminine style.

"Maybe I should grab a bite on the road, Val. I've gotten a little gun-shy about storms since I got stuck in a blizzard in Wyoming," Claudie said, trying to be diplomatic. Val had been a good hostess—taking Claudie out to dinner last night and providing a comfy bed, so Claudie hated to seem ungrateful, but she was anxious to leave.

"I know. This is taking forever. My mom is such a talker, but she's had a rough time of it since Dad passed away." Valery's adoptive mother had called and talked for almost an hour while Val drifted between chopping chives to making a Hollandaise sauce from scratch. Claudie would have exploded with frustration if an old photo album hadn't sidetracked her.

The ratty album—held together by peeling masking tape—was sprinkled with small, square black-and-white photos that slowly segued to murky color shots. To her surprise, the sentimental journey hadn't been as excruciating as she'd expected. Zach was right—there had been good times, too.

One picture grabbed her and took her straight to the scene—a skinny six-year-old holding her little brother's hand as they walked along the shore of Lake Michigan. Her mother, carrying Yancy in her arms, and obviously pregnant with Wesley, held her other hand. What stopped Claudie's heart was the smile on her mother's face. She looked girlish and carefree.

Years later someone—maybe Val—had pointed out that the reason Mother had been happy in Wisconsin was her close proximity to her estranged family. Maybe she thought they might welcome her back into the fold. But that had never happened because Garret got yet another new job and they'd moved to Davenport, Iowa the next spring and Claudie didn't recall ever meeting anyone she could call Grandma.

"Do you prefer ham or Canadian bacon?" Val asked, squatting in front of her refrigerator. "I have both."

Both? Aren't they the same? "Umm, either is fine, thanks. I'm not much of a gourmet."

"I love to cook," Val said with passion. "I plan to open a restaurant after Mom's gone. I'd never sell the video stores as long as she's alive—she likes to come in and throw her weight around once in a while, but commercial retail is not my thing. I'm good at it, but I'd rather be in a kitchen."

As far as Claudie could surmise, Val *was* very good at what she did. Not only was there a new Mercedes in the driveway of her charming older home, but when Claudie had walked into the video shop the previous evening, she'd had a chance to watch Val in action.

"You *will* have my order here tomorrow," Val had barked into the mouthpiece of the telephone headset. Her back was to the doorway where Claudie was standing. "I can't *sell* excuses."

Her strident tone had been loud enough to make several shoppers turn around and look.

"What kind of food would you cook in your restaurant?" Claudie asked, relieved to see Val pull out a frying pan.

Val set it on a burner then refilled her coffee cup. She offered Claudie some, too, but Claudie declined—certain her eyeballs might begin to float if she didn't get some food in her stomach soon. "I haven't narrowed that down, yet," Val said, taking a sip from her cup. "Maybe French. Maybe Scandinavian. There are a lot of folks around here who go for that good Norwegian food," she said, faking an accent that made Claudie smile.

In all honesty, Claudie had enjoyed her visit with her sister more than she thought possible. They had absolutely nothing in common but somehow that didn't matter. The novelty of the feeling made her smile.

"I'm surprised you didn't make more money as a hooker, Claudie," Val said, apropos of nothing. "I mean, you're pretty and thin. Guys go for girls who look like you."

Val's bluntness didn't shock her. It was the Val she remembered. "Prostitution doesn't have a lot of benefits or job security. It's like any other sales job—if you're not out selling, you don't get paid. I got real sick of sellin'." My *soul,* she added silently.

Val nodded sagely as she began cracking eggs into a bowl. "Yeah, I know how that goes. Some days it's all I can do to make myself go to the video store. If it weren't for Mom…"

She didn't complete the thought, so Claudie asked, "Is she demanding?"

Val's shoulder's stiffened. "I prefer to call it high maintenance. The more I encourage her to go out and reconnect with the world, the more she pesters me about settling down and having kids." She gave a derisive snort. "Like kids would be on either of our lists."

Claudie was taken aback by her sister's vehemence. An image of Brady flashed in her mind. "I think I might like to have kids someday," she admitted softly—as much to herself as Val.

Val looked dumbfounded. "How could you even think about it after what our mother went through? Do you remember how she looked at the end? I was only twelve but I can still picture her in the hospital. Her skin looked like waxed paper. Do you know I can't stand to touch the stuff even today?" A shudder passed through her body. "She was as depleted as an empty corn husk."

Claudie didn't argue the point. She'd been with her mother right up to end. She'd watched her waste away like a stream drying up in the summer heat.

Val spun back to the counter. "Nope," she said with conviction, "not me. I don't plan to be anybody's baby factory."

Claudie didn't say anything. The only sound was the snap and crunch of Val breaking eggs into a bowl. Both women jumped when the doorbell rang. "Would you get that, Claud? It's probably Mom. She usually stops over once or twice a day on weekends."

I should have left an hour ago, Claudie thought stifling a sigh. She trudged down the short hallway to the foyer. Plastering a fake smile on her face, she opened the door. "Bo." His name came out as a strangled yelp of shock that brought her sister running.

"Hi, Claudie, long time no see," he said, his voice dangerously soft, deceivingly calm. His eyes burned, a muscle in his cheek twitched, his left hand gripped the threshold as if to block her escape.

What he couldn't know was how glad she was to see him. It was on the tip of her tongue to tell him so when he glanced at Val and said, "You must be Valery. I'm Bo." He reached around Claudie to give Val a quick handshake then said, "Excuse us a minute, but this is long overdue."

Before Claudie could react, his right arm shot out and he hauled her up against his chest and kissed her. Hard. A kiss unlike any she'd ever known. Possessive. Passionate. And, above all, welcome.

CHAPTER FIVE

THEY'D KISSED BEFORE—friendly pecks, one or two tentative investigations. But this kiss was different. Bo was in zero gravity before he knew what hit him. Her arms were around his neck. Her tongue touched his. *Her tongue.* Her sweet, wonderful tongue.

A fake cough blew him right out of orbit. He jumped back like a kid on his first date. When he realized he was looking at an amused sister not an angry dad, he blushed with chagrin. "There," he said, with as much bluster as he could fake, "that'll teach you to run away without telling anybody."

Valery laughed. Claudie looked too stunned to move. *I freaked her out. Damn. Way to go, Lester.*

Bo hadn't planned to kiss her. He'd promised Zach to take things slow and easy with Claudie, but something had come over him the minute he'd seen her standing there looking bright and chipper. He'd had to touch her just to reassure himself she was real.

And she was real all right—real pissed off. He could tell by the way her shoulders stiffened and her eyes narrowed. He'd learned long ago the best defense was to hold his ground.

"Let's get it over with. Do you want to yell at me? Fine. I want to yell, too. But I'm willing to let you go first."

"This sounds like fun. Can I watch?" Valery asked, smiling mischievously.

"No," Claudie snapped. "There won't be any yelling because Bo isn't staying. He can just jump back on whatever white horse he rode into town on and go home."

"They didn't have any white horses at the car rental agency. I got the last thing on the lot, but I'm altogether sure it's a car," he said, looking over his shoulder. "It was the best they had on a Sunday. I guess there's a whole slew of veterans in town for the holiday."

Her lips pursed as if to scold him, so he continued his nonsense before she could speak. Odd, he thought, all this time to think about what he wanted to say and it had never crossed his mind to prepare a speech. "Listen, Claudie, I know you don't want me here, but I'm not leaving. If you and Val are heading to Kansas…" She made a surprised sound and covered her lips with her hand. Bo explained, "My cousin's with the FBI. He helped me put all the pieces together."

She shrank back. "You know? Everything?"

His heart squeezed at the vulnerability in her tone. "Just the basics. Name, date of birth, vaccinations," he said, trying to lighten the mood. "We found bits and pieces and kind of put them together the best we could. The Internet helped."

Claudie looked from him to Valery and back. "Why?"

Now was not the time to blurt out the answer he'd given Zach so he said, "I was worried about you. You're not the kind of person who just takes off without a reason, and I was afraid your reason might have to do with the past—the past that put you on the street."

Her brow shot up. "You thought I'd go back to hooking?"

"Of course not. But whatever made you run away from home had to hurt a lot—I wasn't about to let it hurt you again."

Valery suddenly lifted her chin and sniffed. "Oh, hell," she exclaimed. "My butter's burning." She spun around and sprinted down the hall.

Bo shifted from one foot to the other, waiting for some kind of sign. Claudie was looking at the ground. Bo's jacket felt insufferably warm, despite the chilly breeze whistling through the two tall pines in Val's front yard. Claudie wrapped her arms around her chest and slowly lifted her chin. "I should be mad, but I guess I'm not too surprised. Ren said you'd gone to New York to look for Eve. I think in the back of my mind I knew you might come."

His heart started pumping normally, and he let out the breath he'd been holding. "Does that mean I can hang out with you and your sister or do I have to tail you all the way to Kansas?"

She looked around his shoulder at his humble little two-door hatchback parked behind her station wagon. "Val isn't going with me, so I guess you can tag along."

Bo had to work to keep his jubilation from showing, but she scowled as if sensing it. "I don't know what you're doing here or why you want to come with me, but this is *my* trip and I'm boss. If you don't like it, tough."

He saluted her briskly. "Can I come in? I doubt if Val wants to heat up the outside with her electricity."

Claudie stepped aside so he could enter. Her scent enveloped him the minute she closed the door. It was warmer, more welcoming than the smells emanating from the kitchen. Bo shrugged off the parka he'd bummed from Matt and laid it across the back of a sofa as she led him down the hallway.

"I hope you're hungry, Bo," Val called. "I always make enough for thrashers, as my mother likes to say," Val said when they reached the kitchen.

"Starved," he said. And he was—for Claudie. Her rare and wonderful smile. Her hard-knock sense of humor. Her touch.

Without words she offered him a cup of coffee. He nodded. Their fingers met during the exchange and Bo felt a jolt.

He'd promised Zach to take things slow and easy with Claudie, but that might prove tougher than he'd thought—especially when she smiled that impish grin when she thought he wasn't looking.

CLAUDIE GRINNED. It was hard to keep from grinning when a white knight charged up on his trusty steed to rescue you. Granted the steed was a hunk of junk blocking the driveway, but the knight was hers. Bo. She had to keep staring at him for fear he'd disappear.

Thankfully Val never stopped talking long enough for Claudie's overt attention to become noticeable.

"Claudie was like the big mean sister from hell growing up, weren't you, Claud?" Val asked, her voice retaining a hint of the childhood whine that used to drive Claudie crazy. "I always thought she was picking on me. It wasn't until I got older that I realized she was filling in for our mother."

She paused, her lips pursed pensively. "Mom was sick a lot. One thing after another. Then, the day after Christmas, Dad took her to the hospital and she never came home." She looked at Claudie. "I remember you wouldn't let anybody take down the Christmas tree because you said Mom had a special way of wrapping up the ornaments and nobody else could do it. Remember?"

Claudie gripped her cup a little tighter. "No," she lied, picturing her stepfather standing in the midst of shattered ornaments—green and red shards littering the hardwood floor beneath the scraggy pine. It was early morning, still dark enough that the lights from the Christmas tree filled the room with color. When he'd lifted a shiny silver ball to his face, she'd seen tears, and Claudie had known her mother was dead.

Val frowned as if trying to remember some detail. "Sure

you do. Because after Dad woke us up to tell us, I ran into the living room and the tree was gone and you were sweeping up needles. You were crying. I'd never seen you cry before. I think that scared me more than losing Mom."

She turned back to her cooking. Bo reached out to cover Claudie's hand with his own, but she picked up her cup and walked to the sink. "How much longer, Val? I think I'll run and close up my suitcase."

Val took a plate from the cupboard. "I'll serve Bo first. Yours will be done in a minute." Claudie watched her carefully arrange a sprig of parsley atop the creation then place it before Bo.

He studied it a moment. "This looks better than what they serve in restaurants." He took a bite and groaned in pleasure. "Oh, baby, this…is…sinful."

Claudie pivoted on her heel and marched away. Her heart was beating much faster than it should have been and she tried to tell herself she was just nervous about getting a late start, but she knew that was a lie. She stuffed her nightgown in her backpack as if it were a rag and yanked the zipper closed.

"Yours is ready, sis," Valery called as Claudie plunked her travel-size tube of toothpaste into her cosmetics bag.

Claudie glanced in the mirror and practiced a fake smile. It was pathetic enough to make her smile for real.

Claudie slid into the chair across from Bo, meeting his quizzical look with a nod. Aromatic steam from the plate Val set before her made Claudie inhale deeply. "Umm," she said, her mouth watering.

Oddly put out by its perfection, Claudie hacked down on the three-inch stack of eggs, ham and English muffin with her fork. Hot yolk squirted sideways sending a yellow stream across her left hand.

"Oops," Val said, turning away. "I forgot napkins."

Before Claudie could react, Bo reached out and lifted her hand, bending down as if to gallantly kiss the back of it. Instead, he sucked the egg from her skin, adding a last little lick before her sister returned.

Claudie gaped in shock. She couldn't decide whether to be angry or amused. Bo's roguish wink sealed her fate. She laughed. "You are one sick puppy, Bo Lester," she said.

Val looked between them, a frown on her face. "What'd I miss?"

Claudie took the pretty print napkin from her sister's hand. "Nothing important. I've just agreed to travel with a madman. That's all."

Obviously, upset to be out of the loop, Val turned back to the stove to dish her own plate. Inwardly, Claudie groaned. She didn't want to upset her sister after coming all this way to visit. To her surprise, Bo soon had Val smiling as he regaled them with the horror story of his trip from hell with his cousin Matt.

"First, I swear, there's nothing like four feet of snow to bring out the crazies in New York. The bridges were like skating rinks and every taxi driver thought he was Wayne Gretzky. We were lucky to make it to the airport alive. Unfortunately, our flight was canceled—along with everybody else's, so we ended up sleeping on the floor."

Claudie shuddered. "That's disgusting."

"That's not the worst of it," he said, pausing dramatically. "The woman who was sitting beside Matt had a little dog in one of those plastic carriers. Turns out the dog had the worst halitosis imaginable…and it spent the whole night trying to lick Matt's nose."

Val hooted with laughter. "What'd he do?"

Bo shrugged. "He was asleep. He didn't realize it until he woke up, then he nearly gagged." He gave Claudie a wink.

"He told me he'd been dreaming his ex-wife was trying to seduce him."

"Where's Matt now?" Claudie asked, trying hard not to be charmed.

Bo took a swallow of coffee. "On his way to Kansas—in case you headed there instead of here."

Claudie frowned. She wasn't sure how she felt about the idea of having two men track her movements—one was bad enough.

"What will he do until we get there?"

"Scope things out. He was in law enforcement. He knows the routine."

Claudie rose and carried her plate to the sink. After scraping the leftovers into the garbage can, she reached for the handle of the faucet, but Val said, "Just leave it on the counter, Claudie. You cleaned up after all of us for years. I'll do the dishes later, after you're gone."

"Are you sure you don't want to come along?" Claudie asked, trying not to sound pathetically hopeful.

Val let out a long, heartfelt sigh. "Like I told you last night—Otter Creek is the last place on Earth I'd go to voluntarily. I put that life behind me when I got adopted. And it sounds like you've got a nice life back in Sacramento, Claudie. I really don't understand why you're doing this."

"I told you last night. I don't want the same thing to happen to Sherry that happened to me."

"But why do you care? You haven't seen her in ten years—she probably doesn't even remember you, or any of us for that matter."

"Then she has a right to know. We're her family."

Val's groan twisted Bo's stomach in a knot. "Big whoop. A brother in prison, a sister who's an ex-hooker, another brother who drives a big truck and chases women other than his wife." Claudie's brows shot up in surprise, which prompted Val to add, "That's what Zach told me. Seems Yancy can't quite get his first wife out of his system."

Claudie frowned. "No family is perfect, but she still has a right to know us."

Val's eyes took on a speculative glint. "Are you sure this isn't more about your revenge on Dad? If that Web page you showed me is right, he might have cleaned up his act and your coming along will open a big ugly can of worms that could ruin his life." She smiled serenely. "Not that he doesn't have it coming for what he did to you, but I'm just curious about your motivation."

Rather than answer her sister's question, Claudie started clearing the table, but Val had given Bo a smug look as if she had her answer.

BO TRANSFERRED his bag from the trunk of the rental car to the back of the station wagon, which was idling with the heater blasting in an effort to defrost the windows. He hadn't decided if he truly trusted Claudie to follow him back to the rental lot, but he figured she was too softhearted to take off with his luggage.

He looked toward the small white bungalow where the two sisters were standing on the stoop. Claudie turned to leave, but Val stopped her, then dashed back inside. Claudie looked at Bo and threw up her hands in frustration. Dressed in a purple-and-white ski sweater and black leggings—her blond hair its usual "bed-head" style, she looked like a teenager ready for a day on the slopes.

Seeing the sunlight pick up streaks of white gold in her mop of waves, Bo was struck by how angelic she looked, as if the tragedy and ugliness of her past had bounced off. Bo had defended her without hesitation, but now his trepidation returned. What was she seeking? Revenge? Redemption? Maybe just a simple "I'm sorry"?

Bo wished he had a clear-cut answer, but he doubted if Claudie knew herself. They looked at each other from across the distance. A quick smile touched her lips then disappeared. Bo's heart turned over as giddy as a kid with his first crush. He slammed the rear door of the wagon with more force than necessary. Claudie's chin tilted questioningly, but only for a second. Val returned and Claudie turned to face her.

Bo couldn't hear their conversation, but he headed in that direction when he saw Val hand Claudie a white box the size of a toaster oven. As he approached, he heard Claudie ask, "How'd you get it?"

"Dad sent it to me when I graduated from high school. I don't know how he knew where I lived. We'd moved up here shortly after my adoption was final—Mom wanted us to make a fresh start, and I'd never had any contact with him or the boys after we left town. There wasn't a card or anything, but his name was on the return address. Mom said maybe it was his way of apologizing for everything that went wrong."

Bo joined Claudie on the stoop in time to see her lift the lid of the box, which on closer look appeared to be a cheap jewelry box covered in white watered silk slightly yellowed with age.

"It's Mom's stuff," Claudie said, her voice hoarse with unshed tears.

Bo looked at Valery who lifted one shoulder as if to say, "Whatever."

"Don't you want to keep any of it?" Claudie asked. "You might want to give something to your kids some day…."

Val cut in. "Like I told you before. I'm not going to have kids. Kids make your life miserable. No thanks."

"But, don't you even want something to remember Mom by?"

Bo's heart split down the middle at the little-girl quality in her voice.

Val shook her head. "No. It's *your* mother's stuff, Claudie. My mother lives three blocks away, and, believe me, she wouldn't be caught dead in any of that junk."

The put-down made Bo start to snarl, but Claudie seemed too moved by the unexpected gift to be offended. Bo looked at Val over Claudie's head. *Brat.* She batted her lashes innocently.

"We gotta hit the road, kiddo," he said, taking Claudie's elbow. She was so engrossed by the treasure chest, she didn't even flinch when he put his arm around her shoulders and guided her to the driver's side door. "Aren't you going to tell your sister goodbye?"

Claudie looked up as if coming back to reality. "Oh," she said with a gulp. She shoved the box into Bo's hands and dashed back to hug Val. "I'll let you know what happens," she called over her shoulder as she sprinted to the car. "Thanks for everything."

Bo placed the box in the back seat, fearful she'd be too distracted to drive safely. "You can go through it once I'm driving. Not before," he said sternly.

She gave him a goofy salute and got in the car. "Then let's get going. It's a long way to Kansas, you know."

Her impish grin stayed with him all the way to the rental shop. He and Matt had mapped out the trip before leaving New York. Two days on the road. One night. It wasn't the days that worried him.

"CAN YOU believe this traffic?" Bo said for the second time in ten miles.

The sense of wonder in his tone made Claudie smile. They'd had a brief argument over whether to drive east and catch the interstate or take the same road Claudie had driven. Since Bo had insisted on driving, Claudie had acquiesced to his preference, and she was glad since he seemed so bemused by the lack of cars on the spacious, nicely groomed four-lane highway.

"I'm sure it gets busy on weekdays. And tomorrow's a holiday, don't forget," she reminded him.

"Yeah, I suppose you're right." He was quiet a moment then he swore and slapped his palm against the steering wheel, making Claudie jump.

"What?"

"Today's the little guy's birthday. I forgot to get him a present."

Claudie had to bite her lip to keep from laughing at Bo's tormented tone. "I sent him two T-shirts and a dinosaur from the Black Hills, but I doubt if he got them in time. Ren and Sara were taking him to the coast for the long weekend."

Bo reached between the seats for the navy-blue parka he'd thrown to the back. He handed it to Claudie. "Get my cell phone out of the pocket would you?"

She had to try three different pockets before she found it. Each pocket was an adventure. One was stuffed with bags of airline peanuts, the second with sugar packets—one of which had broken open. She got sticky grains under her fingernails. Sucking her fingers to remove the sugar, she held the small black phone in her other hand. "How do you know where to call? You know Ren won't have his phone on."

When Bo didn't answer, she looked up. He was staring at her fingers in her mouth. Her heart began to race, and she immediately shoved her hand under her butt. His gaze went straight back to the road, but Claudie could tell by his ruddy color he knew she'd guessed what he was thinking.

"If we can't get them on the cell, you can try Babe. She ought to know where they're staying."

Claudie silently groaned. She wasn't ready to talk to Babe Bishop. Although the woman had been nothing but supportive of Claudie recently, she still felt shy around her. And Claudie certainly didn't want to explain this trip.

Holding her breath, she punched in the phone number then listened to the ringing tone. Two rings. Three…

"Hello."

"Ren?"

"Claudie?"

From the background came a loud, shrill cry followed by a muffled curse and thumping sound. "Claudie," Sara cried, the joy in her voice causing tears to fill Claudie's eyes. "It's so good to hear your voice. How are you?"

Claudie wasn't sure she could speak without embarrassing herself so she said, "Bo wants to talk to you," and passed the phone to her left.

Obviously surprised and unprepared, he shifted slightly and took the phone. "Hi, Sara. I found her."

Claudie stared out the passenger window at the rolling farmland now sitting fallow. She'd passed through this country once or twice in her family's many moves, and it felt comforting—like greeting an old friend. But, in reality, Claudie only had two friends: Sara and Keneesha. And she missed them both more than she thought possible.

"I just remembered Brady's birthday and we called to wish him happy birthday," Bo was saying. "Put him on."

Bo leaned toward Claudie and motioned her closer with a nod of his head. She inched sideways until their shoulders touched. She felt the connection all the way to the soles of her hiking boots.

He held the phone so they both could hear Brady's excited

jabber. Since Bo was trying to talk and steer, Claudie reached between them and took the phone from his fingers. A jolt of awareness overrode all incoming messages.

"Slow down, honey boy, I can't understand you. You touched a what?"

"'Tar fish," he cried. "Orange 'tar fish."

Claudie and Bo exchanged a look. "A star fish," he mouthed.

Her mouth went bone dry. *What is wrong with me?*

Sara came on the line and Claudie sat back, giving herself some much needed space. This wasn't like her at all. She'd been with Bo in the car dozens of time and nothing like this had ever happened.

"What, Sara? I'm sorry. My mind's a little out there."

"Understandable. It was probably quite a shock to see Bo. We were afraid you wouldn't be too happy about him joining you." *Happy?* Claudie wasn't sure how she felt, but happy might actually be part of it, she thought. "But, you know Bo, once he made up his mind, there was no talking him out of finding you."

"It's okay for now," Claudie said, aware he was listening to her conversation. "I won't kill him before we get to Kansas. Just in case the car breaks down again."

Bo's lips pursed in a mock scowl.

Sara's voice dropped. "You're not really going to kill anybody are you, honey?"

Claudie started to laugh, but suddenly she understood Sara was serious. In a flash she realized her friend might have thought her intention was revenge. It crossed her mind to be mad, but only for a second.

"Don't worry, Sara. I'm not going to do anything stupid. I already have a brother in prison for vehicular manslaughter. I stopped to see him on my way, and believe me, I'm not in a hurry to go back there."

Sara's sigh seemed mixed with tears. Ren came on the line. "I'm glad to hear you're okay, kiddo," he said. "Put that doofus friend of mine back on the line."

Claudie passed the phone to Bo. She tuned out the conversation, still thinking about Sara's doubt. Did this mean her best friend in the world knew so little about her that she believed her capable of murder? *Bo says I'm like a clam. Maybe it's true.*

When the phone landed in her lap, she looked at Bo. He had a serious frown on his face that made her stomach contract. "Is something wrong?"

He sighed.

"Ren said Eve's old agent called him. Apparently she heard about Eve leaving the network—"

Claudie interrupted him. "She quit her job?"

Bo nodded. "Looks that way."

Claudie shook her head. "I don't believe it. Network was her dream job. She told me so herself when she was back for the wedding."

Bo shrugged. "Sounds like some guy came in and swept her off her feet. The only weird thing is, nobody's heard from her since."

"Do you think something happened to her?"

"Nah," he said, shaking his head. "She's probably shacked up in some tropical love nest."

Claudie frowned. She couldn't picture anyone less likely to succumb to a sweet-talking man than Eve—except herself. "Men always think that, don't they?"

"Think what?"

She started to let it go—after all she was no fan of Eve Masterson's even if Sara was willing to forget the woman had once been engaged to Ren, but instead she turned sideways in her seat to face him. "Men always think women are ready to give up their lives, their careers, their identity for a wedding ring and regular sex. Right?"

"As opposed to no wedding ring and irregular sex?" he asked, shooting a quick glance her way.

She stuck out her tongue. "You know what I mean."

"Not really."

She threw up her hands. "Isn't that what normal people do? They grow up, go to school, meet someone then settle down for a nice, safe life."

"Didn't you leave out the word *boring?*"

She scowled at him even though he wasn't looking at her.

"Claudie, I know you well enough to figure out when you're trying to pick a fight. If you want to yell at me for tracking you down and nosing in on your business, then go ahead and yell. But don't try to confuse me by arguing about normal people. Frankly, I don't give a damn about the normal people of the world. I do care about you."

"And I'm not normal. Is that what you're saying?" She kept her tone even so he wouldn't hear the little kid inside her who'd known from the earliest memory she was somehow different from her brothers and sisters. Different in a bad way.

Instead of answering he hit the blinker.

Claudie looked up surprised to see a rest area sign. She held her breath as the car decelerated and pulled to a stop well away from the other vehicles.

Bo shut off the motor and turned to face her. "Claudie, you know you're not like other people. Neither am I. Frankly, I don't see that as a bad thing. We are who we are, and it gives us character." He took a deep breath and let it out. "Maybe I would have liked things to be different growing up. My dad was a horse's butt as fathers went, and yours was no prize winner, either."

Claudie leaned back against the door. The coolness of the window seeped through her sweater giving her a chill. "My father committed suicide," she said.

Bo's bushy brows collided. "I beg your pardon?"

"My real father. My mother fell in love with the minister's son back in the town where she grew up. It was a small, mostly Scandinavian town in Wisconsin. They were both seventeen. When she found out she was pregnant, he offered to marry her, but his father wouldn't hear of it. He claimed my mother seduced his boy. He sent my father away to a boarding school back east. It was very hush-hush. My mother was left to do the right thing, which in those days meant giving me up for adoption."

He ran his thumbnail along the seam of her leggings. The touch sent squiggly tendrils up and down her legs. "But she didn't," he said, prompting her to go on.

"She was going to, but at the last minute she backed out. Her parents were furious. They told her she couldn't bring me home because they had her two younger sisters to worry about and they didn't want them contaminated by her loose morals."

Bo made a sound of disgust.

Claudie shrugged. "Mother had a hundred dollars. She moved in with one of the nurses from the hospital. The *St. James* School for Unwed Mothers," she added softly.

He opened his mouth but didn't say anything.

"She was working as a waitress when she met my stepdad. Mom once told me Garret asked her to marry him before she could ask, 'What'll it be today?'"

Bo leaned forward. "So she said yes, and your real father heard about it and committed suicide?"

"Who's telling this story? You're as bad as Brady," she scolded. "Actually, Garret, my stepfather, asked her to marry him once a week for four months—he only passed through town on his sales route once a week. She always turned him down. Until the day she talked to an old friend of hers back in Wisconsin and she found out my father had committed suicide in his dorm."

Bo sat back. "Wow. I didn't know any of that."

"I don't suppose it's the kind of thing that shows up on a computer search."

"Did she ever reconcile with her parents?" he asked.

Claudie shook her head. "Not that I know of, but she never blamed them for putting her out. She told me they were doing what they thought best, and as a parent sometimes you make tough decisions for the good of the children." She didn't bother trying to disguise her bitterness.

"You think she was wrong?"

"I think she was weak and selfish. Maybe if she'd given me up for adoption I'd have had a normal life—like Val. Instead I grew up watching her pump out babies like there was some kind of competition to make the most. She was pregnant something like ten times in twelve years. Three were miscarriages, and my little brother Timothy died at birth, but still she had six kids before she was thirty-five."

"Why do you think she wanted so many kids?"

Claudie glanced in the back seat where her mother's jewelry box sat. She felt slightly disloyal sharing her mother's secret with Bo, but she figured it didn't matter any more. "She told me that was the only way she could make it up to him."

At Bo's puzzled look, she explained, "Mom felt she owed something to Garret because he loved her, but she never loved him. Even after giving Garret six kids, she still loved my father." Claudie looked into his eyes and read the compassion she'd never known from another man. "That's why he hated me. I reminded her of my father. Every day he had to live with that reminder." She broke the contact and looked away. "I guess, you can kinda understand why he raped me."

"No," Bo barked, startling Claudie with both the volume and the passion. "I can't understand it, and I can't wait to meet the bastard."

Claudie peeked around to see if anyone was looking. She wasn't used to having someone defend her—it made her nervous. "Listen, Bo, I said you could come along with me because I knew you'd follow anyway, but I don't want you sticking your nose into my business once we get there."

He rocked back, his face still flushed from anger. "Tough."

She blinked. "What did you say?"

"I said tough. I'm here and I'm in it all the way."

"Not if I don't want you there."

"Wrong."

Speechless, her mouth dropped open.

He leaned forward, crowding her space. His breath was warm and smelled of coffee. "I'm here, Claudie, and I'm not about to let you face this jerk alone, even if you throw a hissy fit. People like your stepdad know only one way to operate—they tear you down. They find a way around your good, fine, logical arguments until they make you feel stupid and small and deserving of all the crap they gave you. He raped your spirit, your self-esteem, long before he ever physically touched you. And I plan to make damn sure he doesn't get the chance to do it again."

Claudie couldn't breathe. She couldn't move without crumpling into a ball and weeping, so she sat very still and waited for him to move back. When he did, she opened the door. "I need to use the bathroom," she said, after gulping in a deep breath of chilled air. "I'll be right back."

She got out and closed the door. She walked briskly praying she could make it to the low brick building before she broke down completely.

He caught up with her halfway there. His hand closed over her shoulder. She froze. "Claudie," he said softly. He gently squeezed his fingers. "I'm sorry. That was—"

Without thinking she spun around and threw herself sobbing into his arms. She didn't want his apologies—she wanted something else. Something she couldn't have—an ordinary life with an ordinary past. And with any luck…an ordinary future.

CHAPTER SIX

BO GLANCED to his right. Claudie had reclined the seat as far as it would go and was fast asleep, her head resting on his bunched-up coat just inches from his elbow. They'd stopped for gas and a couple of sodas in the town of Faribault, Minnesota. She'd tried reading the newspaper for a few miles but was obviously having a hard time staying awake so he'd suggested she nap.

"Hey, you're the one who slept on the floor last night. I should be driving so you can sleep," she'd argued.

Bo had insisted he wasn't tired, and he hadn't lied. For some reason, being around Claudie energized him. In New York, he'd had to force himself to trudge through the motions of looking for Eve and conducting his company's business from Matt's apartment. Last week on his trip to Las Vegas, he'd lacked the initiative to check out even one of the fancy new casinos. Life seemed to lack any purpose when Claudie was gone.

That's how Bo knew he was in love with her. He'd known since Vegas but hadn't been ready to admit it until Zach called him on it. But there was no denying it now. The second she'd melted into his arms, her tears soaking his shirt, he was lost. Too far gone to even give a damn. His only problem was how to tell Claudie without totally freaking her out.

His cell phone trilled just as they passed a sign announcing the Iowa border.

"Is this my Welcome-to-Iowa call?"

A familiar chuckle answered. "No, it's the I-don't-give-a-damn-where-you-are call."

"Sure you do. You're my cousin. And my business partner."

"Maybe. We only have our mothers' word on the first and I'm rethinking the second. So far this P.I. business is nothing more than racing around like a headless chicken."

Bo grinned. He checked his speed and eased his foot off the accelerator. "I disagree. I've had an excellent day. Not only was I treated to an aerial view of Minnesota, I found the woman of my dreams and even managed to scarf down eggs Benedict."

"Hey, that's what I had for breakfast, too—mine came in a sack with a little toy. Bet yours didn't."

Chuckling, Bo asked, "So, where are you?"

"I'm at a rest area just past St. Joseph, Missouri," Matt said, the connection fading like a long echo. When it surged back in, Bo heard him say, "…a motel in Kansas City tonight, then head to Otter Creek tomorrow." He made a snorting sound. "I can't believe I'm on my way to a town called Otter Creek. I bet you dollars to doughnuts it has neither."

"If Claudie were awake I'd ask her, but you'll just have to check that out for yourself."

"I can't wait," Matt said, facetiously. He added more seriously, "How she'd take it—your jumping into her life with both feet?"

"She was thrilled to see me."

"Yeah, I bet."

"No, really." Bo noticed her peeking up at him, so he added, "Claudie agreed she needed me along for all the really important things—like pumping gas and washing the windshield. You know, you can't get that kind of service at a lot of places anymore."

Her soft chuckle made his insides percolate. "And neck rubs," she added so softly he almost missed it.

"How far do you think you'll make it tonight?" Matt asked.

"How far will I get tonight? As far as she lets me," Bo quipped, bracing for the slug that was sure to follow. "Ouch!" he yelped. "She pinched me."

Matt's chuckle hummed across the line. "She sounds like a pistol. Speaking of which—she isn't carrying, is she?"

Bo held the phone away from his ear and asked loudly, "Claudie, Matt wants to know if you have a gun?"

She shot upright. "What is it with you people?" she shouted. "You watch too much television, right? No. I don't have a gun and I don't plan to shoot anybody. Jeez." She plopped down turning her back to him.

Bo returned the phone to his ear. "Did you get that?"

Matt was still laughing. "I got it. Boy, Cuz, can you pick 'em. She makes Sonya look like a soft touch."

"But her breath is better," Bo replied.

Matt's hoot echoed in the car. "I'll be sure to tell Sonya you said so when I call home tonight. In the meantime, I'd better hit the road. I'll talk to you tomorrow—unless you want me to check in tonight when I get to my motel."

"Nah," Bo said, "Call me in the morning so we can set up where to meet. Give Ashley my love."

He pushed the disconnect button and dropped the phone into the breast pocket of his flannel shirt. He glanced over his shoulder and saw Claudie looking at him over her shoulder.

"Who's Ashley?" she asked.

"Matt's daughter. She's twelve, I think. A real sweetie pie and Matt loves her to pieces, but he doesn't get to spend a lot of time with her thanks to his ex-wife." He frowned, switching lanes to avoid a convoy of tractor-trailers. "Ashley's the reason we were late following you to Sioux Falls. Matt had the information for me on Friday, but he couldn't leave because Ashley was in some play at school. If we'd have left earlier, we'd have missed the storm."

"Why did you want him to come along?" she asked, her tone puzzled.

Bo sighed. "Matt's mom and my mom are not only sisters-in-law, they're really close friends. And they're both worried about Matt. They think he's sinking into some kind of depression. He was in a bad accident awhile back and can't work on the street anymore. His precinct gave him a desk job—and even loaned him to the FBI because he's so good at what he does, but he feels inadequate not doing what he loves."

"What's wrong with him?"

"His leg got crushed and they had to build him a new knee. He barely limps at all any more, but he's not a hundred percent and never will be."

"That sucks."

"Hey, it's a good break for me. I could really use his help in my business. I've offered him a partnership, which is partly why I wanted him along. He needs to see what the job involves. But like my mom said, he needed someone to shake him out of his rut, too."

She was silent a minute then said, "I liked your mother. We spent a little time together at the wedding. She's smart, but she doesn't rub your nose in it like some smart people do."

"You mean like me?" he teased.

"You're not that smart, Bo."

He pretended to be offended. "I beg your pardon."

Snickering, she repositioned herself so she could draw her knees up and wrap her arms around them. "Okay, you're street smart—like me, but you've got a ways to go to catch up with your mom when it comes to reading books."

He blew out a sigh. "You've got that right." He hesitated

a moment then said, "When I was a kid, I resented her books. I was jealous of them."

"How can you be jealous of a book?"

"Easy, when your mom's busy reading instead of playing with you."

"Oh," she said reflectively. "I see what you mean. My mom never had time to read because there were always three or four kids whining for something, but it was kinda the same thing. She wasn't giving *me* her attention."

"Exactly. I think that was one of the reasons I didn't read for years."

"Ren said you never opened a book in college. He said the only way you graduated was because you were naturally intelligent and you soaked up information like a sponge."

Bo sat up a little straighter. "He told you that?"

She nodded. "Me and Sara. One night when we were sitting around the pool. I don't know where you were."

"Hmm…well, he got the part about not opening a book right. I really regret that now. What a waste! Between the parties and the hangovers I don't know how I ever learned a thing."

Neither of them spoke for several minutes, then Claudie asked, "Where does Matt's daughter live?"

"With her mother and stepfather. He's a plastic surgeon and they have a big, fancy house on Long Island. I think that's another reason Matt isn't feeling too good about himself. He hates it that Ashley has to choose between spending time in his rinky-dink apartment or hanging out in upper-class suburbia."

"It's the pits when kids get caught in the middle," Claudie said. "My brother Yancy told me he has a daughter by his first wife, but he hardly ever sees her. At least your cousin makes the effort to stay connected."

"Matt's a good father, and he was a damn fine husband until Sonya had an affair with the nose doctor. Of course, she blamed Matt because he was never home. She said she wanted more out of life than being a cop's wife."

"You sound like she was unfaithful to you," Claudie said, hearing more than he wanted to say.

"It pissed me off that Matt's job wasn't good enough for her. The same thing happened to a friend of mine when I was on the force."

"Is that why you never married?" she asked in a soft voice.

He kept his eyes on the road—amazed by how easy it was to talk about things he never shared with anyone. "I dated one woman for almost four years. We talked marriage but never got around to setting a date. She worked for a dentist, and she was…" He didn't know how to describe the lack of emotional involvement he'd felt toward Janelle. He'd liked her. They'd had a good sex life. They'd had fun together. But that was as far as it went.

"What?" Claudie probed. "Was she too pushy? Too chubby? Too short? She snored? Her breasts were too big? Her feet were too small?"

Bo flashed her a droll sneer. "I liked her a lot, but I didn't love her."

"Oh," she said softly. "Did she love you?"

"Yes," Bo said with a sigh. "That's why I haven't dated for a long, long time. I hurt her—without meaning to, and I didn't like the way that made me feel."

She pushed the lever to bring her seat into the upright position. It made a clicking sound until it reached the angle she wanted. She turned slightly, her seat belt crossing at her shoulder. "You're a good man, Bo Lester. I guess I always knew that about you."

Bo's heart swelled. "Thanks." His voice sounded gruff

and the fabric of his flannel shirt felt as though it were scraping his neck.

"You're welcome." She took a breath and let it out. "Can we eat soon? I'm hungry."

"DECISIONS. DECISIONS. Apple pie or cheesecake?" Bo said, studying a laminated dessert menu that had been left on their table by their harried waitress. "What are you ordering?"

Claudie's appetite had disappeared the instant he suggested getting a motel instead of traveling on. "Neither."

His left eyebrow quirked. "Are you sure?"

"I think we should hit the road," she said glancing out the window at the black sky. Deep down she know Bo was right—it was foolish to drive any farther when they were both exhausted. But to agree would mean she'd have to voice her request for separate rooms. Bo might think it pretty silly coming from a woman who used to sleep with men for a living.

"Claudie, you told me you didn't sleep well last night and, frankly, I'm shot," he said, his voice reflecting fatigue. "If you're worried about the money, don't be. I'll pay for the motel since I know you're on a budget and I want a good one."

She tried to cover her nervousness with attitude. "Two drivers means one person drives while the other sleeps. I'll take the first shift."

His mouth fell open. "You mean drive all night?"

Nodding with more enthusiasm than she felt, she took another drink of iced tea. Maybe a shot of caffeine would give her the jolt she needed to stay awake.

After a few seconds of stiff silence he let out a big, "Ohhh…I get it. You think if we get a motel I'll expect you to sleep with me. Right?"

Claudie looked away, wishing she could disappear. "No,"

she lied. "I don't have much time off from the bookstore, and I need to get this over with. We're still in Iowa and the sooner we get to Kansas, the sooner I can go home."

When she braved a look, his gaze scrutinized her, making her squirm. "Well, you won't save any time if we wind up in a wreck."

He picked up the bill and slid out of the booth. "Here's the plan. We're checking into the motel across the road. I've stayed in that chain before and they honor my business club discount card, which means I save enough money to afford *two* rooms." He wiggled two fingers. "Okay?"

Unable to look him in the eye, she nodded.

By the time they pulled into the parking lot of the motel she was tempted to tell him one room with two beds would be okay. He was right, of course. They were adults, friends. He'd come all this way to help her. She was an idiot.

But before she could voice her change of heart, he was standing at the registration desk. In a blink he returned with two plastic credit-card type keys and a map with two red circles on it.

"We're right across the hall from each other," he said, looking over his shoulder to back up the car.

He drove around the far side of the building and parked. They unloaded their suitcases in silence. Bo used his key to unlock the outside door. As they headed down the hallway, he stopped to sniff the air.

Claudie recognized the smell. *Chlorine.*

"The desk clerk said they have a heated pool," he said, waiting for Claudie to open her door. "And a spa, too." The childlike excitement in his tone made her feel even more foolish.

"I didn't bring a suit," Claudie said, carrying her suitcase into the spacious, handsomely appointed room.

"Didn't I see a mall down the road?" he asked, his tone too innocent to be real. "It's off season. You could probably get a good deal, if you wanted one."

Sometimes Claudie felt as though arguing with Bo was as futile as trying to change the past. With a sigh, she held out her hand. "Gimme the keys," she muttered. The least she could do was be a good sport.

BO'S NOSE CRINKLED at the strong odor of chlorine. Paradoxically, it made him homesick for his houseboat. His life had been so hectic lately he hadn't had much time to spend on his funky vessel, but he loved the peace it brought him. Water was his retreat—his oasis. Any kind of water—even an Olympic-size aqua-blue rectangle surrounded by white plastic chairs beneath a huge Plexiglas dome. The steamy room reflected the loud chatter of a group of teens laughing and splashing in the far corner of the facility where a sunken spa occupied a raised dais. Surrounded by potted palms, it resembled a small oasis.

He grabbed a towel from a rack and walked to a spot visible from the entrance, in case Claudie came looking for him. Yeah, right, he thought frowning. They'd been getting along fine until he brought up the idea of the motel. It had seemed natural. No sane person drove all night unless it was a matter of life or death. The rationale behind her reaction had been transparently obvious.

Bo dropped his towel and room key on a chaise then yanked off his T-shirt. He dove into the water without hesitation. Its initial coolness startled him but as he lengthened his stroke toward the far end of the pool the water felt pleasantly soothing.

You gotta give her space, man, he told himself as he swam. Given her past, she may never want to be with a man, he thought despondently. He didn't blame her. What good had men done her?

When his fingers touched the wall at the shallow end, he stopped. Standing, he shook the water from his hair and face then sank up to his shoulders back into the now too warm water. With elbows resting on the tiled step he swirled the water with his feet. A sudden thought made him flinch. *What if she just kept going?* It hadn't occurred to him before, but she could have gone back to her room for her bag and taken off without him.

The idea made his stomach churn. He was just about to leave the pool when the door opened and Claudie walked in. "Holy sh—" he softly swore, taking in the cobalt suit, the dazzling expanse of skin and a sinfully provocative wisp of material encasing her hips.

Forgetting to breathe he sank lower until chlorinated water filled his open mouth. Choking, he stood up and waded toward her. "Nice suit," he said, mortified that his vocal cords chose that minute to act like a horny teenage boy's.

She clutched a towel to her chest as if to hide behind it. "It was the only one they had," she said. "How's the water?"

"What water?" He couldn't get over how beautiful she was. Perfect, really.

She gave him an arch look and pointed to the pool. "Oh," he said, feeling his face heat up. "Great. The water's great. I haven't tried the spa yet. I was waiting for the kids to leave."

As if on cue, the noisy group gathered their things and walked toward the door. As they passed, Bo saw the three young studs check out Claudie. Their girlfriends quickly hustled them off. Claudie's gaze followed them until they were out of sight.

"Swimming sounds good," she said, more to herself than Bo. "Work out a few kinks."

Bo gave her space, ordering himself to return to his laps. It took every bit of self-discipline to stay focused on his stroke. And it worked—until he accidentally bumped into her.

CLAUDIE LOVED WATER. As a child, the local swimming pool had been her favorite retreat. The underwater world was one of muted quiet and shimmering beauty—very different from her normal life. She knew Bo liked the water, too, but she'd never seen him attack it quite so relentlessly.

She casually drifted to his side of the pool and *accidentally* bumped his shoulder.

"Oops. Sorry," he said, jerking back in the chest-deep water.

"Are you in training or what?" she asked.

He looked confused.

"That's how Ren swims when he's upset about something. Sara said he put in about three miles a day before he decided to quit the judiciary."

Bo rolled his shoulders. Squarish. Solid. Such fine shoulders, Claudie thought before she could stop herself. She liked the nice even coat of reddish-blond curls on his chest, too.

Bo backed up a step and sank down until the water was up to his chin. "I was in the zone—mindless repetition," he told her, the look in his eye cautious.

She didn't blame him for being suspicious of her new mellower mood. "I'm sorry I was so cranky before. You were right. I was a little freaked about the room situation." She made a face. "You probably think it's stupid for someone like me to worry about where I sleep and who I sleep—"

He stopped her with a hand to her upper arm. A light touch, but it made her gulp. "Claudie, I've been worried about *where* you were sleeping ever since you left. I know how tight money is and I was afraid you might spend the night in your car. That's dangerous," he said sternly. "But it never crossed my mind to wonder *who* you might be sleeping with." He stepped closer and lowered his voice even though they were the only two in the place. "I *know* you, Claudie. I also know that performing sex for money is not the same as making love with someone. When it comes to that, you're practically a virgin."

Claudie's involuntary bark of laughter hid a deeper emotion that ripped through her middle. She backpedaled for breathing space. A tingling sensation under her arms made her want to race away. "That's the stupidest thing I've ever heard, Lester," she said, forcing herself to stand her ground.

"No, it's not. It's the truth."

She snorted her opinion. "I've done things that would make you blush."

"I was a cop for nine years, Claudie. I don't blush easily."

She took another step back but encountered the solid wall of the pool. "I bet you never saw—" He didn't let her finish.

"Forget it, Claudie. You can't scandalize me, or freak me out by telling me some horror story about life on the street. I've been there. It's ugly. Enough said." Claudie's heart was beating so fast she could barely breathe. "If you need to unload some of that baggage you're carrying, I'd be glad to listen, but don't tell me that stuff if you're trying to scare me off. It won't work."

He looked so serious, so intent she almost turned around and fled.

"You know what this is about, Claudie," he said softly.

She shook her head. "No, I don't. It's not about nothin'."

His gaze pinned her to the wall. "It's about love, Claudie," he said slowly. "I…love…you." He said each word distinctively as if speaking to a person who didn't understand the language.

"No," she cried, spinning away. She stumbled up the slippery steps and practically clawed her way to the chair where her towel was. She wrapped it around herself, trying to hide from view. When she glanced over her shoulder, Bo hadn't moved.

With a faltering breath, she sat down in the plastic chair, her knees too shaky to support her. Neither said anything for a few minutes, then Bo waded to the side of the pool and hoisted himself out of the water. Dripping, he sat with his back to her a full minute then he said, still not looking at her, "I'm sorry that came as such a shock to you. I thought it might have been apparent when I raced from one coast to the other and halfway back trying to find you."

She closed her eyes against the tears that wanted to escape. "We're friends, Bo. That means more to me than you could possibly know. Let's not screw things up by making it more than it can be."

He turned and looked into her eyes. "Why can't it be more than that?"

She gaped, momentarily speechless. "Because of who I am. What I did for a living." She let out an epithet she'd promised Sara to banish from her vocabulary.

He held up his hand. "I get the picture. You have your past. I have mine. I was a drunk. Not a classy, pleasantly inebriated sot. An in-the-gutter, can't-remember-my-name barfly."

"Don't, Bo." Claudie covered her face with her hands. She didn't want to hear his confession. It hurt too much.

She heard him stand and walk to her side. He placed his hand on her bare shoulder and the touch went clear through to her heart. "The point is we're perfect for each other," he said, his tone gentle and slightly mocking. "But I'm not telling you anything you don't already know. You're just not ready to admit it, yet." He took his hand away. "That's okay. I can wait."

She wanted to deny his words, tell him to go to hell, but her throat was too tight to speak. When she looked at him, he smiled—his easygoing Bo smile. "Let's hit the hot tub before bed. I don't know about you, but I'm a little tense."

Claudie followed, but she was pretty sure she was already in hot water where Bo was concerned, and probably in over her head as well.

"I BROUGHT a couple of bottles of white wine from the minibar, if you want them," Bo said, carrying two small bottles and one water glass in his hand as he approached the spa. He'd returned to the room ostensibly to call Ren, but in truth he needed to give his libido a break. If he was still drinking, he'd have cracked open a whole row of tiny bottles just to numb his mind.

Claudie, who was already sitting amidst the noisy cauldron of bubbles, gave him a suspicious look. "Why? Are you trying to get me drunk?"

He set the bottles on the green plastic lawn an arm's length from the spa and shrugged off his shirt. Despite the towel he'd wrapped around his middle, the bottom of the shirt was damp. He tossed it over a nearby chair. "No," he told her, stepping down into the near-scalding water. "I thought you might like some wine but wouldn't feel comfortable taking something from the minibar in your room since it might obligate you to be nice to me."

He meant his tone to be light and teasing but she winced as though he'd caught her in a lie. "You don't have to drink it. I just thought it might help you sleep."

She glanced at the wine bottles a second then sighed. "Thank you," she said in a small voice. Drawing her feet up to the concrete bench, she moved incrementally—as if each inch sealed a bargain with the devil. Squatting to keep as much of her body underwater as possible, she reached out, her back to Bo.

Bo couldn't help but stare. Water cascaded down her long, delicate neck to stream over her shoulders. A summer tan line was dissected by the skinny blue tie of her bikini. Her shapely hips and creamy skin invited touch. He sank down immersing his head underwater.

He held his breath as long as possible. When he resurfaced, Claudie was looking at him, glass in hand. "Thanks," she said gesturing in a toast. "You're right. I'd never have opened the bar—even knowing you wouldn't have minded. I learned a long time ago there's no such thing as a freebie."

Bo kept his sigh to himself. He watched her sip her wine and slowly melt in place, head back in pleasure.

He stretched his legs, resting them on the bench beside her. A jet of water pummeled the tense muscles between his shoulder blades. "This feels great, doesn't it?"

"What did Ren say?" she asked, her gaze studying him in a way he wasn't used to.

"He didn't answer. Must have turned the phone off." Bo shrugged. "No big deal."

Neither of them spoke for some time, then Claudie asked, "Will you and Matt room together tomorrow night?"

Bo didn't know what to read into her tone. Was it at all wistful or was that just his imagination? "I told him to try to book three rooms if he could. I can sleep almost anywhere when I have to, but since this trip is more like a vacation than work I figure we should get something nice."

She snorted. "In Topeka maybe, but there's not a lot to choose from in Otter Creek. Val told me last night she went back once to bury her stepfather's ashes and couldn't believe how small it seemed. The only motel had closed up. She and her mom stayed in a bed-and-breakfast that some lady from Boston set up."

As wrapped up as he'd been in the search for her, Bo
hadn't really given their destination much thought. "Well, if
it's not available, we'll get a motel in Topeka and commute.
You don't have any other relatives around that you could
stay with, do you?"

She shook her head. "I never knew my mother's family.
She had two younger sisters but we never met them. My
stepfather told us he tried calling Mom's parents in Michigan after she died, but whoever he talked to said my grandparents had died and her sisters had moved. I don't know if
that's true, but I believed it at the time."

"What about your stepdad's family?"

"He claimed to be an orphan. Mom used to say that was
why he wasn't much of a father—he'd never had a good role
model." She polished off her wine with a gulp and set the
glass behind her.

She looked at him with a peculiar, speculative glint in her
eye and Bo's heart missed a beat. "Want a foot rub?" she
asked.

His feet immediately started itching. "I beg your pardon?"

"You heard me," she muttered, grabbing his left foot so
sharply he almost lost his seating. He jammed his hands to
the bench.

"Sure," he said, trying to be casual—although there was
nothing casual about his reaction to her.

Holding his breath, he closed his eyes and savored the rich,
provocative sensations emanating from her touch. Her
thumbs plied the sole of his foot. Her nails zigzagged across
his instep in a way that made his groin tighten.

"That's nice," he said, gratified by the control he was able
to achieve.

She nodded, seemingly lost in her task. "I knew a girl
who went to massage school. She said massaging the foot is

like giving a minimassage to the whole body because all the nerves wind up there."

"I believe it," he said gruffly.

She looked up. Whatever she saw in his face must have unnerved her because she let his foot drop with a splash and she reached behind her to crack open the second wine. "Just a sec," she said, taking a big sip. She took a second for good measure then picked up his other foot.

"You have nice feet," she said.

"I do?" Bo asked, snorting skeptically. "I don't think anybody's ever told me that."

"You do. I used to be able to tell a lot about a man by his feet. Men who wore ratty shoes and bad socks usually had smelly feet with corns and blisters and calluses. Men who wore good shoes took better care of themselves overall and they had nicer feet."

"Did that make them better men?"

"How could it? They were with me, weren't they?"

Bo sighed. He hated it when she put herself down. "You know, Claudie, there were two schools of thought among policemen when it came to prostitution. One believed hookers were low-life scum out to rip off innocent men." He snorted and shook his head. He'd clashed more than once with the group he considered narrow-minded hypocrites. "The rest of us saw working girls as the victims, doing what it took to get by. The problem came with drugs. There are a lot of junkies out there who sell their bodies to get a fix and if they get desperate, things can get ugly."

She stopped massaging. "I saw a girl overdose once. It scared the living crap right out of me." She shuddered.

She looked so remorseful he automatically reached out and pulled her to him. That she came without resistance spoke volumes. He moved slightly so her body was aligned beside his, but separated by the forceful wash of the jet. She kept her chin down.

"Relax, Claudie," he told her, trying to lighten the mood. "I promise not to make a move on you." He turned sideways. "Here. Let me rub your shoulders. It's hard to get the jets up high enough without drowning."

She took the deep breath of a person facing a firing squad.

The water added a novel dimension to the sensation of touching her. Those rare times she'd tolerated his touch, Bo had been struck by her skin's soft, chamoislike feel. Moisture turned it as fluid as satin.

"You have pretty skin," he told her, his voice husky.

She stilled his hands by placing her fingers atop his.

"Does that hurt?" he asked.

After a minute of silence, she shifted slightly and looked over her shoulder at him. "Would you kiss me? Just once?"

Bo wanted that more than anything, but he'd never in his life been more terrified of the outcome.

What a stupid thing to ask! Claudie silently berated herself.

Even though Bo didn't answer immediately, Claudie sensed his reluctance. She would have jumped out of the hot tub to hide her mortification, but his hands gripped her shoulders, as if suddenly fearful of something. When she looked into his eyes, she caught a glimpse of anxiety. *Bo's afraid? Of what? Me?*

"There's nothing in the world I want more," Bo said, his voice weaving itself into the very fiber of her being. "But I don't want to blow it."

Claudie suddenly felt brave. She turned, balancing one hip on the concrete step. "It doesn't have to be a big deal," she told him, pleased by how normal her voice sounded. "Just a little—"

He cut her off by leaning forward and placing his lips on hers. At the same time his hand went around her back, gently cupping her rib cage. He didn't pull or grasp. His mouth was warm and sweet, tender in a way she'd never known. That tenderness was more seductive than any words or promises—it gave her permission to explore her own reactions and test new boundaries.

She opened her mouth and touched her tongue to his lips and teeth. He tilted his head to give her freer access but didn't engage his tongue with hers. She leaned closer, reveling in the adventure. She'd never liked kissing. This was not only joyful it was sexy. She felt a moist heat between her legs that had nothing to do with the hot tub.

Startled by the intensity of her reaction, she jerked back. Bo's hand kept her from falling off the bench. He opened his eyes. "Are you okay?" he asked.

She nodded, not trusting her voice. It was a lie, of course. She was in bad shape—longing for something she couldn't have and she wasn't doing Bo any favor by leading him on.

"Bo…" she began, but he interrupted her.

"Can we talk about this tomorrow? I'm beat."

Claudie shrugged. A reprieve. She vowed to spell things out in the morning. Bo couldn't love her and she couldn't love him—even if his kiss was the most tantalizing sensation she'd ever known.

CHAPTER SEVEN

CLAUDIE STALLED for as long as she dared. She'd agreed to meet Bo at eight-thirty in the lobby where a continental breakfast was being served. Last night, after that stupid kiss, she would have agreed to anything that got her out of his sight, but now she was sweating their upcoming face-to-face.

The morning after, she thought grimly, *and nothing even happened.*

But it could have. Claudie had to admit she'd been tempted in a way that wasn't good. In fact, it was scary. Lying awake before dawn she'd asked herself if she ought to run away, try starting over where no one knew of her past. She'd done it before; she could do it again. Maybe she'd find a man— someone who didn't know the grim reality of her past. Maybe with a stranger, she could make a life that included sex.

Unfortunately, she thought, he'd have to be someone she didn't care for as deeply as she did Bo. No way could she bring herself to share her used and damaged body with anyone as wonderful as Bo.

But how could she make Bo understand that? How could she get it through his thick head she was doing him a favor by rejecting his declaration of love?

Love. She paced to the window and gazed at the cars in the parking lot. Love was for people like Ren and Sara, not someone like her. Stifling a sigh, Claudie bent down and picked up her bag. She started out the door. No more pussyfooting around, she decided. We're going to settle this once and for all.

She followed her nose to the motel's dining area where Bo sat—a newspaper in one hand, a forkful of scrambled eggs in the other. Claudie ignored the twelve-foot long buffet and marched directly to his table.

"Bo, we're friends. You think you want to be *more* than friends but trust me, it isn't gonna happen," she said, speaking in a strident tone.

Bo lowered his newspaper but finished lifting the forkful of eggs to his mouth. He chewed and swallowed with irritating slowness then flashed her his most heart-stopping grin. "Good morning, Claudie," he said, reaching for his coffee cup. "How'd you sleep? I slept great. Must have been the hot tub."

She frowned. "I'm serious, Bo. You can't pretend you didn't say what you said."

One brow shot up. "Who's pretending? I meant every word. Want me to say it again in front of witnesses?" He started to rise, as if intending to announce his feelings to the neighboring tables.

Claudie rushed forward and put a hand on his shoulder to push him back down. He seemed startled and gave in without resistance. She quickly fell into the closest chair. Leaning forward, she pleaded, "Bo, quit. Just quit."

He cocked his head. "Quit what?"

"Everything." Her heart was beating too hard to think clearly. If only he wouldn't wear that hurt puppy dog look. It got to her every time.

"Bo," she said, wishing his cowlick didn't tweak the hair at the crown of his head in that Little Rascal way. She could hardly resist reaching out to pat it back down. "You know me,

Bo. I don't do the boyfriend-girlfriend thing. I can't. Even if I did, I wouldn't be any good at it. Trust me. The only guy I ever dated dumped me at a truck stop in Oklahoma without even saying goodbye."

She couldn't prevent the twinge of pain that always accompanied the memory of seeing Darren Blains—her first love—hunkered down like a convict at the window of a northbound bus. A sympathetic ticket agent told her he'd confessed that he sold his Chevy Malibu to the garage owner who was supposed to be replacing its fuel pump. "Believe me, honey," the clerk had told her, "you're better off without a weenie like that."

Bo's sudden smile caught her off guard. "What?" she asked, mesmerized by the understanding look in his eyes.

"I just got it. The reason you back away any time I get close is that you're afraid I'll love you and leave you."

Her stomach turned over. "What kind of dumb mumbo jumbo is that?"

He took a sip from his cup. "Not only did I take a psychology course in college, I knew a girl who was a head case. She dated like mad but never stuck with the same guy for more than two months."

"Were you one of 'em?" Claudie asked, despite herself.

Bo shook his head. "Nah. We just frequented the same bars. One night, she spilled out her life story. Classic abandonment issues. Her father killed her mother when she was a baby and she was raised by her elderly grandparents who died before she was out of high school. Her shrink said the reason she couldn't keep a boyfriend was *subconsciously* she didn't trust anyone to love her without leaving, so she left first to avoid being hurt."

Claudie frowned. "What's that got to do with me?"

"You're so sure I'm like every other guy you've ever known, you're afraid to give me a chance."

She sat up straighter. "I'm not afraid of anything."

He looked at her over the rim of his cup. "Sure you are. We all are. When it comes to love it's the nature of the game, but you gotta play."

"Who says?"

He looked momentarily abashed then threw back his head and laughed. "Matt's right. You are a pistol."

His joy was even harder to swallow than his hurt. "Let's go."

"I'm not done with my coffee."

She took the cup from his fingers and finished off the inch of lukewarm liquid in one gulp. Its insipid sweetness nearly choked her. "Good Lord, that's disgusting," she sputtered.

"I like it sweet."

She made a face and shuddered. "Nobody likes it *that* sweet."

He grinned as though she'd just awarded him a medal. "Exactly my point. I'm unique. Which means I'm the one person in the world you *should* date."

He looked so smug she had to laugh—which, for some reason, seemed to be the impetus he needed to move. He picked up the suitcase beside his chair then grabbed hers and started out the door.

Shaking her head, Claudie followed. He had one thing right—there was nobody like Bo.

BO FIGURED they'd make Kansas before dark—well within the time frame he'd given Matt when they talked that morning. Matt planned to spend the day in Topeka putting together a dossier on Garret Anders then he'd get rooms for them in Otter Creek.

Bo glanced at the clock on the dash. He'd offered to buy lunch in Des Moines but Claudie had waved off the suggestion, totally engrossed in exploring her mother's jewelry box. Every once in a while she would exclaim over some bauble with a bittersweet "I remember this!" or an amused "Major ugly!" Twice she'd held up a glittery piece and given Bo a history of its significance in her mother's life.

Bo was actually beginning to feel as though he knew Peggy Anders through her collection of costume jewelry.

"Are you ready for lunch?" Bo asked.

Claudie set aside the box's removable tray and poked her finger into the cluttered jumble below. "Huh?" She glanced up.

Bo made a rubbing motion on his belly. "Feed me."

Her eyes went wide. "Oh!" She looked around. "Sure. Stop anywhere you want."

Her chin dropped and she went back to her mining. "Ooh, what's this?" she said holding up a tattered, dollar-bill sized manila envelope. "Look. It says Claudine on it."

Bo's stomach rumbled but not from hunger. He noticed Claudie's fingers were shaking as they flipped up the metal clasp.

She held open her left hand and poured the contents into her palm. A thin gold necklace spilled between her fingers before a golden heart about the size of a fifty-cent piece landed with a hollow clink.

"It's beautiful," Bo said. "It looks old."

"It's lovely, but I don't remember ever seeing my mother wear it." She held it up to the light. "It's engraved. M.A.R. and J.L.S." She gave him a pensive frown. "M.A.R. Margaret Ann Robertson. My mother's maiden name, but the other isn't Garret."

"Maybe it's your father's," Bo said softly.

Claudie shrugged as if it didn't matter. Using her nail, she had to pry open the stubborn latch. A slight peep escaped from her lips when a gossamer lock of hair fell out.

"Your baby hair, I bet," Bo said. "My mother has a hunk of my hair pasted in my baby book."

"I never had a baby book," Claudie said in a small voice.

Bo would have given anything to pull off the road and hug her, but after her speech at breakfast he didn't think she'd appreciate it. She didn't want their relationship to get any more complicated, and he'd promised her brother he wouldn't do anything to hurt her.

"Is there a picture of you?" Bo asked, craning his neck to peek.

Claudie shook her head and held it up for him to see. A young man's face stared back. Unsmiling. Black and white. Obviously snipped from a yearbook.

"Wow," he said. "Your dad. He's handsome."

Claudie didn't say anything. She hastily pressed the small golden curl back into the heart and snapped it shut. She held it a moment as if trying to decide what to do next.

Bo was about to suggest she put it on when Claudie exclaimed, "Oh, my gosh, look at that!"

Out of the corner of his eye, Bo saw a billboard but he couldn't read the print. "What'd it say?"

"This is where they filmed that movie, *The Bridges of Madison County*. Sara and I read the book." She looked around as if expecting to see one materialize over the highway. When none appeared, she reassembled the jewelry box and dumped it on the back seat. Almost as an afterthought she slipped the golden locket over her head. "Bo, I wouldn't mind seeing the bridge. Sara would really get a kick out of this. I think the sign said something about a park. Maybe it's on the map." She reached under the seat for the atlas.

"You know we're a little pressed for time…." Bo began, but her delighted squeal cut him off.

"It's close, Bo. Really close. Ten or fifteen miles off the highway. I'm sure we could eat there, too. Can we stop?"

Bo couldn't resist the glimmer of anticipation in her eyes. He followed her directions to Winterset, Iowa.

The detour itself wasn't long or even too far out of the way, but once she got there, Claudie didn't seem to want to leave. Bo wasn't sure what was going on in her head.

"Seen enough yet?" he asked two hours later as he followed her toward the red, hundred-foot bridge that somehow seemed vaguely familiar even though he knew he'd never seen it before.

This bridge, the Roseman Covered Bridge, was their second stop. The first had been the eighty-foot Cutler-Donahoe Bridge in Winterset's municipal park where Bo had polished off two hot dogs and one chocolate malt while Claudie explored. Just when he thought they were done sightseeing, Claudie announced her desire to visit the bridge where Francesca, the heroine of the book, left a note for Robert Kincaid, the hero.

They found it without a problem, but the bridge itself didn't seem all that romantic to Bo. However, he decided it was worth the stop to see Claudie strolling toward the weathered red structure, its yawning mouth welcoming her in an oddly benevolent way. In hiking boots, snug jeans and a turquoise sweater, she looked every bit the country girl, fresh and vibrant—and very appealing.

"Will you take my picture?" she asked, glancing over her shoulder.

He held up the small disposable camera.

"This place is wonderful. Just like in the book. Did you read—" she stopped midsentence, realizing her mistake.

He snickered. "Even if I *read,* I wouldn't have picked up that one."

"The Unturned Gentlemen read it," she told him, naming Sara's reading group of which Bo was a fairly recent member.

Bo gaped. "You're kidding. The guys actually read that?"

Her serious nod was negated by a playful grin that gave her away and he came close to scooping her up in his arms and kissing the daylights out of her.

"No, but Ren did," she said, leaning over the white railing to study the autumn grasses below. "He and Sara got in a big argument over it one night. Don't you remember?"

How can I be expected to remember anything when she looks so damn cute?

"Bo?" Frowning, she waited for his answer.

He tried to focus. "Yeah, I kinda remember. Ren called it sappy mush, and Sara thought it was tragically romantic, right?"

She tilted her face upward, squinting into the rafters as if checking for ghosts. "Pretty much."

A thought hit him a moment later. "It seems to me you backed Ren." She turned away, but Bo caught her telltale blush. "In fact, you said they were fools who deserved to die alone because they weren't brave enough to fight for what they had."

She started to step away into the dim interior, but Bo stopped her with a hand to her elbow. "Didn't you?"

She frowned. "Maybe. Something like that."

Bo waited for her to meet his gaze. "Why are we here, Claudie?"

Claudie sighed. "I don't know… Sara liked the book and I thought…" She didn't finish.

He looked at the locket hanging so innocently between her breasts. "Maybe it has to do with your mom," he suggested.

Claudie fingered the locket. "It wasn't the same. My mom

and dad were young. The people in the book were adults. And Robert Kincaid didn't commit suicide."

Bo shrugged. "Living the rest of your life without the woman you love sounds like suicide to me."

She looked momentarily stricken then pivoted and stomped away beneath the famed canopy. "That is such bull, Bo Lester," she yelled. Her voice echoed in an eerie way.

"How am I supposed to know?" he muttered, walking in the other direction. "I didn't even read the book." Of course, a part of him knew neither of them was talking about a book, but he wasn't ready to consider what his life might look like if he couldn't convince her to return his love.

She didn't join him at the car for a good twenty minutes. Bo would have been worried if this were anywhere but peaceful, idyllic Iowa. He looked up when he heard her coming. Her walk was slow and lazy but the way she had her arms wrapped around her middle suggested she was cold.

"Too bad we lost our sun," he said, conversationally. "I hope that doesn't mean we're going to get hit with a snowstorm."

She looked skyward. "God, I hope not. I already lost a day to snow. I guess we'd better get going, huh?"

Bo opened the passenger door for her. "The lady at the hot dog stand said there are five more bridges."

She shook her head. "No thanks. This is just about all the romance I can handle," she said with a self-deprecating chuckle.

"I wouldn't beat myself up about it if I were you. I figured out the real reason you wanted to come here."

She looked up, her chin tilted in a questioning look.

"To put off the inevitable."

Her color rose. "You mean…"

Bo squatted beside the door. He placed her camera in her

lap then reached out to touch her chin. She trembled but didn't pull back. "Claudie, let's just drop this stuff about us for the time being. It was stupid of me to bring it up. I told you how I feel and I meant it, but this isn't the right time to get into it. You came all this way to do something important, and you don't need anything else to worry about. Okay?"

She nodded. "But—"

Her reply was so Claudie he couldn't stop himself. He leaned in and kissed her. Just a soft, sweet peck. At least, that was what he intended. And he'd have managed to keep it platonic if she hadn't let out a small cry and put her arms around his neck.

He sensed her need even if he didn't understand it. He tried to give her what she wanted without taking anything for himself but the sweetness of her taste, the softness of her lips and the low moan trapped in her throat made him deepen the kiss. His fingers toyed with a lock of hair at the nape of her neck. "Maybe this place is more romantic than I realized," he whispered. "But," he sighed. "We'd better hit the road or we'll never find the B-and-B Matt booked." Matt had called while Claudie was on the bridge. The Apple Blossom Inn was just off Main Street in Otter Creek, Kansas. Three of the inn's five rooms belonged to them for as long as needed.

He could hear Claudie's chortle as he dashed around the car and hopped in the driver's seat. "What's so funny about that?"

"You've obviously never seen Otter Creek. You couldn't get lost if you tried. Believe me, I know. I tried."

He started the car and backed around. They weren't far from the highway. With any luck they'd catch up with Matt in time for dinner. As much as he enjoyed spending time with Claudie, he was looking forward to having another person around to run interference.

Maybe that was how he'd been able to sublimate his feelings for her all these months, Bo thought. The two of them had almost never been alone. Between Brady and his parents and the girls at One Wish House, Bo and Claudie had nonstop chaperons. Maybe, deep down, he told himself, that was why he'd insisted Matt join him on this trip. *So much for Mr. Altruism,* he thought dryly.

CLAUDIE HATED to wake Bo, but her purse was on the floor behind his seat and she needed money for the toll. Taking her foot off the accelerator, she leaned to the right, reaching behind the seat. The movement brought her practically face-to-face with him.

He moved—a catlike, lazy stretch that made her smile. She'd once awakened him accidentally on his houseboat when they'd been baby-sitting Brady. She'd inched close enough to study his face—something she'd never dared do if he were awake. Even asleep, she felt as though he might know what she was doing, how she felt about him.

"Hi," Bo said, yawning. "I fell asleep, huh?"

"Twenty miles ago," she told him, moving back to her side of the car. "Can you reach behind the seat and grab my purse? We need change for the toll."

His brow shot up. "We're crossing the river?"

"We will eventually. This is a toll road."

He sat up. "You gotta pay to drive on it?"

She nodded.

"How much?"

"I don't know. Just get some money out, will you?"

The tollbooth was designed for speed. She paid the fee and off they went. "That wasn't so bad."

"Totally un-American," he grouched.

She chuckled. "Like you don't pay taxes."

"I pay my share and half of everybody else's, which is why I don't think I should have to pay to drive on my own roads."

"Yeah, but you're not in California anymore. This is Kansas." Saying the word aloud hit her in a way she wasn't expecting. A rush of memories took her breath away.

Bo sat up suddenly and leaned close. "Claudie. Are you okay? What's the matter, love?"

She hauled in a ragged breath, tightening her grip on the steering wheel. "I'm fine. Just a little reality check."

Bo pointed to the side of the road. "Pull over. I'll drive the rest of the way."

Claudie started to protest. She knew the way, she was the one who should drive, but her arguments never made it to her lips. Stifling a groan, she eased the car to the shoulder. Bo was out and around to her door before she could change her mind.

"This is silly," she said, climbing out.

He pulled her into a quick hug that set her heart racing. "No. It's what I'm here for. Now, you concentrate on telling me where to go—isn't that what you dream of?"

His grin was too infectious to resist. She smiled back then dashed around to the passenger side. She knew at that moment just how glad she was to have him with her. Maybe she'd survive this after all.

AT THE SOUND of a soft knock, Matt looked up from Bo's laptop. "Your other folks just got here, Mr. Ross. I seen the car lights," Mrs. Green said.

The fifty-something owner of the Apple Blossom Inn was a dynamo who'd been running Otter Creek's lone bed-and-breakfast single-handedly since her husband's stroke. Mr. Green, a docile figure with a distant look, followed her around like a puppy.

"Thank you," Matt said. "I'll be right there."

At his inquiry about a local library, the friendly innkeeper had offered him the use of the desk in the study as well as a phone line for his modem. From that spot Matt had been able to amass most of what Bo wanted to know.

He saved his files and exited the program.

Strolling to the foyer, he braced himself for his first glimpse of the infamous Claudie St. James. Matt didn't consider himself a prude, but he couldn't quite fathom how his cousin could be in love with a woman with her kind of past. He'd formulated a mental image of her—and, frankly, it wasn't too flattering.

Matt opened the door and walked outside. The brisk night air was an eye-opener—as was the woman gracefully stepping from the passenger side of the small station wagon. Petite, young and vulnerable were Matt's first impressions.

"Yo, Cuz, we finally made it," Bo called, hauling himself out of the car. Matt thought the joviality in his voice sounded a bit forced.

"'Bout time. Mrs. Green was going to rent your room to someone else," Matt teased.

"Room?" Claudie questioned, her eyes saucerlike in the light from the porch.

Matt heard a tremor in that single word that spoke multitudes.

Bo hurried around the car and stood at her side without touching her. "Rooms," he said, looking to Matt to confirm.

Claudie's apprehension was further broadcast in the look she gave Matt. He walked down the steps, stopping at the gravel driveway. "Your room is on the top floor, Claudie," he said, pointing over his shoulder.

The turn-of-the-century home featured a third story built into the roofline. Three dormer windows were backlit in a soft amber glow; lace curtains added an old-world charm. "Mrs. Green says it's the nicest room in the house in winter."

Claudie stared upward. "Two old maids owned this house when I lived here. My brothers said they kept the dried-up remains of their folks in that room."

Bo hooted. "Bet that's not a rumor the owners want circulated."

Matt couldn't quite get over the fragility he sensed in her. He was expecting brash and brazen, not sad and reserved. "Your room is called the Golden Delicious suite. Bo's in Jonathan, and I'm in Winesap."

Her face—pretty, but certainly not provocative—screwed up as if certain he were pulling her leg.

"No, seriously," he said. "Mine's Winesap. My other option was the Pink Lady. The Fuji was already rented."

She smiled, and for the first time met his gaze. *Oh,* Matt silently acknowledged. He glanced at his cousin who grinned as if reading Matt's mind.

"Claudie, you've just met Matthew Ross, my cousin. Matt, Claudie," Bo said. He didn't give them time to shake hands. "Help me with these bags, Cuz. I need food. Claudie refused to stop for dinner. She said we'd wasted too much time at the bridges." He opened the rear passenger door and withdrew a large white box, which he handed to Claudie.

Matt followed him to the rear of the wagon. "What bridges?"

"Don't ask," Bo and Claudie replied simultaneously.

Naturally, Matt couldn't wait to pry the story out of Bo.

Bo passed Matt the smaller of the suitcases and a small, lumpy backpack. "The place looks great. You did good, Cuz," Bo said, clapping a hand to his shoulder.

"The only other choice was a motel by the highway. This looked more like what you wanted," Matt said, trying to

watch Claudie without appearing to. She stopped at the foot
of the steps to take a deep breath. The wraparound porch was
outfitted with a big swing and half a dozen wicker chairs.
Light from the divided windows spilled out in a warm, inviting way.

When he noticed her shiver, he said, "We better get you
inside to warm up. I picked up some take-out chicken in Topeka, so you won't have to go out again."

"Awesome," Bo said, following a few steps behind.

Matt slipped the strap of the backpack over his left shoulder to free up his right hand for the banister. The small weakness embarrassed him so he covered it by telling Claudie, "I'll
show you to your room."

From the step ahead, she looked back, her expression
droll. "It's up, right? I should be able to find it."

Matt blushed.

"Let him do it, Claudie," Bo scolded playfully. "His
mother was a stickler for manners. Mine wasn't that picky."

She shrugged, her shoulder barely moving the bulky sweater
that looked more college student than reformed hooker. By con-
centrating on his knee, Matt cleared the four steps successfully.

Once inside, there were more introductions when Mr. and
Mrs. Green joined them. Mrs. Green offered them the use of
the kitchen and went ahead to set things out.

Since there was no elevator, they were obliged to trudge
up the wide, carpeted stairs. Each step was a potential prat-
fall for Matt. He tried to cover his discomfort by giving Bo
a spiel about the town.

"Otter Creek was settled in 1886. There are conflicting stories about how it got its name, but legend has it there once
were otters in the nearby waterway, which, by the way, is not
named Otter Creek. Did we bet on that?" he asked, pausing
to look at his cousin.

"Put it on my bill."

"Zach told me he saw an otter in the creek behind our house one day," Claudie said. "Yancy insisted it was a dog. They got in a big fight over it and my fa— Garret made them hoe the entire garden as punishment."

Matt pictured the wealth of information he'd accumulated about the man whose name she could barely bring herself to speak. Sympathy for what she was facing made him say, "Bo told me you met with your brothers and sister. Weren't they interested in coming back with you?"

She flashed him a sharp look. "I started this. It's my problem, not theirs."

He stopped before a door painted a deep burgundy and adorned with a pumpkin-size stenciled apple framing the word, Winesap.

"My room. Bo, yours is over there." A similar door in a different shade of red bore the name Jonathan.

"Cool," Bo said, using his key to open it. He lugged his suitcase inside and dumped it on the bed then poked his head out. "I'm going to freshen up a bit. I'll meet you in the kitchen in ten, okay?" he asked Claudie.

She nodded.

Matt led the way to the small flight of stairs at the end of the hall. Since he still held the key, he went first, trying not to wince.

He opened the pretty yellow door at the top of the stairs and walked inside. He placed the suitcase on a rack beneath the window and set the backpack on the bed. Facing Claudie, he said, "Mrs. Green says there are extra blankets—" He was stopped by the look on her face. "Is something wrong?"

Clutching her odd box as if it were a shield, she said, "I'm not the right person for your cousin, but he won't listen to me. He thinks he's in—" She swallowed without finishing the sentence. "If you care about him as much as he cares about you, you'll make him see that."

Matt's stunned response was an ambiguous nod. It was the best he could do because—for the first time—he understood what his cousin saw in this woman. Honesty. Integrity. And something he couldn't quite define.

CHAPTER EIGHT

CLAUDIE WEDGED the phone under her ear and used the hem of her T-shirt to wipe a tear from her eye. *You're being stupid, girl,* she silently scolded herself. A part of her was thrilled that One Wish House could go on without her, but another was hurt that the residents showed so little concern at her extended absence.

"Take as much time as you need, Claudie," Maya said, her voice a hollow echo from using the speakerphone in Claudie's office.

"Yeah, we'll be just fine. Don't you worry about us," Sally Rae seconded. "Not one of us has missed a single meeting since you left."

Claudie had spoken with Sara a few minutes earlier and been told everybody missed her, but obviously her friend had neglected to add the women of One Wish House were blossoming without her.

"It would be nice if you could make it back in time for the fund-raiser, but, don't worry, we can handle things if you don't," Maya said—although Claudie thought she detected a hint of trepidation. "You're going to be so proud of all the money we make."

"If I don't kill Babe Bishop first, you mean," a voice growled.

"Is that you, Rochell?" Claudie asked. "Is Babe giving you trouble? Do you want me to call her? I could—"

Maya interrupted about the same time a loud "Oof" sound came over the line. "Babe's been great, Claudie. What a trooper! She's really gotten behind the dim sum dinner. In fact, it was her idea to hold an auction, too. She and Rochell have their moments, but that's because they're so much alike."

Claudie choked on a laugh. She pictured Ren's mother's reaction to being compared to a six-foot ex-hooker.

"Claudie," a Hispanic accent cried. "How is your little sister? Did Meester Bo find you?"

He found me and he's treating me like a child, Claudie told herself. *Or a princess.* "Bo's here, along with his cousin from New York. I haven't seen my sister yet—her class was on a field trip to Washington, DC. They were supposed to get home last night. Guess what? Bo got his hands on her school yearbook and Sherry's class president."

Her friends' cheers felt good for some odd reason, even if they were for Sherry—a beautiful, smiling stranger in a one-inch-square photograph. "So when do you think you'll be coming home?" Sally Rae asked casually.

Maybe a bit too casually? Claudie thought with a spurt of hope. "Bo says he thinks we can make contact this afternoon, if I'm ready." *Am I?* She knew she couldn't put it off any longer. Her life was waiting for her back in California.

"Is Bo going with you?" Davina asked.

Claudie smiled. She and Bo had fought long and hard over this issue. In the end Bo had won—or she let him, Claudie wasn't sure which. All she knew for sure was she couldn't face Garret alone. Last night's nightmares proved that.

"Matt and Bo are setting it up so we meet in a public place where they can monitor things," she told them.

The chatting continued a few minutes—each woman doing her best to reassure Claudie that everything was perfectly fine without her. She hung up feeling torn—glad they

were showing the independence and backbone to take on
new tasks but a little sad, too. One Wish House was her baby.
She wasn't ready for it to stand alone.

The sound of crunching gravel drew her to the window.
The rental car pulled in behind her station wagon. Bo burst
from behind the driver's seat with his usual exuberance; Matt
slowly extricated himself from the passenger side.

Matt had intimidated Claudie the first night they met. So
tall and stern—a cop in casual clothing. She could sense his
disapproval. She didn't blame him and had hoped to enlist
his help in deflecting Bo's misguided love. Strangely, Matt
had loosened up in the two days they'd been in Otter Creek
and even seemed to like her. She didn't get a sense he was
making any headway with his cousin, either.

Matt looked up. He started to wave but grabbed the door
when his knee buckled. Claudie saw what Bo chose to deny.
Bo, who loved his cousin like a brother, seemed blind to
Matt's pain, his bad knee, the back twinges that came after
sitting in one position too long and his deep sadness.

Her gaze went to Bo. He also looked up, his smile bright
as the autumn sunshine. Putting both hands over his heart he
mimed a swoon then blew her a kiss. The playful gesture
made her stagger backward, her heart fluttering. Damn, that
man could be infuriating, she thought. She didn't know how
to make it any clearer that she wasn't interested in a long-term
relationship with him. Even though he'd promised to back off
until she had this ordeal behind her, he still showered her with
attention.

Even Mrs. Green commented on his obvious devotion.
"That boyfriend of yours sure does love you," the woman had
told Claudie last night when she delivered clean towels. "Reminds me of the way Mr. Green used to be, back before his
affliction."

A knock on the door shook her out of her reverie. "Come in, Bo, it's open."

"It's not Bo. He stopped to take a leak," Matt said, entering the room. He left the door open. Claudie didn't know if that was gentlemanly protocol or he was protecting his reputation. "Did you get hold of Sara Bishop?"

That had been her excuse for not accompanying the two sleuths on their reconnaissance mission. "Yes. I even talked to Brady. He loved the shirts I sent...and the dinosaur. He calls it a 'T-weck.'" She couldn't help smiling.

"Bo talks about him a lot. I think he'd like a couple of kids himself."

Claudie's stomach turned over. "Then he'd better find himself a nice woman and get married." She pulled together as much bluster as she could muster. "That's how it's done in the Midwest. You meet a woman—someone *appropriate.* You date, then you marry and have kids."

His lips thinned. "Then she meets someone better and you start over from scratch."

His bitterness was unmistakable. She sighed. "I don't think either one of us should apply for jobs at Hallmark," she said dryly.

He looked at her and smiled. "I hate to tell you this, Claudie, but I think it's too late."

The camaraderie in his friendly smile threw her. "Too late for what?"

"Too late to *save* Bo." He said the word with wry inference. "He's a goner. Head over heels in love with you."

"Goddamn it," Bo said, stomping into the room. "I told you not to tell her that. She has enough on her mind without worrying about my feelings. We've already had this conversation, haven't we, Claudie?"

The first time they had this conversation she'd been

tempted to bolt. This time she laughed. "Yes, but you're incorrigible. I should have known you'd blab to the whole world."

Smiling, he strolled toward her. "Not the whole world. Just Matt. And Sara and Ren."

She jumped back before he could touch her. "You told Sara and Ren?" *That would explain Sara's overly cheerful attitude on the phone.*

He grimaced. "Yes. But they already knew."

She noticed Matt was stifling a grin. "How'd they know?"

Bo shrugged. "I'm transparent?"

She barked out a laugh. "You always told me you were invisible. It's not the same." She looked to Matt for confirmation. "Is it?"

Matt chuckled. "In Bo's case it might be." He walked to the chair by the desk and sat down, then said soberly, "If you two could drop the debate for a few minutes, I think we need to discuss this afternoon's strategy."

Claudie looked at Bo, and it took every ounce of willpower she possessed not to run to his arms and disappear.

"DO YOU THINK she'll be okay?" Bo asked his cousin while they waited for Claudie to join them in the parlor.

"She'll be fine. She's strong, Bo. God, when I think of all she's been through…" He shook his head. "She's doing fantastic."

Matt's approval meant a lot to Bo and his endorsement of Claudie was gratifying, even if it surprised Bo a little. "You sure turned around fast," he observed.

Matt looked down to check his watch. Bo thought he detected a blush—something you didn't see too often on Matt. "Yeah, well, maybe my experiences with Sonya left me prejudiced against women. Claudie's a decent person. And you have to respect her motives for coming back here. I give her credit for that—even if I'm not sure it's the right thing."

Bo frowned. "I don't think she appreciated that bit about 'letting nature take its course.'" Word on the street had it that Garret Anders was dying of prostate cancer. Claudie wasn't moved. "Good," she'd said when informed of the rumor. "I hope that means he has erectile dysfunction, too."

Matt shrugged. "It was her call. I only wanted to give her an out if she was having second thoughts. You know what it's like once you open a can of worms." Matt started toward the kitchen where Mrs. Green kept a pot of coffee going at all times. "I'll be back in a minute."

Once he was gone, Bo walked to the window. Pulling aside the lace curtain, he stared unseeing at the yard and the empty street. He wasn't going to argue with Claudie about meeting Anders, but he wondered if he'd done the right thing by not giving her all the details he and Matt had learned about the man. According to the Topeka radio station that sponsored Anders's weekly "Man in God" radio program, Anders was one of their most popular evangelists. "He's a saint, but human," the programming coordinator had told Bo.

When Bo had tried summarizing the results of their investigation last night, Claudie had railed at him. "That's total bullshit, Bo. I knew him for seventeen years and he was a jerk. A pissant, little jerk. He kept my mother barefoot and pregnant. He was a rotten father—cruel and mean and so *un*-Christian it's pathetic."

They'd gone for a walk after dinner because she'd told him she was having a hard time sleeping and he thought the fresh air would be good for her. The air was a little chillier than he'd counted on. "I'm not saying he was a good father," he'd countered, feeling guilty about not divulging the extent of the man's philanthropy. "Zach said the same thing, but—"

"Did Zach tell you about the time Garret hit him with a shovel?" she'd asked her voice as bitter as the breeze.

"No."

Her small laugh sent a shiver up his spine. "One day—we were living in Illinois, I think—we had a snowstorm. It was Zach's job to shovel the sidewalk before school, but we overslept and would have missed the bus if he'd taken time to do it, so Mom said he could do it after school."

Bo had used the slight tremor in her voice as an excuse to hold her hand. Her fingers were like icicles.

"When we got home, Garret was already there. I told Zach I'd help him shovel it real fast. Garret waited until the school bus was out of sight then he came outside and started yelling."

Bo had felt a tremor pass through her body. Since they'd almost reached the inn, he pulled her up the steps and led her to the porch swing where he could wrap an arm around her shoulders. To his surprise, she'd cuddled against him for one brief minute then stiffened, putting an inch between them before going on with her story.

"I was closest to the door when he came outside, but for once he wasn't interested in me. He grabbed the shovel out of my hand as he walked by and marched to where Zach was shoveling. Zach didn't hear him coming. Garret hit him squarely between the shoulder blades with the flat part of the shovel." She clapped one hand to the other in a crack that echoed in the stillness.

"Didn't your mother try to stop him?" Bo had asked, his stomach twisting at the image.

"No. But I did."

Her words chilled him to the bone. "What happened?"

"He pushed me down and held my face in the snow. I couldn't breathe. I thought I was going to die, but Mom saw what was happening and came outside. He let me go the minute she said his name—it was like throwing a switch. Jekyll and Hyde."

Bo had pulled her close and gave the swing a push. The gentle rocking motion seemed to help her relax. "That's why I'm going to be with you tomorrow," he'd told her. "Your mother isn't here to flip switches."

He'd waited for her to argue, but she didn't. Instead, she snuggled a fraction closer and pointed to the night sky.

"Do you see those stars?" she'd asked. "The three in a row?"

He'd had to lean down to see past the roof. The proximity brought him her scent—lemon shampoo and baby powder. "Do you mean Orion's belt?"

"Mom called them the Three Sisters. She said whenever she looked at them she thought of her three girls—Valery, Sherry and me."

"Which one is you?" he asked, brushing his lips over her silky hair.

"The big one, of course," she'd answered with a giggle. "Big and bossy."

He hadn't been able to stop himself from leaning down and kissing her. Her lips were cold but not unwelcoming.

To draw her closer, he'd slipped his hand inside her open jacket and splayed his fingers against her spine. She'd stiffened momentarily then sighed against his lips, a deep throaty hum that made him a little crazy.

He'd trailed kisses along her jaw to her neck, thrilling when she tilted her head back to give him access to the pulse point throbbing at the neckline of her sweater. A kiss, a nibble, a car rumbling down the street.

Claudie had bolted like a shoplifter caught in the act, not stopping until she reached the porch railing. Her angry scowl looked accusatory.

"Claudie," he'd said as equitably as possible, "it was only a kiss."

Stubbornly, she'd shaken her head—the angry, suspicious woman he'd first met ten months ago in Sacramento. "I told you this wouldn't work. Sex ruins things."

Bo's heart had crimped from the pain he heard in her voice. He'd have given anything to take her upstairs and prove her wrong, but he knew she needed time to learn to trust—not only him, but also her feelings.

She'd braced her shoulders for an argument, but he rose and walked to her before she could speak again. After delivering a quick, friendly peck on the lips, he'd told her, "I love Claudie. And if you need time to learn to love her, too, then I'll wait."

As he opened the door of the inn, he'd heard her mutter something about "hell freezing over." Grinning, he'd called over his shoulder, "Lucky me. I packed my ice skates."

"Here she comes," Matt said, bringing Bo back to the present. He hadn't even heard his cousin return. *I must be in love. I'm totally out of it.*

Bo turned and looked toward the open staircase. She'd dressed with care—navy woolen slacks and a burgundy sweater set. Her short blond locks were feathered off her face courtesy of a blow dryer. Her only jewelry was the gold locket.

"You look perfect," Matt said, beating Bo to the punch.

Bo gave him a dirty look and grabbed her jacket from the hall tree. "You'll dazzle him. Are you feeling dazzling?"

She gave him a plucky smile. "Yeah—like a forty-watt bulb."

He held her coat for her and added a quick hug before she could escape. "Don't worry," he whispered. "I won't let him hurt you again."

CLAUDIE REPEATED Bo's promise like a prayer the whole way to Harrah's, the nearby Potowatami casino where Matt had set up the meeting, without telling Garret the true agenda. He'd used the ploy that he was a freelance writer working on a piece about God and gambling.

Claudie had balked at the idea of meeting in such a busy locale, but Bo had convinced her the location worked to her benefit. "Midweek. Midafternoon. It won't be that busy. Besides, we want people around. He's got a reputation to protect. He can't afford to lose his temper in such a public place."

She'd been tempted to argue that the more people present meant more witnesses if she went bonkers and wound up killing her stepfather with her bare hands, but she knew Bo would protect her from her own demons as well as Garret's.

Matt drove. Claudie chose to sit in the back seat. She tried to focus on the rolling landscape, picturing it in spring—her mother's favorite season. The trees would have made lush green ribbons that followed the contours of the creeks and hollows. Farmers would have turned the rich black earth and started planting corn or soybeans.

"Are you doing okay?" Bo asked solicitously. He'd been so kind, so patient. She'd never known a man like him before.

"I'm fine."

He cleared his throat and looked at Matt. "You know, Claudie, Matt has a lot more information about Anders than what we told you. It was my call. Your issues haven't changed even if Anders has. But I could brief you more thoroughly if you'd rather know."

What could Bo tell her? That Garret was a different person than he was ten years ago? So was she, but that didn't alter what he'd done to her.

"No thanks. This is about the past, not the present."

Matt turned toward a large, brightly hued building that hadn't been there when Claudie lived in the area. He pulled under the massive porte cochere so she and Bo could get out. He would park and join them once Garret arrived. A blue-uniformed giant with a broad smile opened the door for her. Bo's hand at the small of her back kept Claudie from barreling in the other direction.

Noise and bright lights bombarded her overly acute senses; the acrid smell of cigarette smoke provoked a wave of nausea. "I need to use the rest room."

As if anticipating her panic, Bo led her to the appropriate door. "I'll wait right here."

Knowing Bo was waiting helped calm her nerves. She washed her hands and dried them, then touched up her lipstick. She looked in the mirror and wondered what Garret would see when he looked at her.

The plan was for Matt to meet Garret at the door and lead him to an alcove where hopefully only one or two gamblers would be. I can do this, she told herself and walked out to join Bo.

"He's here. Matt just gave me the sign. Do you want Matt to bring him over to you or would you prefer to join him and Matt in a few minutes?"

"Let Matt bring him."

Her heart was pounding so loud she barely heard the chatter of gamblers, the whir and spin of machines, the music piped over a loudspeaker.

"We're in luck. Nobody's close by. Matt and I will make sure the place stays that way," he said, his tone forbidding.

She squeezed his hand and smiled at him. "Thanks. I don't think I could have gone through with this without you."

His smile made a funny knot form in her throat. He leaned

close enough to whisper. "I know. It's because you love me, but don't tell anybody. It's a secret."

His impish grin made tears prick behind her eyes. She pushed him away. "Such ego," she tried to mutter, but even to her ears it came out like a caress.

His smile widened, but only for a second, then his game face fell into place. "Show time," he said under his breath.

Claudie spotted Matt, but she didn't recognize the man at his side. Her first thought was disappointment—Garret had sent someone else in his place, and there was a woman with him, too. Claudie glanced at Matt and saw him make a gesture with his hands that seemed to say, "Your call."

Claudie started to turn away when a voice from her past said, "Claudine?"

She spun around, bracing for an attack. Garret. Her arch nemesis. The man opposite her looked old. Gaunt and gray, his legs seemed to give out. He might have crumpled to the ground if not for the support of his companion. "What's this?" the woman asked, helping Garret to a nearby stool. "Is it who I think it is? Can it be Claudie? Praise the Lord, it is."

Her odd way of answering her own questions made Claudie forget this wasn't the way she'd planned the scene.

The woman bussed the man's almost bald pate and exclaimed, "Garret, honey, our prayers have been answered."

Claudie looked at Bo, and they both said, "Prayers?"

"Yes," Garret said his voice sounding stronger than his body suggested. "As Dottie knows, ever since I was diagnosed with cancer five years ago, I've prayed every day that I would have a chance to see you once more before I die."

An unexpected jolt from his simple, matter-of-fact statement made Claudie step backward. "Don't worry, sweetie," the woman said, reaching out imploringly. "He's not contagious. Started in the prostate but by the time they found it, it'd spread to the bone. Ain't no stoppin' it now."

"Who are you?" Claudie asked, unable to help herself.

"His wife," she said, with a beatific smile. "My name's Dottie. We've been together nine years."

A year after I left. A year after he ruined my life. "Did you know you married a rapist?" Claudie asked, the spite in her tone nearly choking her.

"It's the first thing he told me," Dottie said. Her large gray eyes seemed full of sympathy. "You poor girl. I used to work in a hospital and I saw rape victims come in all the time. My heart would just break in two."

"Then how could you bring yourself to marry somebody like him?" She pointed to where Garret sat—his skeletal frame outlined by the neon aura of a nickel slot machine.

"I forgave him," Dottie said simply. "That's what you do when someone makes a mistake—even the most awful mistake in the world. If that person truly regrets it and he gives his life to God, what else can you do?"

Claudie could think of a dozen things—all hideous and painful. "Well, that's easy for you to say. You weren't the one raped."

"No. Not by Garret. But my first husband raped me—right before he took a gun and killed our three-year-old baby girl then turned it on himself. He told me that was my punishment for not being a better wife."

Dottie dropped her chin; tears fell on the carpet like fat raindrops. Garret reached out and took her hand in a gesture of comfort. He slowly rose and advanced two steps closer to Claudie. She felt Bo edge beside her. "Claudie, girl, I accept your hate. I deserve it and I'm not looking for your forgiveness—not for myself, anyway. The Lord knows what I did and why. My anger at losing the woman I loved more than

life and knowing I was to blame for her death consumed me
like a fire. Even before your mother died, I was a poor excuse for a father, but from the day of Peggy's funeral, I went
crazy and drank myself stupid. Instead of easing my pain, it
stoked it until I wanted to hurt somebody else as much as I
hurt."

Claudie backed up, trying to block the memories that
stalked her like a panther on the prowl. "I was in the kitchen
putting away some food the neighbors had brought. More
charity." Her voice sounded miles away.

"Yep. Everybody in town knew I'd lost my job and the
bank was getting ready to foreclose. I was mad about that,
too. Poor pitiful me. Alone with five kids to raise." He paused,
shaking his head slowly from side to side. "I came home that
night and there you were. Mad as a hornet about missing
some dance."

He ran a hand over his face, as if washing away a film.
"That's when I did the most despicable thing anyone can do
to another human being short of murder. And in truth, I killed
something inside you that night. I saw the light go out in your
eyes before you ran away to your teacher's house. I wasn't
just a rapist, Claudie, I was a murderer. First your mom, then
the part of her that was in you—the sweet, loving part."

He broke down, weeping like a child. Dottie comforted
him and helped him back to the stool. For a reason that made
no sense to her, Claudie almost wished she could tell him it
was okay. But it wasn't okay. He'd ruined her life, and he deserved the hell, the cancer and pain he had to endure. She only
wished it would last longer.

"I didn't come to hear your apologies or excuses or whatever this is. Nothing you say can make up for what you did and
what I became because of you. I'm here because I want to make
sure you don't ruin another girl's life the way you did mine."

Garret looked at Dottie. Their mutual confusion angered her. "Sherry," she hissed. "My sister is almost seventeen. That's how old I was when you—"

Dottie gasped as if she'd heard pure blasphemy. "You can't possibly think Garret would hurt Sherry. Oh, goodness, child, no. You're so wrong. No."

Claudie scowled at her. "Why should I believe you? He—"

Garret seemed to rally strength from some deep source. He stepped forward, more the man she remembered and feared. "What I did to you was the last scene in a black chapter of my life, Claudie. At first, I tried to pretend to myself it never happened, but God doesn't work that way. When you told that teacher about what I did, and all hell broke loose, I lied and said you made it up. I was prepared to fight it in court. I cleaned up my act and put on a nice show for the judge.

"But when you disappeared, the truth of what I had done came back to haunt me. Less than a month after you left I ran straight into a brick wall. Literally."

Claudie was struck mute by the honesty she heard in his voice, and something else she couldn't define. Remorse? Salvation?

"I crashed the car, and to be honest I don't know if it was on purpose or an accident. Paramedics had to use the Jaws of Life to get me out, but I was awake long enough to tell them not to bother. I didn't want to go on living. And I died on the way to the hospital."

Claudie looked at Bo, who nodded. He knew about this.

Dottie took over the narrative. "I was on duty when they brought him in. That's how we met." She lowered her chin and said, seriously, "Now, I'm going to tell you something you probably won't believe, but it's God's honest truth. I saw an angel come to Garret and breathe him back to life."

"Breathe him…?" Claudie repeated.

"A white figure—it was glowing and kinda fuzzylike so I knew it wasn't another nurse. It leaned down and put its face close to Garret's and the next second he was breathing. I swear on all that's holy."

Garret nodded his confirmation. "I was dead, then I was alive. All I know for sure is that when I was dead I saw my life for what it was—a barren desert of my own making. My soul was black and shriveled like a dead bug. I'd wasted my chance at love. My greed killed my darling Peggy. It killed the child in you. And it killed me."

"You look fairly alive to me," Claudie said, trying her best to stay unmoved by his confession.

"God gave me a second chance. A chance to change. And I did."

Dottie took a step closer and clasped Claudie's hand with an exuberant cry that made Claudie shrink back. "It's true, Claudie. I witnessed it with my own eyes. He was hurt real bad, and the doctors said he'd never walk, but he did. The lawyers told him not to bother fighting for custody of his kids, but he did and he got Sherry. Valery didn't want anything to do with him, so he let her go to the family she wanted. The boys could have come home but chose to go out in the world instead. You were the only one we never could find."

Claudie yanked her hand free. "Well, I'm here now, but I don't know how much of this I believe. And even if it's true, I don't really care that you're reformed and holy and all that crap. I still wasted ten years of my life selling my body for nickels and dimes because you made me believe that's all I was worth."

Garret swayed. Bo rushed forward. "Do you need a drink of water?" he asked.

Garret nodded. Bo motioned to Matt who slipped away

into the casino. Hunched like a wizened gnome, Garret said, "I feared that might happen, Claudie. I saw a therapist regularly for two years. He helped me come to grips with my anger—a product, we learned, of my foster father's somewhat psychopathic benevolence." His rueful chuckle sent a chill down her spine. "My therapist told me that prostitution was one trap you might fall into given the abuse—verbal, emotional and physical—I'd inflicted on you over the years."

His frank assessment of his behavior seemed too staged to be true. Until she looked into his eyes. The man behind those eyes was in pain. Not the physical pain of cancer but emotional pain caused by guilt and regret.

"He told me rape is an act of violence. I took my self-loathing out on you, Claudine—the child I'd envied for sixteen years."

"Envied?"

"Dear girl, you alone had the one thing I desired more than anything—my sweet Peggy's love. Oh, I know she cared for me, and she proved it by giving me six wonderful children. But I wanted her *love*. The love she felt for the boy who was your father. Unfortunately, it took her death—and mine—to understand she'd loved me the best she could."

Claudie's breath caught in her throat; an ache started behind her eyes.

"I'd sell my soul to take it back—to change what happened, Claudie, but that's not the way God works," he said, his sad eyes boring into her. "I was given a second chance, and I used it to be a good father to Sherry. And I think I can honestly say I accomplished that."

Dottie nodded with verve. "That he did. You can ask her yourself if you don't believe us."

Claudie's mouth was too dry to speak. Fortunately, Matt arrived with a tray of glasses. She guzzled one. Garret took two small sips and handed it back. "Thank you, Matthew," he said politely.

Then he looked at Bo and said, "We haven't been introduced. You know who I am, but I don't know you."

Bo put out his hand. "Bo Lester."

Claudie looked at Garret and his wife. "Bo and Matt are friends. They're also private investigators. I ran across your Web page on the Internet, and they helped me—" The smile the couple exchanged made her ask, "What?"

Dottie answered. "The Web page was my idea. I told Garret you might get curious some day and come looking. I promised him I'd keep the page up and running even after he's gone." Her bottom lip trembled and Garret squeezed her hand. "We like to think his message is important to other lost souls, but we were really looking for you."

Claudie didn't like the way that made her feel. She resisted the softening she felt toward these people. "If I'd have wanted to find you sooner, I would have come looking."

Dottie blinked in surprise. "But we only moved back here last year. Before that we took our ministry on the road."

"How did Sherry go to school?" Bo asked, taking the words right out of Claudie's mouth.

"Home schooling," Garret said. "Dottie's a wonderful teacher. Sherry is at the top of her class. She's class president, you know," he said with a father's pride.

Suddenly Claudie was at a loss for words. She didn't know where to go with her anger, her pain. She couldn't use it to protect a girl who didn't need protecting.

Bo interceded. "I'm sure Claudie would like to talk to her sister at some point, but right now I think we should go."

Claudie didn't resist when he took her elbow.

"Wait," Garret said. "Just one more thing. Claudie, child, I was the worst father imaginable, and I don't expect you to forgive me for what I did to you. But I pray—like I've prayed every day—you'll find a way to forgive yourself."

"For what?" she cried.

"For being human. For loving me as a child loves a father. For whatever it is that you think you're to blame for. Let it go, dear girl. It wasn't you. It was never you. You were the most wonderful daughter a man could ever hope for. You helped your mother without complaining. You took all the guff I had to give with spunk. You protected your brothers and practically raised Sherry those early years. None of what happened was your fault."

Claudie would have sagged if not for Bo's support. She fought the tears that blinded her. In her mind she could see that night. Her sadness, yet there was anger, too. She was tired of being his substitute wife. She wanted to go to the prom and he'd told her they couldn't afford a dress, yet somehow there was money for booze. "If only I'd kept my mouth shut," she said, not realizing the words were spoken aloud until Garret answered.

"If not that night, then some other. My rage was so great, it was just a matter of time."

"But you called me a slut because I wanted to go to the prom with Darren. You said you knew we'd made love and I was a whore and you—"

He shook his head. "I don't remember what I said, but I'm sure it was bad because I had to make you look bad so I could justify what I was doing to you. You were never that kind of girl, Claudie, and I knew it. If you and Darren experimented sexually, it was because you were looking for someone to love you. I'm just sorry you chose someone weak like Darren. He told the police about leaving you alone in Oklahoma."

Dottie nodded sagely. "He's been divorced twice and can't

keep a job. He's a mama's boy—always has been. You were his chance to escape but he didn't have the gumption to go through with it."

"You talked to Darren?" she asked.

Garret nodded. "So did the police. They put out a missing persons report and put up your picture all over the western states. We really wanted to find you." Claudie looked at Bo. Was this the part he didn't tell her about? Would it have made a difference if she'd known?

Garret went on. "Like I said, at first I denied what I did, but after my accident I called the police and told them the truth. A judge gave me probation and ordered counseling as part of my sentence. Dottie was the one who took care of Sherry until I regained custody." He looked at his wife.

Short and round, dressed in her good, Sunday dress and sensible heels. Her scrubbed cheeks were ruddy in color, her cap of permed curls threaded with silver. "My second husband, Bill, passed away shortly after Sherry came to us," she said. "A heart attack. He and I had been foster parents for ten years on account of I couldn't have children. The authorities wanted to move her to another home, but I told them she was the angel sent to keep me from despair. And that she was."

She looked at Claudie. "You did a fine job raising that little girl."

Claudie blinked fiercely, the pain behind her eyes unbearable. Her throat ached with unshed tears. Bo pulled her to his chest and comforted her until the dry silent sobs passed.

"I'd like to see her before I go," Claudie said, her voice low and husky.

"How 'bout you all come for supper tonight?" Dottie suggested.

Claudie shook her head. "No. We're leaving tonight."

Garret spoke. "Sherry gets out of class at three-fifteen. I'll call the school and give them a message to tell her you'll be waiting by the track. Would that be better?"

Claudie nodded. She faced the man who had been her father. There was more to say, but she didn't have the words. "Goodbye."

He put out his hand but stopped short of touching her. "Thank you for coming, Claudie. Now I can meet my maker in peace."

Claudie turned away. Bo's hand never left her back; he paused when she did. She looked over her shoulder. "I can give you Zach's and Yancy's addresses if you want them. I guess you know where Val lives."

Garret gave his wife a look that seemed so full of joy it made Claudie flinch.

Sniffling, Dottie answered. "We'd like that very much. You can give them to Sherry when you see her."

Claudie started to leave, but Dottie gave a small cry and—almost as if she couldn't stop herself—barreled across the short distance to envelop Claudie in a hug. Repelled, yet somehow also comforted by the motherly gesture, Claudie gave Bo a helpless look. He put a hand on Dottie's shoulder and she backed away apologetically. "I'm sorry. I just couldn't contain myself. You truly are the answer to our prayers and you're so much more wonderful than I ever dreamed. I see your mother's spirit in you. From what Garret's told me, Peggy was a beautiful woman who loved too dearly."

Claudie looked from Dottie to Garret. "I have to go," she said flatly. Her anger was gone, but so was her focus. Without her hatred what did she have? A wasted life. An empty shell.

Bo took her hand and led her through the busy casino. Pausing to let a man in a wheelchair pass, Claudie's gaze was drawn to a brilliant Jackpot sign. A revolving board promised her a chance to be a Big Winner.

"A *winner*," she said, bitterness dripping like acid from her tongue. "What a joke! It turns out I raced halfway across the country to save poor little Sherry from squat. I make Don Quixote look sane." Her attempted laugh caught in her chest, doubling her over.

Bo pulled her to him, stifling her sobs. "You're the bravest person I've ever met, Claudine St. James," he whispered fiercely. "If that doesn't make you a winner, I don't know what does."

She swallowed her anguish and pulled back, wiping her cheeks with the shirttail he offered. Beneath the soft plaid shirt she glimpsed a hideous green-and-brown camouflage T-shirt. *Oh, Bo, you are so…*

The understanding look he gave her made her breath catch. He touched her eyebrow and smiled supportively. "Come on, sweetness, it ain't over, yet. Let's get your game face back on—we have one more stop to make."

CHAPTER NINE

CLAUDIE RECOGNIZED her sister the instant the girl stepped through the door of the school. Tall, blond, her carriage proud and graceful, she looked like a young Grace Kelly. Her outfit looked like something a businesswoman would wear—a sober black wool skirt and white turtleneck sweater with knee-high boots. Her calf-length coat of deep teal was topped with a hand-knit scarf of scarlet and gold. She carried a black leather backpack.

She never hesitated on her walk across the paved trail—a path Claudie remembered as mud and gravel. While she'd only attended this school for a year and a half—and had failed to graduate with her class, Claudie still thought of it as her alma mater.

Sherry didn't hail her or display any outward excitement. Her smile seemed curious, but not apprehensive. Claudie surmised Garret had informed Sherry of her sister's arrival.

Claudie rose from the metal bleachers and stepped down to greet her sister face-to-face. "Hi," she said, grimacing when her voice came out garbled. "Do you know who I am?"

Sherry's blue eyes seemed to sparkle with some underlying emotion that Claudie couldn't read. "You're Claudine. My sister."

"Half sister," Claudie corrected. "We had the same mother, different fathers."

Sherry's smile took Claudie's breath away. It was their mother's smile. "You're younger than I pictured. They said you left home when you were my age, and I guess I thought you'd be older by now." She ducked her chin slightly. "You're prettier, too."

Claudie's heart skipped a beat. "Well, that makes us even. You're older than I pictured. My last memory of you was wiping your runny nose. You always had a cold."

Laughing, Sherry exaggerated a sniff. "Allergies. Mom took me to a dozen doctors before they finally pinpointed the problem. Problems. Wheat, pollen, cat dander—you name it. I've outgrown some, but I still sneeze like crazy when the lilacs are blooming."

"Almond trees do me in," Claudie confessed. She took a breath and pointed to the bleachers. "Could we sit and talk a few minutes?"

Sherry frowned. "Daddy said you weren't staying. I don't think it's fair that you just got here and have to leave right away."

For the first time, she sounded her age. "I have to get home to my job." She went on before Sherry could ask her what she did. "Do you have plans for after graduation?"

She took a seat on the cold metal bench—thankful for Bo's jacket and the too big gloves he'd ordered her to wear. Sherry sat down folding her woolen coat around her in a ladylike manner that Claudie found endearing. "I've applied to three schools—two Christian colleges and Kansas State. Partly, it will depend on Daddy's health. I hate to be too far away in case he gets worse. But he's adamant that I go off and live my life, not hang around watching him die."

Her matter-of-fact statement of Garret's mortality struck Claudie as almost too healthy to be real. "Do his doctors give him long?" she asked.

Sherry rolled her eyes. "They told him he'd be dead two years ago. He says the Lord doesn't necessarily consult with doctors when He makes His plans."

Claudie was curious how much her sister knew of her reasons for running away. Oddly, she didn't want to damage Sherry's feelings for her father, so she asked, "Do you know why I left home?"

Sherry looked down. "Yes. It's hard to have too much privacy when you're living in a travel trailer."

This was Claudie's cue to unload her anger and bitterness, but for some reason she asked, instead, "Where have you traveled?"

"Just about everywhere." Sherry made an encompassing motion with her hands. She had the poise and delivery of a professional speaker. *Did she get that from Garret?* "We started in northern Maine and worked our way down the eastern seaboard then across the south and Texas. We spent a year working with the Navajo—that was amazing—then we drove from the bottom of California to the top. It took us six months."

"Did you go through Sacramento?" Claudie asked.

Sherry nodded with enthusiasm. "For sure. I home-schooled, and Mom was a stickler for geography and history, so we'd always spend two or three days in every state's capital city."

Was it possible they were in Sac when I was working the streets? Pushing the disturbing thought aside, she said, "I notice you call Dottie, Mom. I'm not surprised since she's the only mother you've ever known, but I wonder if you'd like to know anything about your real mother."

Sherry tilted her head thoughtfully. Her shoulder-length blond hair curled gracefully against her coat. "I'll probably think of a dozen things once you leave, but…not really. I mean, Daddy's told me a lot about her. How they met, how he talked her into marrying him." Her smile seemed soft and romantic. "Daddy said he took her a different kind of flower every time he passed through her town until he hit on the right one—a yellow rose."

Claudie couldn't remember ever seeing yellow roses in any of their homes.

"We have a big map on the wall at home showing all the places we traveled. The towns where you and the other kids lived when you were growing up are marked in red," Sherry said. Her soft chuckle was full of fondness. "Daddy had the wanderlust even then, didn't he? Only then he was selling appliances and baby furniture and pharmaceuticals. Now, he's selling God." She made it sound like a noble thing.

Claudie didn't want to talk about Garret. She was still having a hard time understanding what happened in that casino. *Who* was she suppose to forgive? *Why?*

As if reading her thoughts, Sherry said, "Daddy told me on the phone the only reason you came back was to find me." Her blue eyes filled with tears. "Claudie, I think that is the sweetest, most wonderful thing I've ever heard. My heart nearly broke in two when he told me."

The thing to do was hug, but Claudie held back for some reason. "I wanted to make sure you were okay. I didn't want you to have to go through any of what I've done. You deserved a chance at a normal life and…"

Wiping her tears with the tips of her gloves, Sherry sniffed and said, smiling, "That's so brave. I'm so glad you're my sister."

Claudie closed her eyes against tears of her own. *Oh, hell.* She looped one arm across the young girl's shoulders. With a small cry, Sherry turned and embraced Claudie with both arms, squeezing ingenuously. "Thank you for coming back, Claudie. You don't know how much it means to me…and my dad."

Claudie stiffened. She couldn't help herself.

Sherry pulled back. She gave Claudie a look too empathic for her age. "I'm sure it's hard not to hate him after what he did."

How does someone so young see so much? Her silent question must have shown because Sherry said, "I'm a peer counselor in school, and we had a girl who was date raped by a college boy. It was awful. She had all kinds of problems afterward dealing with her self-worth."

She smiled. "But now she's got a new boyfriend—he's a junior—a really sweet guy, and she seems happy."

Claudie didn't know what to say. *I've got a boyfriend. I'm happy…some of the time.*

"Dad told me two men were with you today. Is one of them your boyfriend?" Sherry asked.

Claudie swallowed. "He thinks he is." Her answer came out sharper than she'd intended.

Sherry giggled. "Don't they all? I'm going with a guy who thinks he's God's gift to women."

"Have you been together long?"

She shrugged. "Two months. We're at that stage where he wants sex but hasn't come right out and asked."

"What will you tell him when he asks?" Claudie asked, knowing it was none of her business.

Sherry smiled serenely. "Same thing I've told all the boys who want me to do things I'm not ready for—God will tell me *when*—and I'll know it's right because of the ring on my finger."

Claudie shook her head, mystified. "Wow. I wish I'd have had half your poise when I was your age."

Sherry's smile faded. "God gives us our path, Claudie. Yours was much harder than mine has been, but it was the one you needed to travel. Part of who I am is because you loved me and cared for me when I was a baby. I went from you to my mom. You made that possible even though you didn't know it at the time." Claudie blinked against the cold breeze that was making her eyes tear up.

"My mom—Dottie—is a wonderful lady, Claudie. She's an angel, really. You'd like her if you stayed around and got to know her."

Claudie swallowed. "I have to go. My job, my friends…" All true, but she suddenly realized leaving this beautiful young woman wasn't going to be any easier this time than it had been when she was six. "My friends are waiting," Claudie said, rising.

Sherry stood up. Although a good five inches taller, she suddenly seemed small and sad.

"You can e-mail me," Claudie said.

"Really?" Sherry brightened. "Cool. I'm online a lot with my Christian chat groups, and I'm taking an advanced humanities class from K.S.U."

They talked about her plans for college as they crossed the now abandoned parking lot. Sherry pulled out a pen and paper from her pack and wrote down Yancy's address and Claudie's e-mail. In the far distance, Claudie saw a late model sedan with the engine running. Dottie, no doubt. When they stopped beside the station wagon, Claudie spotted her little camera on the dash. "Can I take your picture?"

"Sure," Sherry said, smiling. "Daddy says I'm half ham."

After snapping three shots, Claudie glanced once more at the waiting car then said, "I'm sorry your father's ill. Tell him…not all my memories are bad."

Sherry's eyes filled with tears and she hugged Claudie

fiercely. "You are so wonderful. That will mean so much to him. Thank you. I love you."

"I love you, too, Sherry," Claudie said, stumbling on words she hadn't used for what seemed like a hundred years. "Take care. Keep up those grades, and tell any boy who gives you a problem your big sister will come back and make him very, very sorry he was born male."

Sherry laughed and waved goodbye before dashing across the parking lot. Claudie watched her go. This wasn't the way she'd seen any of this little drama unfolding, but she wasn't sorry her trip had been in vain. Sherry was a beautiful gift, and Claudie felt a tiny bit of pride that she'd helped raise her.

Smiling, she hopped in the car and turned on the heater full blast.

"I'd forgotten how much I hate winter," she said, shivering. "I wanna go home."

STRETCHED OUT on his bed, Bo glanced at the alarm clock. Four-thirty. His bags were packed. The bill paid. Matt was on the phone in his room, trying to arrange a flight to New York. If he couldn't get a plane until morning, he might opt for another night at the inn, but regardless, Bo and Claudie were headed west. And, frankly, Bo couldn't wait.

He didn't know what to expect from Claudie when she returned from meeting her sister. He figured it could go either way. She'd either be a basket case who needed him to comfort her or a clam—her nefarious alter ego.

A swift knock preceded Claudie, who rushed in and slammed the door behind her. She shed her coat and gloves before turning around to lock the door.

Bo sat up, reclining on his elbows. "Are you okay?"

She kicked off her shoes. "I'm fine," she said, strolling forward. "I'm better than fine, actually."

Bo swallowed. "Good," he said, his voice cracking. He cleared his throat and sat up straighter. "Are you packed? We should probably hit the road."

"Not just yet," she said, kneeling at the foot of the bed. She slipped off the dark-plum cardigan leaving the short-sleeved sweater top behind. For Claudie, this practically constituted a negligee.

"What are you doing?" Bo asked, scooting back until his shoulders encountered the old-fashioned beaded headboard.

"Healing. I think."

If she'd have left it at "healing" he might have been able to buy it, but that little quaver in her voice that accompanied the "I think" told him she wasn't ready for this.

"I don't think this is a good idea," he said, even though his body thought otherwise.

She stretched out her hand, lightly brushing the front of his canvas trousers. "A part of you disagrees."

He snorted, crossing his left leg over his right the best he could. "Well, sure, but if I listened to that part of me there's no telling what kind of trouble I'd be in."

"Trouble can be fun, if it's handled right," she said, not so subtly stressing the double entendre.

He shifted positions. "Really, Claudie, after the hell you've been through toda—" He choked on his words when she shifted to all fours, a graceful feline, stalking her prey. The scooped neck of her sweater afforded a great view of ivory lace and peachy skin. The golden locket swung like a pendulum between her breasts.

"Claudie…"

She ran the tip of her tongue across her upper lip.

His damn knees parted without so much as an "Open, sesame," and she moved forward, straddling him.

Bo groaned. "Sweetheart. Please. Don't do this."

She nuzzled the side of his face, her hair tickling his nose. "Why? Isn't it what you want?"

"Yes. Of course. But you need time to get some perspective on what happened."

She sat back, her weight resting in the most perfectly designed position imaginable. Bo felt his control slipping. His mind started charting the fastest way to remove her slacks—until he looked in her eyes and saw the shattering pain and doubt he'd always known haunted her.

"Oh, honey," he whispered, sitting forward to wrap his arms around her. He rolled them to the side so they were facing each other. Without her resting quite so provocatively against his groin he could actually think. "You just got back from hell, baby. It's natural to want to prove to yourself you're still alive, but maybe we should wait until—"

She exploded out of his arms, scrabbling back to the far corner of the king-size bed. "Goddamn it, Lester. Make up your mind. When I don't want you, you want me. When I throw myself at you, you play hard to get." Her chest was heaving and he could see she was close to tears. "What are you?" she growled. "A woman?"

Bo would have laughed but he was afraid she might find his gun and use it on him. He bent his elbow and rested his head on his palm. "I'm a coward."

That shut her up. For a minute. "No, you're not."

He nodded. "Yes, I am. Where you're concerned. I'm so afraid I might screw up I don't know what to do."

Her frown looked doubtful, so he sat up, kneeling across from her. "Sweetheart, there's nothing in the world I'd like more than to make love with you, but a quickie before we hit the road isn't quite what I had in mind."

Her eyes narrowed. "Men are supposed to want it any time, any place."

"I don't just want your body, Claudie. I want you."

She looked down. "I thought this would prove—" She gulped. "I don't know what I thought it would prove."

Bo reached out and pulled her to him. She laid her head on his shoulder and put her arms around him. Nuzzling her neck, inhaling the fresh outdoor smell in her hair, he whispered, "Can you tell me what happened?"

When she nodded, he moved them backward to the plump eyelet lace pillows. She snuggled into the space beside him, her head still on his shoulder. Bo closed his eyes and listened to her relate the news of her sister. His heart swelled with her joy, twisted with her pain. He tried to keep from thinking too far ahead—the long drive home where they'd spend three nights on the road. Time he planned to use to convince her to marry him.

"Will you marry me?"

Claudie leapt to her feet as if a bomb had gone off beside her. The mattress jiggled as she danced from foot to foot. "What? What did you say?"

Bo felt a rush of heat to his face. "Oops," he muttered. "Did I say that aloud?"

"You didn't mean to say it?" She stopped dancing and gave him a suspicious glare.

"Well, yeah, but not right this minute. Damn." He put his hand to his head.

Her giggle caught him totally off-guard. When she bent over laughing, he didn't know whether to be hurt or laugh, too.

She collapsed to her knees, tears in her eyes. "That is too funny," she sputtered. "An accidental proposal." Wiping her cheeks with her hands, she looked at him and asked, "What would you have done if I'd said yes?"

He sat up, facing her. "I'd have considered myself the luckiest man in the world." Her smile faded. He touched her damp cheek. "I wasn't kidding, Claudie. I want to marry you and start a family. I want to help you open a second and third halfway house. I want to be at your side when the governor awards you a plaque for your contribution to society."

Her eyes spoke the words he knew she couldn't say to him. Not yet, anyway.

He leaned forward and kissed her. "They call those dreams, Claudie girl. Now that you've kicked the bogeyman out of your nightmares, you can dream, too."

She tilted her face to kiss him. Her tears added a salty flavor to her taste. When her hands moved to his shoulders, he hauled her to him, his pulse racing with hope, love.

The knock on the door shattered the moment. She pulled back guiltily.

Bo silently cursed his cousin, the only person it could be. "What?" he barked.

"Let me in. I just got a call from my mother. It's about your dad, Bo. He's in the hospital."

CLAUDIE'S OPINION of Matt skyrocketed as she watched him handle Bo with a stalwart calm she couldn't begin to match. Not that Bo flew off the handle, but Claudie could tell he was upset and not thinking as clearly as usual. For one thing, he was under the mistaken impression she would let him fly off to New York without her.

"It makes perfect sense," he told her for the third time. "I'll switch Matt's ticket to my name and he can drive you home."

She rolled her eyes. "No way am I spending three days on the road with Matt, even if he is your cousin. No offense," she said, looking at Matt who seemed equally serious.

"None taken." He looked at Bo. "She's right. That wouldn't work. I can't just jump into your life, Bo. This is my weekend to have Ashley."

"What's three lousy days, you jerk?" Bo growled. "I'd do it for you."

Matt's complexion darkened a degree. "I'm not saying I won't help out. I just think we should think things through. You haven't even talked to your mother yet. You know my mother—she's an alarmist."

Bo's mouth fell open.

Matt ducked his head, sheepishly. "Well, maybe not, but it still might not be that bad."

The sound of a phone made them jump. Bo clutched his chest pocket, where he'd put his cell phone after retrieving it from his briefcase. "Hello," he cried. "Mom. How is he? Aunt Irene called a few minutes ago."

Claudie watched his face, her nerves skittering along the top of her skin. She couldn't believe anyone could go through so much emotional turmoil in one day and survive. She'd already decided if this was a false alarm, she'd ask for her room back so she could go to bed. California could wait.

Bo walked to the small desk on the other side of the room and scribbled something on the rose-embossed notepad. "I got it. I'll be there as soon as possible. How are you doing?" He paused to listen. "Well, don't let yourself get too run-down. Listen to Irene, she's a nurse." He nodded, already on the move with that purposeful, focused style of his.

A chameleon, he called himself, able to blend into a crowd. Also, as forceful and dynamic as Ren or Matt when he chose to be. "I'll call you when I get in, Mom. Take care. I love you."

He pressed a button and pocketed the phone. "He's in intensive care. Pretty much touch-and-go for the next twelve hours. I gotta go. Will you two stop fighting me on this so I can get out of here?"

Matt rose. "My flight's the only one out and it leaves at

nine-forty-five. That's four hours from now. The airport's an hour away, so we might as well take it down a notch. There's nothing you can do at the moment."

Bo's upper lip curled. "There should be."

Claudie started to the door. "I'll get packed. Matt, would you see if there are two more seats on that plane?"

Bo swore.

When the phone rang, Claudie spun on her heel and picked up the receiver by the bed. The voice on the other end wasn't one she was expecting.

"Hello, Claudie? It's Garret."

She sat down abruptly. "Yes," she said, mouthing the word *Garret* to Bo. "What do you want? We're in a bit of a hurry here…."

"I know. You're anxious to leave for home, but there's something I forgot to tell you this afternoon. I'm so glad I caught you."

She didn't like the softer feelings his raspy voice provoked. She couldn't seem to draw up the image of him she'd held for ten years—drunk, slobbering, stinking of sweat and booze. Over the years, she'd added features of other men, other cruelties and coarseness until he was a demon too hideous to conjure in the daylight hours. Now he was none of those things. Somehow he'd become nothing more than a pathetic shell of a man waiting for death.

"We're leaving soon."

"Well, I won't keep you. I just wanted you to know about the insurance money. I thought it might make a difference to you, if you broke down and needed it for anything." His odd hesitation made her look at Bo, who'd walked to her side.

"What insurance money?"

Garret cleared his throat. "Your mom's folks bought her a paid-up insurance policy when she was a girl. After you were born she made you the beneficiary. She never changed that, so when she died, you inherited it."

"How much?"

"It was for 2500. Of course, it's worth quite a bit more now."

Claudie frowned. Bo's inquiring look made her reach out and touch his arm. Matt appeared with a piece of paper and a pen upon which she scribbled a dollar sign.

"I don't get it. Why is it worth more now?"

Garret coughed again. "Well…Peggy never told me about it. After she passed away, I found it in with some papers." He paused. "I was really upset and hurt that she— There were a lot of times we could have used the money if we'd have cashed it in, but she never mentioned it." He paused as if to catch his breath. "It's possible she just forgot about it, but at the time I was consumed by rage."

Claudie closed her eyes. She understood that kind of anger.

"Anyway, after you left home I cashed it in. Since I was your legal guardian, nobody questioned it. I'd planned to spend it, but then I had my wreck. By the time I got out of the hospital, I knew I couldn't live with myself if I touched a dime of it, so I gave it to a friend who was an investment banker."

This pause was different. Expectant. She gave Bo a tentative smile. "Did he run off to Brazil?" she asked.

Garret's laugh ended in a painful-sounding cough. When he had his voice back, he said, "No. Glen's as honest as the day is long. He did pretty well for you, Claudie. I just got off the phone with him. It's a nice tidy sum. Enough to put down on a house if you and Bo were to get married."

"Married?" she choked out, unable to contain herself.

Bo looked up, a quizzical expression on his face.

Garret stuttered. "Umm…er…I'm sorry to have presumed. Maybe you could use it to buy a new car. Dottie said yours was—"

"Car," Claudie cried, vaulting to her feet. "My car. What am I going to do with my car if I go to New York?"

She looked at Matt, who shrugged. Bo gave them both an "I-told-you" look.

"What do you mean?" Garret asked.

She recounted Bo's news.

"Just leave your car right there," Garret said. "Give the keys to Mrs. Green. Dottie and I will come get it first thing in the morning and keep it here for you until you can come back for it."

"That's very nice of you to offer, but—"

Bo groaned.

"No, buts, Claudine," he said severely. "I've waited a decade to be able to help you in any way I could. I don't think I've got another decade left in me, so you'd better let me do this."

Claudie took a breath. "All right. Tell Sherry she can drive it. A girl needs her own wheels from time to time."

When Garret answered, his voice sounded thick with emotion. "That's very good of you, Claudie. She will be thrilled to pieces." Claudie hated to admit how nice his praise sounded to her ears. "Now, about the money. Do you need any to help you get to New York? I'm sure Glen could advance you some—"

She smiled. "No. Bo can buy my ticket and I'll pay him back later." *Some way or another.*

She told her stepfather goodbye and hung up the phone. To Bo she said, "The car is taken care of, and I'm independently wealthy." To Matt, she said, "Go make another reservation. I'm going to New York."

MATT TUCKED his carry-on bag beneath his knees, glad to find three seats together in the small waiting room. Claudie took the spot beside him. Bo, still restless as an edgy lion, turned on his heel. "I'm going to the john."

Claudie put her bulky leather purse on the empty seat to save it.

They sat in silence surrounded by the low hum of other passengers and an occasional flight announcement. Compared to JFK this airport was low-key, but Claudie peered around like a kid in a museum.

"Is this your first time?" he asked.

She gave him a droll look that made him blush. "On an airplane," he qualified.

"Isn't there a law against doing it on an airplane?" she asked impishly.

"Claudie," he snapped. He wasn't in the mood for teasing. He was rarely in the mood for teasing these days. Although Matt had enjoyed the stimulation of working in the field, he still felt unsettled and useless. He couldn't even deliver the one thing his cousin asked for—an extra few days to drive Claudie home. He'd been so damn relieved when she insisted on going to New York that he'd almost kissed her.

She lightly brushed her hand against his sleeve. "Sorry," she said. "I get a little goofy when I'm nervous. And, yes, this is my first plane ride."

The way she said it made him smile.

"You should smile more often, Matt," she told him. "It's a lot less scary than your big, bad cop frown."

He gave her his toughest squint. She shrank back in her seat. "Sorry," she peeped.

He shook his head, and heaving a sigh, slumped down in his chair. He closed his eyes. "You're a good person, Claudie. I'm glad you're here. Bo's gonna need you."

"Tell him that. I think he's really pissed," she said.

Matt turned his chin to look at her. He wasn't easily impressed, but the way she handled the confrontation with her stepfather had been something. Now, jumping in blindly to help Bo took guts—especially considering the way Bo was acting. "You gotta understand. Things between Bo and his dad were never good. Robert B. is a cold man. He used to scare the hell out of me."

She looked doubtful.

"Scout's honor. One time in college, I bumped into him at some family function and asked him about an investment opportunity some friends of mine were all hot about." He grimaced. "The man had me backed up against the wall before Aunt Ruth rescued me."

"What'd he say?"

"Basically, he told me to keep my money in my pants because I was too damn dumb to invest it in anything more complicated than beer."

"What'd you do?"

"I bought ten thousand shares of my friend's stock. Which, basically amounted to pissing it away, because the market crashed and the company folded. Uncle Robert was right. I'd have been better off with the beer."

She smiled uneasily. "He sounds complicated. How'd he wind up with a son like Bo, someone so…real."

Matt looked toward the main corridor, which was visible through Plexiglas partitions. It took him a minute to find Bo, who moved in and out of the crowd like a wraith—unnoticed, Matt guessed, by the majority of the people he passed. For as long as Matt had known him, Bo had gone out of his way to blend in—understandable, Matt thought, given Bo's larger-than-life father. But Bo was far from ordinary.

"This is probably a dumb thing I'm doing," Claudie said, slumping down lower than Matt.

Matt shifted enough to face her. "Cool it. Here comes, Bo. And he's going to need you in New York. I guarantee it."

She looked to the scanning machine where Bo was waiting for a lady and her dog to pass through. "But he doesn't want me here," she said.

"Right. Just like you didn't want him to find you. But he did, and you're glad, right?"

She smiled. He closed his eyes. He didn't begrudge Bo and Claudie any happiness they could find, but as far he was concerned, love was for fools.

BO PULLED OUT the in-flight magazine from the seat in front of him and tried to focus on the pictures—words were beyond him. His mind bounced from one topic to another like a golf ball on pavement. One second he was thinking about his father, the next Claudie's stepfather and her sudden windfall.

Craning his neck, he looked around to see if he could find her. Since they'd booked so late, none of their seats were together. A full house, but no sign of Claudie.

Shaking out his hands, he depressed the button to recline his seat and loosened his seat belt. No way around it, this was going to be a long flight.

To his left, in seats A and B, was a young couple nestled against the window like baby lemurs. Behind him, the drink cart began its tortuous rumble up the aisle.

With a sigh, he closed his eyes. His mind jumped to Claudie—its favorite topic. He couldn't believe she'd insisted on accompanying him to New York. That Matt had refused to back him up still irked a little, but he understood why Matt wasn't anxious to drive to California. And, secretly, the idea of his handsome cousin spending three or four days with the woman he loved didn't exactly thrill Bo, either.

Chagrined by his unwarranted jealousy, he looked down.

To his amazement, a hand slipped between his seat and half-empty seat B. Curious, he leaned into the aisle to look behind his seat.

"Claudie?"

Grinning, she jerked her hand back. "I was going to pinch you."

Her mischievous smile took his breath away. "Why?" he whispered.

"To get your attention."

He motioned her closer. "I thought you didn't like my attention."

"That was before."

"Before what?"

"Before I was rich."

Her little-girl tone unloosened something painful inside him. "Honey, I hate to tell you this, but forty grand isn't all that rich."

She rolled her eyes. "Maybe not by Ren Bishop's standards, but it is by mine. It's enough to make me an entirely different person."

His happy mood slipped away. "I like the person you are."

She scooted closer. "Do you?" she softly asked.

He nodded. She was almost close enough to kiss, but of course he couldn't. Not in public.

"Then maybe I won't change," she said, her gaze pinned to his.

Bo's heart thudded in his chest. He swallowed and glanced over her shoulder where a nine-year-old boy watched them intently. He cleared his throat. "How'd you manage to switch seats?" he asked.

Her pout was followed by a pensive look. "I saw the man in this seat go to the rest room, so I followed and asked if I could sit here."

"And he agreed?"

She nodded.

Bo didn't buy it. "Why?"

Her gaze slipped from his. "I told him we were eloping."

The lie took Bo's breath away. It took him a minute to put together a comeback. "Claudie, nobody elopes to New York City."

She made a face—so Bradylike he almost laughed. "We're only flying to New York. From there we're taking the train to Niagara Falls. A *sleeper,* remember?" she teased.

Bo had to duck back into his seat to avoid being mowed down by the drink cart. *Niagara Falls? Where did that come from?* He would have loved to ask her, but for the moment all he could do was stew.

When the flight attendant asked him for his order, it was on the tip of his tongue to ask for scotch—until a slim hand materialized between the seats and pinched the fleshy part of his arm. Snickering, he said, "Orange juice, please."

CHAPTER TEN

CLAUDIE PEERED through the hospital's glass doors to the street beyond. The steady drizzle that had accompanied her and Bo on the taxi ride earlier that morning was beginning to turn solid. The weather forecaster on the television in the waiting room predicted a severe winter storm. If she wasn't feeling quite so tense, Claudie might have enjoyed the snow. But she couldn't relax—not when Bo was acting so funny.

She sighed and squinted, trying to make him out. He'd escorted his mother downstairs from the eleventh floor where his father remained in intensive care. Although Ruth had protested that she was perfectly capable of obtaining a taxi without his help, Bo had insisted. Claudie had tagged along without being asked.

Talk about a fifth wheel. She rubbed a spot on her forehead trying to alleviate the ache. Hanging around a hospital would have been difficult enough even if Bo was acting normal, but Claudie barely recognized the man she'd joked with on the airplane just days earlier. Ever since he'd learned that his father's medical emergency wasn't a heart attack at all but a concussion from a fall he'd taken while in-line skating, Bo had turned inward—as rigid and unapproachable as the urban towers that surrounded her.

Claudie opened her purse and took out a bottle of water. She wanted to help, but Bo wouldn't let her in. *If he'd just talk to me—tell me what he's feeling…* she thought, jumping aside as two men in blue jumpsuits hurried past. She took a gulp of water and replaced the bottle in her bag.

A moment later, Bo appeared—his shaggy, un-combed mop wet with snowflakes. His haggard appearance made her ache to comfort him, but his somber demeanor didn't invite closeness.

Claudie scooted sideways. The bleak but determined look in his eyes made her uneasy.

"I need a magazine before we head upstairs." She pivoted and walked to the gift shop counter.

Bo followed. He stood close enough for her pick up his scent—coffee, a hint of fresh air and that familiar, comforting essence that was pure Bo. "Claudie, we need to talk," he said, his tone serious.

She blindly grabbed a *People* magazine and dug in her purse for money. Bo slapped down a five-dollar bill and took her elbow. "Now."

If anyone else had acted that bossy she'd have leveled the guy, but Claudie sensed the depths of Bo's frustration. She shoved the magazine in her purse. "Do you want to sit in the lobby or go outside?"

"Not down here. It's a madhouse," he said, his tone flat. His fingers tensed on her elbow. The contact felt good even though she wasn't certain what he wanted from her.

"Upstairs, then," she suggested. This giant city within a city fascinated her as much as it repelled her. Certain gross smells could ambush without warning. Loud noises were prone to explode in any direction. Pathos seemed to outweigh hope.

Bo ushered her toward the bank of elevators. Moments later they stepped into the medicinal-smelling chrome box. Side by side they squeezed into the closest corner. Bo pushed the appropriate button.

The elevator shimmied and Bo's shoulder brushed hers. Claudie tensed.

"Most muggers stay out on the street," he said—a faint touch of the old Bo in his voice.

Confused, Claudie glanced at him. His eyebrows wiggled and he nodded toward her hands. White knuckles gripped her pocketbook. She loosened her grip but kept her chin down to keep Bo from seeing her embarrassment. Never had she felt more like a hick from Kansas.

"This can't be much fun for you," Bo said. His voice was low to avoid being overheard by the other occupants.

"I didn't come here for fun."

"Why did you come, Claudie?"

Claudie's distress level rose. She wasn't sure she could answer that in the time it took to ascend eleven floors. "Payback," she mumbled, refusing to meet his gaze.

"I beg your pardon?"

She inched closer to the wall, taking care not to bump the bandaged foot of the man in the wheelchair behind her. Bo moved, too. His arm brushed against hers, and Claudie had to fight not to react. She no longer loathed touching—especially Bo's touch—but she didn't trust herself not to wrap her arms around him and try to pretend this medicinal-smelling world didn't exist.

"You were there for me in Kansas. This is my chance to pay you back," she said softly.

His harsh curse was uttered under his breath. "You don't owe me anything, Claudie."

She closed her eyes and sighed. She had too much to say—and too little—to get into it here. She changed the subject. "Matt told me Ashley's overbite is going to cost three thousand dollars. Apparently, that's cheap. His ex-wife's husband's cousin is an orthodontist, so they get a family discount."

Bo stuffed his hands in the pockets of his wrinkled Dockers and eyed her as if she'd just changed colors. Her cheeks warmed under his scrutiny, but she continued, "And he's spoken to Mrs. Kriegen several times. You'll be glad to know she's decided he's not the anti-Christ out to usurp your business."

A flicker of emotion touched his lips. Encouraged, Claudie said, "It sounds like the business is running pretty smoothly without you, but Matt said things could get hairy if you don't get back to work soon."

Bo shrugged with a carelessness she knew he didn't feel.

Claudie also knew she was to blame for Bo losing a week away from his business. "It's my fault, Bo. That time you spent chasing after me—"

He didn't let her finish. "Don't." His voice was unusually stiff and stern. Businesslike. "Matt just got a call from an old friend in the D.A.'s office. They're throwing some work our way. A couple of the cases include some decent rewards. I'll send a couple of my guys out here after the first of the year to work with Matt. That should keep us solvent."

The acrid twist he put on the last word made her flinch. "Bo, what's going on?"

He glanced at the display panel—two more floors. When the doors opened, Claudie started toward the waiting room, but Bo took her elbow and led her to one of the long narrow windows away from the nurses' station.

Feeling overcome with dread, Claudie pressed her forehead against the cool glass. Below her a panorama of white sparkled as fresh and pristine as a child's snow globe. "Wow, that's kinda pretty."

Behind her, she heard Bo's droll, "Tourist."

It was the first glimpse in days of the Bo she knew—and possibly loved. She didn't peek for fear he'd be gone—his bleak alter ego returned—so she stared outside. *I wonder if it's snowing in Niagara Falls?*

BO WATCHED the wind drive waves of fat white flakes against the window beyond Claudie. Gusts curled upward shaping a miniature drift along the building's ledge. If he focused on the weather, he could almost block out the image of his father lying helpless and diminished in the room down the hall. Almost.

"Has there been any change?" Claudie asked, not turning around.

Her breath steamed up the window like a ghost track. Bo felt surrounded by ghosts. The only way to keep them at bay was to stoke the fire of his anger.

"Nope. Whacking your head on a curb will do it every time. I know. Tangled with a few curbs myself. Although that was from drinking. Even *I* wasn't dumb enough to go in-line skating without a helmet." He snorted. "Wait. I forgot. This was a *heart attack.*"

Bo flinched inwardly at his snide tone but found himself powerless to summon one iota of the compassion he'd initially felt when learning of his father's hospitalization. He'd completely lost it when he arrived at the hospital and Trisha—his father's girlfriend—told him the truth. Bogus headlines were one thing, lying to your son was another.

"Trisha told me she lied to the media to protect your father's image," Claudie said softly.

Bo pictured the five-eleven, model-thin blonde. At least she was thirty, not nineteen as he'd first pictured, and she worked for a public relations firm, but that did little to ease Bo's prejudice. Tricia was the first lover his father had publicly acknowledged by moving into her condo. Did she mean more to him than the others before her? Bo didn't want to know. He didn't care.

"What kind of woman takes a sixty-eight-year-old man in-line skating?" he muttered. "I can't believe I fell for it. I should have known better—after all, you need a *heart* to have a heart attack."

Claudie turned sharply. Her brow was wrinkled with concern. "I don't think he did it on purpose, Bo."

Her mild censure annoyed him. She was supposed to be on *his* side. "Yes, he did. He waited until I fell in love to take up in-line skating and screw up—"

She interrupted. "What do you mean? What's screwed up? Isn't that why you followed me to Kansas? Isn't that why I'm here? Because we—we're there for each other."

Her reluctance to name her feelings infuriated him. Bo knew he was being childish and irrational, but he couldn't help it. And anger helped justify his decision. "Speaking of being here…I think you should go home. The doctors won't say when—or if—Dad will come out of this coma. *I* can't leave Mom to deal with this alone, but it's ridiculous for you to hang around."

Her sweet lips pursed in a frown. "I don't mind, Bo. I mean, it would be a little easier if I had a feeling you wanted me here, but—"

"That's just it, Claudie. I don't want you here. I have too much on my mind to deal with your needs, too."

Her eyes grew wide—a flash of hurt evident before she righted her shoulders regally. "I'll get my things and leave. My coat's in the waiting room." She turned away before Bo could move.

He closed his eyes and leaned into the window. The glass sent a shiver through his body as if part of his soul had been ripped away. His stomach clenched at the shot of acid that hit full force. Frustration, anger and fear duked it out as he followed her down the hall.

"I'll take a taxi to your mother's then call the airport to see about a flight," Claudie said, not looking at him. She was seated, gathering her *stuff*—a paper cup, a crossword puzzle book, playing cards and several candy bar wrappers. "I hope this storm doesn't get worse. They had to close the airport last week, remember?"

Was that only a week ago? Bo thought, sinking into the chair beside her. How could he possibly have gone from the person tracking down the woman he loved to this empty, disconnected shell in so short a time?

She reached for her parka—the one his mother had lent her to replace Claudie's woefully inadequate West Coast jacket.

"Wait."

Her hand hovered—trembling—above the jacket.

Bo closed his eyes, suddenly drained. How had his life gotten so screwed up? "I'm sorry, Claudie. I know I've been a jerk."

He felt her hand on his forearm. His skin was clammy with sweat. Despite the chilly weather outside, the hospital kept the rooms just above boiling. "Don't beat yourself up about it," she said. "I know how to roll with the punches. I thought I could help, but it's obvious I'm just in the way. No biggie."

He recognized that voice. It belonged to the woman he'd met six months ago—cool, contained, streetwise and world-weary, not the woman who had joked with him about going to Niagara Falls. He opened his eyes and looked at her. "Claudie, I don't want you to leave." The instant spark of hope in her eyes made his stomach turn over. "But it's crazy for you to stay."

She shrank back as if struck.

Turning in the chair to face her, he said, "I should never have let you come. This place is like the twilight zone of my life. I walk into my father's room and leave *me* behind—the Sacramento me, the person I am when I'm with you. Gone. History."

Her obvious concern twisted his gut in a knot. *What's wrong with me? Why can't I take what she's offering?*

She put her palm to his cheek. Her scent brought comfort at a primal level, but his brain rejected the succor. "Tell me what to do, Bo. Go or stay. It's up to you."

A disturbance in the hall made him look away. Matt leaned in the doorway and motioned him to come. Bo shot to his feet. "Go." Her shattered look made him hesitate. "No, stay." As he hurried to the door, he called over his shoulder. "I don't know. We'll talk about it tonight."

SEVERAL HOURS LATER, Claudie stomped her boots on the inch-thick mat inside the door then unlaced them and set them to one side to dry. Her stockings were soaked from the ankle-deep slush she'd encountered on her walk from the subway. Dashing on damp tiptoes she sprinted across the glossy marble floor of the apartment's foyer to the carpeted hallway then hurried to the guest bedroom where she'd spent two sleepless nights. Maybe a bath and a glass of wine would help, she thought. With any luck, she might even sleep.

She grabbed her sweatpants and flannel nightshirt from her suitcase and walked to the bathroom across the hall from her room. A palace of topaz-veined marble—its pristine beauty was softened by two dozen wax pillars in various shades of lavender—all with blackened wicks. That lived-in look took the edge off the distress she'd felt when she saw for the first time the great disparity between her childhood and Bo's.

She turned the two golden handles of the jetted tub and went in search of a glass of wine. Two open reds waited at the discreet bar just inside the book-cluttered living room.

Bo's mother obviously indulged in her literary passion. Claudie checked the label on each bottle, selecting the one that looked the cheapest.

Carrying her glass in one hand and a book on painted-lady architecture in the other, she returned to the bath. As she stripped, she studied the instrument panel on the side of the tub.

With a sigh, she added a measure of luxuriant lavender-scented bath crystals to the water. After lighting six candles, she turned off the overhead light and slipped into the fragrant water. She took a sip of wine—rich and smooth—and closed her eyes. Slowly, the tension that had been building all day melted away.

Fortunately, Bo's father had pulled through his most recent medical crisis. Mr. Lester's heart had stopped for several minutes before a team of doctors and nurses was able to revive him.

Her confrontation with Bo that afternoon lingered. Suddenly Claudie knew what she was going to do. If the weather cooperated, she'd grab the first plane for home in the morning.

Home. "Where is home?" Claudie muttered, polishing off her wine. Not Kansas—even though both Sherry and Garret made it clear she was always welcome there. Not Minnesota or Wyoming.

She sighed, her breath sending a ripple across the water. Even though she'd reconnected the pieces of her past, Claudie felt more alone than ever. Home was with Bo, but he didn't want her.

BO FOLLOWED his nose. He wasn't surprised to find Claudie in the kitchen—his mother had ordered him to go home and "have a nice bite to eat with Claudie," but he hadn't expected her to look quite so domestic.

"Hi, there," he said softly. She wheeled about, nearly spilling her wine. "Whatever you're cooking smells good. Did you make enough for two?"

She nodded, her eyes big. He didn't blame her for being cautious after the way he treated her that afternoon.

"Is your dad better?" Claudie asked, her tone somber.

"Stable, but Irene said this afternoon's crisis might be a precursor to other little episodes before his body eventually shuts down."

Her face showed profound sadness, and he knew it wasn't for a man she'd never met. She's here for me, Bo thought, and all I do is push her away. Am I as stupid and callous as my father? Am I?

He opened the refrigerator and grabbed a can of soda. He'd face those questions when he got back to Sac—*one identity crisis at a time.*

"What's cookin'?"

Stirring the pot on the gas range with the intensity of a witch from *MacBeth*, Claudie said, "Clam chowder. From a can, but I doctored it up."

Bo walked to the counter and pulled out a stool.

Claudie filled a bowl at the stove and carried it to him. Her bottom lip was caught between her teeth in concentration. The childlike mannerism hit him below the belt. Why was he acting like such an idiot? This was Claudie—the woman he loved.

Once the bowl was safely in place, she looked at him and smiled. "Matt told me Thanksgiving is the busiest air travel holiday of all, so I'm thinking of leaving tomorrow if possible."

"When's Thanksgiving?"

"Thursday."

"No way."

She nodded toward the calendar.

He ran a hand through his hair; it felt dry and coarse like a clown's wig. The soup smelled inviting, but his mouth tasted as though he'd been on a three-day binge. He wanted a drink.

Claudie filled her bowl and joined him at the counter. "Sara wants me there for Thanksgiving and we've got the dim sum fund-raiser the following week," she said, taking the stool next to him.

Sacramento seemed a million miles away. Another dimension.

"What exactly is dim sum?" Bo asked, idly stirring his soup.

Claudie made a face. "I'm not sure. Maya said the name means 'little treasures.' I guess it's like won tons and egg rolls but more involved."

He swallowed a spoonful of soup. The heat loosened the knot in his chest. "Sounds like a lot of work."

"It's keeping them out of trouble. And Babe's *soliciting*— Rochell's term—things for a charity auction. The girls got a big hoot out of that."

They ate in silence until Claudie asked, "Are you going back to the hospital tonight?"

Bo shook his head. "Nope. Trisha's going to be there."

He didn't want to think about the woman or her place in his father's life. Bo didn't understand how his mother could tolerate the woman's presence. Bo sure as hell couldn't swallow it.

He looked at Claudie. "How come your hair's wet?"

"I soaked in the tub." She closed her eyes and sighed. "A luxury I won't have once I get home."

She whispered the word. *Love and home—stumbling stones in the road of life,* he thought sourly.

"This tastes great," he said striving for sincerity.

Her weak smile seemed as disingenuous as he felt.

He pushed back his stool and stood up. "I think I'll take a shower and go to bed," he told her. "The storm's getting worse, but Mom said she'd call if anything changes."

Claudie rose and began to gather up their dishes. Bo's gut churned. "Matt told me he talked to Ren today," Bo said, not able to keep from following her with his gaze. "Sara wants Matt to go to Atlanta."

"Why?"

"They still haven't heard from Eve." Bo shrugged. He hadn't been listening too closely to what Matt told him. "Sara's convinced the South is a black hole. Life goes in but never comes out."

She looked over her shoulder and smiled. "I know. I think it has something to do with her time in the military, but Keneesha lives in Georgia and she's doing great. You'd think Sara could show a little forgiveness."

Forgiveness. That was the main tenet of what his mother was preaching tonight before he left. *If I can forgive him, son, I would think you could show a little compassion.* But Bo didn't forgive his father. Not for cheating on his mother. Not for valuing work over family. Not for being a pathetic excuse for a father.

Bo spun on one heel and stalked out of the room. He marched through the living room to the corner bar that he knew would be stocked with every kind of booze available—a good New York bar. He filled the ice bucket from a tray in the mini refrigerator, then dropped two cubes in a crystal highball glass. As he surveyed the gold mine of choices before him, he caught a glimpse of Claudie in the doorway.

"What are you doing?"

"It's been a lousy day and I feel like a drink." He grabbed a red-label scotch.

"Life sucks, right?" She stopped a few steps away. "You hate your father, and he might die before you can tell him off. Is that it?"

"Close enough," he snarled, wrenching the cap off the bottle. "But let's not forget that the bastard's soon-to-be ex-wife is solicitously wailing by his bedside along with his current girlfriend who just happens to be ten years *my* junior." He dumped amber liquid into the glass.

He picked up the glass and drew it to his lips. The smell almost choked him, and he had to pull back to catch his breath. A sudden movement made him look toward the couch. Claudie's sweatpants flew through the air to land on the floor beside him.

He turned his head sharply. Her oversize plaid flannel shirt stopped at midthigh, only bare leg continued. Her toes curled in the plush carpet. She started unbuttoning her shirt.

"What the hell do you think you're doing?"

She shrugged. The shirt gaped, displaying the tops of her breasts. "This is what we do, right?"

Confused, furious, he watched another button succumb to her nimble fingers. "What are you talking about?"

"Vices," she said—her voice flat. "Yours is booze. Mine is sex. When things get tough, we fall back into the old patterns." Bo cringed at the resignation in her tone. "I'd kinda figured that might happen, which is why I didn't think you should get involved with someone like me."

"Claudie, this has nothing to do—"

She didn't let him finish. "Bo, think about it. If this is enough to push you over the edge—after twenty years of sobriety, how long will I last?" Her mocking laugh hit him like a punch in the gut.

She freed the final button.

Bo swore. The glass slipped from his fingers, landing haphazardly in the sink. Whiskey splashed everywhere—the smell a toxic flashback to the floor of a college bar where he once spent the night facedown in his own vomit. Wiping his hand on his pants he started toward her just as she shrugged out of the chamois-soft shirt. It pooled at her feet.

"Oh, God, Claudie," Bo whispered, taking in her naked form. Beautiful. Breathtaking. And Bo couldn't have been more furious. "Put that back on."

"No."

He reached for the shirt, but she jumped back and sent it flying off the tip of her toe. "Don't worry," she said flippantly, hands on her hips. "I won't charge you."

Bo's stomach heaved. "Claudie, stop it. You're scaring me. You're not a prostitute anymore."

She turned to face him. Her hands dropped to her sides. "And you're not a drunk."

Bo closed his eyes against the tears that hit him.

"I'm not the same girl who was raped by my stepfather— a man who could never love me no matter how much I wanted him to. And you're not the same boy whose father failed you in ways you can't even talk about. We're not those people any more, Bo. Are we?"

"No love, we're not." He put out his arms. She flew to him, wrapping her arms around his neck, kissing his wet cheeks.

"Then who are we, Bo? Do you know?"

Kissing her eyes, her nose, her lips with feverish need, he whispered, "We're two people who love each other."

Her sigh was the only answer he needed. Bending down, he scooped her into his arms and started toward his room. Right or wrong, there was no turning back this time.

CHAPTER ELEVEN

WHEN HE PICKED HER UP, Claudie's heart almost jumped out of her chest. The gesture was so romantic—such a long-held image of the romantic hero—tears sprang to her eyes.

As if sensing her sudden disquiet, Bo nuzzled his lips against her hair and whispered, "I need you, Claudie. More than I've ever needed anybody, but we won't take this any further if it doesn't feel right to you."

His hands, so big and hot against her skin felt connected— not invasive strangers taking, but old friends, giving.

She dropped her head back to look at him. "I'm fine, Bo. Really."

She framed his face with her hands and kissed him with the same fire she sensed burning inside him. "My place or yours?" she asked, trying to sound sexy.

To her surprise, his step faltered. "Where do you prefer?"

She threw back her head and laughed. "It's not the where that matters—it's the who. I'm with you. That's what counts."

His smile had a Harrison Ford quality, as if he couldn't quite believe his good fortune. "My room, then. I packed a few—you know—just in case."

That he couldn't say the word made her smile inside, but she nodded seriously. "Good. Playing it safe is what kept me healthy."

He flinched, and Claudie realized there were still things

that needed to be said. When they reached the bedroom, she closed her eyes as he carried her across the threshold, imagining herself a new bride. In a way, she was. Their first night together would be her first time since leaving her old life behind. Her excitement was tempered by a voice that asked, *What if this is no different? What if I can't feel anything?*

When he set her down on the bed, Claudie kept her arms around his neck reluctant to let go.

"They're in my bag," he said, his eyes questioning.

She pushed away her fear and released him. Bo walked to the closet where his bags were sitting, still half-packed. He unzipped his leather shaving kit and pulled out a strip of three foil-wrapped disks.

When he turned around, he was frowning. "Claudie, maybe this isn't—"

A sudden shiver made her look down at her naked body. Even her mother's locket was missing—safely stored in her travel bag while she'd soaked in the tub. Spotting a cashmere throw at the foot of the bed, she grabbed it and looped it across her shoulders. The fluid material provided instant modesty, but oddly she felt herself blushing, as if her true feelings were even more visible.

She patted a spot beside her on the bed. "You're right. We should talk first."

His wiry brows collided above his nose. "Talk about what?"

She took a deep breath. "Like how many men was I with? Were they any good? Did they all have dicks the size of a horse and is it true size doesn't matter? How long could they last? Did I ever come? Am I going to see their faces when I'm with you?"

Bo's stricken look made her yank the silken cloak over her head and pull her knees to her chest.

"Claudie," Bo whispered. She sensed him dropping to his knees in front of her. "Look at me."

She shook her head. How could she ever have thought this would work? They might be adults and her hooking life was history, but he was still a man and men were weird about things like virginity and virility.

He looped his arms around her back and cuddled her as a father might a small child. His warm breath penetrated the fibers of the material near her ear. "We can do that if you want," he said softly. "I'll even go first. I'll tell you everything I've ever done with other women—the ones I can remember, at least. The size of their breasts. The way they moaned or screamed or barked."

She drew her chin up sharply. The blanket slipped to her shoulders.

One corner of his mouth twitched.

"Oh, you—" If her arms had been free, she would have slugged him.

"The point is," he said, laying his cheek against hers, "we can do all that crap if it will make you feel better, or we can leave it behind us and see what happens."

He pulled back to look into her eyes. "I don't have any answers, love. To tell you the truth, I'm scared spitless, but that has nothing to do with other men. I only care about you. What if I hurt you? What if this is the right thing, but the wrong time?"

His empathy loosened her inhibitions. She worked one arm free and touched his face, running her index finger over his lips—manly lips, a little skinnier on top, but well-shaped and usually full of humor.

"Oh, Bo, I've missed your smile." Closing her eyes against a rush of sudden, unexpected tears, she threw her arms around his neck and leaned into him. Her knees parted and she locked her ankles across the tops of his buttocks.

The blanket disappeared, no longer needed once Bo's hands replaced it. He laid his head against her chest and pulled her to him. His long sigh connected with something deep inside her.

Lowering his chin, he nuzzled the tops of her breasts, first one then the other. "You are incredibly beautiful," he whispered.

She arched her back as his mouth closed around one nipple. When he suckled, shock waves vibrated through her center core. A soft moan slipped from her lips. Silence had always been her credo—never give anything away—even pain, but with Bo she couldn't keep still.

He cupped the other breast and gently kneaded it, working loose emotions she'd never allowed into her world. "Oh…" she shyly volunteered, "that feels…nice."

His low chuckle caught her off guard. Were lovers supposed to laugh? Did she already do something wrong? "Just 'nice?'" he asked. "I was hoping for something like *wonderful, fabulous.* You're tough."

His playful tone further unlocked the rigid control she'd always kept in place. She pushed him away and scrambled back, moving to all fours. "And here I always thought I was easy," she teased.

Momentarily stunned, his gulp of laughter was followed by a frontal assault like something she once saw when she'd worked as an usher at a professional wrestling show. Before she could so much as scream in mock outrage, she was flat on her back with Bo stretched out on top of her.

"How come I'm naked and you're still dressed?" she asked, her nose touching his.

His rumbling chuckle jiggled his belly against hers in a most provocative way. She felt a buzzing sensation that triggered a warm moist response. Her wiggle was automatic, unplanned, but it provoked a kiss that took her breath away. A lover's kiss. Possessive, demanding.

Comforted by his weight, yet reassured by the fabric separating them from actual consummation, she reveled in the sensation of his kiss, the taste and texture. She freely explored his mouth before giving him access to hers.

As the pressure of his erection intensified against her pelvis, she lifted her hips, grinding them upward. His low groan sent a shot of adrenaline through her veins. She played her hands down his back, pulling the tails of his shirt free so she could touch his skin—moist with sweat, yet smooth and taut. His muscles worked at her touch, reminding her of his strength.

Lifting up on his elbows, Bo lowered his head and looked into her eyes. "You're torturing me and you love it, don't you?"

The humor in his gaze was tempered by the fire she felt ripple through him. She contracted her abdominal muscles to lift her pelvis higher. "You're on top," she said, watching him grit his teeth for control. "What does that say about you?" She ran the tip of her tongue over her top lip. "You like a little pain with your pleasure?"

His hoot made her heart soar. He wrapped his arms under her back and rolled them both to one side. "I love you, Claudie St. James. You are incredible."

She started to say something about it being too early to tell, but the words died on her lips when Bo ran his tongue from her clavicle to her bellybutton. He pressed his face against her belly.

Claudie worked her fingers through his hair, content to have him holding her—not sure she was ready for him to go any lower. As if hearing her silent debate, Bo pulled back. His understanding smile took away her tension. She suddenly knew she could trust him to hear her, to know her.

"I don't expect my mother back any time soon, but just in case…" he said, slipping off the bed. He crossed the room and locked the door. On his way back, he stripped off his shirt and belt then sat down on a cane-back chair opposite the bedside table to remove his shoes and socks. Before standing, he leaned over and unplugged the phone.

Claudie levered to one elbow. "Is that a good idea? What if something happens?"

Bo happened to be looking down, carefully guiding his zipper past the bulge in his pants. When he looked up, he grinned. The pants fell to the floor. "Didn't you hear? There's a blizzard out there. Even the phones are down, and the battery on my cell phone needs recharging." The impish glimmer in his eyes made her smile back.

He stripped off his Jockey shorts and walked toward her. "Besides, Dad's got two worshipful women at his bedside. Don't you think I'm entitled to one?"

"Did we say anything about worshipful?" she teased.

He gave her a hurt look then shrugged. "I'd settle for tolerant and forgiving of my middle-aged love handles."

She looked at his fit, trim midsection and couldn't help from noticing his very erect penis. "I don't see anything worth complaining about," she said. "In fact, on a scale of one to ten, I'd say you're a twenty."

His soft chuckle brought a grin to her lips. He stopped to pick up the foil-wrapped condoms that had fallen to the floor. When he looked up, their eyes met. "You're too kind, but I appreciate that in a woman. Especially when she's the woman I love."

His words hit her deep. He'd said the words before, but for some reason, it never truly registered at a gut level. This time she felt it—in her gut and below. "I love you, too, Bo," she said, her voice hushed with the power of her emotions.

Fear, loss, hope and joy warred within her breast. Her heart beat so fiercely she had to turn on her side and cross her arms to keep the pain from consuming her.

Bo was there in a flash, molding his body into the curved C she formed. His breath against her neck and shoulder was warm and soothing, his body a shield from external forces. But who would protect her from the demons within? Too many memories, so much pain.

"I never wanted to love anyone, Bo," she choked. "Love sucks. It killed my mother. She loved my father and never got over him. It ruined her life. What if—"

His strong arms tightened around her. "I won't let that happen. We'll figure out a way to get past all this bullshit. I know I've been a jerk since we got here, but that's all about me and my old man. Not you, Claudie." He kissed her ear. "You are my one reality."

She believed him, and she trusted him, but could she trust love? She rolled over to face him. "Could we say we're just a little in love?" she asked, trying to make sense of her fear. "For now at least. We could do this—make love, and it won't be like any of the others because we care about each other, right? But the idea of being totally, forever in love, scares me."

He pulled back enough to look into her eyes. He didn't answer right away. Claudie held her breath, wondering if she'd blown it.

"You just love me a little bit?" he asked.

His tone told her how much she'd hurt him. He sounded like Brady. "No," she said, hugging him fiercely. "I love you more than I dare. I love you so much it terrifies me because I have no control over it and I don't want to wind up like my mother."

She felt him relax. He stroked her back in a way that almost made her purr. "You're afraid to love because you think it's what killed your mother." He made her look at him. "Claudie, negative emotions kill people, not positive. Love is what gave her you. How could that be bad?"

Her sudden tears seemed as inappropriate as her earlier laughter, but Bo held her and kissed her and when the moment passed she found she was still naked and in the arms of the man who loved her and obviously wanted to make love with her. And to her amazement, for the first time in her life she felt ready. Truly ready to make love, too.

IN THE IMMEDIATE aftermath of their lovemaking, Bo felt a high unlike anything he'd ever known. His heart seemed to swell to the size of his chest cavity and that was good. Very good. Claudie's head on his chest, her breath floating across his chest hair felt very right.

But out of nowhere came a voice, a harsh hurtful voice that said he probably totally screwed up not only Claudie's life but also his own. He knew it wasn't true. Anything as wonderful as making love with the woman he'd spent his whole life looking for couldn't be bad, but the old voices knew just where to dig.

What happens if Dad dies? What if he lives? Either way Mom's going to need me. For how long is anybody's guess. But Claudie's life is back in Sacramento. People are depending on her. She needs the validation the halfway house gives her. She deserves to revel in its successes.

"Bo?" her sleepy voice asked, interrupting the chaos in his head. "Is that you in the picture on the mantel? The little boy in a cadet's uniform?"

Bo pushed aside his dark thoughts to bring the photo in question to mind. He smiled ruefully. Grindham Academy. Elite, pretentious, expensive and bleak in every sense of the word except structurally. "You mean the fat kid in the neo-Nazi drum major suit? No. That wasn't me. That was my twin brother Mike. We sold him to the gypsies when he was eleven because he wouldn't even try to learn to play rugby like the other rich kids." He snorted. "I mean, come on, what the hell good was he?"

She was silent a long time and Bo wondered if she'd fallen asleep when she suddenly asked, "Do you ever hear from him?"

"Who?"

"Mike." The way she said the name made him realize she was holding back tears. He didn't want his past to intrude on what they'd just shared so he tried to keep it light.

"Sure. All the time. He's a big used-car dealer down in the Keys. Smuggles a few cigars on the side. Never been married but he's got three kids."

"Do you ever wish you'd been the one they sold?"

Bo closed his eyes against a sudden shaft of pain. It took him a minute to regain the use of his vocal cords. "Why would I? I had it good—three squares, finest education money could buy, enough pocket money to score booze off the doorman. I couldn't complain," he finally said. But in truth, he'd dreamed of running away so often, in a way, a part of him was that imaginary brother living on some balmy Caribbean beach.

She sighed, her breath whispering across his chest. "Maybe we could go visit him someday."

He kissed the top of her head. "Before or after Niagara Falls?"

She lifted her head. "It's your call. He's your brother."

Bo tried to smile but his mouth wouldn't work right. She moved to take his face in her hands, and she told him, "You just gave me something I didn't think I'd ever find—my heart. Maybe someday you'll let me return the favor."

He squeezed his eyes tight and nodded, not trusting himself to speak. With a light sigh, she kissed his lips then sank back down. Bo held his breath, afraid any movement might create a ripple in the calmness. His heart was fine, thank you. As was his libido. His conscience was another matter, but he was just too damn tired to get into that.

Pulling her closer, like a shield, Bo gave in to sleep.

MATT RUBBED the sleep from his eyes and stumbled out of the elevator. It wasn't that late—probably about ten, but he'd fallen asleep watching some lame sitcom and might still have been curled up in his recliner if not for the phone call that jolted him awake.

His mother had been short and to the point. "Robert's being taken into surgery. They need to relieve the pressure in his brain. It's highly risky and we can't reach Bo."

He hadn't bothered arguing with her that if Bo didn't answer the phone it was probably because he was dead to the world and needed his sleep. More than likely the phone lines were down in that part of Manhattan and the cell phone's battery was low. Whatever, Matt knew his duty. As his Jeep negotiated the slippery streets and slush-covered potholes, Matt realized the storm had blown itself out. Stars were visible as moonlit clouds scattered before an icy wind.

Stalled cars, idiot drivers and a couple of impassable streets combined to slow him down. When he reached his aunt's apartment building, he had to use his badge to secure the okay from the building's doorman to leave his car in the loading zone. Stomping snow from his feet, he pushed the doorbell and waited.

When no one answered, he used his fist. "Bo, open up. It's me, Matt."

Concern was starting to build when he finally heard a noise on the other side of the door. "Matt?"

"Claudie. Open up. The phones are down and I need to talk to Bo."

Two locks clicked and he hurried in. To his utter shock, Claudie was standing to one side, wrapped in a blanket—with quite obviously nothing under it. Her hair was tousled, and she had that just-loved look about her.

He felt his cheeks grow hot and he looked down the hall toward Bo's room. "Is he here?" *Well, duh?*

She nodded. "He's asleep. I'll get him."

Matt had to force himself to stare at his boots to keep his eyes off the fetching figure she made tiptoeing down the hall. *Angelic* was the word that came to mind.

Bo joined him moments later, zipping his pants as he walked toward the foyer. "What's going on?"

Matt gauged the changes he saw in his cousin's demeanor. More the old Bo than the bitter man of late. Maybe she was an angel, he thought.

"Your dad's having some kind of crisis. Mom didn't go into the details on the phone, but the bottom line is they're taking him into surgery. Sounds touch-and-go. Your phone's out, so they sent me."

Bo swore. He ran a hand through his hair impatiently. When he looked at Matt, he said, "I'll be right back."

The bedroom door slammed behind him and Matt walked into the living room. A trail of clothes littered the carpet, but before he could analyze it too deeply Bo returned. "There's no need for both of us to go. I can call a cab."

Matt handed him the keys. "It's stopped snowing but the roads are a mess. There aren't many cabs running. I'll just crash here."

"Okay." Bo took his jacket from the coat closet and felt around in his outer pocket. "Damn," he said, producing his cellular phone. "I meant to plug this in the minute I got home."

He tossed it to Matt. "Take care of it, will you?"

Matt nodded, but Bo had already turned away. "I'd better tell Claudie goodbye. This will probably be an all-nighter. No telling—"

Before he could finish the words, she appeared, wrapped in a too big robe, obviously borrowed from Bo's closet. Barefoot, she dashed to him and threw her arms around him. "Are you sure you don't want me to come with you?"

Bo shook his head.

"Call if you need me, okay?" She kissed him.

Matt looked away. The tender scene hurt. He loved his cousin and was glad he'd found someone to help him through this turbulent time, but a part of him was bitterly jealous.

"Go back to sleep," Bo whispered, kissing her. "I won't call, unless—"

"Call," she ordered sternly. "I won't be able to sleep until I hear."

Bo nodded then took a deep breath and left.

Matt and Claudie stood in silence a moment. He sighed. "Well, hell, I'm awake now. Want some ice cream? Aunt Ruth always keeps ice cream in the house."

CLAUDIE HEARD Matt's question, but it didn't register. She stared at the door, kicking herself for not insisting on going along. Did his refusal to include her signal a reversion to the stranger she'd been seeing for the past two days instead of the tender, caring lover she'd been with an hour earlier?

"Umm, here," Matt said, tossing something to her. Claudie reacted instinctively, catching the soft bundle to her chest. Looking down, she saw her sweatpants and flannel shirt. Heat instantly consumed her cheeks.

"You might need these," he said. "The snow stopped, but now it's colder than hell."

"I suppose it's pretty obvious that we—"

Matt cut her off. "Bo and I have an agreement. I don't make up stories about my nonexistent sex life and he doesn't tell me about his. If something happened between you two, I'd say it was about time, but I'd really prefer not to talk about it. Envy isn't a pretty emotion."

She couldn't help but smile. He returned it with a wink then headed for the kitchen. "I'm a top-notch sundae maker. Wanna risk it?"

Claudie took a deep breath and let it out. "Okay. I doubt if I can sleep. I'll be right back."

"Take your time. A perfect sundae is a work of art. It can't be rushed."

Hugging her bundle of clothes, Claudie returned to Bo's room. The sight of the bed—a jumble of blankets and pillows—made her sigh. She sat down on the side Bo had occupied and reached beneath the sheets searching for any residual heat. His smell—soap, body talc and something intangible that seemed to define him in her mind—made her flatten her body against the covers.

"You are a treasure chest of wonders," he'd told her. "Glittering gold baubles, sparkling jewels. I feel like the richest man on earth when I'm in your arms."

She'd believed him. How could she not when he took her over the brink of the most glorious feeling her body had ever known? Their connection was too special, too perfect to be anything but love. For the first time in her life, she understood what her mother had felt for her father.

Propelled by an impetus she couldn't name, Claudie pulled on her warm clothes and dashed across the hall to the bathroom where her toiletry bag sat on the marble counter. She fished inside—impatient to find the one tangible link she had with her mother.

"Ah," she sighed, pulling the golden chain from the bag. Claudie faced herself in the mirror as she placed the necklace over her head. "I'm sorry it didn't work out better for you, Mom. I truly am," she whispered.

With that concession came a sense of pity for her stepfather. "Poor Garret," she said, drawing the locket to her cheek. "I'd be bitter, too, if I couldn't—"

Superstitiously, she bit her tongue. Things were too unsettled to predict what would happen between her and Bo. What if his father doesn't make it? she wondered. What if Bo never gets the chance to tell him how he feels?

She couldn't predict what might happen because, despite what they'd shared and how much she loved him, she didn't know him well enough.

With a sigh, she turned off the light and went to find the one person who did know Bo—maybe even better than Bo knew himself.

"How's the art project coming?" she asked, poking her head inside the doorway of the kitchen.

"The bowls are on the coffee table," Matt called back. He was standing in front of the microwave, his back to her. "I decided to make some tea, too. Do you like sugar in yours?"

"No, that's Bo's cup of tea."

Matt snickered, glancing over his shoulder. "I forgot napkins, grab a couple, will you? They're in the buffet by the liquor cabinet."

She took two from the top drawer of a built-in buffet. She wondered if Matt had noticed the mess. She tucked the napkins in the waistband of her sweatpants and hastily cleaned up the spilled whiskey. The smell almost sent her racing for the bathroom.

"Close call?" Matt asked, walking past her with two steaming mugs.

Frowning, she rinsed the rag. "You could say that."

"I've been worried about him the past few days, but I honestly didn't expect him to turn to booze," Matt said conversationally. "Once Bo makes up his mind about something, that's it. I haven't seen him take a drink in ten years."

Claudie joined him at the cozy grouping of overstuffed furniture. Two damask upholstered sofas faced each other while a pair of pale-yellow leather recliners sat side by side facing the fireplace. She took the chair at right angle to Matt.

Claudie laid a napkin beside one giant bowl of ice cream then reached for the bowl Matt had scooted toward her. Art was an understatement. Wavy lines of chocolate syrup drew to mind a child's painting, but strategically placed cherries gave it more a Picasso look. "This is gorgeous."

"Thanks."

She swallowed a bite of ice cream and sighed with pleasure.

Matt cleared his throat then said, "You know, Claudie, Bo's a great guy and I love him like a brother, but he *is* a guy."

"No argument there," she said, unable to keep from grinning.

Matt's swarthy complexion darkened. "What I mean is that's why Bo's been such a jerk lately. He's tweaked about his dad, but he can't talk about it. Guys don't talk about their feelings."

He sounded so sincere Claudie asked, "To each other or to anyone?"

"Pretty much anyone. Used to drive my ex-wife crazy. She was sure I was holding out on her—you know, keeping my inner thoughts private. Truth is, men don't have inner thoughts."

Claudie burst out laughing. "That's not true."

"It is. They might exist, but we're genetically programmed not to hear them."

She almost choked on a cherry. "Baloney. We sell a ton of books at the bookstore about men getting in touch with their feelings. Just because you're a little deaf to those kinds of emotions doesn't mean you can't learn to hear."

He gave her a horrified look that made her sit back laughing—until the little twinkle in his eye let her know he was putting her on. "You're just as bad as your cousin," she said, taking a sip of tea.

He scraped the last bit of ice cream from his bowl. "I know. But it's nice to see you smile. It's been awhile." He set the bowl down and leaned back. "This has been a pretty crazy week, huh? First, your family, then Bo's. I guess you could call this trial by fire."

"I guess." Claudie fingered her locket, trying to picture the image of her father. She wondered what her life would have been like if he'd been strong enough to disobey his father and marry her mother.

Suddenly, something Sherry said came back to her. This was her path. If the misery of the past hadn't happened as it did, she wouldn't have known Bo.

Sighing, she looked at the cluster of photos on the mantel. "Matt, do you know who Mike is?"

"Mike?" He frowned as if racking his memory banks. "What's his last name?"

Claudie shook her head and rose. "Never mind. It's not important. I'm going to try to sleep. Are you staying?"

He nodded. "Yeah. I'll hang out in case Bo calls."

Claudie smiled, but deep inside she knew he wouldn't call. He'd shared his love with her but not his demons. And what that meant for their future was anybody's guess.

CHAPTER TWELVE

THE MUTED HUM of a vacuum cleaner shook Claudie out of her dead-to-the-world sleep. She leapt from her bed, confused and a little dazed. The unfamiliar surroundings momentarily brought a burst of panic—*some guy's hotel room,* but the sight of Bo's suitcase with his shaving kit spilled open gave instant relief.

"Whoa," she murmured—the adrenaline in her system slowly dissipating. "I actually slept."

She grabbed the robe she'd used the night before and left the room. Somehow, the normalcy of a vacuum seemed out of place given all that had happened. She and Bo had made love. And it was good. Very good. Claudie couldn't repress the grin that spontaneously blossomed.

Her smile faded when she saw Matt and Ruth standing at the living room window against a backdrop of blue sky. Brilliant sunlight poured across their shoulders. They were speaking in low tones, their body language tense. The vacuum switched off and Ruth turned to say something to the maid. She spotted Claudie.

"Claudie, you're awake. I'm sorry if the vacuum—"

Claudie shook her head, walking forward to join them. "No, that's all right. I didn't mean to sleep so long, but I had a hard time falling asleep last night. Did Bo call?" she asked Matt.

Matt glanced at Ruth before answering. "Yes. I told him you were asleep, and he ordered me not to wake you."

"How's Mr. Lester?"

Ruth reached out to pat Claudie's arm as if she were the one whose husband was in critical condition. "He came through the surgery fine, but they've got him heavily sedated—a sort of precautionary coma this time. Irene said the doctors are optimistic."

Claudie's initial relief was tempered by a sense of underlying tension. "Is Bo at the hospital? I'll grab a shower quick then…"

She started to leave, but Matt's look stopped her. "What?"

Matt started to speak but Ruth cut him off by reaching out and taking Claudie's arm. "Would you care for a cup of coffee? There's pastry and fruit in the dining room. Let's go sit down." Ruth's smile was so like her son's, Claudie almost hugged her.

"I have some calls to make. I'll join you in a few minutes," Matt said, excusing himself.

Claudie watched him walk away. *Something's wrong.*

When they were seated, Ruth handed Claudie a cup filled with dark, fragrant coffee. Claudie sipped the bitter brew then set down the cup and pushed back the wide sleeves of the robe. "Okay," she said, "tell me what's going on?"

Ruth closed her eyes a moment and sighed. She'd aged since Claudie met her last summer. "I hate nosy people, Claudie. I've always made every effort not to intrude in other people's lives, particularly my son's. But I don't feel as though I have a choice in this case."

She drew in a breath, then said, "Claudie, Bo loves you. And I'm guessing that you love him, too."

Claudie looked down. Her feelings were too new to share in public. Especially like this.

"I'll take that as a yes," Ruth said, her tone gentle. "And, Claudie, I'm very glad because you've done something no other woman ever has. You've gotten under Bo's skin—touched his vulnerable underbelly."

"Is that bad?" she asked, glancing up.

Ruth shook her head. "No. It's wonderful. You've exposed the Bo that exists beneath all those silly disguises he's so fond of. Have you ever asked yourself why Bo chose to become a policeman and then a private investigator?"

Claudie shook her head.

Ruth made an encompassing motion. "As you can see, he didn't want for much growing up. He led a very entitled life—the kind of upbringing that usually spawns lawyers and doctors and investment bankers, not private investigators."

Claudie didn't bother looking—the *old-wealth* opulence had been the first thing to hit her when she'd walked in the door.

Ruth smiled. "I'm sure you've wondered about that, too. Well, I believe Bo purposely chose a career he thought his father would detest."

"There's nothing wrong with being in law enforcement," Claudie said, although Ruth was right. The thought had crossed her mind.

"Of course not, but Robert B. Lester, God love him, is a very pretentious person. He was raised that way and truly can't help himself. If it weren't for his amazing intellect and an almost childlike need to be loved, I never would have looked twice at him."

Claudie didn't want to be rude, but she couldn't help wondering what this had to do with her.

As if reading her thoughts, Ruth said, "Claudie, dear, the point I'm trying to make is that my son is a smart man, but he's never looked very deeply into what drives him. Bo has a number of issues to deal with where his father is concerned, and I'm afraid he won't do that if you're here."

Claudie sat back. *She wants me to leave.* "Have you talked to Bo about this?"

It was Ruth's turn to look away. "I wanted to speak with you first. If you're determined to stay, I won't stand in your way. As I said…" She reached out and touched Claudie's hand. "I want what's best for my son, and I honestly believe you're that person—just not at this moment."

Is she right? Is my being here keeping Bo from dealing with his problems? Maybe that's what Bo meant when he asked me to leave.

Claudie looked at Ruth's hand still resting on her own. Deep down she knew Bo's mother was right. Hard as it would be, Claudie had to let Bo deal with his own problems first.

She rose. "I'll call the airport about a ticket. But," she looked sadly at Ruth, "I can't just leave without talking to Bo."

Ruth nodded in agreement. "Of course not. Matt's going to the hospital, so he can take you there as soon as you're ready."

Claudie rose. "I should get organized." She started to step away, but paused and impulsively asked, "Ruth, could I borrow that photograph of Mike, uh, I mean, Bo? The one on the mantel? I'll make a copy and send it back."

Ruth cocked her head, curious no doubt about Claudie's gaff. "Of course, dear. Keep it. I've been trying to give all my photos to Bo for years, but he wouldn't take them."

Claudie started to leave but stopped at the doorway. "I really hope Mr. Lester gets well soon."

"Me, too, dear," Ruth said, softly. "For all our sakes."

BO LIKED his father's new room. Without the wall of high-tech equipment behind the bed, Bo felt reassured his father's health was improving.

Not that you can tell by looking at him, Bo thought.

Robert was still unconscious. A new bandage had replaced the old. Bigger, but more evenly conformed. His face looked bruised, with dark smudges beneath each eye. His long narrow cheeks were sunken, but the breathing apparatus was gone, as were the many tubes.

The doctors predicted a full recovery—although none would speculate how long that might take. What that meant for him and Claudie—whose lives were in California, Bo didn't have a clue.

Claudie. An image of her, naked in his arms, her breath coming in short, sweet bursts as she climaxed, caught him in the solar plexus.

He'd just talked to his mother and she said Claudie was on her way to the hospital. With any luck they could grab a few private moments in the coffee shop or the chapel. Maybe they could…

The sound of the door opening interrupted his wayward thoughts. And the focus of those thoughts walked in.

"Hi, there, sleepyhead," he said walking to her. Her hair was messy from the breeze and her cheeks still held a kiss of winter. "How are you?"

He started to put his arms around her, but she sidled to the left. She crossed to the window and stood with her back to him. She kept her jacket on, he noticed, despite the locker room heat.

"What's wrong?" he asked, starting toward her.

"Matt's driving me to the airport, Bo. My plane leaves in two hours."

Baffled, Bo shook his head. "What are you talking about?"

She took a deep breath; her hands fluttered nervously. "I called the airport and apparently the Thanksgiving rush has started, plus the storm last night compounded things. The

only seat available before Friday leaves in two hours. I…
took it."

A panicky sensation made his underarms tingle. "Why?"

Her shoulders lifted and fell.

Bo cleared the distance between them. He put out his hand
but didn't touch her. "Claudie, is this because I left so abruptly last night?"

Her eyes flashed in anger. "Of course not. I know what an
emergency is. You were…you are needed here. And I have
to get back to work. To One Wish House."

Bo threw his hands out. "Now? You're leaving now?
Didn't last night change anything?"

She flinched. "For me, it did," she said softly. "I'm not sure
what it meant to you."

He blew out a sigh of relief. Jitters he could understand.
They'd missed that whole waking up in each other's arms
thing. He took her by the shoulders. "If we could find a quiet
corner, I'd show you what it meant to me," he said playfully.

She jerked free of his touch. "Bo," she said, sharply. "This
is a hospital. That's your father."

"Yeah, I know. Don't remind me. They're starting to de-
crease his medications. He'll be back on his feet in no time—
although it may be a while before he goes skating again."

Bo was watching Claudie's face; he swore he saw a flicker
of sadness or regret that reminded him of their time in Kansas. "Claudie, what's this about? Really?"

"I talked to your mother this morning. She's worried about
you—your feelings toward your father."

Bo shrugged. "I'm here, aren't I?"

"Yes. And we both know you'll stay as long as your mother
needs you, but she thinks having me here will be a distraction."

Bo snickered and pulled her close. "She's right. A beautiful one."

Her sigh warmed his chest, but a shiver passed through his body. Instead of melting against him, she held herself back.

"That's what I was afraid of." She touched his cheek. "Bo, last night was the most wonderful experience of my life. But every moment we're together is one less chance you have to fix this thing between you and your dad." She took a breath. "You can't keep putting this off, Bo. I know what I'm talking about."

Bo pulled back. A heavy weight pressed on his chest. He spun on his heel and strode to the window. "This isn't the same as with you and Garret." He gestured toward the figure on the bed. "That man was a lousy father and a pathetic excuse for a husband but he never smacked me around or anything. Hell, half the time he acted as if I didn't exist. Besides, what does that have to do with us? It's ancient history."

"Is it, Bo?" she asked. "I don't think so."

Before he could go to her and take her in his arms, the door opened. Matt popped his head in and looked around. "Claudie, if you want to make that plane, we have to go. Traffic'll be a bear."

She nodded and started to leave, but Bo intercepted her. "Wait. You can't go. Not after last night."

She kept her chin down. "I have to."

The scent of her cologne filled his nostrils, bringing with it a memory of her uninhibited response to his lovemaking. "You can't just leave me, Claudie. Good Lord, woman, I tracked you all over hell to be by your side when you needed me. Now you want to take off like a scared rabbit the minute things get too intense."

"That's not why I'm leaving, and you know it."

He ignored the pain he heard in her plea. "No, I don't. Last night was real, Claudie. Maybe too real for you."

He thought for a moment she might change her mind, but

instead she reached up and removed her locket. She held it out to him.

Bo kept his fists tightly clenched at his sides, but she reached down and took his hand in hers. "Open," she ordered.

When his fingers unfurled, the gold chain spilled into his palm. The locket felt warm and heavy. His heart lifted and fell. His sinuses prickled from the emotion churning within.

"I'm trusting you with my heart," she said, rising up on her toes to press a quick kiss to his numb lips. Then she left.

Blinking at tears that refused to go away, he closed his fist around the talisman. He clasped it to his chest, as a racking pain drew out a long groan.

A noise made him look up. His father's eyes were open and he seemed to be staring at Bo.

Bitterness rose up like bile and Bo growled, "Are you satisfied now? You weren't content to ruin the first forty years of my life, you had to screw this up, too."

BO WAS SITTING AT THE FOOT of the bed dully threading Claudie's necklace between his fingers when his mother walked into the room.

"She's gone," he said flatly.

Ruth took off her coat, laying it neatly over the back of a chair. "Yes, I know. Matt took her to the airport. Both Matt and Claudie care a great deal about your welfare. You know that, don't you?"

He shrugged, not really listening.

"Robert B. Lester, Junior," his mother said sharply. Bo so rarely heard that tone of voice he almost jumped to attention. "I'd appreciate it if you'd listen when I'm talking to you."

Bo called that her librarian's voice. "I'm sorry," he apologized. "What did you say?"

She pulled up a chair beside the bed and sat down. "Do you remember when your Grandmother Lester passed away?"

Bo shook his head. "No, I can't say as I do."

"Pity. It might have helped you deal with this."

Puzzled, Bo looked at her. "Why?"

"Your father acted the same way you're acting right now. He pushed me away when I tried to help him. It wasn't six months later that he had his first affair."

Bo gaped. "You knew about it?"

She gave him a droll look. "Just in case you're ever tempted to cheat on Claudie, let me tell you—the wife is *not* the last to know. Not if she's paying attention."

Bo couldn't have been more stunned if his father suddenly jumped up and started dancing a jig. "I don't get it. Why'd you stay with him all these years?"

Ruth sighed and looked at the man in question. "I loved him, son. I still do. The heart doesn't always listen to what the head says."

Bo knew that for a fact. His head had been telling him for years that he hated his old man, but here he was—waiting, hoping, caring. He couldn't say for sure what he expected once his dad opened his eyes—they'd been strangers to each other for years.

"Who's Mike?" his mother asked.

Bo's nerves scattered like quail. "What?"

"You heard me. Claudie asked if she could take Mike's picture with her when she left. It was a slip, but it made me wonder."

Bo smiled. "It's nothing. We were joking around."

He could tell by her look anything short of the truth wasn't going to fly. "I was kinda chubby in that picture, and she couldn't believe it was me, so I told her it was really my twin brother, Mike." Talking about Claudie and last night brought him perilously close to panic. *She's gone.*

"I always regretted that we couldn't have more children," his mother said wistfully. "I think it would have made your childhood so much easier. Growing up the way you did probably made you feel like a bug under a microscope."

He lifted one shoulder. "It wasn't so bad, Mom."

"No, but it wasn't so good in some ways. I remember the day you were born. Your father was so proud. He called a buddy of his at the Times and asked for a whole column to announce your birth."

Bo snorted skeptically.

Ruth sighed. "Bo, your father and I both made mistakes. In our marriage and with you."

"You've been a great mom."

She reached out and patted his hand while shaking her head. "I've always been more comfortable around books than people, but your father thrived on public attention. Sometimes I wonder if I acted out of pure selfishness. When he wasn't around, I was free to read, to study, to escape into my books. Perhaps, I'm the one who was unfaithful first."

Bo was stunned by her confession. "Mom, it's not the same…"

She cut him off with a sharp gesture. "Yes, it is. If you love someone, you try to meet their needs, and you hope they'll meet yours. If you don't meet them halfway, you have no right to expect them to be there when you're ready."

Her words sounded ominous, a portent of the disaster he'd created in his own love life. Claudie had tried to help him in the way she thought best, and he'd yelled at her. Accused her of being a coward.

When he started to rise, Claudie's locket slid to the stark

white blanket. Claudie's mother's locket—the most precious thing she owned.

"She gave me her heart," he whispered—his voice cracking.

"So you could find your way home to her," his mother said softly.

Blinking at tears that refused to go away, he closed his fist around the talisman. He clasped it to his chest, as a racking pain drew out a long groan. His mother enveloped him in her arms. "It's okay, baby. Everything will be okay."

MIDWAY THROUGH the movie she wasn't watching, Claudie grabbed the glossy in-flight magazine from the seat pocket in front of her and flipped through it searching for a map. She used her right index finger to mark New York, then traced one of the myriad lines to San Francisco.

If this is us, we fly right over Kansas.

As discreetly as possible she opened the plastic window shade beside her. She was tucked in a corner and no one grumbled when she opened it so she guessed she was safe. Pressing her nose to the window she peered below. Nothing but a gray blur. Either they were too high or low-level clouds were blocking her view.

With a sigh, she closed the shade. She felt restless, yet lethargic. Anxious and tense, but numb. She couldn't identify her problem. *Lonely? Lost?*

People without family or friends were lost. But she had both—somewhere a mile or so below her.

Impulsively, she reached out and took the phone attached to the seat ahead of her out of its plastic receptacle. She dug in her purse for her credit card, then followed the instructions to place a call. This would cost her a fortune, but she didn't care. She found the number she'd tucked in a secret pocket of her billfold and punched in the sequence.

The voice that came on the line was so clear Claudie almost dropped the phone. "Sherry?"

There was a pause. "Yes. Who's this?"

Claudie's mouth went dry. "It's me. Claudie."

Her sister's loud wail seemed to echo in the cabin. "Thank the Lord. He heard my prayers."

Claudie blinked in confusion. "What?"

"I was just praying you'd call. We had a really bad night last night and I'm home alone and I was feeling really blue and—"

Claudie could hear her sadness. "What happened?" *Boyfriend troubles?*

"We had to take Daddy to the hospital. He was in a lot of pain the past few days, but he wouldn't go to the doctor. Finally, it was just so bad I started crying and he gave in."

Claudie's stomach twisted. "What do the doctors say?"

Her sister's voice became soft and childlike. "They've contacted the hospice, Claudie. I just came home for his Bible. We left in such a rush last night, we forgot it."

Claudie heard her start to cry. "Oh, honey, I'm sorry. I'm probably pretty close to you right now. I'm in a plane on my way home. Do you think they'd care if I opened a door and jumped out? Maybe I'd land on your house."

Her silliness brought a giggle on the other end of the phone. "I'd catch you in my butterfly net. Daddy and I used to catch all kinds of bugs and butterflies for my entomology studies. I always caught the prettiest ones."

Claudie swallowed against the lump in her throat. "Sherry, I'm sorry Garret's taken a turn for the worse. Give him my…tell him I…" She didn't know what to say. It was too soon.

Sherry rescued her. "I'll tell him you called. It will make his day."

Claudie's eyes filled with tears. "I'll call again as soon as I'm home."

They exchanged a few more words then Claudie hung up the phone. She peeked out the window again. The man she thought she hated was dying, and she felt like crying. The man she loved was half a continent away.

Claudie glanced at the movie screen and saw the beautiful leading lady in full bridal regalia kiss her groom. If she'd had anything in her hand, she'd have thrown it. Happy endings were for movies and romance novels. Real life was a whole different story.

CHAPTER THIRTEEN

"CLAUDIE," A VOICE CALLED the instant she stepped into the terminal of the Sacramento airport.

Totally unprepared for a greeting party, it took Claudie a few seconds to pinpoint the sound. Sara and Brady rushed to meet her.

Brady barreled into Claudie, nearly knocking her over. She scooped him up.

"Oh, Brady-boy, I missed you so much," she cried, emotion choking her almost as much as Brady's arms around her neck.

A moment later, he wiggled free, and she set him down. He rattled off something too fast for her to catch then beamed at his mother expectantly.

"He wants to know if you'll read to him tonight. He missed you. We all did," Sara said, giving Claudie a warm hug.

Claudie's heart expanded but she still couldn't figure out how Sara knew to meet her plane. Had Bo called?

As if reading her mind, Sara said, "Matt called. He was worried about you. He sounds like a nice guy. Brady…" Distracted, she dashed after the little tyke. "Let's get your bags. We can talk in the car."

Brady was asleep before they hit I-5. Claudie couldn't keep from smiling at his cherubic face. She definitely wanted children. She hoped Bo felt the same way. *If he was still speaking to her that is…*

"Could I use your cell phone?" she asked, suddenly desperate to hear his voice. "I should let Bo know I got home safely."

"Sorry. It's in the diaper bag which I left at Babe's," Sara said. "Do you want to stop somewhere or can you wait until we get home?"

"Sure. No problem."

Sara gave her a sidelong look. "Well, something's wrong. Did you and Bo have a fight? Is that why he isn't with you?"

Claudie regretted not spending more time preparing an answer to that question instead of spending most of the flight second-guessing her decision to leave. "Bo's mom and I talked about it and we decided he needed to spend some time alone with his dad."

Sara made a face. "How'd Bo take that?"

A fluttery sensation akin to panic made Claudie reach for her locket—her touchstone. But it was gone. Her one tangible proof of her journey. Then she remembered something. She fished in her purse for the little disposable camera. She'd used the last shot to get a picture of Matt at the airport. "Sara, could we drop this off at the one hour photo place on the way home?"

"Sure," Sara said. "And Ren can pick them up when he gets done with class. When I told him you were coming home, he insisted on a welcome home party. A little barbecue. Then a dip in the hot tub. Okay?"

Soothing water and a glass of wine sounded tempting. So did the idea of talking to Ren. Who better than Bo's best friend to tell her if she did the right thing?

ON THE FOLLOWING THURSDAY, as the residents of One Wish House were preparing to join the Bishops for Thanksgiving dinner, Claudie ducked into her office. She sat down at her

desk and picked up the handmade Thank You card that had
been waiting on her desk when she got home Monday night.
Beside it, Claudie's photos lay scattered, including the three
shots of Sherry that made Claudie's heart soar.

"You saved her," Maya said softly, taking Claudie by surprise. She hadn't heard her approach. "I knew you would."

Davina and Sally Rae joined them before Claudie could
respond.

"She's so beautiful. And tall. Are you sure she's your sister?" Davina asked.

"Did she like you?" Sally Rae asked. "I mean, you know,
did you tell her about ..." Her expressive complexion turned
bright red.

"What I want to know is why'd you have to give her your
car?" Rochell complained, sweeping into the room in an impressive African caftan. "How're ya gonna get around?"

Claudie chuckled. "I didn't actually rescue Sherry. I told
you—my stepdad's dying of cancer. They're moving him to
a hospice Saturday."

The low cheers were meant to be supportive, but Claudie
was saddened by the image of Garret that came to mind.
"The important thing is Sherry's great, and I gave her my car
because my mother left me enough money to buy a new one.
I'm going to start looking as soon as Bo—" she bit off the
thought. "As soon as we get past this dim sum thing."

This, of course, set them all off on their favorite topic, but
Claudie held up her hand for silence. "Let me finish. As to
whether or not Sherry really is my sister—yes. She has our
mother's eyes and smile. And, Sally Rae, she's going to come
visit after graduation. I can't wait to introduce her to all of
you."

Claudie had received two e-mails from Sherry—including
an update on Garret's condition and had forwarded both to

Val, hoping to reconnect those two. And Claudie planned to keep in touch with her brothers, too. Particularly, Zach. In fact, she hoped to talk to Ren today about Zach's postprison options.

Ren had already helped Claudie by giving her some perspective about Bo's situation. "One thing I know," he'd told her that night in the hot tub "is, no matter how much you love a person, *you* can't fix him. Ultimately, that has to come from within. Give him time, Claudie. He'll understand that you did what you thought was best for him."

Claudie hoped so. But so far, he hadn't returned any of her calls.

Something Sally Rae was saying suddenly sank into Claudie's consciousness. "Wait. Did you say Babe has a date?"

Sally's blush returned. "I overheard her on the phone. She said it isn't really a date. He's an old friend, and he asked Babe to help his church serve Thanksgiving dinner to the needy, so they're only coming to Ren and Sara's for pie."

Rochell hooted and rolled her eyes. "I swear all this do-gooder stuff is going to come back and bite her in the butt. Rich people can't mingle with us common folk for long without something bad happening."

Claudie would have argued the point, but Sally beat her to it. "Hogwash. Money sets people apart, but a good heart can overcome that. Babe told me her father was a grape farmer, Rochell. She was the Grape Queen before she met Ren's dad. And I'll tell you a secret, but you have to promise not to tell her I blabbed."

The room fell silent.

"Babe's real name is Beulah. Beulah May Smith."

Rochell's gaze met Claudie's. "My grandma's name was Beulah."

"My father's name was Smith," Claudie said softly.

On the way to the airport Matt had handed her a computer printout with a name and a bunch of dates on it. "I know this isn't any of my business," he'd said apologetically. "But it's what I do."

Claudie smiled picturing that paper. Her father's name was John Lowell Smith. Knowing that meant more to her than she ever could have imagined. Sadly, the one person who would most appreciate the significance of it wasn't speaking to her.

A car horn sounded in the driveway. Everyone scattered to collect last minute items to take to the feast. Claudie hurried, too, but she'd have been more thankful if Bo would have called that morning.

Maybe he'll call Sara's, she thought trying to smile. Maybe.

THE SMELL OF roasted turkey warred with the antiseptic smell of the hospital room. Matt had dutifully carted three plates loaded with all the traditional Thanksgiving fixings to the hospital to share with Bo and his mother. Bo's father was on a restricted diet and showed no real interest in food. In truth, Robert showed no interest in life, and Bo found his meager supply of compassion sliding beneath an overwhelming sense of frustration.

"Your mother is the best cook in the world," Ruth told Matt, wiping the corner of her mouth with a floral napkin. "I love her yams."

Matt smiled. "That's what Ashley said when she found out she wasn't having dinner at my mom's."

Bo thought Matt looked inordinately pleased by that. "Is she at Sonya's parents' today?"

Matt shook his head. "Alan's mother's place in Connecticut. I just talked to her on the phone. She said there are a million little kids around but nobody her age, so she's bored out of her mind."

Bo eyed him thoughtfully. "Tough break. Guess she'll look forward to next year with you, right?"

Gnawing on a drumstick, Matt nodded grinning.

Bo's low chuckle was interrupted by a sharp, unintelligible outburst from his father. The first time Robert had tried to make himself understood, only meaningless sounds had burst forth—guttural and strange. Irene explained that this was common for a man whose brain had suffered such an extreme trauma, but the knowledge made it no less unnerving.

Bo rose from the corner table where they were eating and walked to the bed. "Awake? Good. I think they have pureed turkey for you today. I'll call the nurse." Bo realized his formal tone probably sounded phony, but he didn't have the first clue how to talk to this man—a stranger in his father's body.

He started to turn away, but his father suddenly grabbed Bo's hand in a grip far stronger than Bo would have imagined. "Whoa, somebody's been pressing iron when our backs were turned." He leaned toward his father. "What can I get you, Dad?"

"Scotch."

The clarity, as much as the word itself, took him aback. "Mother, did you hear that?"

Ruth and Matt joined him. Bo felt his father's grip lessen. "He answered my question. He wants a drink."

Ruth frowned. "That's not possible, dear. You're on a lot of medication."

Robert's eyes closed. His fingers went slack.

"I don't think he was serious, Mom," Bo said. "But he sure got our attention."

She pressed a kiss to her husband's slack lips then said,

"I've made up my mind. Tomorrow we start looking into rehab centers."

Bo was shocked. They'd discussed the timing of this decision at great length but not in front of his father. "Matthew, you may start moving into Robert's loft tonight, if you wish."

"Are you sure Uncle Robert's going to be okay with that?" Matt asked, eyeing Bo's father nervously.

Ruth patted her husband's shoulder and smiled. "It's for the best. We're both too old for any more nonsense, and the location will be perfect for your new office."

Bo agreed wholeheartedly. "It'll be great, Matt," Bo said. The disposition of his father's apartment had been bothering him until his mother suggested renting it to Matt. There was still the matter of boxing up his father's personal items, but at least this relieved Bo of having to find a renter.

They returned to the table and sat down to finish their meal.

"I don't have to move in right away," Matt said, taking a bite of mashed potatoes. "I could wait until after the first of the year."

"The sooner the better as far as I'm concerned," Ruth said. "Once we get Robert settled, Bo will be free to return to California. And Claudie."

Bo rubbed his thumb across the bump in his pants pocket. Her locket. The one tangible reminder of their night together. The longer they were apart, the less real their time together seemed.

Matt pushed his plate away and crumpled his paper napkin on top of it. "I guess you're right. I'll go home and start packing." He rose. "If you're not too tired, Cuz, stop by and give me a hand. Or are you going out to my mom's, too?"

It had been decided that Ruth would spend the night with her sister-in-law. Bo planned to stay until his father was asleep for the night then go back to the apartment. "Mom? Is it too late to change my mind and go with you?" he teased.

Matt gave him a light poke on the shoulder. "Don't come empty-handed. Bring boxes."

Once he left, Bo and his mother ate in silence until she said, "How's Claudie?"

A bite of stuffing lodged in his windpipe. "Umm…I haven't actually talked to her."

Ruth's brow rose. "And why is that? It's been three days."

Bo let out a raspy sigh. "I…don't know what to say."

She snorted. "I doubt that very much. You're the product of two people who never shut up. Robert once said the thing that kept us married so long was our ongoing dialogue—and the fact neither of us listened to a word the other one said."

Bo chuckled, but his smile faded when she gave him a stern look. "Call her. Now. Wish her a Happy Thanksgiving and tell her you miss her." She stood up. "Enough nagging. You'll pick me up at Irene's in the morning, right? The first rehab place I want to visit is on Long Island."

Bo was dreading that almost as much as calling Claudie. What could he say? I'm sorry? For what? For having a father like his? That went without saying.

After his mother left, Bo rose and stretched, stiff from so much inactivity. He glanced at his watch and subtracted three hours. "So, whatcha doin', Claudie girl?" he said aloud, drawing her image into his mind. "Just sitting down to eat?"

A moment later a voice said gruffly, "Crazy. Talk. Self."

Bo spun to face the bed. "God!"

His father shook his head. "Dad."

Bo laughed. He couldn't help himself. The shock of hearing his father speak rivaled the realization he'd just laughed out loud at something his father said—a miracle that hadn't taken place in twenty years.

Bo stepped closer. "Must have been that turkey juice they gave you. You look better."

Robert closed his eyes and breathed in. On the exhale he said, "Still want drink."

Chuckling, Bo walked to the moveable bed stand and poured some ice water into a plastic cup. "Here you go. Whiskey and water. Light on the whiskey."

Feeling awkward, he put one hand behind his father's bony neck and helped guide him to the glass. A trickle made it past Robert's flaccid lips. Excess drops fled down his cheek, getting caught in the bristly white stubble. When Robert closed his lips to indicate he was finished, Bo gently placed his father's head back on the pillow and used a towel to wipe up the spills.

"Not bad," Robert said.

Bo placed the cup on the tray and moved back, resting his hip on the bed near his father's thigh. "Mom and I are going to look at a couple of extended-care facilities tomorrow," Bo said, feeling a need to say something.

Robert's eyes flew open, a look of panic visible in his gray green irises.

"It's temporary, Dad. Just until you can walk and talk again. One of the places has a hydro pool and offers Swedish massage. I'll ask to meet the massage therapists. I know you prefer tall, buxom and blond." Bo tried to keep his tone light, but even to his ears it sounded snide.

As his father's breathing evened off, Bo picked up his coat and left. He planned to call a cab from the lobby, but once he picked up the receiver he made the impulsive decision to call Claudie. His mother was right. He was making a bad problem worse. He knew she made it home safely because she'd called his mother's and left a message on the machine. He'd played it a dozen times, alternating it with the recording he'd saved from his office.

"Twisted," Matt had said, catching him in the act. "Severely twisted. Maybe that old lady you told me about on the plane was right. Maybe you are a stalker."

"Shut up."

"You know, you deserve it if Claudie never talks to you again. Notice she called your mother, not your cell phone."

"You have my cell phone," Bo pointed out.

"She hasn't called it."

"I only have your word on that. Aren't you supposed to be picking up your daughter from her riding practice?" he'd snarled, hating the way Matt could provoke him. Matt was even more annoying than Ren.

Matt had left, but the disquiet his observations raised lingered.

Bo punched in his memorized calling card code, then Ren and Sara's number. He knew from Ren's call that Claudie and the girls from One Wish House were spending the day with the Bishops.

"Happy Thanksgiving," a deep masculine voice answered.

"Yeah, whatever," Bo returned.

"Hey, Bo, what's happening?"

"Not much. Is Claudie around?"

His attempt to sound casual came off as cool as a teen asking for his first date.

"Nope. She's not here. After we finished eating, Claudie and the others offered to take Brady to rent a movie."

"Damn."

"Can I have her call you back?"

Bo sighed. "I'm helping Matt move into my dad's loft tonight. We'll be in and out. And my mom took my cell phone in case the hospital calls."

Ren was silent a minute then said, "You know, Bo, this is none of my business, but Claudie was trying to do the right thing by giving you time alone with your dad. How's he doing, by the way?"

Bo briefed his friend on his father's progress, ending with, "He seemed more like his old self tonight." Then trying for levity, added, "I guess that personality transplant thing is still in the experimental stages."

Ren's laugh sounded good, but it made Bo homesick. He missed his friends. He missed Brady. He missed Claudie.

Bo's gut churned. "Do you know where she'll be tomorrow?"

"She and Sara are going to be at the bookstore all day because Daniel's skiing in Utah. You know how busy the day after Thanksgiving is for retailers. It's the start of the Christmas rush."

Damn! Just what I need—another lousy holiday to add to the equation.

"Just tell her I called. Monday I'm getting a second cell phone for Matt, so she can call my number if she wants to get hold of me."

Bo hung up feeling more conflicted than ever. His mother needed him, and for the first time in Bo's life his father needed him; but he needed Claudie—who was back where she belonged.

STILL A BLOCK from the video store, Claudie squeezed the little hand she held, smiling down at the curly crown of the child walking beside her. She'd missed Brady so much when she was gone, but it hardly compared to what she was feeling at this moment for Bo. His presence had been glaringly absent from the long, festive dinner table in Sara and Ren's recently remodeled dining room.

Claudie thought she was doing a good job hiding her true feelings until Sara cornered her in the kitchen. "We miss him, too, Claudie. But Ren says Bo's father's prognosis is good. Bo will be home in no time," she'd whispered. Nearby, Maya and Sally Rae were mashing potatoes—a joint effort since neither seemed too familiar with the process.

"I know," Claudie had tried assuring her. "I'm fine."

"Yeah, right. Me, too. Except I'm pregnant and you're miserable."

Claudie had patted her friend's rounded tummy. "How are my godchildren?"

"Bo's kid is great. Yours is only so-so."

Claudie knew Sara was joking, but she blanched at the thought that something was wrong with one of the twins— babies she and Bo felt they'd had a hand in conceiving. After all, Ren never would have met Sara without Bo's investigative skills, and Sara wouldn't have moved in with Ren without Claudie as a chaperon. Close to tears, Claudie had grabbed a napkin just before Sara scooted her out the patio door.

Claudie refocused on the present when Rochell ushered them into the brightly lit video store. She absently picked up a video.

"Claudie?" Brady asked, tugging on the leg of her khaki slacks to get her attention. "For me?"

She glanced at the four other women who were looking at her expectantly. Claudie looked down and saw she was holding a movie. She hadn't even realized she'd picked one out. When she read the title, she laughed. "I guess this will do. What do you think, ladies?"

She held up the box with its highly recognizable title.

Maya gave an inscrutable shrug.

Sally Rae sighed wistfully and said, "I used to watch that with my big brother. He always reminded me of the cowardly lion." She frowned. "He got hit by a car and died when I was fourteen."

"Let's get it," Davina said with enthusiasm. "I never got to watch the whole thing. Ever."

Only Rochell gave it a thumbs-down. "Those flying monkeys give me the creeps," she muttered.

While Sally Rae took Brady up to the counter to pay for *The Wizard of Oz*, Rochell hunted for a second—more *adult*—selection. As she waited, Claudie resurrected a memory of lying elbow to elbow on the floor in front of the television with her siblings while Dorothy skipped down the Yellow Brick Road toward Oz. Claudie didn't know if the image was real or imagined, but she could vividly picture Garret and her mother on the sofa, holding hands. Kissing.

"The past speaks to you," Maya said quietly.

Claudie didn't dismiss her observation. She'd sensed the older woman's concern since her return. "Not everything was bad. There were good times, too, but I guess those memories got lost in the pain."

"You wish to go back again? Be a family once more?"

I'd like to spend time with Sherry...and Zach. I'm sorry Garret's sick, but... Before Claudie could formulate an answer, Brady ran up to her and grabbed her hand.

"Home, Claudie?" he asked, his blue eyes glittering with love and affection.

Claudie blinked back her sudden tears. She picked him up and squeezed him tight. Settling him on her hip, she followed the others out the door. Maya brought up the rear. Over her shoulder, Claudie softly called, "This may not be Kansas, Maya, but it *is* home."

CHAPTER FOURTEEN

RESTLESS AND TENSE, Bo prowled the confines of his father's new room at the Pennington Institute, an extended-care facility renowned for treating all kinds of neurological-motor disabilities. His father was going through an in-processing evaluation; Matt and Ruth would be along soon with Robert's personal items and clothing.

Tricia had appeared at the hospital that morning to tearfully announce that the whole situation was "too intense" for her. For some reason, her brief, awkward goodbye had left Bo feeling more unnerved than he cared to admit.

For the first time in his life Bo understood the frustration of wanting to be in two places at the same time. He was needed here—his parents needed his help and business-wise no one else could get the ball rolling with Matt—but Bo wanted to be with Claudie.

And she would have been here if not for her misguided belief about his needing to fix things with his father. *The past is ancient history* he'd told his mother. And Bo meant it—except when he looked at his father. Then all the old hurts had a way of zapping him.

He'd tried to discuss his feelings with Claudie. Unfortunately, long distance phone calls did little to promote empathy. For one thing, it had taken half a dozen attempts to finally connect with her. His first try on the Saturday after Thanksgiving had ended in a shouting match with Rochell, whom he'd woken up at seven in the morning.

"You've been off the streets for months, Rochell. Aren't you acclimated to a new schedule, yet?"

"I'll give you acclimation, Mr. High and Mighty," she'd countered with a growl. "Aren't you the fool who raced off to find the woman he loves only to send her back with her tail between her legs like a whipped pup?"

Her graphic metaphor almost made him lose his breakfast. "You don't know anything about it, Rochell. Let me talk to Claudie."

"Not before I tell you why she outta dump your ass." Rochell made it to number six on her list—All men suck—when she finally admitted that Claudie and Sally Rae had started a new exercise program and were out jogging.

Bo finally caught up with Claudie at the bookstore later in the afternoon, but his timing was off there, too. Sara had just left and Claudie was swamped with customers. She'd promised to return his call that night—which according to the answering machine she'd done while Bo was packing up his father's belongings at the loft.

The three-hour time difference seemed to conspire against him no matter when he called. Either she was running errands or attending a city council meeting with Babe Bishop or giving an interview to a reporter about the upcoming fund-raiser. To her credit, Claudie never failed to call back. Her voice on his mother's answering machine was like candy—sweet little morsels that whet his appetite for something more substantial.

Even getting back his cell phone hadn't helped. He was out of the loop. On those rare times he'd managed to catch Claudie, she'd sounded distracted, overwhelmed by the last-minute details involved with hosting what had become a large-scale fund-raising event.

Bo sat on the edge of the bed and pictured his conversation with Claudie the night before. Even three thousand miles apart he could hear her fatigue. "You sound wiped out."

Her sigh was very un-Claudie. "I thought it was jet lag, but Maya calls it 'life lag.' Everything is catching up with me. Plus I'm worried about Sherry and Garret. I told you he's in hospice care, didn't I?"

Bo didn't want to think about Kansas...or New York. He only wanted to hold Claudie and feel her cuddle against him in her shy, sweet way. "You have too many irons in the fire. If I were there to be a buffer, they'd have to come through me to get to you."

"Any idea when you're coming back?" she asked. Before he could answer, she'd added, "Not that I'm trying to be pushy. I know this is really, really hard for you."

He sighed. He had a few too many irons of his own. "I'm shooting for Saturday, but I can't promise anything."

"I wasn't asking for promises," she said testily. "I was just curious."

They were both silent a moment then Claudie told him, "I'm covering for Daniel on Friday and Saturday. The dim sum thing is Sunday. Then I'm off Monday through Thursday—if I survive."

"Do you need a place to hide out?" Bo suggested, wondering if they'd ever get back to the easy repartee they shared in Kansas. "I happen to know where you could find a quaint—some might say, charming—houseboat on the delta."

Her long pause had been enough to make him twist the phone cord into a knot. "I promised Sara we'd go Christmas shopping in the city next week—maybe even stay over. And I have to start looking for a new car, too."

Her excuses confirmed Bo's fears. "You're really mad at

me, aren't you? For the way I acted when you left. Especially after the night we shared."

"No. Of course not," she said quickly, too quickly. "I'm a big girl, Bo. I knew what I was doing and I'm not trying to hold you to anything. What happened that night was just one of those things."

"No, it wasn't." He couldn't prevent the desperate edge in his tone. "Claudie, tell me you don't believe that. I love you. You know that, don't you? This stuff between me and my dad doesn't have anything to do with us."

Bo listened to her breathing; it seemed to catch in her throat. Before he could say anything else, she said, "I'm really wiped out, Bo. Can we finish this later?"

"Sure," he said, grimacing at the despondency he heard in her voice. "I miss you, Claudie. I love you."

He wasn't certain she heard since the only answer was the echo of her yawn. "Good luck tomorrow," she said. "Bye, Bo."

A noise at the door made him jump to his feet. Two orderlies pushed a wheelchair into the room. It had taken Bo a while to get used to seeing his father in a wheelchair. A strap around his chest kept Robert upright, but his head lolled weakly to one side.

Even at a distance Bo could tell Robert was exhausted. The gray shadows beneath his eyes seemed far more pronounced. Bo hurried forward to help. One attendant removed Robert's leather slippers while the other unfastened the chest strap and worked Robert's striped silk robe over his shoulders. Bo turned down the burgundy print bedspread while the men swiftly, effortlessly transferred Robert's unresponsive body to the bed.

"Thanks," Bo said, taking the robe from the taller of the two. He hung it in the closet. "We appreciate your help."

"No problem," the man said. "I'm Jake and this is Francisco. Any time your dad needs something, just give us a holler."

Francisco parked the wheelchair to the right of the bed and they left. Bo stepped to his father's side. The bed, while as functional as a standard hospital bed, was lower, more discreet. The room itself was large and light. In addition to the recliner and armoire, there was a small settee and a coffee table.

Before the movers had arrived at Robert's loft apartment, Ruth had chosen a few of his favorite things she hoped would make the place more homelike. But Bo doubted the Baccarat vase and the couple of Boucher drawings would do the trick.

He checked his watch. Matt and his mother should arrive soon. "Not stay here," Robert said, suddenly.

The lack of inflection in his father's voice still bothered Bo. All words were delivered in a robotlike cadence, emotionless—sometimes clear, sometimes garbled.

Bo noticed his father's fists clenched at his sides.

"Sorry, Dad," Bo said, trying to sound sympathetic, "but you don't have a choice. This place comes highly recommended. I'm sure you'll do fine here."

The answer must not have been what Robert wanted to hear. His eyes closed, fingers relaxed. These mercurial mood swings threw Bo for a loop, too. His father had always had only one mood—serious.

Bo studied his father's face. Daily physical therapy had helped him regain some color. Although Robert still lacked most fine motor skills, the therapists had been impressed with his recuperative powers.

Bo looked up as a nurse entered the room. She carried a small tray with three tiny plastic cups.

"Good afternoon, gentlemen. Welcome to Pennington," she said, smiling to include Bo as well. Small, dark and in her midfifties—her accent sounded Philippine. She moved with quick, economic motions. "I've got some medications for you, Mr. Lester."

Without warning, Robert's arm swung wildly and caught her just below the shoulder. The tray crashed to the floor. She would have fallen, if Bo hadn't reached out to steady her.

"Sorry," Bo said.

Her look held no malice. "It's okay. Patients are often upset and confused when they first arrive." She kneeled to pick up the pills. "I'll try this again a little later. We can always go back to an IV if he doesn't settle down."

Robert's eyes were closed giving no indication whether or not he heard her, but once she was gone, Bo saw his father unclench his fist.

"I remember you telling me once that a bad attitude was no excuse for abusing the help," Bo said softly.

"Hangover," Robert said, taking Bo by surprise.

"I beg your pardon?"

"Bad hangover."

When it dawned on him what his father meant, Bo couldn't keep from grinning. "You're right. You did say 'hangover,' not 'attitude.' But in my case, the two were practically interchangeable."

His father let out a deep sigh. Bo knew that sound: exasperation—a signal Robert was ready to throw up his hands and stalk away from whatever argument they were in the midst of.

This time Bo did the walking. He picked up a large, lush hothouse plant—a gift from Sara and Ren that had just arrived—and carried it to the window.

"Carmen," his father barked, almost making Bo drop the plant.

Bo placed the container on the sill and walked back to the bed. Bo didn't know anyone by that name but the fact his father was calling out for someone other than his mother infuriated him.

Before he could respond, his father spoke again. "Serves right."

Serves right? "I get it," Bo exclaimed. "You mean karma, not Carmen. You think this is payback for what you've done in your life."

Robert's head nodded fractionally. When he opened his eyes, there were tears. Not the tears of frustration that Bo had seen off and on all week. Tears of anguish. And fear. The kind of fear that awaited the less-than-righteous on judgment day.

Something twisted in Bo's gut. His first impulse was to turn around and walk out, but he couldn't make himself go. Instead, he stepped closer and put his hand on his father's shoulder. "Dad, that's not how it works. I think you have to die first, then you come back as an anteater or something."

Bo regretted his flippant answer when Robert's chest heaved with silent sobs. Tears ran into his pillow. Bo's fingers squeezed. "Dad, what happened was an accident. This place is going to help you get your life back. That's a good thing, right?"

Bo sensed his father struggling to speak, but was obviously hampered not only by his physical disabilities but his emotions. "Bad…father," he finally spewed out.

A flood of emotion cascaded over Bo. He pictured Claudie facing Garret—the man who'd robbed her of her self-worth. What had Robert done so wrong by comparison? Worked too hard? Been self-absorbed and demanding? Failed to keep his loved ones close?

Bo lowered his head and looked into his father's eyes. "Yeah," he said softly. "You were a lousy father…at times.

But, believe it or not, I think I always knew deep down that you loved me."

Something in his father's eyes changed. Hope tempered by caution. "Always," he whispered.

Bo's heart swelled with emotion. He blinked back tears of his own. "I remember telling Ren Bishop one time that no matter what a bastard you were, I could count on you for anything. Was I right?"

Robert nodded.

"Then prove it."

"How?"

Bo pulled up the wheelchair and sat down. He rested his elbows on the mattress and said, "Get well. Soon."

His father's left brow rose—a semblance of his old self.

Bo suppressed a grin. "I don't know if Mother mentioned it, but I've met someone. Her name is Claudie. She's not like anyone I've ever known. She's totally honest, absolutely straight with the world. I love her and I'm going to ask her to marry me."

His father's smile was a little crooked but it was definitely a smile.

"Knowing Claudie, she'll undoubtedly insist on waiting to set a date until you're well enough to attend. So, the sooner you get well, the sooner I can get married." Knowing how much his father loved a challenge, he added, "Now that I think about it, you ought to pay for my wedding."

His father's wiry gray brows shot up. "Why?"

Bo bridged his fingers trying to look stern. "Well...there's still that matter of your gambling debt."

His father's eyes went wide.

"Oh, sure, try to give me that cracked-my-head-on-the-sidewalk-and-can't-remember-anything excuse. You know what I'm talking about. That Christmas I came home from college. Mom was helping Aunt Irene with Deborah's twins. Remember? I invited those guys from the bar to the apartment to play poker, and you joined us."

Robert scowled. "Crooks."

"I had them right where I wanted them until you bluffed me out of my straight flush. If I hadn't folded, I would have won. Instead that loser dude with the tattoo won." In truth, Bo had been drunk on his butt and probably would have lost his shirt, all the good silver and the vast majority of Christmas presents under the tree if his father hadn't come home and rescued him. "I figure I lost about six hundred bucks. Invested wisely—which you would have, no doubt—we'd be looking at something in six figures by now. So, I think it's only fair that you pay for the wedding."

Robert looked at him squarely. He didn't blink. After a moment of stiff silence, Bo saw the corner of his lips twitch. "Done," his father said.

Bo smiled. "Good. I'll keep you posted on the details. There is one small problem." *Please let it be small.*

Although obviously exhausted, his father said. "Tell me."

Bo let out a long sigh. "Claudie was here with me for a few days. We were in Kansas together when we heard about your…accident. She left so I could…" Bo made a face. "She tried to do the right thing, but I was a jerk."

"Dumb."

Bo flinched. "It gets worse. We'd actually been…uh… together the night before." He felt himself blushing under his father's unblinking scrutiny. "It was the first time, and—"

Bo couldn't quite believe he was talking about this with his father.

"Tell her."

Bo cocked his head. "Tell her what?"

His father's mouth worked at forming the words. "Only…one…love."

Even given the state of his father's memory, Bo couldn't let that kind of hypocrisy go unchallenged. "Dad," Bo said, striving to keep his long-held bitterness in check, "have you forgotten about Trisha? She wasn't exactly your first extramarital affair, you know."

Robert's eyes squeezed tight. "Bad husband." Bo didn't argue. "But. Just one. Love," he said, choking on tears.

Bo caught the slight emphasis on the word *one*. He leaned forward, his elbows on the armrests. "Mom?" he asked softly.

His father nodded.

A sound made Bo turn. His mother stood in the doorway, one hand covering her lips.

"Dad, if you love Mom so much how come you had those affairs?"

Robert's lips worked at forming a sound, but in the end no words came out—just a low, raspy moan. Tears dripped into his pillow before he turned his face away.

Bo felt his mother at his side. She leaned down and took her husband in her arms. In a soothing voice, rich with emotion, she told him, "It's okay, honey. I know you love me, and you know you're the only man I've ever loved. We need to put all that foolishness behind us. We have a tough road ahead, Robert Lester, and we aren't going to waste time worrying about things that can't be changed. Do you hear me?"

Her librarian voice. Stern and commanding.

Robert looked at her. Tears glistened in his eyes. He nodded.

Bo pushed backward with his feet; the wheelchair rolled to a stop a few feet away. He watched his parents with a sense of awe and wonder. Was it possible that thirty years of hurt could be wiped away just like that?

As quietly as possible, Bo slipped away. He started down the hall but stopped when his mother called his name. He returned to her side. For her small stature, she suddenly seemed like a miniature dynamo. Her eyes glowed with an inner fire.

"Thank you, dear heart, for giving him that," she cried, taking Bo's hand.

"What do you mean?"

"The wedding. That's just what he needed to hear. Now, he truly has something to aim for in his rehabilitation."

Bo swallowed painfully. "I…uh…I didn't necessarily think he'd take that seriously. I mean…Claudie and I…we haven't really talked about…uh…I think I hurt her."

Ruth squeezed his hand. "You'll be home tomorrow. You can make things right. Claudie's a smart girl and I know she loves you. Together, you can fix it."

Bo sighed and enveloped her in a hug. If his parents could reconcile after so much marital strife, surely there was hope for him and Claudie.

CLAUDIE ADDED a sprinkle of cinnamon to the frothy cappuccino and handed the cup to the customer on the other side of the counter. She seldom worked the coffee bar, but Sara was handling the book side of the store while their two new employees—both young prostitutes who were struggling to leave their pasts behind—were on break.

"How did we ever handle this business without outside help?" Sara asked, clambering awkwardly onto a stool.

"We had Keneesha," Claudie said.

The two exchanged a look and burst out laughing. "Claudie, Kee's a great friend, but she thought the espresso machine came off the starship *Enterprise*."

"I know," Claudie agreed, smiling at the memory. "But she was terrific with Brady."

"True. And at the time we didn't have Ren to baby-sit."

Claudie prepared a fruit smoothie in the new blender they'd installed for the popular iced drinks. "Here," she said, setting the old-fashioned parfait glass on the counter in front of Sara. "Drink up. It's peaches and cream. The babies will love it."

Sara beamed. "You take such good care of me. Mmm," she murmured. "Yummy."

Keeping one eye on the door at the far end of the building, Claudie said, "Sara, I'm worried about Rochell. I think she might be doing drugs. What should I do?"

Sara took a long draw on her straw before answering. "One Wish House's policy on that subject is crystal clear. She wouldn't be the first who couldn't make it, Claudie."

Claudie nodded. Of the twelve women Claudie had tried to help, only six were still off the streets—the four at One Wish House and two who'd married and moved to other cities. Five had gone back to hooking. One died from a drug overdose.

"If you'd seen her eyes this morning…" Claudie began but couldn't finish. It killed her to give up on anyone, but she knew the futility of trying to help someone who didn't want help. "I'm sure she's using. I should have busted her this morning. I don't know why I didn't."

"I do," Sara said. "She reminds you of yourself. I thought so, too, the minute I saw her."

Claudie made a face. "Sara, Rochell's black."

"That has nothing to do with what I'm talking about. She's alone and angry and smart and touchy. Just like you were."

"Touchy?"

Sara nodded. She gingerly lowered herself off the stool and stepped away from the bar. "Come here."

Claudie groaned. "I'm busy. I still have to unpack the FedEx box."

"Come."

Claudie did as she was told.

When they were standing shoulder to shoulder, Sara said, "I remember a time when the only person who could touch you was Brady."

Claudie's laugh was supposed to sound ironic, but it came out forced and harsh. "Sara, I don't know how you and Ren do it, but, believe me, what I did for a living involved a whole lot of touching."

Sara stuck out her tongue. "I don't mean that kind of touching. I mean hugs. Like this." She wrapped her arms around Claudie and squeezed. Sara's rounded tummy kept them slightly apart, but Claudie automatically hugged her back.

Claudie laughed. "You are so nuts. What does this prove?"

Sara pulled back slightly, but didn't let go. "It means you've evolved, my friend. You're not afraid to let yourself touch or be touched...by someone who loves you."

Just then, the two new clerks walked past them toward the coffee bar. Both girls gave them a sideways glance, then looked away.

Sara dropped her arms and Claudie stepped back, embarrassed.

Claudie looked at Sara and they burst out laughing.

Wait till I tell Bo, Claudie thought, then sobered. *When, Bo? When are you coming home?*

BO LOOKED at his watch. He'd known he was cutting it close by stopping at Pennington on his way to the airport, but he'd needed to tell his father goodbye in person.

"What time do you get to Sacramento?" Matt asked from the driver's seat.

"Ten."

"Did you let Claudie know you're coming?"

Bo nodded. "I left two messages—at the bookstore and at One Wish House. I'll try again from Denver if I have time. My car's in long-term so I don't need a ride, but I'm anxious to see her." *What an understatement that is!*

"One Wish House sounds like a pretty cool place. I'm impressed that Claudie's trying to help other women. I knew a few hookers when I worked vice. It's a tough life."

Looking out the window, Bo sighed. "It still amazes me that she survived in that business for as long as she did without giving up."

"Yeah, I know what you mean. Underneath that tough exterior is a very soft heart. She proved that in Kansas." He glanced at Bo and added, "Did I tell you I talked to Sara this morning? Doesn't sound like Claudie's stepfather is going to be with us much longer."

It was on the tip of Bo's tongue to say "Good," but the memory of the shattered look on Claudie's face when she told her family goodbye made him swallow the thought. He'd learned a few things himself about fathers in the past week. Even the worst was forever a part of your heart.

Neither man spoke for several miles, then Matt said, "I keep forgetting to ask—do you know some guy named Mike?"

Bo's stomach lifted and fell as though the Jeep just hit a bump. "I know half a dozen Mikes. Why?"

Matt shrugged, turning the wheel to take the airport exit. "Just curious. Claudie mentioned the name before she left. I thought he might be someone from her past. I could check him out if you want."

Bo's relief was conflicted. His mother had said Claudie took *Mike's* photo with her. "No. I'll take care of it. You're gonna be busy looking for Eve."

Matt snorted. "Piece of cake. She's a celebrity. They don't

fall off the face of the earth without someone knowing something."

They talked business the rest of the way to the airport where Bo had Matt drop him off without waiting. He lugged his suitcase to the ticket counter only to discover his flight had been delayed one hour.

"Mechanical difficulties, Mr. Lester," the ticket agent told him.

"Will it affect my connection in Denver?" Bo asked.

The woman entered data into the terminal then smiled. "No problem. You should make it with time to spare."

TIME TO SPARE, Bo thought ruefully, as he watched his Sacramento-bound connection taxi away from the gate. Cursing under his breath, he tracked down a ticket agent who spent twenty minutes trying every configuration known to man to get him on the next available flight.

"Six-sixteen," the woman chirped.

Bo looked at his watch. "Eleven minutes from now?"

She shook her head. "Tomorrow morning."

"No way. There's got to be something else tonight. Did you try Salt Lake? Seattle? L.A.?"

She nodded. "Everything. There have been fog problems in San Francisco impacting all West Coast flights. I'm sorry, but that's the best I can do." She gave him a sympathetic look. "I can give you a voucher for a motel room, but in all honesty, you might want to stay put. You're going to be on standby and it pays to be the first one here."

Muttering his disgust, he took his new itinerary and headed for the bank of phones in the center of the concourse. Denver's new airport was sleek, modern and efficient, but it was still an airport, and he wasn't a bit happy about spending the night there.

His mood didn't improve after four phone calls. Neither
Matt nor Ren answered, so he had to leave messages, but he
couldn't tell them to call his cell phone because he'd mistak-
enly packed it in the suitcase he checked through. A woman
named Mary answered at the bookstore, but she refused to
call either Sara or Claudie to the phone, telling him they
were in a very important meeting and couldn't be bothered.
He tried One Wish House, planning to leave a message for
Claudie but the line was busy.

*Someone's online, I bet. We've got to get a second phone
line in there,* he thought.

Sighing, Bo found an empty chair in a nearly deserted gate
and sat down. He pulled out his laptop, thinking he could at
least play catch-up on business, even if his life was hanging
in limbo. He released the latch and pushed the power button.

He frowned. Does it always take this long to load?

The screen saver appeared—along with a little symbol
telling him he was out of power. "Damn," he swore out loud.

He snapped the lid closed in disgust and slumped down in
the chair.

"Low battery?" a voice asked.

Bo glanced up. A well-dressed businessman gave him a
friendly smile. "There's a place over in the main terminal that
gives you a power hookup, Internet access, the whole thing.
They charge by the minute, but it's pretty reasonable—compared to the price of beer, anyway."

Bo sat up. "I'm interested. Tell me more."

Eleven minutes later, Bo was breathless from his trot to
the far end of the main terminal. Laptop Lane, he read, checking out the small storefront. The posted hours told him he had
forty-five minutes to get his battery recharged.

"Feel free to send e-mail," the cheerful clerk told him,
handing him the key to his private office cubicle.

E-mail, he thought. E-mail. That might be the perfect way to tell Claudie his feelings. It beat the heck out of stuttering and stammering on an answering machine, and he certainly wasn't about to trust his inner thoughts to any of the residents of One Wish House.

E-mail. Fast. Private. Personal. Perfect.

CHAPTER FIFTEEN

"TRY THIS ONE, CLAUDIE," Davina said, forcing a small, dumpling-shaped morsel into her mouth. "Spinach, shrimp and peanuts in won ton dough. It's *muy bueno*."

Chewing, Claudie nodded. "Uh-huh."

Claudie looked around at the throng of people crowded into One Wish House's backyard. A steady stream flowed in and out of the gate, some looking anxiously ahead to the striped awning where Maya and her cooks were dispensing the tasty little offerings, others triumphantly carrying their aluminum-foil-wrapped paper plates to their cars or to the tables set up along the fence.

"Can you believe we pulled this off?" Davina asked. Her tone of awe matched what Claudie was feeling.

"I wouldn't have bet on it last night." Claudie shuddered recalling the chaos in the small kitchen well past midnight. Fortunately, Maya had subcontracted a dozen of the dishes so Claudie and the girls were limited in what they'd had to prepare.

A tall man carrying a messy-faced child split away from the crowd and approached them. At his side was an older woman, petite and elegant in white woolen trousers and a colorful sweater. "If I'd have known you were going to need the backyard I'd have hired a grounds crew to come in," Ren Bishop said apologetically. As a landlord, he was a tenant's dream.

Claudie shrugged. "The grass would have gotten trampled

anyway. I had no idea this would go over so big. Hello, Mrs. Bishop, how are you?"

Babe's reply was cut off by Brady's yell. "Ninjas."

Claudie grinned. Maya had arranged for a troupe of Korean dancers and drummers to perform.

Ren let Brady down but kept his eye on the rambunctious youngster. "I'd better not lose sight of him. If his mother didn't kill me mine would." He winked at Babe then looked at Sara who was perched on a stool taking money from eager buyers. "I just wanted to tell you I'm very impressed, Claudie. You've done an amazing job and from what Sara said you're making money hand over fist."

Claudie tried to smile but only one thought came to mind: *I wish Bo were here to see it.*

Ren patted her lightly on the shoulder. "He'll be here soon, Claudie."

Claudie started, not even aware she'd spoken out loud.

"Knowing Bo," Ren added with a grin, "he probably hogtied some passenger in the bathroom to be sure to get a seat out of Denver this morning. He'll make it."

Ren turned suddenly and let out a low groan. "Brady, come back here, you little imp. Bye, ladies, see you later." He took Babe's elbow. "Mother, another dim sum goodie?"

Davina followed them with her gaze. "What a hunk! You and Sara are both so lucky. Meester Bo's not bad, either."

Claudie made herself smile. Everybody seemed to assume Bo would show up and they would magically be a couple. Only Claudie doubted it would be that simple.

For one thing, there was the matter of the message on the answering machine.

Claudie excused herself to go inside—ostensibly to check the indoor cooks, but she slipped past the kitchen and dashed upstairs to her office. She wanted to hear his message one more time. She hadn't noticed the little flashing light last night until almost 1:00 a.m. on her way to bed. Sara had already called to tell her Bo's flight had been delayed leaving New York and he was stranded in Denver, but Claudie hadn't heard from him directly—until she checked her machine.

"Hi," his disembodied voice said. "I'll keep this short and sweet. I wanted to be there tonight but that isn't going to happen, obviously. Save me some dim sum—whatever the hell that is—and I'll see you tomorrow. By the way, have you checked your e-mail?"

Claudie hadn't had time to go online, but now seemed as good a time as any. She slipped into her padded chair and pushed the envelope icon on the keyboard. A minute later, Claudie's breath caught in her throat. "A poem."

She scooted closer to the desk; her fingers were shaking so badly she could barely manage to move the mouse to scroll downward. She read:

Silver wings took you away, but your
golden heart remained—an amulet of love
to guide the way home. Do you wait with open
arms in the almost-memory of a honeymoon
beside the roaring waters? Or did my callow act
forge a river of sorrow too wide to span
with poetry or electronic prose?
A kiss might be a vow unspoken. But the question
has yet to be asked or answered.
Will you marry me?

"Oh, my God. It's a proposal," she said dumbfounded.

"A proposal? Of marriage? From Bo?" Sara cried rushing to Claudie's side. "Let me see."

With a shaking hand, Claudie pointed at the screen.

"It is!" Sara squealed a moment later. "He wants to marry you. This is so romantic."

"Romantic?" Claudie wailed. "Sara, we've barely even spoken since New York. Now, I'm supposed to say okay, let's live happily ever after? Just because he sent me an e-mail?"

Sara's smiled faltered. "Y-yes?"

"I don't think so." Claudie tried to sound stern but knew she'd failed when Sara whooped with joy. She also knew her friend was a cockeyed optimist who lacked the pragmatic objectivity she needed. "Where's Ren?"

"He just took Brady home. Daniel's coming over to stay with him while Ren handles the auction." Sara turned back to the screen. Her long sigh made Claudie cringe. "Ren doesn't write me poems. Oh, Claudie, this is so beautiful. Let's print it and frame it."

Claudie pushed the exit key. "No."

"Why? Don't you want him to propose?"

Claudie rose and paced to the window. Below, a mass of cars filled the street, taking up every spare parking place for three blocks on either side of One Wish House. No primer-gray Mazda in sight.

"Sara, my mother married a man who loved her more than she loved him. I let Bo into my life back in Kansas, but when I tried to return the favor, he closed up." She sighed and closed her eyes, her heart heavy with regret. "I love Bo, but I refuse to live my life like Garret—bitter and angry because the person I love doesn't love me the same way."

BO CLIMBED OUT of his car and stood for a minute just soaking up the December sunshine. The crisp breeze made him want to sing. *Home.* I'm finally home, he silently rejoiced.

Well, not quite home, he amended, trotting to Ren Bishop's back door. He tried the knob. It opened.

"Anybody here?" he called out, walking into the kitchen. He'd planned to go right to One Wish House, but after a night on a bench in the Denver airport he needed a shower.

"Is that you, Lester?" a voice replied.

Bo opened the refrigerator and snatched a cold wiener from an open package. "You got it."

"Unca' Bo," Brady squealed, racing through the swinging door that connected with the dining room. The little boy launched himself into Bo's arms, barely giving Bo time to chomp down on the hot dog.

"Hey, superkid, I missed you," he said, chewing. He hugged the little body as tight as he dared then let him drop to his feet. Kneeling in front of him, he looked the child over. "You've grown a foot. What are you feeding this kid?" he asked, looking up at Ren.

"Tofu dogs. Like the one you're eating."

Bo's stomach lurched. He scrutinized the remaining half-eaten object then looked at Brady. "Not bad. I think I like 'em."

Rising, he shook hands with Ren. "It's good to be home. I thought I should clean up before I head to Folsom. Mind if I use your shower?"

"Make yourself at home. I'm heading back over there as soon as Daniel gets here. He's going to read to Brady while I handle the MC duties at the auction."

Bo shouldered his tote bag and started toward the stairs. "What kind of things are you auctioning off?"

"Mother strong-armed a couple of dozen businesses into donating items and services. Some artwork, tai chi lessons, a cord of firewood, a couple of trips…" He snapped his fingers and abruptly veered toward his office. "That reminds me—I almost forgot something." Glancing over his shoulder at Bo he added, "Make it snappy. I'm due onstage in fifteen minutes."

BO'S MOUTH dropped open when he saw the number of cars on the street. One of the One Wish House residents—Bo couldn't remember her name—moved a barricade to let Ren park in the driveway behind his mother's car.

"Wow! Good turnout," he said, getting out.

"It's been like this all morning, hasn't it, Sally?" Ren gave the blonde a friendly smile. When Bo looked at her, she gave him a stern frown.

Bo sighed. "This ain't gonna be a cakewalk, is it?"

Ren cuffed him lightly. "Nothing worthwhile ever is."

They entered the side gate, which had been propped open with a garbage can, and Ren took off to find Sara. Using his skill as a sleuth, Bo melted into the crowd, on the lookout for Claudie. He felt her presence before he saw her. Her back was to him. He didn't recognize the long-sleeved wine-colored wool dress, but its simple sheath cut made her look taller. Sheer gray hose set off her shapely calves, and platform heels gave her an extra three inches of height. Instead of the spiky curls he loved, her hair had been tamed to a sophisticated cap of waves.

Bo's heart leapt in his chest but a bittersweet bite of fear made him hesitate. She was engaged in an animated conversation with Rochell. Bo saw Claudie put out her hand and squeeze the other woman's shoulder. When Rochell looked up, there were tears in her eyes.

Bo knew the moment Rochell realized he was watching. Their eyes met. Hers took on a shuttered look and she dropped her chin. Claudie glanced over her shoulder. Her spontaneous smile was replaced by a cautious nod.

Adrenaline pumped through his veins. He hurried to her side.

"Hi."

Claudie looked at him a long time, her eyes checking out his face, his clothes, his hands. Bo glanced down. "I should have brought flowers," he said stupidly.

She blushed. "No. It's okay. I...um..." She suddenly looked at the woman beside her. "Bo, you know Rochell, right?"

"Hell, yeah, he knows me. He came to the house looking for you."

Bo didn't want to talk to anyone. He wanted to pull Claudie into the most private corner around and kiss her. Instead, he put out his hand and smiled. "Nice to see you. Could we go somewhere and talk?" he asked Claudie.

Claudie frowned. "I'm in the middle of something here, Bo." She turned to Rochell. "I'm sorry for assuming the worst."

Rochell shrugged. "Don't sweat it." She turned and left.

"Claudie, I—" Bo started.

She interrupted him. "I made a mistake, Bo." His stomach flip-flopped. "I thought Rochell was using drugs. Her eyes were red—she seemed really out of it." Claudie sighed. "She's been studying for her GED—burning the midnight oil. I'm such a fool."

"No you're not. You care about these women. Isn't that what all this is about?" He made an encompassing gesture. "The women of One Wish House are making good things happen, and I like being a part of that." He nodded at a man he recognized as a prominent attorney. "So do a lot of other people, apparently."

Something in Claudie's eyes softened. "If you're serious about pitching in, they could use your help in the kitchen," she said, her tone teasing.

Bo's heart skipped a beat. "Only if it'll get me some time alone with you." He moved to close the gap between them, but bumped into someone who muttered something in Spanish, then exclaimed, "Meester Bo," Davina chirped, "you came home. I knew you would. They all say you are never coming back, but I know different."

"Why wouldn't I come back?"

"If I had a rich papa who wasn't doing too good, that's where I'd be," Davina answered, nibbling on something that looked like an egg roll.

Bo stepped back as if struck. He looked at Claudie. "Is that what you think?"

Her cheeks turned the color of her dress and she looked around self-consciously. "No. Of course not. It's just that…" She shook her head. "Let's not do this here. Ren's about to start the auction."

Her diversion worked. Davina wiggled her fingers at Bo in a cute wave. "I gotta go," she said. "I'm biddin' on the Hawaii trip. Sandy beaches and mai tais, here I come."

Claudie started to step away but Bo stopped her with a hand on her arm. "Claudie, I know I was a jerk when you left but we can talk about this, right? Did you get my e-mail?"

"Uh-huh," she said, softly, her gaze not meeting his. "It's a little hectic right now and I need to talk to Ren before he starts the auction. Will you be around later?"

All Bo could do was nod. This wasn't at all what he'd planned. He grabbed the closest folding chair and sat, his gaze following as Claudie melted into the crowd.

"Hello, Bo," a clipped voice said.

Bo looked up, his heart sinking another inch into the soft ground. He dragged himself to his feet. "Hello, Mrs. Bishop. How are you today?"

She studied him a moment then took the chair beside his. "I wanted to tell you that I'm very impressed with the way you handled things with your father," she told him, motioning for him to sit.

Bo's shock must have been written on his face because Babe added, "Family is the most important thing there is in the world. Family…and love. Sometimes those things are the most painful, too. But you didn't let your antipathy stand in the way of doing the right thing—where your parents were concerned, anyway."

Bo swallowed. "Thank you."

She gave him an odd look. "I never would have guessed you to be a poet. Isn't it odd how we so often keep the most interesting parts of ourselves hidden from view? Even from those for whom we care the most," she said softly, then rose and walked away.

Claudie showed Babe my poem? His shock was almost as great as his humiliation.

"BO'S HERE," Claudie whispered in Sara's ear.

Sara finished making change for the last dim sum customer then whipped a fat rubber band around the cash box and stuffed it in her purse. "Tahiti or the Virgin Islands? Which one do you want? I figure there's enough cash in this box to live on for a year."

"Tahiti. And I doubt if the Virgin Islands would take me."

Sara's smile didn't quite make it to her eyes, which seemed filled with sympathy. "Have you talked to him?"

Claudie gave a noncommittal shrug.

"You're going to have to, you know."

Claudie took a deep breath, rallying her spirit. "Yeah, I know. I can run, but there's nowhere to hide. He's too good a P.I. to let me get away with that."

She turned to leave, but Sara stopped her. "Um…Babe knows about the poem. She read your e-mail. Not on purpose, but—"

An odd kind of expectation made her ask, "What'd she say?"

Sara smiled, a bit wistfully. "Something about underestimating poorly dressed men." The two friends looked at each other and grinned, but Sara quickly sobered. "What are you going to say to him?"

"I don't know, Sara. My heart almost jumped out of my chest when I saw him. I've missed him so much. But I'm afraid, too."

Sara rose and gave her a quick hug. "Sometimes, you have to gamble, Claudie. A lot of people—you included, if I remember correctly—told me Ren was only interested in me because of Brady. But, I knew deep down he was the only man in the world for me."

"Ladies and gentlemen," an amplified voice said, "If you'd be so kind as to lend me your attention—and your wallets."

Claudie watched as Ren drew in the audience with his easy banter. As everything from clock radios to fancy dinners went for top dollar, she scanned the crowd looking for—but not finding—Bo. She happened to look toward the stage when Ren paused dramatically to pull an unmarked envelope out of his pocket. She'd personally tagged all the items up for auction and couldn't recall seeing that one.

"Now, here's an interesting item," Ren said, waving it back and forth. "Personally, I love this one, but then, I'm a hopeless romantic. As some of you might know, I was married recently. My lovely wife, Sara, is right over there. Sara, take a bow."

Blushing, Sara rose and waved as the audience applauded.

The crowd laughed when Ren added, "As you can see, our honeymoon was quite successful."

Sara ducked behind Claudie, trying to hide.

"Claudie!" Ren exclaimed, as if remiss in his duties. "Ladies and gentlemen, I forgot to introduce Claudine St. James, founder and administrator of One Wish House." He walked to the edge of the small deck that was serving as a stage. "Claudie, come up here a minute."

Claudie shook her head. "No thanks, Ren. I'm fine right here."

Sara placed her hands firmly at Claudie's shoulders and pushed her toward the steps. "Go. He's not going to let you off the hook."

Letting out a sigh, she trudged up the redwood steps. She gave him her most ferocious glare, but Ren smiled smoothly and put his arm around her shoulders to lead her to center stage. Claudie used the time to try to read the writing on the envelope in his hand. It looked like Sara's writing.

After the applause died down, Ren handed her the envelope and said, "Since you're up here, why don't I put you to work? Would you like to read the next item up for bid?"

Claudie slipped her finger under the tab and looked inside. A single sheet of creamy paper. Ornate calligraphy—Sara's latest hobby—made it hard to scan, but two words jumped off the page and Claudie almost dropped the paper.

Ren smoothly took it from her, saying, "You're right. This is my job. But you hang tight so we can give this to its rightful owner, once it's purchased."

Claudie looked for Sara, who was beaming like a beacon. *Oh, my friends what have you done?* Desperately, she glanced around. *Where's Bo? What if he left?*

"Now, as I was saying. As a recent newlywed myself, I can tell you the most—and I mean most—important part of a wedding is the honeymoon." The crowd guffawed. "So, what we have here is a paid trip to the honeymoon capitol of the world—I don't know that for a fact but that's what this paper says—Niagara Falls." A loud cheer went up.

Ren rattled off all the details; a stay at a bed-and-breakfast; boat trip under the falls; sleeper accommodations by train. To start the bidding, he said, "I'd say twenty-five hundred dollars isn't too much to pay for the trip of a lifetime."

A youthful voice sang out. "Twenty-five hundred."

Claudie spotted the man. A yuppie MBA with his girlfriend at his side. *Bo, where are you when I need you?*

"Three thousand," she said without thinking.

Ren stepped back in amazement. "Excuse me?"

She glared at him. "You heard me. Three."

He looked over her shoulder at his wife. "Okay." He cleared his throat and continued, "The bid's been raised. Do I hear any others?"

The man at the edge of the crowd called out, "Four thousand."

Claudie couldn't look at the couple. It made no sense, but she knew she couldn't let someone else have her honeymoon—even if she didn't have a fiancé. "Five thousand two hundred," she said, naming the portion of her inheritance she'd planned to use as a down payment on a new car. She'd worry about that later.

Ren grimaced. "The bid is now five thousand two hundred dollars. Going once, going…"

Out of the corner of her eye, she saw the woman clobber the man with her purse. "Fifty-three hundred," he yelped.

Claudie didn't dare go any higher. She needed a car. Niagara Falls was a pipe dream. She reached deep for her best what-the-hell face, but it just wasn't there. Ren's eyes were filled with sorrow as he said, "Five thousand three hundred dollars. Going once. Going twice…"

"Six," another voice said. "Oh, what the hell, make it ten. I only plan to do this once."

Bo cleared the railing of the deck with a clean vault. He walked past Ren and stopped in front of Claudie. "Can we talk now?"

She nodded. There was no way she could speak, her heart was in a million pieces.

Bo put out his hand. She gave him hers.

"Going, going, gone," Ren said, hastily, as they left the deck and entered the house. A tumultuous cheer followed them inside.

The parlor was empty so Claudie stopped, turned and threw herself into Bo's arms. "I thought you'd left."

He kissed her hair and hugged her tight. "Never," he whispered. "I was getting bawled out by the tall blonde for letting you leave New York without me. What's her name? Sally?"

"Sally Rae," Claudie said looking up.

Bo kissed her forehead. "Were you really going to blow a big chunk of your inheritance on a trip?"

She caught her bottom lip between her teeth. "It's a trip of a lifetime," she said.

"Only if you're with the person you love. I love you, Claudie, marry me? You know it wouldn't be a honeymoon without you." His impish smile made her burst out in tears. He gathered her close. "Oh, babe, I'm sorry. I say the stupidest things when I'm nervous."

"You're never nervous," she corrected.

"That was before I fell in love. Now, I'm nervous all the time. I'm afraid I'm gonna blow it with you. Like I did in New York."

She moved back to give herself space to breathe. His hands skittered up and down her back like nervous cats looking for a place to settle. She laid her head against his chest. The sound of his heartbeat brought back a flood of memories— tenderness, tears, breathless passion she'd never expected to feel.

"I don't know, Bo. Do you honestly think we can get beyond our pasts?"

He kissed her hard, then led her to the settee. He dropped to the cushion beside her, never letting go of her hands.

Gazing into her eyes, he said gravely, "I know we can as long as we talk to each other. I'll even introduce you to Mike."

Her breath stopped. "Really?"

He nodded. "But only if I can meet Yancy."

This time Claudie saw through his humor to the sad inner child behind his quip. "Can you tell me what happened in New York?"

His broad shoulders sagged. "When there was a chance Dad was going to die, I thought I could handle my feelings, my anger. For some reason dead was doable. But when it looked as though he'd pull through, all these conflicting emotions hit. Anger. Sympathy. Bitterness. Grief. And, with you, love."

She cupped his jaw. "That scared you, right?"

He nodded. "Yes, but not for the reason you think. What I felt for you was so real, so pure, I was afraid it would get sullied if Dad were in the picture. Do you see what I'm trying to say? Dad lived his life without any respect for love, and I didn't want him to make what I felt less than perfect."

"How could he do that, Bo? You're not your father. You feel things differently."

"Am I really that different? It's easy to tell yourself that when you're three thousand miles apart, but the more time I spent with him, the more I wondered. I'm forty years old, Claudie, and I've never been in love until I met you. My dad slept with women left and right, but I wouldn't call that love."

"But your mother—"

"She loved him, and he put her through hell."

Claudie understood what he didn't say. "Bo, I'm not the type to put up with that kind of thing. You even look at another woman and I will hurt you. Believe me, it's something a hooker learns how to do early on."

He eyed her. "You mean that, don't you?"

She nodded. "Bo, you're not your father. And I'm not your mother. I'm not my mother, either. I want two kids, not ten. Preferably two years apart."

"A boy and a girl?" Bo asked, smiling.

She shrugged. "Sex doesn't matter."

He lowered his chin and waggled his bushy brows. "Oh, yes, it does, my love. I'd be happy to prove it to you, if you'd care to accompany me to my houseboat."

She plunged into his arms. "I'll go anywhere with you, but, first, I think we should talk about…the poem." His body tensed.

Babe and a distinguished-looking gentleman started into the room until they caught sight of Bo and Claudie. Mumbling their apologies, the couple backed away.

Claudie sighed. She cupped Bo's smooth, recently shaved jaw and said, "Okay. Let's go, Cookbook Man. We can talk at home…I mean, the boat."

Bo let out a loud whoop. "I heard that Freudian slip. You love me, Claudie St. James, and you're going to marry me, aren't you?"

A movement in the doorway caught Claudie's eye. Four familiar faces were peeking around the jamb. Ren and Sara stood to one side. "Maybe," she said, trying not to give away the flood of joy she felt inside.

"That's a yes," he cried, pumping his arm as if he'd just scored a touchdown. "When? Tomorrow?"

"No! Absolutely not. Good grief! I have a life, you know," she said, too flustered to think. "Garret's dying. Your father's in the hospital. I have two hundred people in my backyard."

Bo sobered. "Garret's worse?"

Claudie nodded, her chest suddenly tight with emotion. Bo dropped to one knee in front of her. "Oh, baby, I'm sorry. For everything. But most of all for blowing up when all you wanted to do was help with my dad. I was a coward. I didn't want you to see the real me."

Claudie blinked back her tears. "I've always seen the real you, Bo. Those disguises you wear wouldn't fool Brady. You're good and strong and kind and very brave when it comes to taking care of other people, but you're too hard on yourself. And you're not very forgiving when someone you love lets you down." She swallowed the lump in her throat. "That scares me, Bo. I'm afraid I won't live up to the person you think I am."

He wrapped his arms around her and pulled her close. "You're right. I blamed myself for not being the son my father wanted. But that's behind us now. Thanks to you…and what happened in Kansas."

Claudie blinked, questioningly.

"Oh, sweetheart, I'd have to be pretty petty to whine about my life when you were able to get past your anger at Garret."

He dug in his pocket and withdrew her mother's locket. As he slipped it over her head, he said, "You gave me your heart, Claudie. But you've always had mine."

"Oh, Bo, I love you." She pulled him to her. Through her tears, she saw her friends sniffling and hugging each other. Sara's face was buried against Ren's chest. Babe, who stood a little off from the rest, remained tearless, but she smiled warmly and nodded her approval.

Claudie couldn't wait to call Sherry and Val.

It was a long and winding road—and not a single yellow brick on any part of it—but, somehow, Claudie had found her way home.

EPILOGUE

THE SUN—barely past its zenith—failed to mitigate the effect of the chill December wind that swept across the rolling hills of eastern Kansas. Blue-black spruce—hump-shouldered matrons bowed from the forces of Nature—encircled the hallowed grounds. Fifty-some mourners crowded around a vivid patch of artificial green carpet with a rectangle of hothouse flowers at its core.

Garret had passed away the night of the fund-raiser. Sherry had called the following morning to tell Claudie the funeral was set for Saturday. Claudie couldn't get over the number of people who'd packed the tiny white church then followed the hearse to Otter Creek's cemetery. Sherry had tried to prepare her the night before, but Claudie hadn't envisioned this kind of support.

"In the end, Peggy came for him," Dottie said softly as they waited for the service to begin. "I know because he smiled—that very special smile he saved for Sherry, and you."

"Me?" Claudie choked.

The older woman, her kind eyes red from crying, nodded. "You were so like Peggy, how could he not love you, too?" She took Claudie's cold, numb hands in her own and said, "Brave, generous, loving Claudie. You truly are your mother's daughter. You proved that by coming back to heal the rift between you and Garret. He died in peace, and I can never thank you enough."

Claudie squeezed her hand and looked at the casket. Oddly, she felt no anguish, no bitterness—only regret.

"My parents wanted me to tell you that instead of flowers they're sending a check to Garret's foundation," Bo whispered, joining her when Dottie left to take her assigned seat.

She looked at him and her heart swelled with joy. The Bishops stood beside him.

Claudie hadn't been able to talk Sara and Ren out of joining them on this journey. And Claudie would be eternally grateful for the support. Sara's sweet smile and Ren's easy manner diverted many curious, if well-meaning, friends and associates from inquiring too deeply into Claudie's past. This freed up Claudie to concentrate on her siblings.

Yancy had driven in the night before with his wife and sons, who'd reveled in Dottie's warmhearted attention. Valery, who had balked at making the trip until Bo got on the phone and applied his sweet-talking charm, arrived in her Mercedes. Sherry—overwhelmed by both the loss of her beloved father and the convocation of so many estranged siblings—was slowly finding her footing.

"Friends and neighbors. Brothers and sisters," a gruff, but dignified, voice said to those gathered. "Please join us in prayer."

Claudie gazed at the man in the ill-fitting suit, bare hands folded around a worn Bible. Around his neck was a beautiful, hand-stitched stole of Lakota design. Zach. His presence here was Ren's priceless gift.

As her brother solemnly gave their communal goodbye, Claudie stared at the simple casket. Squeezing Bo's hand, she felt the reassuring pressure of the engagement ring on the third finger of her left hand. Their wedding was set for the first weekend in June—two weeks after Sherry's high school graduation. Bo's father vowed to be well enough to dance up a storm. And Sara was happy that she'd have a full month after the birth of the twins to get in shape. Everyone in Claudie's family, even Dottie, promised to attend.

Claudie looked skyward. She wanted to think Garret and her mother were somewhere up above smiling down on them. A perfect family they weren't, but, in the end, the bonds among them were strong enough to bring them all back to Kansas.

Everything you love about romance...
and more!

Please turn the page for Signature Select™
Bonus Features.

Bonus Features:

BONUS FEATURES

WINDOW TO YESTERDAY

Author Interview:
A conversation with
DEBRA SALONEN

It's hard to imagine, but Debra was a history and geography major in college! Read on to discover more about her.

4

Did you always intend to write about two connected stories? If not, what led you to write about connected characters?

Actually, the answer to this question is one that I usually don't discuss outside of writing circles. Mainly because non-writers look at me as though I'm crazy when I tell them that I had no intention of writing a spin-off from *His Daddy's Eyes* until Bo appeared on the scene. He virtually demanded his own book. Honest. I'll never forget the moment he showed up in the scene I was writing. I knew that Ren needed a best friend, and I was pretty sure this person needed to be a P.I. So, early in chapter one, Ren gets called out of court and waiting in his office is Bo. From the first moment I "met" him, I felt a tingle of awareness. He was frank, funny and completely different from Ren, whom I'd already fallen in love with. Within a few pages, I threw up my hands and said—out loud—"Okay, which one of you guys is the hero?"

See? This is the kind of stuff that gets people put on medication. And to make matters worse, Bo answered back. "Well, obviously, I am," he said, "but not in this book." We haggled a bit and finally agreed that if he settled down and behaved as a well-rounded and integral secondary character, I'd write his story next. Which turned out to be *Back in Kansas*.

Were your heroines equally as pushy?
Of course not. They're ladies. In fact, one was a lady of the evening. (Sorry, Claudie.) Actually, Sara was a sweet soul from the very beginning. Kind and generous. She'd made a life for her young nephew that included her eclectic group of friends—society's castoffs, which is pretty much how Sara regarded herself. From the hand of friendship she extended, hope blossomed, and Claudie found the strength to start a new life away from the streets. When I talked to my editor about the possibility of writing Bo's book,

she was very receptive until I told her I planned to pair Bo with Eve, Ren's ex-girlfriend.

She said, horrified, "But Bo's in love with Claudie."

I responded, "Yes, I know, but Claudie's a reformed prostitute."

My editor pointed out quite succinctly that romance readers had evolved and were certainly able to accept that "not all heroines come into a relationship with an unblemished past."

True, but there's blemished and then there's selling your body for money. I agreed to try, but until I actually got to *know* Claudie, I was scared to death of her and her past. Once we started her heroic quest, I began to understand just how strong, yet fragile, she was and how much courage it took to return to the source of her pain. I came to love her as much as Bo did, and if I'd listened to him in the first place, I'm sure I never would have doubted that their story would make a compelling one.

Tell us your favorite road trip story.
Spring, 1973. South Dakota State University. "Classroom on Wheels." Hard to believe I actually got college credit for two weeks of touring the west with fourteen other students. Privately we called this "Dr. O's Traveling Show," named after Lee A. Opheim, Ph.D., the history

and geography professor who led us on this fabulous journey. I still recall several surreal moments—like tasting nickel-size snowflakes in Yellowstone in May and peering over the edge of Wild Horse Canyon, imagining the thunder of hooves just before the crazed animals plummeted to their deaths. We had a snowball fight standing on either side of the Continental Divide, and braved the bridge across the Royal Gorge. It was an adventure that I doubt could be replicated given the price of gas and insurance today, but one that I will always treasure. Claudie's journey hit a couple of the same spots as my "Classroom on Wheels" trek: Salt Lake City, Utah, Cheyenne, Wyoming and the Black Hills of South Dakota.

Were you an English major in college? Did you always intend to become a writer?
Actually, I became a geography and history major after completing two years studying foreign languages with an emphasis in Spanish. I love language and languages but couldn't see myself teaching *español,* so I switched to geography—partly because...well, frankly, the students and teachers seemed to be having so much fun. I also enjoyed the challenge of working with spatial relationships in cartography and researching the human element in history.

Even then my professors would shake their heads when I took liberty with certain dull, dry facts and tried to add a human face to my research. I eventually graduated with a master's degree—just in time to give birth to my daughter.

And while I always thought of myself as a writer, it wasn't until my children were in school full-time that I actually tried submitting stories to my local newspaper. Eventually, this led to a position as a feature writer. I was blessed with a wonderful editor, Barbara Hale, who taught me about craft, style and self-editing. I also learned to ask the right questions and listen, really listen, to the answers.

However, my first love has always been fiction, and newspapers tend to frown on you making things up. So, with the support of my wonderful husband, I was able to quit my day job and start writing full-time. My first effort met with several rejections, but my second manuscript was bought and published by Harlequin Superromance in 2000. *His Daddy's Eyes* and *Back in Kansas* were my second and third books, respectively.

Someone asked me recently if I regretted not pursuing my doctorate when I had the chance. I answered, "No, absolutely not. How can I have any regrets when my life has been so richly blessed?" Writing is my happily-ever-after.

Story-wise, what constitutes a happy ending for you?
Of course, the standard answer is the heroine and hero winding up together, but for me, that's the tip of the iceberg. I want to feel a sense that they've each learned from what happened in my book and have grown as people. I expect them to retain their individual values but appreciate what the other person has brought to their relationship. I try to picture them years and years down the road, not in matching rocking chairs, but hauling their grandchildren cross-country, hitting all the silly stops no one else would have the patience to visit. I hope my readers will know that nothing is a given in my characters' lives, except each other. The rest is work, but work is a good thing. These aren't fairy tales, you know.

Many of your books are about families, particularly siblings, like your upcoming SISTERS OF THE SILVER DOLLAR series. What is it about family dynamics that makes you keep coming back to the concept?
Families fascinate me. I grew up an only child— with four brothers and sisters. My siblings are

quite a bit older than me. The one closest to me in age had enjoyed baby-of-the-family status for ten and a half years before I showed up. Fortunately, my older sisters were around to make sure he didn't kill me. I've always been intrigued by the workings of families, the good stuff and the bad. Grace, the heroine of the first book in the series, and her sisters grew up in Las Vegas. Their family was a little "different" given their Romany heritage and the large extended family that surrounded them. Each sister is a strong, unique person, dealing with life, loss and their widowed mother, who in the past had been revered for her ability to see into the future. I was intrigued by how the girls related to each other and the world at large. I hope I've done them justice as they follow their *tacho Romani drom*, their one true path.

What is the one thing you don't have enough of and wish you had more of?
Time, of course. Doesn't everybody want more hours in the day? When you are very young, you never think the day will arrive when you finally turn twelve, or twenty-one. Then suddenly, the time-space continuum speeds up. I don't know why someone hasn't researched this phenomenon and put an end to it. I would...if I had more time.

No, seriously, I think women who write for a living have, in Ricky Ricardo's words, "a lot of explaining to do." Most non-writers—this includes the writer's family—have a difficult time understanding the creative process. To the casual observer, writers seem to spend a lot of time in loungewear doing "stuff" on the computer. Who's to say that stuff doesn't include eight hours of Spider Solitaire?

My response is, of course, don't you realize how similar playing Spider is to plotting a book?

Do you believe in inspiration or plain old hard work?
Both. I cherish inspiration. It's a bit like falling in love: the sparkle, the clarity of vision, the driving need to spend time with your new project, the hope this new story imparts. But without plain old hard work, I'd never see a book through to the end. That early flush of perfection soon gives way to doubts, questions, even animosity. I've been known to snarl at my characters and ask, "Why did I think I loved you?" That's when hard work comes in—reinforced by contractual deadlines. If you stick with the story and trust that the initial promise will deliver, inspiration—accompanied by satisfaction—does return, just as you type "The End."

What happens after you finish a book? What do you do?

There are two parts to this answer. The technical side involves several steps: print the manuscript, head to FedEx, wait, revise said manuscript, head to FedEx, wait, review line edits, read galley proofs, wait and finally, after FedEx delivers your author copies, promote. The creative side has several options. If you're contracted for another book, you take a few days off to vegetate and catch up on life, then plunge into research, which, you hope, triggers that inspiration we covet. If you're not contracted for another book, you take as much time off as you need to refill your creative well. For me, this involves reading, gardening, cooking, shopping, watching movies and doing nothing. Doing nothing is highly underrated as a leisure activity, but I'm quite good at it. Since I have five more books under contract at the moment, it will be a while before I can practice this art again. I just hope I won't have lost my edge.

Marsha Zinberg chatted with Debra in the summer of 2005.

The Writing Life:
When Readers Write Back

Have you ever finished reading a book and wanted to write to the author to say how much the story touched you, impressed you, irked you, reminded you of your own story or moved you to pick up a pen and do better? Well, I've gotten a wide range of reader letters over the years and thought I might share a few—both the good and the bad—because I firmly believe that you shouldn't embrace positive accolades if you can't appreciate negative criticism, as well.

One of my most vivid reader letters came in response to *Back in Kansas*. A young mother wrote to say that Claudie's story mirrored her own. She'd been abused as a child and had run away from home in her teens. My initial reaction was pure panic. Had I done justice to the anguish this kind of violation might produce? What right did I have to let my imagination lead me into such a dark and terrifying place? Had I in any way added to this woman's pain by bringing up bad memories? She didn't go into detail about her time as a runaway, instead she focused on her new life. Her children. Her hope for the future. She thanked me for writing this book and said that reading Claudie's story had been cathartic for her. She closed her letter saying she hoped that one day she might be strong, like Claudie, and confront the man who had molested her—not to punish him, but to forgive. This is a letter I will treasure forever.

But, I also had several letters from readers who took exception to the story and quoted Bible passages about redemption, apparently fearing that Claudie's story was a thinly disguised version of my own life. I wrote back thanking them for their concern, but I tried to assure them that my research into prostitution had been handled from afar. I am lucky to have a great many resources within my family. My nephew had just completed his master's degree in social work when I was writing *Back in Kansas*. He'd interned in a Welfare To Work program and had counseled many prostitutes looking to rebuild their lives. We talked about Claudie's self-esteem issues, the choices she made that led her to the streets and the drive and desire needed to break old patterns.

A frequent theme in the letters that I receive concerns the correspondent's desire to tell his or her own story, or, rather, for me to tell that story for them. I understand, believe me. Writing is a lot of work. There are times when I wish I could hire someone to write my stories for me, but I can't. And neither can you. No one else can tell your story because nobody knows it the way you do. You've lived it, felt it, tasted it. Honest tears deserve honest effort. If you want to share your personal truth, then you need to take the time and effort required to put the words on paper. I didn't go to college to become a writer. I learned the mechanics of writing over time. I wrote badly at first, but I got better. Life is a marvelous teacher, and if you're open to learning what you need to know to get started, there are fabulous resources available to new authors online at eHarlequin.com. Tell your story. Please. I'd like to read it.

Now, for the bad stuff. Fortunately, there haven't been any really brutal letters. One person took exception to the coarse language my teenage character used in my first book. I understand, but this is how that particular character talked. She was angry—and had good reason to be. She'd just found out how unfair life could be. I wrote to explain. The reader wasn't appeased and vowed to never pick up another of my books. Obviously, I wasn't the right author for that reader.

Another person took me to task because the town of Gold Creek (from my SULLIVAN SISTERS trilogy) "does not exist." He'd apparently checked every atlas his library had to offer and could find no trace of the town. My initial reaction was to dash off a note saying "Duh, they call this *fiction* for a reason." But then I read on. He mentioned that he read romances because his wife was bedridden and could no longer see, so he read them aloud to her. Because this was the kind of book she enjoyed. Duh...of another kind. In my reply, I thanked him for taking the time and effort to write and explained that I'd chosen to place my story in an imaginary locale so the citizens wouldn't be upset when I had their corrupt sheriff arrested. I also commended him on his compassion and love for his wife. He never wrote back, but I like to think he's still out there reading romances aloud to his wife. It's the kind of thing one of my imaginary heroes in some imaginary place might do someday.

Which reminds me, I have a T-shirt that says Warning: Anything You Do May Appear In My Next Novel. I guess the same might apply to letters, just in case you were thinking about writing to an author.

Here's a sneak peek...

Betting on Grace
by
Debra Salonen

18

**The prophecy: You will marry a prince—
but you will have to save him first.**

*Las Vegas restaurateur Grace Radonovic is
more than a little surprised when her late
father's friend proposes marriage.
Wanting to be true to her father's memory
and burdened by the wieght of her close,
but overbearing Gypsy family, she accepts.*

Who is she to turn her back on the dynasty?

CHAPTER 1

THE NOISE LEVEL within the small, crowded detective quarters was almost enough to mask the sound of the phone, but the flashing light, which blinked in time to the pulse in Nick Lightner's temple, caught his eye. The beat seemed to say, "Going, going, gone."

The festive celebration was in honor of his father's long and distinguished career in law enforcement. Today was Pete's last day as chief of detectives in Clarion Heights, a Detroit suburb that Nick's family had called home for twenty-eight of Nick's thirty-four years.

But in Nick's book, *retirement* was a four-letter word. He'd seen too many good cops turn into couch potatoes with circulatory problems and bad tickers just months after handing in their badges. From the minute his father announced his plan to step down, Nick had started nagging his parents to "look ahead."

His preaching must have worked because just last week, Pete had said, "Your mom and I have decided we're through with winter. We're selling the house and moving to Portland, so we can be closer to Judy and the girls." Judy was Nick's sister. His parent's *real* child.

Nick knew that his adoption played no part in Pete and Sharon's decision to move. They'd loved him and provided for him as if he were their own child from the moment they took him in. They had every right to want to be closer to their grandchildren. In the offspring department, the best that Nick, whose last serious relationship had ended nearly a year earlier, could give them was Rip, a five-year-old collie mix named after Richard "Rip" Hamilton, the Pistons' star shooting forward.

In his head, Nick knew this move wasn't about him. But the four-year-old inside him—the little kid whose father gave him away to a friendly cop after Nick's mother was struck by a bus and died—hated losing anything, from a silly bet to a major case. That tenaciousness worked in his favor on the job but was hell on relationships.

As was his habit, Nick hid his disquiet behind a short temper and withering scowl.

He picked up the phone and growled, "Nick Lightner."

The slight hesitation on the other end of the line had Nick's instincts perking up. "Oh, yes, of course," a woman's voice said. Unfamiliar, with just a hint of an accent Nick couldn't place. "I'm sorry. Your name threw me for a moment. I've always thought of you as Nikolai. Nikolai Sarna. But you would have a new name, wouldn't you?"

Tingles of apprehension skittered through him. No one other than his parents and the attorney who'd handled the adoption in Los Angeles knew his birth name. He'd been Nicholas Lightner since the day before his sixth birthday.

"Who is this?"

"My name is Yetta Radanovic." The name meant nothing to him. "I'm your father's cousin. Your *birth* father, I should say. Jurek Sarna. Most people know him as George. He was…is, I mean…my father's sister-in-law's nephew. That doesn't really make him my cousin, I suppose, but he's family, all the same."

Nick's mouth went dust dry. He'd seen his birth certificate. His mother and father had been honest with him from the start about his adoption. Partly because they figured at four and a half, he'd remember his past, partly because that's the kind of people they were. Upfront. Honest. Responsible. Unlike Lucille Helson and Jurek Sarna, the exotic dancer and ex-con who had given birth to him then handed him off to another family when things went sour.

"I don't know about your mother. I never met her. But your father was a Gypsy," Pete had told Nick when Nick was about ten.

"Romany," Sharon had corrected. "I believe that's the proper term these days. Linguists have proven that the Romany came from Western India. The name

Gypsy stemmed from a mistaken impression that the people were from Egypt." Sharon was a teacher and never passed up an opportunity to share information.

Nick had no time for the past. He knew who he was—a thirty-four-year-old cop, no wife, no kids, no commitments. He lived ten miles from the house he grew up in. He loved his job, his dog and the Pistons. He had no interest in the hazy memories that crept into his dreams on nights when he'd had one too many beers.

He hadn't given his background more than a passing interest since his eighteenth birthday when his mother suggested they try to locate his birth father. Nick had turned down her offer of help. "He decided fourteen years ago to let me go. I don't have any use for a person like that."

A truly kind woman, Sharon had reminded him of the mitigating circumstances. "Your mother had just passed away. A tragic accident. I'm sure your father was reeling from the loss and didn't have a home or job to return to after he got out of jail. Maybe he thought he was doing you a favor by giving you to us."

Nick hadn't even tried to see her point. A decision had been made. Nick had been given away. Like a stray cat that was too much work to feed. Nick hadn't wanted to know this man sixteen years ago, and he didn't want to know him now. He assumed that was what this call was about.

22

"How did you get this number?" Nick asked the woman who patiently waited while he collected his thoughts.

"From Jurek, of course. He has connections on both sides of the law that we don't speak about. I could be wrong, but I believe he's always known where you were."

The very notion made Nick's skin crawl.

"What's this about?"

"I—I'm not sure that calling you is the right thing to do, but Jurek said you were a policeman. Normally, that would make you um, suspect. We Romany tend to solve our own problems without involving the law enforcement, for a number of reasons."

"You don't trust cops."

"Exactly. But since you're family…"

Nick's bark caught the attention of his father who was lifting a glass of champagne as someone toasted him. Nick waved to signify the call wasn't anything serious. "Madam," he said, lowering his voice for maximum impact, "I am not anything to you or to the man y—"

"Of course, you are. Just because Jurek made a bad decision thirty years ago doesn't change who and what you are. You're Nikolai Sarna. You're Jurek's son, which makes you half Romany. That blood runs through your veins, whether you choose to admit it or not. And your Romany family needs your help."

Nick started to laugh. The woman's audacity impressed him. She sounded regal, as if used to giving orders and having people tow the line. "What kind of help? Money? I gotta tell you, I don't make enough—"

"Don't be absurd. I wouldn't call a stranger and ask for a handout, even if I were destitute. The simple fact is my youngest daughter, Grace, is in danger. She's considering a business relationship with a man I'm convinced wants more than just her money. In my dream, he appeared as a snake that swallowed each member of my family whole."

A dream snake? What kind of bullshit is this? Maybe it was some kind of prank, he decided. "Where are you calling from?"

"Las Vegas. Where you were born."

He'd never denied the fact.

"On July 29, 1970. At four in the afternoon. I was the third person to hold you. You had such fine blond hair, I thought you were bald. My girls all had dark black hair."

Nick looked at the people grouped around his father. The plan was to move the party to The Grease Monkey, a popular watering hole where Nick's mother and the other spouses would meet them. He wasn't in the mood for a party, but at the moment it sounded better than this nonsense. "Yes, well, that's very interesting, but I'm a cop, not an exterminator and your…um, snake is two thousand miles away from here."

His sarcasm must have come through loud and clear. She said haughtily, "Jurek warned me not to expect your cooperation. I seriously thought twice about calling you, but in addition to this matter of Charles Harmon…"

Charles Harmon? How do I know that name?

"…a mutual friend told me that your father is entering the hospital next week for an operation. I'm sure Jurek would rather you didn't know that, but I learned the hard way that it's much healthier to clear up unresolved issues before a person dies than—"

Nick sat up abruptly. His feet hit the floor with a snap that made several heads turn his way. "Did you say Charles Harmon?"

He pawed through the files on his desk for a fax that had come through a day or two earlier from his counterpart in Toronto.

"Yes. Grace insists he's just a friend…and, to be fair, he was my husband's lawyer when Ernst was alive, and Charles helped me handle some financial matters a few years back. But he's changed since he bought into that casino. And I've seen the way he looks at Grace—like a gambler counting his chips before a high-stakes bet."

What was that alert about? White slave trade? A

possible link to an international drug... "Ha," he said, snagging the sheet from the middle of the stack.

The woman on the other end of the line made a huffing sound. "Well. If you're not interested in helping us and meeting your father before it's too late, then I'll leave you with my good wishes and say goodbye." She hesitated for a fraction of a second then added, "You've been in my prayers since the day I learned of your mother's passing, Nikolai."

The name rattled him, but Nick ignored the odd flutter in his chest. He scanned the bulletin. "Wait. Hold on. I didn't say I wouldn't help."

"Yes, actually, you did."

Nick started to grin. "Well, maybe I changed my mind." He could care less about his long-lost relatives, but a chance to nail a scumbag like "Lucky Chuck" Harmon was too sweet a gift to pass up. "Tell me more about your daughter and the snake."

"GRACE, GRACE, GRACE, tell me you're joking."

Three Graces. Never a good thing. When her eldest sister Alex, short for Alexandra, started repeating herself, Grace Radanovic knew it was time to change the subject.

"So, what do we know about this long-lost cousin of Mom's—other than the fact that I'm supposed to pick him up at the airport in an hour?" Grace asked, cramming a too-large wedge of Danish in her mouth. "And why can't he take a taxi?" she mumbled, chewing and talking at the same time. "You know what traffic is like in February. Every snowbird in the country has descended on Vegas in their giant RVs."

Alex reached across their mother's lace tablecloth to grasp Grace's hand. "Sweetie," she said. Her melted-chocolate-colored eyes were filled with gravity and concern—a combination that resulted in what Grace and her other sisters called Alex's teacher look. It always made Grace feel about five. "Don't change the subject. No one is knocking your ambition, but you have to be realistic, too."

"She's right," another voice said from across the room.

Liz. Sister number two. The most imperial and dogmatic of the four Radanovic sisters, but also the kindest. A true healer, Liz was a physical therapist, who, until recently, volunteered with WorldAide, a Doctors-Without-Borders kind of group.

"I can't believe you're even suggesting this. We're spread too thin, as is," a third voice chimed in.

This came from Kate. Third-born, just two years older than Grace. Together, they owned Romantique, a neo-Mediterranean restaurant located in an upscale strip mall on West Charleston. Kate, an accomplished chef, ran the kitchen; Grace handled the marketing and bookkeeping.

Not giving up on the hope of deflecting her sisters' attention from her impetuous—and, obviously, premature—announcement, Grace said, "Delicious pastry, Kate. Maybe we should hire Jo full-time. I know you're finicky about who you let into your kitchen, but she does have a way with cream cheese." She spoke so fast a bit of raspberry filling lodged in her throat, causing her to cough.

"Don't talk with your mouth full," Alex scolded, giving Grace a look designed to stop even the most fearless four-year-old in his tracks. "Besides, diversion isn't going to work. You can't casually toss out 'Oh, by the way, I'm thinking of opening a second restaurant with Charles,' and not expect us to say something."

Grace knew that. She'd planned to share her idea in full once she had the details ironed out with Charles, but his call this morning had left her wondering if she'd made a mistake by suggesting they could do business together.

Charles Harmon was an old family friend and Grace's occasional dinner date. He was also a lawyer and part owner of the Xanadu, a small, shabby off-Strip casino where Grace had hoped to locate her new venture. She'd been in the shower when he called and he'd left a message asking her to drop by the casino to discuss her plan. Nothing in his tone could have been construed as ominous or threatening, but a chill had passed through her body as if she'd been dunked in Lake Mead in January.

"If you didn't want our feedback, why'd you say anything?" Liz asked, filling the electric tea kettle

28

with water. Four sisters, four beverages of choice: coffee, tea, cola and whatever strange brew Liz was currently into.

"Because…well, because you know me. I have a bad habit of speaking before I think things through, right?"

Her sisters agreed with a mixture of groans and sighs.

Before anyone could comment, she continued. "Last week, I floated an idea past Charles. Why not remodel the Xanadu's ridiculous excuse for a coffee shop into a satellite operation of Romantique? Can't you see it as a hip bar with an exposed kitchen where Kate could really show off her stuff? I even came up with a name for it. Too Romantique."

Alex and Liz, who were respectively six and four and a half years older than Grace, exchanged a look Grace had seen many times.

"It's a very clever name, Grace," Alex said. "But I have to go on record as being against this. I'm not comfortable with you doing business with Charles. There's something about that man that makes me nervous."

"Yeah," Grace said, snickering softly. "We know. That's why you set him on fire."

The standing joke for years had been that their father, Ernst, brought Charles home to meet Alex, who'd accidentally dropped the cherries jubilee and singed Charles's beard. Charles had been clean shaven ever since.

"I agree with Alex," Liz said, tapping her foot as she waited for the water to boil. "You're talking major remodeling. That isn't going to come cheap. Where are you getting the seed money? I know Charles is pretty well off, but he does have two partners. Are they part of this?"

Leave it to Liz to ask the tough questions. Everything about Liz was functional, from short-sleeved denim blue shirt with a rainbow embroidered just above her name to khaki pants and thick-soled shoes. Her shoulder-length ebony hair was pulled back in a ponytail.

She poured boiling water over several scoops of some greenish powder resting in the bottom of a juice glass. Grace didn't bother asking what medicinal properties the concoction contained. Liz went through health fads the way some people did diets.

"Well—" Grace stalled "—that particular issue didn't come up. But since I'm the one who brought the idea to Charles…I thought I'd ask Mom to let me invest the money in my trust fund."

Alex shook her head. Liz choked on her partially swallowed swill. Kate let out a sound of pure disgust.

"Are you nuts?" they said simultaneously.

Grace felt her cheeks burn. "Like I said, this is just in the chatting stage. I tossed the idea on the table last week when Charles took me to dinner. His call this morning is the first I've heard back from him. Didn't MaryAnn tell us he was wrapped up in some pro bono insurance claim business or something?"

MaryAnn Radanovic, their cousin Gregor's wife, had been Charles's personal secretary for just over a year. Gregor, who was Liz's age, was the girls' paternal uncle's son. In addition to being cousins, Gregor and MaryAnn were also neighbors, living just two houses down from Yetta.

Liz blew out a sigh and turned to the sink to rinse out the green residue in her glass. "I can't vouch for the pro bono aspect of his business, but we've been seeing a lot of referrals from Charles's group at the chiropractic office. But you're trying to change the subject again and it's not going to work. You know what Dad had in mind when he set up the trust accounts for each of us."

Grace knew. A wedding. As old-fashioned as it sounded, Ernst had always referred to the four trusts he and Yetta had established for their daughters as dowries.

"Well, none of you used your trust money for that purpose. Why should I have to?" Grace asked.

She'd known the question would come up and she'd given the matter some serious thought. Alex's money had been earmarked for a wedding until her plans fell apart at the last minute, then she'd drawn from the fund to buy a house and set up The Dancing Hippo DayCare and PreSchool. Liz's nest egg had paid for college, several trips abroad and the down payment on her home. Kate's money had been invested—and lost—by her scoundrel ex-husband. Only Grace's trust remained untouched.

"Listen," she said, trying to sound businesslike, "Mom has final say on how I spend the money since she's the trustee. I just thought I'd feel you guys out, first. You know how distracted she's been lately."

"Boy, that's true," Alex said. "I wonder how much of that has to do with our new guest."

"Yeah," Kate said after taking a swig of Coke, which, as usual, she'd tried to disguise by putting it in a coffee mug. "I have to say I'm not wild about some stranger moving in next door."

"Did anybody do a Google search on him?" Liz asked.

"I did, and nothing came up. Nada. Which is probably a good sign, right? But I still don't know why *I'm* the one picking him up," Grace said, relieved that the focus of conversation had shifted away from her obviously premature declaration. While she might have come from a long line of Gypsy fortune-tellers, Grace felt most comfortable with facts and figures. If the bottom line on this new project looked feasible, then she would approach her mother about accessing her trust fund—regardless of her weird, inexplicable dreams.

...NOT THE END...

BETTING ON GRACE is available in stores November 2005.

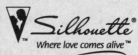

SPOTLIGHT

"Delightful and delicious...Cindi Myers
always satisfies!"
—*USA TODAY* bestselling author Julie Ortolon

National bestselling author

Cindi Myers

She's got more than it takes for
the six o'clock news...

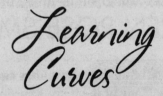

Learning Curves

Tired of battling the image problems that her
size-twelve curves cause with her network news
job, Shelly Piper takes a position as co-anchor on
public television with Jack Halloran. But as they
work together on down-and-dirty hard-news
stories, all Shelly can think of is Jack!

Plus, exclusive bonus features inside!

On sale in October.

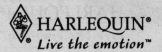

HARLEQUIN®
Live the emotion™

...there's more to the story!

Supperromance.

A *big* satisfying read about unforgettable characters. Each month we offer *six* very different stories that range from family drama to adventure and mystery, from highly emotional stories to romantic comedies—and much more! Stories about people you'll believe in and care about. Stories too compelling to put down....

Our authors are among today's *best* romance writers. You'll find familiar names and talented newcomers. Many of them are award winners—and you'll see why!

If you want the biggest and best in romance fiction, you'll get it from Supperromance!

Emotional, Exciting, Unexpected...

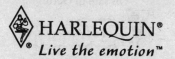

COLLECTION

Somewhere between good and evil…there's love.

Beyond the Dark

Three brand-new stories of otherworldly romance by…

Linda Winstead Jones

Evelyn Vaughn

Karen Whiddon

Evil looms but love conquers all in three gripping stories by award-winning authors.

Plus, exclusive bonus features inside!

On sale October

Where love comes alive™

SAGA

USA TODAY bestselling author

Dixie Browning

A brand-new story in
The Lawless Heirs miniseries...

FIRST TIME HOME

Reeling from the scandalous ruin of her
career and love life, Laurel Ann Lawless
escapes to North Carolina and turns to
relatives she's never met. She soon feels
a strong sense of belonging—with her
newfound family and her handsome
new landlord, Cody Morningstar.

*Available
in September.*

Bonus Features:

**Author Interview,
Recipes
and
Lawless Family History**

Where love comes alive™

Starting over is sweeter when shared.

What else could editor Elisha Reed do when
she suddenly goes from single workaholic
to mother of two teens?

Starting from Scratch
Marie Ferrarella

HARLEQUIN®
Next™

SHOWCASE

Two classic stories in one volume
from favorite author

FAYRENE PRESTON

**In one house, secrets of past and
present converge...**

SWANSEA LEGACY

Caitlin Deverell's great-grandfather had built
SwanSea as a mansion that would signal the
birth of a dynasty. Decades later, this ancestral
home is being launched into a new era as a
luxury resort—an event that arouses passion,
romance and a century-old mystery.

PLUS, exclusive bonus features inside!

Available in November 2005.